THE BEST OF FOOLS

MARILYN GREY

WINSLET
PRESS

WINSLET PRESS

No, Not that Jane Austen
The Best of Fools
Copyright © 2015 by Marilyn Grey

To learn more about Marilyn Grey, visit her Web site:
www.marilyn-grey.com

ISBN-10: 0990353877
ISBN-13: 978-0990353874

This novel is a work of fiction. Names, characters, places, and incidents either are the product of the author's imagination or are used fictitiously. Any resemblance to actual events, locales, organizations, or persons living or dead is entirely coincidental and beyond the intent of either the author or the publisher.

Printed in the United States of America

First Edition: September 2015
15 14 12 11 10 9 8 7 6 5 4 3 2 1

To:
Laura Dobb

Amazing how two people can meet, live across the ocean, never hug or laugh together over a cup of tea, yet be so closely linked together that you wonder if this friendship was somehow always a part of your life. I couldn't have written this book without you. Literally. You helped with little words and odds and ends to make Alistair a bit more realistic, since I've never been to England although we all know it's my dream. :-) Laura, you are such a beautiful person. So devoted and caring and compassionate and lovely. I love your humour. I spelled it with a U for you. :-) And I love the way you care for your son and your family. I love your joy and your "can do" attitude. You're a lot like Jane to me. You don't give up, no matter how hard it gets. And you try to keep going. To smile. To Live. And to love. You remind me of this book. The message at the heart of it.

Carpe Diem

I wish you a long, joyful life like that of The Best of Fools. And I hope our friendship only continues to grow until one day I am your neighbor and we can have a cuppa with a tea cake. :-)

Love you, duck!

You'll never know if you can fly,
unless you take the risk of falling.

Nightwing

MARILYN GREY

The Art of Falling

IT SEEMS THAT IT IS A TRUTH UNIVERSALLY *UNKNOWN* that every girl in the world is not looking for a romance.

I clicked my pen and stared at my bedroom wall. Every one of my girl friends—and I do mean every.single.one—went to see the latest Nicholas Sparks flick. I stayed home as usual. Not my thing, really. I preferred intense dramas or maybe even a little action. Plus I majorly procrastinated on my English essay.

I wrote my name at the top of the paper and shook my head. The idea of marriage didn't appeal to me, at least not any time soon, but I can tell you this ... the idea of changing my name appealed to me.

Tomorrow I'd turn eighteen and, against the oh so old-fashioned ideals of my parents, I planned to get a few tattoos I'd been dreaming about. Or ... spend that money to change my name. The decision consumed me.

I tried to finish my homework, but Donovan kept interrupting me with his hilarious text messages, then finally he rang my phone.

"I'm trying to finish this paper," I said. "Aren't you supposed to be doing the same? I know you haven't started either."

"I finished it last week." He laughed. "Come on, let's hang out one last time before my trip."

"I really should finish this paper, but it does sound tempting."

"I need to give you a gift for your birthday anyway."

"I'm taking you to the airport tomorrow morning, remember? You can do it then."

"All right, all right. Finish the paper and if it's early enough maybe we can get a coffee?" He paused. "Wait, never mind, I forgot. You're Jane and you start your start your essay's the night before they're due and stay up until sunrise to finish them."

I smiled. "Exactly. Except it's due Monday and today is Friday, but there's no way I'm spending my birthday weekend writing this."

And that's exactly what happened. I stayed up until the light poured into my room and as much as I wanted to pull the covers over my head and go back to sleep, I shoved them off of me, rolled out of my fluffy cloud, and rubbed my eyes. I skipped a shower, ate breakfast as fast as humanly possible, and drove to Donovan's house. I was early, but I wanted to see him for at least thirty minutes before he left.

He jogged to my car and flopped down in the passenger's seat, stuffing a backpack between his legs as he buckled up.

"Happy eighteen." He reached over the armrest and pulled me into a hug. "How does it feel?"

"You tell me." I backed out of his driveway. "You experienced it five days ago."

He tapped the door. "Eh, we'll see."

"Sounds hopeful."

He tilted his head and stared at me.

"What?"

Shaking his head, he turned his gaze back to the passing trees and smiled. He was fresh out of a breakup with a girl who cheated on him. He didn't really love Megan. It was a relationship built on convenience. She was there. He was there. And it just happened before anyone could say no. Now he was on his way across the ocean to meet a Russian girl he met through some kind of online dating site. You can only imagine my disapproval of a dating site, but I tried to be as supportive as possible. One day, he'd find someone amazing. Someone nice and soft and beautiful. He deserved that.

After a comfortably quiet drive, I parked in the airport's garage and turned the car off. He looked over at me and reached his hand into his backpack.

"So, I got you a birthday present," he said, his voice oddly shaken. "I know there's only two things you want for your birthday. To change your name and get some tattoos. So, I thought I'd help you out with one."

I smiled. "You got me a gift certificate for that tattoo joint, didn't you?"

He pulled a small jewelry box out of his bag and stared at me. I tried not to look at the familiar shaped box in his palm or make eye contact with him. He was going to meet this girl ... right?

"I thought I could give you my last name, Jane." He opened the box to reveal a sparkly ring. "If you'll have me. I know it's weird and everything, but I love you. I need you. I've got an extra plane ticket for you and we can elope right now if you want to."

I raised my eyebrows and choked on my words.

"You had to see this coming." He set the box on my lap. "I love you. Always have."

"I ... I..." I suddenly needed to open the window to breathe. My pulse quickened so fast I felt it beating in my ears. Everything around me—the dashboard, the steering wheel, his face, my hands—blurred until I closed my eyes.

He slapped my arm and laughed hysterically. "You totally bought it."

I looked back and forth. "What?"

"It's a fake ring." He kept laughing and handed me a wrapped gift. "This is for real."

I held up my hands. "Slightly freaked out to open it."

His little boy smile replaced the mischievous grin. "You'll like it."

I slowly unwrapped the paper and set it neatly on the floor of the car as he smiled. How did he remember? It was so long ago. I didn't even remember telling a soul. Not even him. Running my fingers along the edges, I tried to thank him but the words refused to make an appearance.

"It took me years obviously, but I finally found it a few months ago. Thought I'd wait until your birthday though."

"Where did you ... how?" I opened the box and felt the familiar smooth velvet. "How do you know it was mine?"

He shrugged. "Who else buried a box in the woods in the exact area you said it would be?"

"You just went out there and dug it up? This is really it?"

"When I had time every few months or so. It's been years. I just didn't want to give up because you always talk about how you wish you had never gotten rid of it. Thought I'd surprise the hell out of ya if I found it, so I dug around until I did. Found some jewelry and other stuff in my search." He pulled out a bag. "Some of it you might like."

Don't cry, don't cry, I said to myself, but my eyes already stung with joy. "Thank you, Donny." I pulled him into a hug. "I can't thank you enough."

"You could by accepting my proposal."

I hit his arm and sat back, staring at my box. The box that held my dreams. Underneath the velvet was a secret compartment. I looked at him, wondering if he searched it. Not that I'd really mind. The guy knew me inside and out. Still though. The secrets under there would tell him things about me I hadn't told even him, things I didn't know if I could face again after all these years.

"I better run in there." He couldn't erase his smile. "I'll miss my flight."

"I'll walk you in."

We walked fast and it didn't take him long to find where he needed to go. His family traveled far more than mine. The only major vacation I remember was our trip to England. Mom and Dad and their ridiculous obsession with all of that stuff. Jane Austen and everything related. Made me want to turn my fork upside down and lower my face on it until I punctured out my eyeballs. Okay, maybe not that bad, but it overwhelmed me to the core.

Donovan stopped when I could no longer follow.

"Time for a little radiation exposure," I joked, only he knew I wasn't really joking.

He ran his fingers through his messy dark hair. Typical lacrosse player with hair flipping out at the ends. It's a wonder we stayed so close with all of our differences.

"Happy birthday, Jazzy." He gave me one last hug as my mind drifted back to the first time he called me Jazzy. We were playing in my basement while our parents talked upstairs and he thought the way I played with Barbie's was "jazzy." I guess in his little kid world that meant weird or crazy. True though. I hated Barbie's. So I guess I gave them mullets and dyed their hair with Kool-Aid and well, yeah, that can be a tad weird to some people.

"Thanks again, Donny," I said. "I'm serious. You're the best friend I've ever had. I love you."

"Love you too, girl." He looked over his shoulder. "Gotta go. Talk soon."

I watched him check in and disappear, then took a step back. My foot bumped into something and I almost lost my balance. I turned to find a guy flat on his face, cheek pressed against the cold, dirty airport floor

"I am so, so sorry," I said. "Are you okay?"

He stood and shook his head as though he were waking from a dream he was still trying to figure out. "How embarrassing." English accent. Sounded like Yorkshire. "I am so sorry. I didn't see you there and ... you're okay?"

"I'm not the one who fell." I quickly took in his details. Brown and caramel Asics shoes. Fitted, but not too fitted, jeans with a few not-so-deliberate worn spots. Plain black t-shirt. Nice arms. A few tattoos peeking out from his sleeves. Defined jaw line. Sandy hair. Attractive in a normal way. Not the type of guy to stand out in a crowd, but certainly not one most girls would ignore.

"I'm sorry. Mind if I buy you a cup for the trouble?" Especially the totally clich English accent. Most girls wouldn't be able to miss it. How romance novel-ish. How ... Jane Austen-ish. I never understood why women immediately gave a man fifteen bonus sexy points just for having a foreign accent.

"I'm okay, really. I should be the one apologizing."

"You could buy me a cup then." He held back a smile. "I've only just missed my flight and I could use a bit of company. If you don't mind, that is."

"What are you here for?"

He glanced around the busy airport. "I suppose the same thing every one else is here for. To fly on a plane?"

I almost laughed, but it came out as a puff of air. "I mean, why are you in America?"

"Um, nothing important really." He swung his bag to the other shoulder. "Coffee? I could use the company."

I nodded and followed him. He didn't seem to be flirting, just friendly and apologetic, I guess, even though it really was my fault that the poor guy fell flat on his face.

We stood in the Starbucks line when he asked the inevitable. "So, what's your name?"

"Jane." I nodded as the line moved.

He stepped forward. "I'm Alistair. And no, people don't call me Al."

"Just Alistair, huh?"

"Only just? Not at all."

I laughed, not quite understanding but decidedly going with the flow. "What am I doing here? A stranger ... in an airport. Recipe for disaster."

He glanced at the cashier who called us over to her. "I believe you are getting a coffee, Jane." He ushered me in front of him. "Anything you like."

"No, no," I said. "I'll get it myself."

He didn't object as I opened my wallet, but gently pushed it away when I reached for my card.

"It's my apology," he said, then turned to the girl. "I'll have a coffee with plenty of cream and just a bit of sugar please."

The girl's eyelashes fluttered at him until she caught me staring at her. "And for you?" she said, trying not to look at Alistair as her face flushed with pink.

"Just a vanilla latte is fine. Thanks." I scooted behind him. "And thank you, Alistair."

He paid the girl without making eye contact, then touched my back as he edged me toward the counter where our drinks would soon appear. Touchy kinda guy.

"Jane Austen?" He laughed. "Your name really is Jane Austen?"

I looked away and rummaged through the straws.

"It really is, is it not?"

"You saw my license." I shook my head.

He nodded. "So ... that's pretty weird, but what's weirder is that you people here in the States put marshmallows on your sweet potatoes, yams, whatever you call them."

"Random." I almost smiled. "What's weird about that? Not everyone does it that way, though."

"So." He took his coffee as a girl sat it on the counter, then he handed the second cup to me. "You're really named after Jane Austen?"

"Takes all I have not to roll my eyes when people ask this." I sipped my coffee and nearly burned my tongue off. "My parents are weird, like marshmallows on sweet potatoes. What can I say? I'm lucky like that."

He laughed and pointed at an empty table. I nodded and sat down.

He sat across from me and reclined into the chair. "Does your boyfriend like your name?"

"Nice try."

"What?"

"Oh, you know. Typical cheesy way to find out if a girl has a boyfriend. Or vice versa." I set my cup on the table and leaned forward. "Let's bypass all of the awkward stuff and just be realistic. No, I don't have a boyfriend. And yes, that's by choice. I don't want a boyfriend any time soon."

He took another sip and squinted his eyes. I turned my head to the left and watched people rush by, then checked my phone. Fifteen minutes until Donovan's flight was supposed to take off. My birthday wouldn't be the same without him, but maybe one of the girls would come with me to get a tattoo.

One of the girls.

If they weren't with one of their guys.

Alistair cleared his throat and tapped his cup. I forgot about him for a second.

"You ever had a boyfriend?" he said.

I mouthed, "Nope."

His eyebrows shot toward the ceiling. "Never? What about a kiss?"

"Had a few of those."

He laughed. "No boyfriend?"

"It's just not something I'm interested in. People fall in love too easily and it's all fuzzy and surfacey, then what happens? They get cheated on or they break up or they lose interest. Does that sound appealing to you?" I picked up my drink. "Way too much drama for me." I shook my head. "Way too much."

He finished his coffee and tossed the cup into the trashcan beside us, then folded his hands on the table and smiled.

"I know, I know. Jane Austen, the paradox."

"Fascinating."

"It's not that fascinating."

"Not at all."

"I'm not trying to be negative, just honest."

"No." The sunlight beamed through the windows and highlighted his hair. "Honest is good. It's perfect."

I glanced in my lap as my phone screen lit with Donovan's text. *Signing off for now. See you in a few days. Happy birthday girl. Smile for me! Miss you.*

I typed back, *Love you. Be safe!*

Alistair ended up doing something on his phone too. I watched his fingers move for a few seconds, then noticed two men gawking at me from the table beside us. I looked away. Did other girls actually enjoy being nothing more than someone's eye candy? Sometimes I wished I were completely unattractive just to avoid weird and creepy stares.

I decided to stare back at them and make them feel uncomfortable. They looked away and refused to make eye contact with me. Alistair looked up, confused. He shot them a look and turned his gaze back to me. First time I noticed his eye color. Same as mine, only less green and more gold. Normally I noticed eye color as soon as I met someone. In fact, I already knew the girls to our left had blue and brown eyes and the creepy men to the right both had brown eyes. Why didn't I notice Alistair's?

"Wait ... what?" he said.

"I didn't say anything, but I should probably go now." I smiled and stood up, only to bump into a woman with a nasty look on her face.

"Watch where you're going." She huffed and blew by me.

I sat back down and raised my eyebrows at Alistair.

"Is it just me," he said, "or do most people in the world have a natural propensity toward impatience?"

"Definitely not just you."

I nodded toward his phone. "Who were you texting? You looked a little upset."

"My girlfriend."

"Nice try. You don't have a girlfriend."

"How do you know?"

"Wild guess."

"No, really?"

"You aren't the type to sit with another girl if you're taken."

"And what makes you think that?"

"Well, first of all, you offered me a treat as an apology for being there when I turned and tripped you. Wasn't your fault, but you insisted and then insisted on buying me a drink. The cashier was flirting with you majorly, and you were as oblivious as can be. You handed me my drink, tried to pull the chair out for me but I sat down too fast, and didn't look at your phone when it was beeping until I looked at mine. Want me to keep going?"

"I don't understand what this has to do with my relationship status."

"You're a nice guy, Mr. Alistair. Nice guys don't entertain other girls in airports while their girlfriend's wait anxiously at home. These guys with rings on their fingers. The ones next to us, you know. They, on the other hand, may be that type..."

He shrugged. "Fair enough."

"Why are you here?"

"Dropped my best friend off. Now"—I stood—"I really should be going. It's my birthday and I need to figure out what I'm doing today."

"I'll walk you to your car." He stood beside me, heating my arm with his. "Since I'm a nice guy it shouldn't be creepy, right?"

I walked toward the door and he followed. Odd start to my birthday. I felt bad asking him to leave me alone, but wanted to get in my car and drive away without some strange guy trying to give me his number. That is what he'd do after all. I just knew it.

We finally reached my Jetta and I clicked the button on my keychain to unlock the car doors. He glanced at his phone and sighed.

"Thanks for the coffee and everything," I said. "I better—"

"Can't believe this." He looked down at his phone and shook his head.

"I better get going." I opened the door. "Hope everything goes well with your friend there."

"I procrastinated. Changed my flight and decided to stay a few extra days. Came from Nashville, but my flight stopped here to board for London. But I missed it because of a delay from Nashville. I suppose I need to find a hotel. You mind taking me to—wait, it's your birthday. I don't want to intrude." He stepped back and turned to walk away, then looked over his shoulder and waved. "Have a great birthday."

No phone number. No flirting.

Color me shocked. He really was a nice guy.

I sat down and turned on my car, then looked at the box on the passenger's seat. Still couldn't believe Donovan found it. I held it in my lap and opened the top, then slipped a credit card under the velvet and pulled up. The tape didn't have the slightest tear. Donovan didn't see it, then.

I set the box back on the passenger's seat and backed up, then drove away only to find Alistair holding his thumb out along the main road.

I slowed down and pulled over. He motioned for me to keep going, but I parked and stuck my head out the window.

"Come on," I said. "I'm not letting you hitchhike in Philadelphia."

He settled into the passenger's seat and closed the door. "Are you sure?"

I laughed and pulled back on to the highway. "Stop being so nice.
"

He exhaled, barely laughing under his breath.

I started to speak, but stopped when I realized he was saying something at the same time.

"You go first," he said.

"What were you saying?"

"Just that there's a hotel about three minutes up this road." He pointed over the dashboard. "That will be fine. Thank you so much. I feel rubbish messing up your birthday."

"Rubbish. That's cute." Did I actually just say *cute*?

He didn't seem to notice. "Turn right here."

"You know what?" I ignored the turn and drove straight. "You obviously know a thing or two about tattoos. That was my birthday present today from my friend. Pretty much the only thing I wanted besides a different name. Want to come with me? You seem like you could use a distraction from whoever is bothering you with those texts."

"You really want to change your name?"

I nodded as emphatically as possible.

"But it's who you are."

"No." I pat my chest. "Who I am is in here, not out here."

"I don't know. It's your name."

"So I can turn around and take you back to your hotel of choice or you can hang out with me and I'll bring you back tonight." *What am I doing?* "This is a bit strange, isn't it?"

He inhaled slowly and exhaled even slower. "It is a bit, but comfortable too." He rubbed his face, then dropped his hand back to his lap. "Then again, I'm rather used to hanging out with strangers."

I didn't ask what he meant. Not that I didn't want to, but my mind fell into a hole when he said it was comfortable. Of all words, he said *comfortable*. I only experienced that kind of comfortable with

Donovan and Autumn, but there was something about this Alistair, something that made him seem new and familiar all at once. If he lived here we'd become instant friends.

That worried me.

"Like that," he interrupted my thoughts. "I don't have silent moments like that with most people I've only just met. That just happened."

I wanted to respond, if only to prove that I wasn't contemplating it as much as I was.

"I don't mean to scare you, Ms. Austen." He laughed. "Contrary to your assessments of me, I am not looking for love and I live across the ocean. It wouldn't make sense to..."

I stopped at a red light and stared at him.

He stared back. "I don't start things I can't finish."

The Picture in Our Minds

WE CROSSED OUR ARMS AND ANALYZED THE TATTOO designs on the wall. Occasionally his voice sent waves through the silence with a, "This one is nice," or a, "This is okay." Then finally his finger landed on a beautiful design. "That's mint," he said, finger trailing the art. "You should get this one."

"What? Are they mint leaves?"

"Mint leaves?"

"You said, 'That's mint.'"

"Right..." He squinted. "Is that not something you say?"

"Is what?"

"You know, like that's awesome, or cool, or crackin'."

I nodded. "Cracking?"

"Anyway." He pointed. "That's my favorite one, but this is your body. What do you fancy?"

Did I really want to tell him that I had my eye on that one from the start?

"This your first tattoo?" he said.

"Yeah."

"Eighteen today?"

"Yeah."

He nodded. "Maybe something simple, then?"

He moved toward me as we examined more images on the wall. Not the slightest hint of cologne came with him. Surprising. Most guys had enough scent emanating from their deodorant, plus the extra cologne on top of that, to instantaneously make me sneeze.

His breath landed on my neck as he leaned over me and pointed to another design. I stepped back and ignored the shiver making its way to my fingertips.

"Any ideas?" Phillip, the tattoo artist, said from behind me. "Need some help?"

"I have a few ideas." I really wanted the one Alistair liked—or fancied—but...

"Do you know where you want it?" Phillip said.

I turned to face him. "Thinking my arm. Down the side here. Or maybe my back or shoulder."

"Show me a few you like." Phillip stepped forward as I pointed a few out, then he continued, "Okay, I can see your style pretty clear here. How about we start small with this one"—he gestured to my second favorite design—"and then you can always come back and build from there to the vine down your arm." He paused. "You're not nervous, are you?"

I shook my head. "No, no. I'm ready."

The next hour, or however long it took, dripped by like water from a sink left on the absolute lowest setting. If I experienced pain along with the vibrating sensation on my arm, I didn't notice. My mind was far too distracted by the boy sitting across the room, scrolling through an iPad and laughing at the screen every few minutes. He carried with him a simple charm. Not that typical ladies man charm, but a distant charm that conveyed depth and passion. Mystery. He had mystery. That's what it was. And I dare say ... he intrigued me.

But...

The inevitable *but.*

It wasn't unlike me to make friends fast or to associate with strangers, but becoming distracted by a boy was not on my list of acceptable actions.

Especially one like him. My parents would have a field day and there was absolutely no way I'd allow that. Jane Austen would not marry a British man on the hills of an English countryside. She definitely, definitely would not do that.

Marry? I asked myself. *How did we jump to marriage already?*

I closed my eyes and hummed Tchaikovsky in the quiet of my mind until Philip said, "That your boyfriend?"

Eyes still closed, I said, "No. We just met."

"Oh, really? You seem pretty close for just meeting."

I didn't respond.

A few minutes later, he said, "Feeling okay?"

I nodded and continued humming songs in my mind.

Finally, he wrapped it up and told me to look. I opened my eyes to Alistair smiling down at me. Then quickly closed my eyes again.

Something about....

"I'm famished," Alistair said. "Mind if we stop and get something for lunch?"

Phillip helped me sit up. "What do you think?"

I analyzed the simple design on my left shoulder. "It's perfect. Thank you." Definitely sore though. "What do I do next?"

"Let me just bandage it up. Then it's important that you don't mess with it, touch it, pick at scabs. Keep the bandage on for a few hours and try not to get the tattoo wet." He began to bandage my arm. "Also try to stay out of the sun until it's completely healed. Ice packs do wonders for redness and swelling."

The tattoo didn't excite me as much as I thought it would, but I liked it. We all sat in silence as he finished his job. I paid for my new body art at the front desk, feeling a little more thrilled about it, and turned to Alistair. "What are you hungry for?"

"Anything," he said. "My treat since it's your birthday. And yes, I insist."

"When is your birthday?" I said as we walked out the door.

"September 15."

"Hm." I analyzed the slight lines forming around his eyes, so subtle. "You're about twenty one?"

"Twenty two." He almost opened the car door for me, but I beat him to it. We both sat down and he continued, "You're a queer one, huh? Perceptive."

"I take in details other people don't see right away. It's probably my love for mystery novels."

"Man, I think it's been years since I read a novel." He pulled the visor down when I drove out of the parking lot and into the blazing sun. "Music has consumed me like I'm about to consume whatever we eat."

I laughed. "Music? Is that why you were in Nashville?"

He answered back with silence and a slight nod of his head. I didn't want to pry, even though I desperately wanted to.

"You into music?" he asked.

"I am, but probably not the kind you're thinking."

"Yeah? Like...."

"Like Brahms, Sebastian, Haydn, Liszt."

"Fascinating."

"Why?"

"I can't quite figure you out. Wearing a pretty little sundress with pearls hanging from your ears. You just got a tattoo that you wanted to go all the way down your arm and you like classical music. Any other music you like?"

"Not really. A little here and there, but I prefer classical."

"Just peculiar, that's all I can say. Not to mention your obvious aversions to romantic relationships."

I located an empty space a few feet from a local pizza shop and parked.

"I'd take you somewhere nicer," I said. "But it would take longer and I figured you're probably starved already. And, just to drill it into your head, I do not have aversions to romantic relationships. I have precautions. It's different."

"Pizza is great." He ignored my speech, opened his door, and bolted down the city sidewalk to the pizza shop. Hungry guy. He did, however, wait for me while holding the door. I plopped a few coins in the meter and jogged to him.

"You really like the chivalry thing, huh?" I walked through the door and brushed his arm, which felt surprisingly ... never mind. I would not be that girl. It felt normal. Like Donovan. That's all I felt. That's all I would feel.

"I was raised to treat others with kindness." He touched my back as I walked through the next set of doors. "My father always told me to be a gentleman to everyone, even other men, regardless of how unfashionable it becomes."

"It has become unfashionable." I peered up at the menu. "And I'd like to know why it's so gentlemanly to open doors for people, but not gentlewomanly? Why can't girls get away with doing that stuff for guys?"

The tasty aroma of homemade rolled dough and melted cheese smacked me in the face. Best smack ever. I hadn't eaten since my rushed breakfast. When I closed my eyes I could almost taste the salty, crispy fries and fresh out of the oven pizza. His hand warmed my back again as he guided me toward the counter. Was that a shiver crawling down my spine? What the?

"Can I help you?" the cashier said.

"Want to split a cheese?" Alistair said. "And some chips?"

His touch. His hand. Although now in his pocket, the warmth of his fingers remained on my back. "Sure. I'll take some fries and a Dr. Pepper too."

"We'll get a large cheese pizza, an order of ... fries, and two Dr. Pepper's," he said, then looked at me. "I meant fries when I said chips. Always forget that."

I excused myself for the bathroom. He did the same, although

I bet he really needed to go. I just needed to collect my thoughts and berate myself. Pacing the empty orange-scented bathroom, I told myself not to get tingly sensations or enjoy the way his skin felt against mine. My hormones wanted to ruin me and send me into a full-fledged reel of tawdry romance. I couldn't allow it.

"But I'm not anti-love," I whispered to myself.

The other me chimed in, "He lives in England. It wouldn't work anyway."

"Yes," Less Reasonable Me agreed. "And I don't like to start something I can't finish either."

"Exactly."

"But—"

A toilet flushed. I jerked my head to the left as a lock on one of the stalls jiggled, then dashed into the empty stall before she saw me.

She will see you come out after her, I thought inside, then thanked myself for reminding myself that I wouldn't escape the embarrassment.

I waited until the hand dryer stopped and the door swung closed, then another minute before walking out. I didn't see any women sitting anywhere, thankfully, so I continued on toward Alistair. Starved as he was, the poor chivalrous fellow sat in front of the untouched food. Patiently waiting for me.

I sat down across from him and apologized for the wait. He clasped his fingers together and brought them to his lips, shaking off my apology as though it were unnecessary, then his phone rang. He lifted it, tilted his head back, and exhaled, nodding to me to see if I would mind if he answered the call. I shook my head and wondered if I should also wait to dig in. Be the gentlewoman and what not.

A young girl smiled at me from behind the counter as she lifted a slice of pizza from the steaming vegetable pizza on display. I smiled back and she giggled. Ah, the girl in the bathroom. I stared into my lap.

"Seriously, there's no way I can do that," Alistair said. "Colin, this is ridiculous. You know this isn't the way I wanted to do it. That's the last thing I care about." He paused and noticed me. Yes, I was candidly listening. "Sorry, but I'm not doing it." Another pause. "Give me a break, Colin." Another pause. "This is total rubbish." He ended the call and picked up a slice of pizza. "Let's eat."

"Thank you for that."

"For what?" he said between bites.

"For showing me that you're not always so nice."

He laughed. "I guess I'm prone to agitation as much as the next person."

"It's good. I mean, I'm all about being kind, but it's nice to see that you can also stand up for yourself. It's good to have opinions."

"Of course this is coming from a highly opinionated and therefore biased perspective." He smiled.

So did I. "So, you've already noticed." I laughed and nodded toward his phone. "What was that all about?"

"My manager." He gulped his soda. "Trying to force me into gigs I'm not interested in."

"What are you? A guitarist?"

"Do I look like a guitarist?"

"Not sure." I tapped his hand. "You're fingers are calloused though."

"Nice work. I do play a bit of guitar, but that's not what I do in this band."

I realized my hand was still on top of his and I quickly yanked it back. "Sorry."

He laughed. "Don't be."

"So ... bassist?"

"Drummer."

"Wow." I slurped the last of my soda and wanted more. "Didn't expect that one."

"Stereotypes. I didn't expect you to be the tattoo or classical music type either. More like a country music fan."

"What?" I gasped. "No way. Country? Why country? Not that there's anything wrong with country, but ... why country?"

"I haven't the slightest clue. You seem pretty normal on the surface. I bet you're popular in school, huh? Did you really just inhale more of that pizza than me?"

I picked up another slice and widened my eyes as I brought it toward me. "At least I?m careful not to get it all over my face.? I dabbed my mouth with a napkin. ?I?m not popular as in cheerleader and homecoming queen kind of popular. I do have a lot of friends from different cliques. I get along with a lot of different types of people, I guess. Is that popular? But normal ... I don't want to be normal."

"That's just the thing. You absolutely are not even close to normal." He brought a fry to his lips. "Rest easy."

We finished eating in silence until we ended up licking our fingers and dabbing crumbs. At the same time. We laughed, cleared the crumbs, and shoved our mess into one large pile on the empty pizza tray and stood. "Ready?"

"You want me to take you back now?"

He leaned closer to me. His eyelashes blinked only inches from mine. "I'm not sure *want* is the right word, Ms. Austen."

I sincerely hoped my face did not look as red as it felt. "And what would you want exactly?"

He tossed everything in the trash, placed the tray in its designated return spot, and held the door open for me. "How about a walk?"

"Oh! How I shall fancy a delightful stroll about the town," I teased him with my best impression of his accent.

"That was pretty good," he said. "A little too posh for my accent, but good for an American."

We rounded the city corner. I watched him take in the surroundings. I'd never been to Nashville, but I couldn't imagine it being like Philly. I'm sure he wanted to see something nicer than a few boarded up houses and mini marts.

"Let's go left up here," I said. "We aren't in the best area for sightseeing, but there are some more romantic streets over that way."

"Ro ... mantic?" He nudged me with his elbow, and I'm sure he intended to aim for my arm, but instead he jabbed my boob. "I am so ... what I ... oh, what a daft cow. I'm sorry."

"Daft cow?" I laughed. "It's fine. Not much here to fondle anyway."

"There's enough."

I pretended not to hear that. "So ... I meant romantic as in beautiful, lovely, pleasant. I'm not completely anti-romance, you know."

"But you're a little anti-romance? Parents divorced?"

"Not in the slightest. Their love story is too sappy for the cheesiest of Hollywood."

"That must be nice." He shoved his hands into his pockets. "My parents are divorced. Happily so. It's a bit awkward, but they parted on fairly civil terms."

"You'd think it would be nice to have cheesy parents who haven't released the honeymoon stage yet, but it's overwhelming. They named me after Jane Austen because they fell in love in high school when they were partners for a *Pride and Prejudice* reading project or something. Everything since then has been perfect for them. They never fight. They always stare dreamily into each other's eyes while I'm trying to get through breakfast. And the worst part is they gave me this ridiculous name."

"At least it's authentic cheese and not that artificial stuff."

I laughed. "What?"

"Your parents. Better to have real cheese than fake cheese." His left foot stepped forward in line with mine, then the right. "It's not that bad, anyway. Your name."

"It's not so much the name as it is the expectations that come with it. Jane Austen, child of insanely intense romance gurus, destined to fall in love and live happily ever after, staring blindly into her husbands eyes every morning." He started to speak, but I had to finish with, "I'm not cynical."

"I feel the same actually."

"What?"

"There's too much emotionalism and sensationalism expected in relationships, so it sets a lot of people up for not having their happily ever after. Maybe for you, it's not worth it to try. I sometimes wonder that about myself."

"I didn't say that." *Did I?* "I'm not anti-love."

He raised his eyebrows.

"I'm really not. If it happens, it happens, but I don't like this pressure girls are given from the age of two to dress up like princesses and pine over a prince, only to grow up and date way too many guys or get depressed because they don't have a boyfriend. Life shouldn't revolve around romantic love. There are other kinds of love in life, but when you're name is freaking Jane Austen it becomes a joke, really. A lifelong joke that drives me nuts."

"Have anything positive to say on the matter?" He nudged me again, this time careful to hit my arm instead. "I'm kidding. I completely understand."

"No you don't."

"Sure I do. You think I've watched my parents fall apart only to walk away looking for the first girl I found?" He took his hands out of his pockets and his arm touched mine again. I didn't want to notice, but it took all I had to stop noticing. "There's a reason I'm not flirting with you."

"What's that supposed to mean?"

"You're obviously aware of your looks, or at least the several blokes who have been staring at you today, but you're also intelligent and unique. I can't say I've ever met a girl like you before."

"You're pretty interesting yourself."

We reached a nice block of houses with flowers and vines pouring from window planters. The sun painted the bricks a golden hue, as though it were already nearing sunset, but it couldn't had been that late already, could it?

He stopped walking and held my arm, securing us in a band of light that covered his fair skin with a hazel glow. Gazing down, I focused on the freckles dotting his hands. I couldn't look into his eyes. One, I feared he'd try to kiss me. And two, I worried I wouldn't stop him. Then that would lead to three, four, five, and so on of consequences I did not want right now.

Precautions. Not aversions.

He stepped back and stuffed his hands into his pockets again. Slightly relieved in a disappointment-tainted way, I finally allowed my eyes to settle on his. He stood completely still. Not even a hint of a smile toyed with his lips. Just ... stood there. Staring. At me.

If I stopped staring, I'd seem shy. And shy would seem interested. So I continued to stare without staring, if that makes sense. Instead of staring into him, like I assumed a lover would do, I stared through him like a laser beam passing through his eyes, in and out of his skull, and back out into the city street behind him. Yes, that worked. That erased any hint of interest. At least I thought so, until he stepped forward, hands still in his pockets, and said in a hushed voice, "I hope you don't mind. I only wanted to take a picture."

A picture without a camera. How clever. A picture with his mind.

His declaration splashed watercolors on the blank canvas I worked hard to maintain. Blank. I wanted blank. Now, I stared at my feet as the colors swished and curled around me, dying my tidy little world with its vibrant fever and pulling me into something unexplainable, something I couldn't control, something I didn't want as much as I wanted it.

He continued walking. It took me a second to gather the pieces of myself and catch up with him. I looked over my shoulder, back at the exact place on the sidewalk that he stopped me. The colors were already fading. Then a car sped by and the moment we had was lost in a cloud of exhaust. Lost forever.

The picture was only left in our minds.

The Big Day

HAD I REALLY GONE THE ENTIRE AFTERNOON without checking my phone even once? I shot everyone a quick *I?m sorry, I?m alive* text as the sun dropped behind the buildings, making its way toward the other side of the world. The side Donovan was still traveling to. I hoped everything would go well for him, but somehow doubted it. Online dating never seemed to work out the way it should. At least not in any cases I'd seen first hand. Although there was Molly, Autumn's older sister. Three years out of high school and desperate for love, she tried one of those dating sites, found the man of her dreams, and within months they already had a honeymoon baby on the way. Thankfully Autumn thought it was just as crazy as I did, even amidst her love for everything Nicholas Sparks and yes, Jane Austen. Shudder.

It's not that bad, really. *Sense and Sensibility* at least had some sense. Had Marianne wallowed in her tears or chased after Willoughby I may have taken away a star or two, but she married the Colonel and for that I am happy.

Alistair and I walked back to the car without talking. In between thoughts I'd listen to the sound of our feet tapping the sidewalk, the songs passing from open car windows, and the endearing tunes of the ice cream truck traveling to fingers that would soon be covered in sticky sugar.

Autumn texted me back: *What are you doing?? I thought we were meeting for dinner??*

I responded: *I'll be there soon. Got held up with something. Explain later.*

Then my brother texted: *OK, mom was worried cuz she didn't hear from you, see ya later, happy bday sis.*

I responded: *Thanks, be back later around 10 ... I'll text mom too.*

Alistair walked with his hands in his pockets almost the entire time. His hands seemed most relaxed there, but it left little room for his arm to sway into mine. Not that I wanted that or anything....

In only a few minutes we would be sitting in the car, driving to his hotel. We would say goodbye forever and I shouldn't have cared. I'd only known him, well, not even a full twenty-four hours and I had my ... precautions.

I'm only eighteen, I said inside. *It wouldn't be the right time anyway. Not for me.*

Yet, being with him made a hectic city feel peaceful. He was right. It was comfortable. And it seemed different than Donovan or Autumn. It wasn't just comfort. There was excitement bubbling under the satisfied stillness. It was there. I know he felt it too, but I couldn't lead him on.

"Deep in thought?' I said, interrupting the quiet air between us.

He kicked the ground as he took a step and brought his hands out of his pockets. "Do you ever feel like your life is passing and there's nothing you can do about it?" His hands made various motions as he talked, passionately. "I mean, here I am, I planned everything so precisely thinking, gee, perhaps life will be like this when I am in my twenties and here I am. It's nothing like I planned or imagined and sometimes I wonder if I'm being tricked into a bland life I never wanted."

I tried to understand, but he lost me. "Tricked?"

"Life feels fake sometimes, doesn't it? As though we're passing through without a choice in the matter."

"I don't think so. I mean, maybe it feels that way right now, but you have choices."

"Like I could choose to stop you right here on this sidewalk and kiss you until you can't breathe?"

I ran my hand through my hair, letting it drop into my face to hide my expression.

"Kidding," he said, laughing. "Well, sorta, you know."

We finally sat down in my car and my legs thanked me a hundred times. Did he really want to kiss me?

"What kind of music do you play?" I asked as I turned the car on.

"It's hard to classify." His tone suggested that he didn't want to talk about his band for some reason.

So, I shifted subjects. "What do you listen to?"

He jumped at the bait. "A lot, but mostly classic rock, blues, that sorta thing."

That fit him.

"I've pulled the hotel address up on my phone here," he said. "I'll tell you where to turn."

"I'll just head back toward the airport and you tell me when it says to do something different. I think I remember where it is."

"It's been nice." He turned his face toward the window. "A bit strange, I suppose, but it has been nice, hasn't it? Today, I mean."

"Strange and nice about covers it."

I stopped at a red light and danced my fingers along the steering wheel. He took my hand into his and pulled me toward him.

"Jane, I'm sorry, but I really do want to kiss you right now."

I pulled back and exhaled when I saw the light turn green. Foot on the pedal, I accelerated the car and tried to slow down my pulse. I would not, could not, kiss him.

Dr. Suess, anyone?

Eyes on the road, I felt his gaze burning a hole into my head, but it most certainly would not burn a hole into my heart. Trees on the side of the road, fading sun to my right, two solid yellow lines—*focus, Jane, focus.*

"I'm not asking to be your boyfriend. Just a kiss, like the others." He rubbed his legs and looked from the window back to me. "I know it can't work, but I ... I don't know ... do you know what I mean?"

"Alistair." I shook my head. "It's not you. I know you're not some whacko trying to get in my pants. I guess there's always that chance, I mean, I don't know you very well. You could be a whacko and I really hope not, but I'm ... I can't kiss you."

"It's trousers."

"What?"

"I believe you meant trousers, not pants. Although you could very well mean pants too." He stopped and looked at me. "I'm not in love with you."

I laughed.

He smiled. "There's something between us though. I know you feel it."

"It's not real, Alistair. It's just our emotions eating us alive. British boy and American girl meet in an airport, spend the day together, and by the end of the day they've fallen in love." I glanced at him, expecting a smile but he looked as serious as possible. "It has all the necessary elements of a sweeping romance, but it's our emotions. It can't be anything more. It's not possible to fall for someone when you've only just met."

"A relationship has to start somewhere," he said and pointed. "Turn there. Not saying this should be a relationship, but it's something, don't you think? There's something here."

"What's the point?" I nodded toward the road. "Which way do I go?"

"Left and then it's there on the right. Days Inn." He ran his hand along the open window. "What's the point in anything?"

I laughed. "That's vague."

"The point is I want to kiss you. You said we have a choice. Well, I'm making a choice for once. A choice for myself. I may not love you or know you inside and out, but when I watch your lips move I want to kiss you. What would it hurt?"

"It's weird."

He laughed. "It is a bit queer, that's true." He repositioned in the seat and unbuckled himself. "Still doesn't change the fact that I want to kiss you before I leave. I won't ever see you again and the least I could give you for your birthday is the best kiss you've ever had in your life."

I shot a stunned look at him only to find him leaning toward me with exaggerated and dorky puckered lips. Laughing, I parked the car and left it on. Tchaikovsky's *1812 Overture* with full cannons played quietly in the background. I bet he didn't notice, but I did. Quite dramatic for the moment, but I thought it was funny so I left it on.

I glanced in the backseat at the box Donovan gave me. The box that would explain one of the many reasons why I am the way I am. Why I developed my precautions. I couldn't wait to go home and open it, as much as it scared me, but for now I needed to send off a sweet boy without the kiss he so wanted.

The kiss I half wanted.

"One minute," he said, pulling out a scrap of paper, tearing it in half, and grabbing a pen. He cupped his hand over the words and wrote something way too long to be a phone number, email address, or even mailing address.

Intrigued, I tried to peek, but he glanced at me, pretending to be agitated but failing. He leaned back against the door so that I couldn't possible see what he wrote on the paper hidden by his hand. I tried and he flashed me a few grins. He obviously liked tormenting me with his mysterious ways. Finally, he finished writing and ran his fingers through his hair and ... okay, maybe I sixty-five percent wanted to kiss him.

The distance tempted me. No last names, phone numbers, or addresses. No strings. No attachments. No arguments and jealousy and break ups.

Just a kiss. A once and done kiss.

Couldn't hurt, right?

"You're thinking about it," he said. "I can tell. My winsome accent has won you over."

"Right." I laughed. "Winsome, all right. Speaking of accents, what do British people think of American accents?"

"Everyone always asks this."

"And?"

"We don't think about it the same way American's do." He held my hand again. "So..."

"This is so strange! I can't kiss you when you ask. It's weird, awkward ... queer."

He smiled. "You really don't want to?"

"I do and I don't."

He inched toward me until his breath touched my neck. Funny how warmth can send chills down your body. I closed my eyes, allowing the heated shivers to cover me. His breath smelled like spearmint and if he moved closer to my lips I wouldn't be able to deny tasting him.

I opened my eyes as he kissed my cheek.

"Was that okay?" he said.

I nodded, now eighty-nine percent wanting his kiss.

"Well." He opened the door and swung one leg out. "Thank you for entertaining me today. It's been a day of all sorts, and you've made it a bit less dreadful." He swung the other leg out. "And happy birthday."

The cannons erupted at the end of *1812 Overture* and I nearly jumped out of my seat. Hilarious timing. A quizzical look appeared in his eyes as the end of the song burst forth. I shrugged. He smiled and stood outside of the car.

I liked that he didn't force himself on me. And I liked that he didn't give me his phone number or email address or even try to draw out the conversation to stay in my car longer. I liked it so much I wanted him to stay.

"Thank you," I said as he shut the door.

He leaned into the window, smiled, and held my gaze for what felt like minutes. Then he tapped the door and walked away, disappearing behind glass doors without so much as a nod back in my direction. His hands-in-the-pocket stride carried him out of sight. Out of my life.

My pulse should have slowed, but it quickened again.

And so that's it....

I almost—not quite almost, but *almost* almost—went after him for that kiss, but More Reasonable Me said, "No, let it go. It was nothing more than an interesting afternoon and now it's time to go back to normal life."

"Yes," Less Reasonable Me said. "But?"

I shifted the car into drive and noticed a ripped paper on the passenger's seat. I turned it over, pulled off a mint candy taped to the paper, then read:

*If we are meant to kiss one day, let's call it The Big Day, then we will meet again. This day, May 17th, four years from now. **The Big Day**. You'll be 21 then. That should be enough time to consider a kiss, yes? If you are willing and we are both as single as we are now, I will be at the airport on May 17th, your 21st birthday, and you will be there too, and I will kiss you like I want to right now.*

Let's see where life takes us...

Till then, Alistair Anonymous

I glanced back at the glass doors, hoping to see him standing there, but he was gone and you know, I kind of liked it. Autumn and Donovan would never believe me. I'm not sure I even believed it myself. Did I really spend an afternoon with someone I just met?

I drove away, smiling as *1812 Overture* ended with full-bodied emotion.

Yes, four years. That was plenty of time to consider falling in love. And I would ... I would at least consider it before The Big Day.

THE BEST OF FOOLS

MARILYN GREY

Chapter 1

I STARED AT THE BOX ON MY BED. DONOVAN GAVE IT TO ME two days ago and I still didn't have it in me to open it, so I found a good hiding place in my closet and tucked it away. Then, on days like today, I'd stare at it and wonder. Maybe after graduation I'd open it. Only a few more weeks. Donovan could come over and be with me just in case it dredged up old memories I didn't know how to process.

Autumn knocked on the door and walked into my bedroom. "Heard from Don?"

"He emailed." I plopped on to my bed. "So far, so good. He said she's wonderful."

"Still can't believe you're letting him do this."

"Me? Letting him?" I laughed. "I told you, Autumn, I don't know … fifty seven times now … I am not in love with Donovan."

She tapped a picture of Donovan that I had taped to my mirror. "You guys are perfect for each other. I don't get it."

She continued looking at all of my photographs. Autumn and I had only been friends since junior year. She transferred to our school from Mt. Claymont, some private school up north, when her dad got a new job down here. Her guidance counselor, who happened to be mine as well, assigned me to be her "Welcome Buddy." We still joke about the title today. Instant friends, though. Just like Donovan and

47

I eleven years earlier. Just like Alistair and I two days ago. Alistair Anonymous. Would I see him again?

Probably not. Life changes too much in four years. He'd probably forget anyway.

"Daydreaming about your British lover again?" She tapped the note I taped to my mirror, then double-looked. "Um, did you realize he put the wrong date?"

I walked over to her. "What?"

She pointed. "He said four years when you're twenty one. You'll be twenty two then."

"So did he mean four years or my twenty first birthday?"

"What if you pick the wrong day?"

I laughed. "It was a fun day, but not the best day of my life. I don't plan on actually showing up."

"You could always show up both years."

I shook my head. "Oh, right. That's so like me."

"I could show up for you."

"Go right ahead." I smiled and grabbed my purse from my dresser. "Let's go."

"You were dreaming of him, weren't you?" She poked my shoulder. "You didn't deny it."

"I wasn't dreaming of Alistair."

She let out a fake laugh. "Right."

My brother popped out of his room before we reached the stairs. Figured he would. He had a thing for Autumn and really, who wouldn't? Long, soft blonde hair that always seemed perfectly in place, topped off with completely unique and bright, bright green eyes, like emerald or something. She'd look amazing in a trash bag.

"Where you guys going?" Eddie—yes, after Edward from *Sense and Sensibility*—said. "Can I come?"

Autumn smiled. "Just going to the craft store so your old lady sister can get some more yarn for her knitting projects."

I lightly backhanded her arm. "I'll convert you to a knitter one day and you know it. You can come if you want, Ed."

Poor sixteen-year-old and heavily hormonal Eddie looked utterly confused. Craft store. Autumn. Tough decision.

"You coming back after?" he said.

I nodded.

"I'll see ya then." He disappeared into his room and Autumn and I walked out to the car.

"That's so cute," she said.

"Don't get any ideas."

"He's like two inches shorter than me."

"So are most guys."

"True, but he's a sophomore. I'd never...."

"Never say never. I spent my birthday with??

"Amorous Alistair."

I laughed and opened the car door. "Exactly."

AUTUMN WASN'T INTO KNITTING OR SEWING OR ANYTHING crafty, but she suffered through my hour long journeys as I perused every aisle of JoAnn Fabrics. That's what friends are for.

I ran my fingers along a beautiful chiffon fabric and pondered using it for my prom dress, which I so predictably waited until the last minute to make.

"Not that one." Oh, Autumn. Reading my mind again.

"You sure you don't want me to make yours too?"

She shook her head. "I love your work and totally trust you for my wedding dress one day, but I already found the perfect dress."

"Can't wait to see it." I thumbed through a few more colors of possibility. "What color did you get? At least tell me that."

"Red. Deep red."

"That's going to look amazing on you."

She ignored the compliment as usual and stopped in front of a gorgeous green fabric, nearly the color of her eyes.

"Ooh!" I jumped in front of her and pulled the Emerald City sparkly fabric out, standing it between us. "This is it. This is totally one-hundred percent the one."

"No," she said. "It's pretty, but we'll be like a Christmas tree. If you're going to be my date there's no way I'm showing up looking like we belong at the North Pole."

I laughed. "That's hilarious. Good call. Hmmm..."

"How about this?" She pulled out a sparkly ivory chiffon. "Red and ivory would go well together."

I scrunched my face and slipped it back to the shelf.

"Black? Gray? Blue? Purple?"

"Gray could be interesting." I found a nice one and pulled it out, imagining what I'd create. "Yeah. I think I could do something cool with this. Just need a little white, black, and maybe a dash of red to match yours."

"I can't believe we're going to prom together." She smiled. "Not exactly the way I imagined it."

"It's not like you didn't have other options."

"Eh. I won't see any of those guys ten years from now. It's a special night. I know we'll always be friends and I'd rather remember having fun with you."

"I so love you."

I stuffed the fabric under my arm and perused the aisles for the other things I needed. Autumn followed, looking deep in thought. I knew what she was thinking, but didn't want to bring it up. I'm a huge fan of not poking and prodding people. They'll open up when they're ready as long as you're there with open arms.

My phone beeped. I pulled it out of my purse and opened the new email from Donovan.

Hey Jazz,

Hope everything is well there. Maria and I are having an amazing time. I can't believe how much we've hit it off. I'm actually looking at colleges here now. I think she might be the one, Jazzy.... I'll be home tomorrow. See ya at the airport. Love you... Donovan

"What was that?" Autumn said.

I reread the email and lingered on that line. The line. She might be the one.

"What's wrong?" she said.

"What?" I slipped my phone back into my bag. "Nothing's wrong."

"I may have only known you a year, but you know you are my best friend and I can definitely tell something's wrong."

I grabbed the black fabric I wanted. "Nothing important."

Chapter 2

SATURDAY MORNING I FUMBLED OUT OF BED AND WENT
back to the airport to get Donovan. I'd be lying if I said I didn't look
around, wondering if Alistair was somehow still there. The memory
of him hadn't left me, but it felt too unrealistic to be real. It reminded
me of the guys you meet at the beach, kiss once under the stars, then
say goodbye to and never see them again. So fun, but so important
that you forget their name by the next summer.

"Guess who.? Donovan's hands covered my eyes.

I turned and hugged him as tight as possible.

"Miss me much?"

I squeezed harder. "That answer your question?"

He laughed. "Let me see the tattoo."

I revealed my arm.

"Nice."

"You like?"

He nodded. "Of course I do. It's part of you."

"Well, technically it's not part of me. Just ink inside of me. Kinda
creepy now that I think of it that way."

He smiled. "Let's go. We have a lot of catching up to do and I'm
starving."

"Starvin' Marvin."

He laughed. "Your old nickname."

"I didn't realize at the time what a disastrous thing it would be to wear that Marvin the Martian shirt."

We laughed.

"Yeah, and I rescued you from ridicule," he said. "I can't remember how though."

"Neither can I. So funny though. I was mortified."

"Yeah, but look what those things did to you. Now you're turning into a woman who doesn't need the world's approval to be who she wants to be."

"I hope so." I wanted to tell him that I looked for his approval, but suddenly I felt weird.

We got in my car and drove to Wendy's. His request. Then ate in the car as we drove back home. We didn't talk much for a while, then he randomly said, "So, tell me about your British lover, Jane Austen."

"Don't even." I threw my empty sandwich wrapper in his face as I stopped at a red light.

He threw it back.

A few minutes later I parked in his driveway. He grabbed the strap of his bags and looked at the house.

"I'm exhausted, Jazzy." He looked at me.

Why did my heart just stop beating for a second? Why did his eyes—out of nowhere—look ten times more amazing, like pools I wanted to jump into and explore. "Don't go home," I wanted to say. It felt like forever since we talked. Really talked. Plus, the box. I wanted to open it with him beside me.

"Want to go catch the sky?" he said. "Let me just go put my bags inside."

I laughed. "I never said yes. Won't it be a little weird now? I mean, aren't you taken now?"

"No." He looked down. "More on that later."

I followed him inside. Alyssa ran and jumped into his arms. He twirled her around as she buried her head in his neck and cried happy tears.

"Oh, come on, Lyssa. It wasn't that long." He set her down and she hugged his legs.

"Look who's back.? Mr. Slovak hugged Donovan, then turned to me. "And you too." My body disappeared in his bear arms. "You two hungry? Mom's making your favorite dinner."

"We just ate," Don said. "But I think we're gonna go for a quick drive and by the time we're back I think we'll be ready for that dinner."

I nodded.

Mrs. Slovak entered the living room as she wiped her hands on her "Kiss Me or Don't Eat" apron.

"Son," she said. "So glad you're back. Hi, Jane. How's your family doing? I heard your dad got a new job."

"It's not official yet."

She looked at Mr. Slovak. "We'll have to get together for dinner soon." She waved us away. "Go on and have fun for a bit while I finish up."

Donovan disappeared upstairs and jogged back down with a huge smile on his face. He was ten seconds from teasing me about my British lover boy. I just knew it.

We plopped back into the car when he finally made my guess a reality.

"So, when will you be moving to your English cottage with

Alistair?" he said with his best English accent. Pretty much the worst version you'd ever hear.

I elbowed him. "Drop it."

He shrugged. "You aren't going to go back to the airport, are you?"

"Doubtful. He got the year wrong anyway. Said four years when I turn twenty one, but I'll be twenty two in four years."

"I don't like math either."

I stopped at the stop sign. "Usual place for sky catching?"

"You bring the box?" he said.

"No. Did you want me to?"

"Well, I want you to open it before we die."

I laughed and accelerated. "Guess it's the usual place, then."

We arrived after a short drive. I parked and met Donovan on the hood of my car. We reclined and watched the clouds stretch into long streaks across the blue background.

"You know," he said.

"Uh oh. A Donovan lecture is coming. Let me hide!"

He laughed. "Just saying one day you'll need to stop avoiding everything."

"Maybe tomorrow." I flashed him a smile.

He smiled back.

"So what happened with what's her name?" I said.

"Glad what's her name made such an impression that you remember her name so clearly."

"Hey, it's not like I met her!"

"Yeah, yeah. Everything was perfect until I was saying goodbye. She got real serious and told me it wouldn't work. She hates long distance. I was willing to move there, but I don't know. I get the feeling she still loves her ex."

"But then why..." I cut myself off and tousled his hair. "It'll be okay. Plenty of girls would love to be yours, Don."

"I don't want just anyone." He put his arms behind his head. "We're young. Plenty of time to figure things out. I had a great time though and it did help me figure out what I want in a woman."

I swallowed. Why was my mouth dry all of a sudden? "And what would that be?"

He tapped the roof of the car. "Can you believe we still come here as adults?"

"That's right, we're adults now. Eighteen. Wow. I feel like a kid still."

"I hope you always do." He pulled my wrist. "Come.?

Why did I suddenly feel trapped in a movie of my own life? Reeling on by as I watched from the couch.

He wrapped his arm around me and pulled my head toward his chest. We were weird best friends who for years had odd platonic cuddle sessions. This one made me nervous though. Shy, even.

He held my head while I listened to his heartbeat. Then his breathing slowed. I watched my hand rise and fall on his chest until he did his twitchy thing. That's how I knew he was either asleep or very close to it. He fell asleep so fast. It always took me way longer.

He jerked and woke himself up.

"Whoa," I said. "You okay?"

"Plane was falling."

I laughed. "Do you think it's weird that we do this?"

"Do you?"

"I asked first."

He laughed, bobbing my head with his chest. "I don't know. I guess it could be to some people, but we've been doing this for years."

I perched myself on one arm and stared at him. He looked back. We were so comfortable together, even inches from each other's lips. But since my day with Alistair something changed. Something in me. Maybe my hormones were reawakened.

Just fantastic.

"You aren't in love with me?" I said. "Seriously. Are you?"

He looked at me for a few seconds, calculating his response, then finally said, "Do you want me to be?"

I slapped his arm and sat up.

"What?" He sat beside me and pulled his knees to his chest, then hung his arms over them. "What's the right answer? Does Jane Austen want me to fall in love with her?"

"You are so annoying." I shook my head. "No, she doesn't. I just wonder how we can do this year after year, in between your girlfriends, and not have feelings for each other. It is kinda weird, isn't it?"

"I'm not complaining." He pulled me toward him. "I love you. Our friendship might be a little strange, but it works for us."

"You don't get the slightest bit turned on when you're here with me?"

He laughed.

"What?"

He shook it off and changed the subject, "You're in a bizarre mood."

"Are you saying I'm not attractive to you?" I teased.

"You're pretty much the opposite of beautiful."

I laughed. "I don't know. This Alistair thing has me screwed up. I mean, I felt things. His arm brushed mine and I felt things. When he walked away I almost went after him. Seriously, Donovan. This is sickening."

"Normal."

"Sickening."

"Normal. Welcome to the world of normal people with normal feelings."

"I don't want to be welcomed. Take me back to my world of abnormal feelings."

"Want to go get the box and open it?"

OH, THERE THEY GO AGAIN.

Donovan and I walked into my house to find my parents gazing into each other's eyes in the living room. Maybe even doing some kind of slow dance to music only they could hear.

"Hello," I chimed in. "Other people exist in the world."

They laughed and turned to us while holding hands.

"Oh, Donovan," Mom said. "You're back. How was your trip?"

He leaned back on his heels. "It was good, thanks."

"Missed you around here, son," Dad said. "I had a project and could've really used the extra hands."

"Oh yeah? What project?"

Mom interrupted, "It's a surprise for Janie."

"Mom, don't call me Janie."

She laughed. "You're still my baby Janie."

"Okay, okay," I said, walking toward the stairs. "Come on,

Donovan, before they brainwash you and sweep you into a BBC film."

They all laughed. Donovan followed me to my room and sat on the bed. I pulled the box out of my closest and sat beside him, staring at the ... the thing in my lap.

He glanced at the box, then me, then the box, me, the box. "Want me to open it for you?"

I waved his hand away and opened the top. Then stared at it. And ... stared some more.

"Uh." He reached for it. "Let me handle this for you."

I swatted his hand. "Patience, my friend. Patience."

I stared.

"You're kidding, right?" He reclined on my bed. "I'll just take a nap. Wake me next month when this is finished."

"Do you ever feel like you're in a glass box?" I ran my finger along the inside and lifted the hidden compartment. "There on the other side is everything you want and it seems so easy to touch, but when you reach out with a smile on your face, ready to wrap your fingers around it ... you hit glass. "

He sat up and looked at me, but I didn't look up, only felt his eyes on me as he cleared his throat and said, "What are you reaching for?"

I shook my head, not wanting to tell him. Or myself. I didn't want to admit what my dreams were. They seemed so childish. So stupid in a world full of starving families and destitution beyond my wildest imagination.

My dreams were petty. And I knew that. Which is why I shoved them in the box and buried them years ago.

I flipped it open and took a deep breath.

Donovan peeked inside. "It's ... a paper? A note of some kind?"

I lifted it in my hand. The paper shook like the last fall leaf on a sleepy tree. I fanned myself with it, inhaled again, then handed it to Donovan.

"You want me??

I nodded.

"Okay."

The paper crinkled as it unfolded and the Polaroid slipped out on to his lap. I looked away, embarrassed to even have it. What would Mom and Dad think?

Mom and Dad.

Donovan lifted the photograph and turned it to the back side. No writing.

"She looks like you," he said. "What is it?"

He looked over the paper for some kind of hidden note, but there wasn't a note. Just the picture. The picture I buried, but never forgot.

"It's my mother," I said, finally exhaling.

"Your...."

I pat his knee. "Yup."

This is the point where Autumn would ask for every last detail in the known universe. She'd stop at nothing and ask questions I never knew the answer to and probably never would. And she'd try to convince me that I knew, somewhere deep inside, if only I just thought harder. For her sake, you know, because she liked stories and she liked to turn everyone around her into one.

But honestly, I didn't always know.

And sometimes what you need isn't a friend who wants details, but a friend who sits there, in the opaque silence, listening to you breath while feeling—yes, feeling so deeply and so intensely—every last good or bad emotion coursing through your mind and heart.

That is why Donovan would forever be my best friend. That is why I wanted him there when I saw the picture for the first time in over a decade.

He set it on my lap and I touched her face, then my eyes rested on her stomach. My first home. The place where it all began.

No matter how many times I played the situation over in my head. The fifty thousand possible scenarios that could have been the story of *why*. Why? Why didn't she want me?

"See, Don," I said shyly. "I'm not really Jane Austen anyway."

Chapter 3

AUTUMN AND DONOVAN SAT NEXT TO EACH OTHER IN Honors English and I sat right behind them, next to Joey, our ultra strange class clown. I secretly hated sitting next to him because he would randomly stand on his chair and blurt out weird random movie quotes no one could figure out. Not that I cared much about that, but he did it so fast that he'd jerk my desk and I'd end up with a huge line of ink down my paper or a notebook with the rings popped open as it hit the floor. Not really my idea of funny, but the guy had some kind of major ADHD going on and I kinda felt bad for him so I'd laugh even if it wasn't funny.

Like, oh I don't know, right now as he jumped on top of his desk and yelled, "Badges? We ain't got no badges! We don't need no badges! I don't have to show you any stinking badges."

I held my desk in place as Mr. Granger lowered his glasses and huffed.

"Joe, please have a seat."

Joey took a bow and landed back in his chair.

Yes, my friends, this is Honors English I'm talking about.

Donovan slipped me a note. I pulled my notebook onto my lap and propped it against the desk, unfolded the note, and smoothed it over top of my notes from class.

TWO THINGS, well, make that three actually.

1.) Ready for finals tomorrow?

2.) Go to prom with me?

3.) Busy tonight? I have an idea.

I wrote back:

1.) Ready as I'll ever be.

2.) I'm going with Autumn. You don't have a date??

3.) Meet me at the ice cream place. 5pm.

I tapped his shoulder and his hand twisted behind his back, grabbed the note, and disappeared. A few seconds later he handed it back.

No date. Guess I need to find one. Any ideas? Ice cream place it is.

The bell rang. Everyone stood as Mr. Granger tried to speak above the squeaking chairs and yapping faces. Not a clue what he said. Something about tomorrow's finals that I dreaded.

Donovan had taken off and vanished. His next class was at the complete opposite end of the school, three floors up, and being the good boy that he is ... he just couldn't be late. So Autumn and I walked to our next class together. She had Psych in the same wing that I had theatre. Worked out well. She went on about prom dresses and prom song and prom prom prom.

"Glorified homecoming." I popped her bubble. "Chill out. It's not that special."

"It is though, if you want it to be."

"Eh."

She shook her head. "And the award for most cynical of all goes to...."

"Funny." I laughed. "Does one need to have an affinity toward dancing to be considered optimistic?"

She smiled. "Nice come-back."

I stopped at the door to the theatre. "I'll see you tomorrow. Mr. McShea wants me to stay after class today for some reason so I won't be out right away."

"Kay. Love you. Text me."

"Will do."

OH. MY. DELIGHTS.

The ice cream melting in my mouth and running down my fingers could not have been more amazing. I mean, imagine the deepest, richest, creamiest chocolate you've ever had in your life, times that by, oh, about seventy million, then top it off with swirls of crispy caramel bits. Heavenly delightful mess.

"I have never in my life seen a girl your age eat ice cream like a two-year-old," Donovan licked the peach ice cream as it dripped down his pretzel cone. "And I mean that as a compliment."

I smiled and licked my fingers. "So. Good. How's yours?"

"I'm guessing not as good as yours." He handed me a napkin. "So, I've been thinking."

"Ladies and gents, he's been thinking!" I held my finger in the air and laughed.

"It's miraculous, I know." He shoved my finger back to the table. "How about we take a road trip this summer? I was thinking, if you're up for it, we could try to meet your, um, your biological mother." He crunched into his cone and watched me for a response, but I didn't give one. "So...?"

"I don't know, Don. Really? Is that a good idea?"

"Why not? You obviously still think about it. I don't know what you're thinking or feeling, but you have to be curious. It couldn't hurt, could it?"

I wiped my face. "That's just the thing ... it could hurt a lot."

"It could." He crunched again. "But it also could hurt to never try."

"Ladies and gents." I held up my finger. "He has a point!"

He laughed. "You and that finger pointing."

I finished the last of my waffle cone and wiped my face. "Did I get it all off?"

He shook his head and dabbed my chin with his napkin. "There."

"How would we find her anyway?"

"Well, you probably need to ask your parents what her name was. From there it should be easy, especially if they know which state she lives in."

"I can't ask my parents. No way."

"How else will you find her name?"

"I won't." I picked apart a sugar packet. "My parents have never talked to me about her. There's no way I'm bringing it up."

"Never?"

"Never."

"How'd you find out?"

"Overheard them talking one night when they thought I was sleeping."

"But the picture...."

"Found it in a box in the basement that was stuffed with baby clothes and toys. I'm not even sure it's her, but I look a lot like her so I just assumed. Kept it tucked away in my room for years after that. At first I hid it under a corner where the carpet came up from the floor a little. When I got older I wanted to stop obsessing over it, so I buried it in that box."

"And then tried to dig up the entire woods in an effort to find it again?"

"Thanks." I laughed. "I guess there's still a part of me that wants to know. It's weird."

"Normal."

"Find a date to prom?"

"I think I'm going to stay home. What's the point?"

"Don't say that around Autumn."

"Yeah, she's freakishly into the whole thing."

"She has more friends than we do. Probably counts for something."

"Hey, speak for yourself. I have plenty of friends."

DONOVAN OFFERED TO COME OVER ON SATURDAY TO BE there when I asked my parents about ... my parents, but I told him I'd rather be alone. So alone I was, and kinda regretting it, as I approached Mom in the kitchen. She finished drying a dish with a towel, set it in the cabinet, and turned to me. With that look.

"How do you always know when something's wrong?" I tried to smile.

"I wouldn't say that," she said. "Something isn't wrong right now, it's just not right."

"Yes, and it's even weirder that you know that."

"Mother's intuition, I guess." She put her arm around me and led me to the table.

I sat. She sat next to me. And she waited.

Mother's intuition.

I cleared my throat. "Um...."

"What's bothering you, Jane?"

I slid the picture on to the table because I had no words to give. She touched it with the tip of her fingers, held my knee with her other hand, and looked at me. I stared at the table, but she pulled my chin up and forced me to look at her as her eyes reddened and tears pooled near her lashes. She blinked and one fell.

"I didn't mean to upset you. I found this a long time ago after I heard you and Dad talking about her."

She covered her mouth with her hand and leaned into it.

I squeezed my eyes shut and sighed. "I'm sorry. I should've left it alone."

"No, honey." She took my hand. "You have every right to ask and to know."

"Why didn't you guys tell me before then?"

"It's ... complicated. There's a lot to it and we wanted you to be old enough, but then time slipped through our fingers and I never knew what to say or how to say it."

"So, you're not my mom?"

Her shoulders lurched forward and she let out a soft whimper.

"I mean...." What did I mean?

I put my hand on her shoulder and she covered it with her own. Dad walked in, contorted his eyebrows, then caught the photo on the table. He knelt down between us, one hand on my back, the other on

Mom's thigh. Mom stared at him while sucking in her lips. I stared at both of them. Dad nodded his head and stared at the floor.

Can we say awkward?

"I'm sorry," I said. "I didn't mean to start something. I just wanted to know the truth about myself."

"The truth is you're our daughter. I've never thought any differently about it."

"But why was I adopted? Who was she?"

Mom squeezed my hand. "Honey, I know it's going to eat away at you until you know the details, but it's complicated. We don't know where she went."

"Why did you adopt me? Is Eddie adopted too? Can you have kids?"

Dad finally stood, then leaned against the kitchen counter. "We adopted you unexpectedly. The opportunity arose and we felt the need to take it, but yes, we can have children and Eddie is our biological child."

"So it's just me then."

"It's not just you," Dad said. "It's all four of us. We're a family, Jane. Whether or not you came out of Mom's womb or another woman's doesn't change the fact that she's your mother and I'm your father. Eddie is your brother. We're a family. There's more to it than blood."

"What's her name?"

Mom handed me the picture. "Her name is Julia. The last we knew she was living in Boston."

"How old is she?"

"Younger than us."

"Who's my da?I mean, who's my biological father?"

"We don't know."

I looked at Dad. He shook his head and shrugged.

"Does Julia even know the father?"

"I believe she does," Mom said, then pulled me into a hug. "I understand your need for answers and I'm here if you need anything."

"Does Eddie know?"

"No. We thought it would be best if you talked to him whenever you found out."

I pulled away from her hug. "You could've told me. Earlier, I mean. You know, save me from the emotional breakdown that happens when you find out you aren't who you think you are."

Dad laughed. "You always have been one to exaggerate. Even when you were a toddler."

"I'm serious. Not about the emotional breakdown, but I don't know who I am anymore."

"This doesn't change who you are, honey," Mom said. "Or who we are."

I knew that, in essence. My mind totally understood what she meant, but still. My heart couldn't come to terms with it. Was I always Jane Austen? Or did my parents change my name? Does my anti-sensationalism thing come from my other mom, since it obviously didn't come from my parents?

I wanted to know.

I excused myself from the table. As I started up the stairs I stopped and heard Mom say, "See."

See what? I wondered.

I sent a quick text to Donovan, asking him if he liked Boston. He shot a response back within seconds, *Boston it is!*

Chapter 4

I HELD THE RAILING AS I WALKED DOWN THE STAIRS. ONE of those typical prom moments, except I was walking down to Autumn who stood by the couch looking amazing. Then he appeared with a smile on his face, wearing a dirty Adidas t-shirt and shorts with holes in them.

I was most definitely not going to blush.

"Look at you," Donovan said. "Blushing and everything."

I touched my face as I stepped off the stairs and he pulled me into a hug. "You look incredible."

"So do you. Even a little sweat to compliment the outfit." I laughed. "And Autumn. Wow!"

She spun in a circle and Eddie's jaw pretty much attached itself to the floor. I walked over and lifted it back to his other lip. "Better watch that thing. Someone might trip."

Mom wrapped her arms around me and sniffed.

"Oh, no, not again," I teased, then turned to hug her. "No crying. It's just a dance."

"Soon you'll be married and have children and I'm just going to miss all of this." She held my shoulders and moved one of my stray hairs back into place. "You look beautiful."

Someone tapped my shoulder. I turned to Dad's glowing face. He pulled me into him and held me there longer than the others, then whispered, "I'm so proud of you. You look so pretty, darling, but what I'm more proud of is the beautiful woman you've become. I couldn't have asked for a better daughter."

"Thanks, Dad."

Mom took a few pictures of Autumn and I together by the fireplace mantle, then outside by the garden.

"Can I jump in?" Donovan asked. "I didn't get dressed up for nothing."

He stood between Autumn and I for a few pictures, then asked for a few with just me.

"Remember homecoming?" he said.

"Yeah. When you talked me into taking pictures with you on my back."

"Wanna try that now?"

"No. You'll break me in half now."

He laughed. "How about you jump on my back?"

"Are you guys done?" Mom said.

"One more, Mrs. Austen." He turned his back to me. "Come on. For the sake of old times and good memories."

"I'm in a dress."

"Oh, come on." He pretended to whine. "It won't hurt anything."

"Fine." I placed my hands on his shoulders and jumped up. He grabbed my legs and .... RIP!

"Donovan!" I yelled and slapped his shoulder. "I told you!"

He lowered me back to the ground.

"Um...." Autumn said. "Your dress is completely exposing your naughties now."

Donovan laughed. "Naughties?"

"Guys!" I snapped. "This isn't funny. I have nothing else to wear and I spent so much time working on this dress."

"Don't you have something somewhere?" Autumn whined. "We need to leave within thirty minutes or we'll be late. Can you fix it real quick on your sewing machine?"

"Seriously, Donovan. I told you!"

He looked at the back of my dress. "It's not that bad."

Mom put her arm around me. "Donovan, it's not gentlemanly to look."

Could this get any worse? "Okay. I'm going to try to fix this."

"Just put on something casual and I'll go with you like this."

Autumn laughed. "I'd love to see that."

"Then you won't have a date," I said.

"Nope, I'll have two dates."

Mom walked back inside.

"Come on," Donovan said. "We can be the weirdos of senior prom."

"Just what I always wanted, but you don't have a ticket."

"Yeah I do. I can get it before we go. I got two to have an extra if I found a date."

"You couldn't find a date?" Autumn said. "Why not?"

"Guess I forgot about it."

"What would you have me wear?" I said. "If I decide to be weird with you, that is."

"How about I wear the dress and you wear my clothes?"

"No way. Next choice."

"Okay. Let's dress like homeless people."

I laughed.

"Now, get your naughties in there and change before the wind gets frisky on you." He pushed me toward the door. "I'll go get ready too and be back to pick you ladies up within ten minutes."

"Well," Autumn said, "Things are always unusual when you two are involved."

DONOVAN DROVE TO THE BEAUTIFUL HOTEL IN DOWNTOWN Philly and pulled up in front near the valet parking sign. Autumn stepped out first and Donovan and I just looked at each other. Smile on his face, nervous twitch on mine. What was I *thinking*? It wasn't too late to turn around and go back home.

He wore an oversized sweater from the eighties. Complete with holes and stains he probably created before he left his house. His pants were equally as nice and his hat was a rather interesting multi-colored hat—ketchup stain prominently placed on the bill—with a spinning helicopter on top.

"Ready, gorgeous?" Donovan opened his door and stepped out, then walked to my side and opened. "Come on, dahling."

I took his hand and revealed my lovely outfit to the valet who seemed to get his words caught in his bow tie. He readjusted the bow, cocked his head, and took the keys from Donovan. What was probably more alarming than my oversized, sloppy clothing was the hair Donovan insisted on giving me. He teased my hair with a comb, sprinkled flour in it, then stuck a toy bird inside. It was funny, absolutely hilarious, until I stepped out of the car and got a few sideways-turned-full-on-awkward glances. At least I didn't have that many friends at school. I probably just solidified that even more. But that's okay, the few friends I did have would laugh their asses off. Donovan and I always managed to swim upstream and those close to us loved us for it.

We walked inside with Autumn and it took all I had not to laugh or turn red.

Donovan held my hand. "Be serious. Play the part."

A girl from history class stopped in her tracks. "Did you bring homeless people to prom?" She said to Autumn as her finger hovered in the air at us.

Autumn smiled. "Just doing my charitable duties."

I turned my face to hide my snicker.

"Man," Donovan grumbled like an old man. "Any food up in here? I'm steerved."

Autumn linked her arm with his. "Right this way, fine fella."

A group of classmates stared at us as we walked toward the steps. I thought I'd feel ridiculously stupid, but Donovan and Autumn made it so funny that I almost forgot I was part of the act.

"I don't even think they recognized us," I said.

"Think we'll be voted king and queen tonight?" Donovan said.

"Maybe." I scratched my head. Flour was getting to me. "We definitely have a good chance, I'd say."

"What would British lover boy think of you like this?" Autumn asked.

"Why do you guys call him that? He's not my lover boy."

"He'd like her best like this," Donovan said. "Especially the bird in her hair. That's mint."

I sighed. "This is never going to end, is it?"

We finally made it to the hall where our classmates gathered around tables. Some sat down already, but most people were still standing and talking. So many gorgeous girls with perfect hair and dresses and shoes. Autumn fit in. Donovan and I ... didn't.

So funny.

When we entered the room that became pretty obvious. About seventeen faces gawked at us, while seventy more whispered and laughed. Autumn held her head high and played the charitable card well as she introduced us to people who should've recognized us from class, but didn't. Until Zoe came over to us all hunched over and laughing so hard tears were pushing mascara down her face.

"You guys." She leaned into Donovan's chest and his arm wrapped around her. "What on earth are you doing?"

"We've come to eat," Donovan said. "What else?"

She laughed. "Come sit at my table. This is just too much."

We followed her to her table. Or Donovan did. Like a kid chasing a kite. Autumn and I lingered behind them and she elbowed me.

"Are they a thing?" she whispered.

"Doubt it. You know him. Flirt to the core. He likes attention from the ladies."

"One day that'll get him in trouble."

"Nah. I've never seen him flirt when he has a girlfriend. He's as faithful as they come."

"What about Alistair? He's willing to wait years. That takes the cake."

"He didn't say that. He said we'll see what happens and if we're both single we'll meet up. Key word: if."

"Well, we know you will be unless I get to you."

"I will be. No doubt about it. I'm not dating anyone until I'm twenty five."

"You're so weird, but I love you." She sat down and helped me sit beside her. "I so cannot wait to see you dance like that."

"Uh, this lady is off limits in the dance department."

"I'll talk you into it."

"I'd like to see that."

I LET HER THINK SHE TALKED ME INTO IT, BUT REALLY I FELT stupid sitting alone like a bum while all the pretty people danced the night away. For some odd reason I thought I'd blend in and feel better on the dance floor. Bad, bad, very bad thought. Wrong as I was, I had fun at the expense of everyone else's bewilderment.

A slow song started. Some popular new song I never heard before. Autumn and I danced together until the next song started. "I've Had the Time of My Life," from the *Dirty Dancing* soundtrack. I so badly wanted to stay for that song, but my bladder had other plans. Autumn stayed behind and continued dancing alone, but I knew within seconds some guy from some dark corner would come and snatch her up.

I jogged out of the hall and almost bumped into a couple kissing.

"Sorry," I said, then covered my mouth with my hand. "Oh, Donovan. I see you've been enjoying your night."

Zoe pulled his face back to her lips and I almost kept watching as a subtle pang of jealousy agitated me.

Nope.

Not going to be jealous. Especially of Donovan. Why would I be?

I didn't like him like that. We'd never work anyway.

By the time I got to the bathroom I had already come up with fifty-eight reasons why I was being crazy, but when I walked back to the hall and had to pass their make out session ... I realized I was crazy. I was. Because for the first time since forever, I couldn't stand seeing his hands in another girl's hair.

So being the strange-o that I am, I stared at them for a few seconds until Zoe stopped and peeked her head around his. He turned, then looked back at her. I don't know why I didn't take that as my cue to go back to being a normal person, but I didn't. I stared at them. Hands at my sides. Alone. My heart beat thumped slowly in my ears like a tender drum beat in the back of the orchestra and a lump formed in my throat. The kind you get right before a speech in front of a bazillion people. I swallowed.

She peeked around again and he turned, gave me a what-the-heck-are-you-doing kinda face, and turned back to her. She smiled and nodded and he walked over to me.

"Do you need something?" He pointed over his shoulder. "Cuz if not...."

"I'm okay." I walked around him and smiled at Zoe. "Take care of that boy. Hurt him and you die."

She blinked fast. "Um ... I ... okay."

"She's kidding," he said as his arm flipped over her shoulder.

"I am." I smiled and walked back into the hall. Autumn waved me over. The music couldn't have gotten anymore obnoxious. Whew. Something about kissing a girl. Seriously?

I didn't go back to her on the dance floor. Instead I sat down and took a drink of water. Alone.

Why did that word suddenly bother me more than ever before?

"Are you okay?" Autumn asked as she parked Donovan's car in front of her house.

"Yeah. Why?"

She unbuckled her belt. "Sure you don't want to come to the after party?"

I lowered my chin and gave her *that* look.

"Well, I'm going. You're just going to take Donovan's car back to your place, right?"

"Yeah. Why?"

"Just don't want you walking home alone in the middle of the night."

"Okay, Mommy." *Speaking of Mom....*

Would Zoe be coming to Boston too?

"I'll call you tomorrow," Autumn said.

"Kay."

"And maybe then you can tell me what's been bothering you."

"Kay."

She lunged toward me as she grabbed my arm. "Tell me now. What's going on? I can't go out when you're upset about something."

"Autumn, I'm fine."

"Fine. I get that. Fine. But there's a reason you're not more than fine and I want to know what it is."

Hanging from the rearview mirror was a necklace I gave Donovan when we were seven. He always kept in his room, dangling from the side of his bunk bed, then his desk, then inside his pillow case. Now he kept it in his car. I never asked why.

It swung there in the moonlight, glistening as it caught the head-lights of passing cars. I don't know why he loved that thing so much. It was just a toy necklace made of plastic. Easily replaceable.

"Um." I cleared my throat and looked at my lap. "It's weird. I don't know."

"Is it the Alistair thing?"

I almost laughed.

"Then something happened to you tonight?"

"It's not a big deal."

"I'm one of your best friends, Jane. I consider you my only sister. The sister I wished I always had. You mean the world to me and when something isn't right with you it isn't right with me, okay? It is a big deal. A huge deal. So what's going on?"

I rubbed my neck. "I love you."

"I love you too."

"Well, there's a few things. One, I was adopted. I've never met my real mother or father. I don't know why they gave me up and it sounds stupid of me, but it makes me question who I am. Am I really Jane Austen? I've never quite felt like I fit in with my family and I don't know ... I just feel weird about it, like I need to know the truth."

"Wow." She held my hand. "Are you going to find her?"

"Maybe. Donovan wants to help me."

"So that's what's been bothering you?"

"That's been on my mind a lot, yeah. But I guess what bothers me is being alone. Feeling alone. I don't think I want to fall in love or go hunt down Alistair, but I just feel alone and it's the first time I've felt that as a negative feeling. I don't know what's wrong with me."

"We all have our down moments. Don't beat yourself up about it."

"This isn't a down moment though. It's a complete questioning of everything I am and everything I want to be. We're eighteen now. It's time to start preparing?I mean, really preparing?for our future. I'm trying to figure out what that looks like for me."

"One day at a time. You majorly, majorly overthink things girl-friend."

"Understatement."

Chapter 5

DONOVAN WENT THROUGH GIRLFRIENDS LIKE LITTLE KIDS go through shoes, so when he'd say, "I really like this one," I rarely paid attention to him. The girl he traveled to see ... for a second I thought it would work out, but I should've known better. I had a love phobia as he called it, but he had a commitment one.

So when he tapped my hand after graduation and pointed to Zoe while saying, "I think she's it," I just smiled and said, "We'll see."

"No, really," he said. "I think I'm going to marry this one."

"And I said we shall see."

"You don't believe me."

"No."

He smiled. "I have a surprise for you."

I raised my eyebrows.

"It'll be ready after we get home from Boston."

"I still can't believe we are really doing this."

He waved to Zoe. She lit up.

"Such a ladies man," I joked.

"Effortlessly."

I shook my head and pushed him toward her. "Go get your girl, I need to find my parents. I think they brought Granny."

"Give her a hug for me."

"Come over and give her one yourself."

"I just might."

Head held a little too high, he walked back to Zoe and lifted her up in his arms. She wrapped her arms around his neck and kissed him like something out of a chick flick. I never thought I could be that girl, and maybe I still couldn't, but since Alistair things had changed. Suddenly I'd picture myself as the girl wrapping her love around a guy, kissing him until the sun went down.

I wondered how he was doing as I spotted my family in the hallway. They waved me over. Granny's smile couldn't have been any more enormous. I walked toward them as I thought of Alistair, wondering what he was doing, if he was happy, if he found someone else.

Three years—or four, whichever he intended—was a long time. There was no way he'd still be single and wondering about me. Better chance of me enjoying *Fifty Shades of Gray*.

Granny pinched my cheeks and pulled me into her shaky arms. Her glasses fell to the tip of her nose as she wiped a tear and forced my head to her shoulder.

"I love you," I whispered.

"Oh, honey," she whispered back. "I'm so proud of you."

Mom and Dad cut in and gave me warm hugs too, then went back to holding hands and staring into each other's eyes. They seriously reminded me of a couple in their early puppy love days. How could I ever compare with that?

Mom never told me I needed to find what they had. And as much as she loved everything about love, she never pressured me.

But the name. The name pressured me enough. I don't even know why. It was just a name.

Eddie gave me an awkward pat on the back and said, "Good job, sis."

I forced him into a hug and kissed his cheek. "Thanks, bro."

He wiped his face and darted his eyes around, probably making sure no one saw him get kissed by his big sister. Eddie was undoubtedly the shyest person I had ever known. Getting a word out of him or some kind of expression of life was an extremely difficult task. He tried, but he'd fumble over words until his eventual moment of defeat where he'd stare at his shoes, chew the inside of his cheek, and kick the ground.

Kinda like now.

"Ready to go home?" Dad said. "We have a surprise for you."

I looked around the school hallway one last time. So many memories. First day of school. First kiss in the stairwell by the left wing. First detention for passing a note to Autumn after being reprimanded three times. Or maybe it was because she forgot to study and the note had all of the answers to our quiz. Lots of firsts. Lots of lasts. These halls would one day be a distant memory and although I thought I was elated to strut outta that place, it left a bittersweet taste in my mouth.

I followed my family out to the parking lot and piled into the backseat of the car. Eddie and Mom sat beside me. Granny sat up front with Dad. Lots of small talk until we pulled up at home and went inside. Knowing Mom, I expected streamers and cake and food. So I was pretty surprised to find the house just as it was when we left.

"Take a seat on the couch," Dad said. "I'll be right back."

Granny sat beside me and held my hand. Eddie stared at his phone while reclining on the other couch.

Mom stood next to me. "We didn't make a big deal out of this with a party and everything because we know how much you don't like all the attention, but we have something for you."

Dad came back into the room with an envelope and a smile. He handed it to me and everyone watched as I peeled back the flap and slipped my hand inside. I pulled out a card. A handmade card. Mom's handwriting on the front said: *Because we love you.*

I opened it up and read:

More than you know. We saved this money since you were a baby. Buy a new car, an apartment, a college tuition, or save it! It's up to you to use it however you see fit as you embark on the next chapter of your life.

We love you,

Mom & Dad

I turned the check over and gasped, nearly falling out of my seat. Everyone smiled when I looked at them, except Eddie who was completely oblivious.

"I can't take this much," I said, still in shock. "It's too much. Don't you guys need it?"

Dad laughed. "It's yours, sweetheart. We saved a little with each paycheck for you and your brother. Ninety dollars a month for eighteen years is two-hundred and sixteen months of saving. We wanted you to choose what you'd like to do with the next few years of your life and to have the money to begin on the right foot. Now it's up to you to plan the next steps."

"Or I could blow it all on clothes."

"Oh, Jane," Mom said as though she believed me.

"I'm kidding." I stood and hugged them both. "I have no idea what to say. I'm still in shock."

Dad chuckled. "Now, no special party here today, but we have dinner planned. Do you want to invite Autumn or Donovan over?"

"I would, but they're busy."

They walked away smiling at each other while Granny watched me stare at the check on my lap. A million possibilities ran through my mind. I still couldn't believe it.

$20,520.

WHAT?!

I took a picture of the hefty check with *my* name on it and texted it to Donovan.

Five minutes later he sent me this:

???

I texted: *Still. Taking. Deep. Breaths.*

Him: *Bahamas!!!!*

Me: *Call me tonight.*

Him: *K.*

Ten seconds later: !!!!!!!!!!!!!!!!!!!

Chapter 6

THE CHECK SUCCESSFULLY WENT INTO MY MEAGER BANK account. I had only worked Saturday's at Jump In Swim School for the last two years, making a modest $205 a month after taxes. So, as you can imagine, my bank account had never been so happy. Every twenty minutes I'd pull up my banking app, login to my account, and stare ... just sit there and stare at the number on the screen.

I had saved up a little over the last few years, but not enough to do much of anything. Now the possibilities were most definitely endless. Endless, I say!

But endless as they were I knew what I wanted to do with it. College wasn't really my thing, didn't care for a new car since mine got me from point A to point B without issues, and although traveling sounded fun it wasn't as appealing to me as starting my own fashion design business or clothing line.

I had been sewing since I was seven. Mom taught me as part of my proper Jane Austen life skill sessions, but she never imagined how far I'd run with it. I got by for the last ten years on a dinky cheap Shark machine, but I really wanted a nice Brother. Maybe even an antique Singer for kicks.

I couldn't wait to get the business going and surprise everyone. First step, Internet search galore.

I spent an entire two days looking up how to establish a legit business, plus any tips I could find on fashion design. By the end of my research spree I had mailed in a sole proprietorship registration form and a fictitious name form. My new clothing line would be called Adrian Elyse. Adrian based off of my favorite non-Batman movie, *Rocky*, and Elyse for no reason. Just looked and felt good after Adrian.

It was really happening.

Next step, Mom would not appreciate, but probably saw coming.

Autumn came over to help. She drove while I navigated. We pulled up in front of the building and I could already tell that I wanted it.

"You sure you can do this?" Autumn said. "I know that's a lot of money, but not that much. What if you rent this and realize it's too much? What if the business doesn't take off?"

"A girl after my own heart." I laughed and pat her knee. "You know I've already thought about every single question imaginable."

"And?"

"And I'm renting. Worst thing that could happen is I have to move back out, but come on, have a little more faith in me than that. Plus, if you decide not to go away to college you could always rent with me."

"Unlike you, I don't have a various assortment of creative talents to pursue. College it is!"

"You have plenty of talents." I opened the door when the landlord showed up in front of the building with a folder tucked under his arm. "Let's go."

Autumn and I greeted Jerry and he allowed us to go inside.

"The first floor was used as a pet grooming spa for a few years, but they moved to a different part of the city last month." Jerry walked toward the center of the room. "You said you were starting a clothing line?"

I nodded.

"Impressive for a girl your age." He gestured toward the front desk. "If you want, you could get rid of this desk here. We just need to talk through logistics and any improvements made to the building will be paid by you, but I will reimburse them by crediting your rent."

I looked around the room. Light wood floors. Glossy. Beautiful. Sleek. I could easily see the room as a gorgeous boutique filled with my custom clothes and the excitement made my heart flutter like crazy. Kinda like it did when Alistair's arm touched mine. I pictured him on the sidewalk, giving me those eyes.

Autumn snapped in front of my face. "Come back to reality," she said, drawing out her words to emphasize my spaced outness.

"Sorry," I said. "Could I see upstairs, please?"

He led us up the stairs to a modern-looking loft apartment. I gasped. So did Autumn.

"This is amazing," I said, taking in the light that poured in through the windows. "I didn't expect it to be so modern in such an old building." I walked to the back windows. "These windows are incredible."

At the back of the building the windows covered the entire wall and faced west, so the sunset would paint my room at night. Right now sunshine beamed through and lit the entire room. Light wood floors. Clean, modern kitchen with new stainless steel appliances. I walked up the cute little stairs to the bedroom area that sat above everything and realized it extended back further than I thought, even had a second room that could be used as a spare bedroom if anyone wanted to room with me. It felt more like an exposed attic than a one-bedroom loft.

"I absolutely love this," I called down to Jerry. "Let me guess, it's out of my budget."

He cleared his throat. "What's your budget?"

I thought for a second. Did a quick calculation of everything I needed to buy and yeah, Autumn was right, I probably wouldn't have enough, but I was determined to try.

"A thousand a month?" I should've said it without the question mark.

He nodded. "Well, you know this is a prominent and popular part of the city and includes the storefront downstairs."

"You're saying it costs more than a thousand."

"I've been renting it out for three thousand, but I would be willing to allow you to stay for the first six months at fifteen hundred, then if all goes well and your business improves we can move up to the full price."

"And what if it doesn't improve?" I said. "Six months isn't a lot of time."

"We can talk about it then." He rummaged through some papers in his folder and handed them to me. "If you're interested we'll need to do a credit check and have you fill out this paperwork."

I nodded. "My credit is perfect. Have barely done much with it yet."

"Okay." He handed me a few more papers. "That should be all you need. Would you like to take the next step?"

Autumn stood behind him and waved her hands like a referee while she mouthed, "Don't do it."

"Yes." I flipped through the papers. "I would love that."

He went over a few details as I glanced around the room, imagining my own furniture and art on the walls. My own place. My own store.

Really?

Donovan texted me: *Hey, let me know when you're free. We need to talk.*

Me: *Yes. We. Do!*

Donovan: *No... I mean... we need to talk.*

Me: *Tonight? Our spot?*

Donovan: *5pm.*

Me: *K.*

I took one last look around the loft, inhaled the clean, fresh paint smell, then followed Jerry and Autumn downstairs. Soon this would be my home. In the city. Alone.

Maybe it wasn't such a good idea. "So," I said. "I can think this over a few days if I want and get this paperwork back to you when I'm ready?"

"Sure," he said. "I do have quite a few people coming to look at it today, so I can't guarantee that'll still be here, but you're more than willing to think it over and see."

Hm. I didn't like the idea of losing out on the opportunity of a lifetime. "Can I fill the paperwork out right now?"

He laughed. "I'm not allowing anyone to do it right here, so go ahead and take your time."

"What's the deposit?"

"One month of rent, plus your first month of rent is also due upfront."

"So ... three thousand?"

He nodded.

I reached into my bag and grabbed my check book, wrote out a check for three thousand buckareenos—which I never in a million years thought I'd ever do—and handed it to him. "Just in case. I don't want to miss it if I want it."

"Okay, I'll hold on to this and rip it up if it doesn't work out."

I smiled. "Thank you. Thank you so, so much."

With one last pivot, I was on the floor staring at Autumn's shoe and ... thinking of Alistair.

His face was fading in my memory now and it had only been weeks. I should've taken a picture. Why didn't I take a picture?

Wait a minute. Why did I care?

"Jane." Autumn tugged on my shirt. "Are you enjoying the smell of the floor or something? Let's go."

Jerry helped me stand with a smile on his face. Autumn's face was as red as a Tarantino film set. I brushed my jeans off and laughed. "Sorry. Got deep in thought."

Jerry pat my back as he opened the front door for us. "That can happen while pressed against linoleum."

We laughed. Autumn didn't. Oh, great, I thought. The lecture was coming in like a storm cloud.

I thanked Jerry and got into the car. He walked back into the building as Autumn sat down, threw her hands into the air, grabbed the steering wheel, and glared at me.

"That look haunts me in my dreams," I said.

"Jane!"

Here it comes. The epic lecture. Wait for it. Wait for it. And....

"Do you realize what you're doing? I mean, this is Philadelphia. The city. Alone. Young girl. Pretty girl. Alone! Not to mention the price tag. Fifteen hundred a month. Really, Jane? You're gonna blow all that money your parents spent eighteen years saving and then end up moving back in with them with nothing. And"—finally she took a breath—"what in the world were you doing on the floor in there?"

I did my best Bill Cosby impression. Shaky face, pursed lips.

"I'm serious. Do you really wanna blow all of that money? Some people would kill for that kind of graduation gift."

"Oh, don't make me feel bad. I was going to wait until you left for school, but I'm giving you some of it. Donovan too."

"No." She waved her hands around. "I don't want your money, Jane. I just want you to use it wisely."

"So, apparently I have not one, not two, but *three* mother's. I'd say I'm lucky, buuuuut...."

"I know, I know."

"I'll be okay. You need to tone the responsibility dial down a few notches. If it doesn't work out within two months I'll ask Jerry if I can leave."

"That's if you get the place." She pointed to a fancy couple walking into the building and greeting Jerry. "Those people might beat you to it."

DONOVAN IS ALMOST ALWAYS LATE, BUT SO AM I. SO when we decided to meet somewhere I normally planned to get there ten minutes later than he said, then I ended up twenty minutes later, and by the time he would get there it would be thirty minutes passed our planned time. Never failed. Well, I guess sometimes it failed, but not most times. I like to try to be accurate if I catch myself. Never is a strong word.

I sat on the hood of my car and he pulled up ten minutes later. The sun was still pretty high up there, not quite ready to wake up the other side of the world. Donovan sat beside me, pulled his knees up to his chest, and sighed. Bad sign. I waited for him to speak first, but he sighed again and that meant he wanted me to ask.

"Don't make me ask." I poked his knee. "I know there's something you need to say."

His lip quivered as he squeezed his eyebrows together.

"What's wrong?"

He gasped for air, then let out a soft cry. Last time I saw him cry he was ten and had accidentally ran over a baby bird with his bike.

"Donovan?"

Awkward. I wasn't experienced in handling boys that cried. Sappy Mom's and Dad's, check. Boys? Not even a half of a check.

I poked his knee.

He buried his face into his elbow and wailed.

I, um, I poked his knee again, feeling more mature by the minute.

He reached into his pocket and whipped out a box. A ring box.

And laughed hysterically. "Got ya again!"

I swatted him. "You're such a jerk."

He opened the box and the ring sparkled in the sun. "What do you think?"

"You already tried this one on me."

"No. This one is real. I got it for Zoe."

I raised my eyebrows. "Zoe? You've been together, what, a week?"

"Two."

"Two weeks." I shoved the ring box closed. "No way. You're not proposing."

"I am." He put the box back into his pocket. "But I need your help to pull it off."

My nose stung a little, almost as though chlorine had snuck its way through my tear ducts, into my nose, and wanted to come back out. My eyes burned. They burned. What? I was not about to cry. I wouldn't. But why was I?

I played it off. "I'm so happy for you."

"Thanks." He stared dreamily into space. "Getting all emotional on me, huh? Alistair really did a number on you."

Thank God the burning water dried up and my eyes went back to normal. Nose too. "It's not Alistair." Or was it?

"You don't want to look him up? Not even the slightest bit?"

"Haven't thought about it much. How could I find him anyway? No last name."

He pulled his phone out and set it on his thigh, clicked a few things, then showed me the screen. "This him?"

"Nope. Nice try."

He did it again. "This?"

I was all geared up to prove that I was right when Alistair's eyes looked at me. Well, his eyes on the tiny phone screen.

"Guess so. Just looked up his name, put the word band in, plus added where he's from. Cake work."

Those eyes were still there.

"You done drooling yet?"

"What's his bands name?"

"Kitten Corner."

I laughed. "What is it, dork?"

"Jingle Jam."

"And his last name?"

He clicked around on his phone. "Alistair Anonymous."

"Can't you be serious for one minute of your life?"

"No." He showed me the phone. "That's what it says on his band's page."

"Must be a stage name." I shook my head. "All this time I had his name."

"See, you wanted to look him up."

"Noooooo. Just saying. Weird, that's all."

"Uh, huh. As soon as we leave your lips are going to be pressed against your phone."

"Anyway, about the proposal."

"About that. Let's brainstorm."

"You realize you're brainstorming with the most unromantic person in the universe, right?"

"Exactly. That's what'll make this proposal unique."

"Or terrible."

"Brainstorm?"

"Kay."

He leaned back on the car window and didn't pull me into him this time. Cuddles were off limits when he was taken. Which would be forever now. I'd never press my ear against his heartbeat again.

Burning nose.

I crinkled my face and shoved the sensation away, then reclined next to him and stared at the sky. I was supposed to brainstorm proposal ideas, but all I could think about was Donovan's heart beating over there without my cheek against it.

Something was dreadfully, dreadfully wrong with me.

BRAINSTORMING SESH WAS AS UNEVENTFUL AS IT GETS. And, hate to say it, but Donovan was totally right. As soon as he pulled away, laughing at me, I grabbed my phone and looked Mr. Alistair Anonymous right up. Who makes their stage name Alistair Anonymous anyway? Talk about weird.

I found his band page. Alistair Anonymous, drummer and backup vocals for Hatchenfield. So moody in his pictures. I searched his name again and scrolled through the results, hoping maybe to find a Facebook account or something. Not that I'd contact him. If I wanted to I could just send a message through Hatchenfield's website like a regular old stalker. But I didn't want to. If I ever saw him again, which I probably wouldn't, it would be when he said and how he said. No sooner. No messages. No stalking. No desperation from my side of the ocean.

Because I wasn't desperate.

But I was curious....

And so maybe I was a stalker. I kept looking for a Facebook account to no avail. Kinda gave me hope that maybe his last name was fake. Not that it mattered. Why did I keep thinking things that freaked my own mind out?

I tossed my phone into the other seat, cranked my car into drive, and drove away with Alistair's moody pictures and Donovan's sparkly ring competing for attention from my tired mind.

I ignored them both and thought of the apartment. What would I do? Could I swing it? Did I want to try?

And most of all ... when would I tell Mom?

Chapter 7

SO, NOT ONLY DID I HAVE TO TELL MOM THAT I WOULD BE moving into my own apartment in one week, but I also had to tell her about Boston. I guess I could've tried to hide it, especially if I no longer lived there, but Mom had this sweetness and deep, amazing love for people and pretty much any living thing from a plant to an unhatched egg, that it was kinda hard to lie to her. I did once in tenth grade and I expected a major punishment like my friends. Grounded or something for weeks. But nothing like that happened. Instead Mom came to me all teary and said it hurt her feelings that I didn't feel like I could be honest with her, then she hugged me and apologized. For some reason that kinda bothered me, so I shrugged it off and told her she has nothing to apologize for and she looked me right in the eyes and said, "But I do, sweetie. If you don't feel comfortable enough to tell me the truth, then I must not be the mother I want to be."

Truth is, it was me. All me. Mom had a tendency to be so hard on herself, especially with parenting. I remember one time when I was about six and she had to work part-time from home to help with bills. She came into my room thinking I was asleep and knelt beside my bed, wet my sheet with tears, and told me she was sorry for being a bad mommy and for not paying attention to me enough that day, but I didn't think a thing of it. In my mind she was perfect. The best.

And always would be.

I still felt that way, even if I wanted to meet my real Mom.

So, yeah, about that.

I couldn't lie to the woman, so I needed one of those beat around the bush easy methods to break the news. Why was it so hard? Honesty is one of those things. It's so necessary, so healthy, so needed for any kind of functional relationship, but it's very, very hard. My tongue always seemed to hide in my throat when these situations would come up.

But I had to do it. So I stayed up late and waited for Dad to take his nightly shower when Mom finished cleaning up the kitchen. She pulled out a freshly baked loaf of banana bread just as I walked in the room.

"That smells so good." I reached for the warm, delicious, lovely bread to snatch a corner from the top, but she gently put my hand back down.

"Wait until it cools," she said in an English accent. "Then we can make a cuppa and have some treats together."

"That sounds nice," I said. "A cuppa. Is it English accent week?"

She nodded and turned the stovetop on to boil the kettle of water. My parents spoke only with English accents once a month. There was a time when Eddie and I were too young to realize how weird it was and we tried to play along. Then we realized how weird it was. And we did not play along.

It reminded me of Alistair. Mr. Anonymous. Who I looked up again only ten minutes before coming into the kitchen. American tour coming up. This summer. Cities and dates to be posted soon.

Yes, I considered it.

No, I wouldn't be a stalker.

But with Donovan head over heels—for now—and Autumn going away to college in September my life was beginning to err on the side of loneliness and while I'm totally fine with being alone, I'm not fine with *loneliness*. Any perceived negative emotion with a *ness* on the end didn't settle well with me and I have no idea why. Sadness seemed worse than sad. Sad is like ... definitive. Hey, here I am, I'm sad. But sad*ness* ... doesn't that sound so tragic?

"What are you thinking about?" Mom laughed. "You looked pretty entranced."

"Oh, nothing." I took the warm mug from her hands and held it to my chest. Ahhhhh. I did actually enjoy my cuppa. "Just realizing I have something against nouns, but not adjectives."

She smiled. "You've always had an interesting mind. You were never the kid to ask why the sky is blue, instead you told me your own theory with quite a bit of persistence."

"Do you remember what I said?"

"Of course." She tilted her head back as she remembered. "You told me that God ran out of silver paint, because if he had silver he definitely wouldn't have chosen blue."

I laughed. "Of course not. I mean, who would want a blue sky when you could have silver?"

"How does it feel to be done high school?"

"Normal."

I was hoping she'd ask me what I wanted to do so that I didn't have to bring it up.

She sipped her tea, then stood and served us both an amazingly thick chunk of that amazing bread she perfected in a way no one else ever had. I devoured it a little too fast and desperately wanted to eat the entire loaf, but I controlled myself and finished my tea instead.

"Has Donovan decided what he's doing yet?"

"Getting married, I guess." I swirled my finger in the bottom of my cup and licked the milky sugar off of it.

"Really? I didn't know he had a girlfriend."

"Donovan? Girls practically wait in line for him, Mom. He's oh so swoon worthy."

"But you don't swoon over him?"

"No." I laughed. "And somehow no one ever believes me when I say that. He's not perfect. Those girls just don't see the other sides of him. Like how he farts when he laughs and always clanks the spoon on his teeth when he eats cereal."

She smiled. "You sure you won't marry him?"

If only she knew about Alistair Anonymous, these Donovan conversations would end. "You just say that because he's the only male species I've ever allowed into my heart."

"Precisely." That accent. Man. So weird.

I wonder what Alistair would think of my parents doing their English accent week.

Why? I reprimanded myself. *Why do you do it to yourself? Just stop with the Alistair thing.*

"You can have a totally platonic friendship with someone of the opposite sex, you know," I said. "Doesn't need to turn into wedding bells."

She squeezed my hand, then stood.

"Mom." Pretty sure that barely escaped my mouth.

She washed the cuppas that held the cuppa.

Deep breaths. Big deep breaths. Fill the lungs, Jane. Fill 'em up. Okay. Last deep breath. Aaaaand ... GO!

"Mom," I said louder.

She turned, but kept her soapy hands over the sink. "Yes?"

Eddie walked in and sniffed the air.

Great.

She wiped her hands and gave him a slice of bread, then put the kettle back on. He moaned and grinned as he bit into the warm deliciousness that I was now reaching for again. Mom moved it away.

"Save some for your dad." She dipped her hands back into the sink. "Now, what were you saying?"

I glanced at Eddie. "Um. Was I saying something?"

She nodded.

"Oh, just that I wanted more bread."

Three days went by and I still didn't tell Mom anything I wanted to tell her and I felt like a complete idiot. I mean, here I was, eighteen. Newly adulted. And ... still acting like a nervous child. In many ways though, I still felt like a kid as much as I hated that I did.

I stared at the calendar above the sewing desk in my room. I was officially three thousand dollars less rich and I'd be moving into my new place in two days.

Two. Days.

Donovan popped up on my phone.

"Hey," I said.

"Tell your mom yet?"

"Nope."

"Really?"

"It just hasn't worked out."

"You need to tell her though. She'll be upset if you don't, you know how emotional she gets."

"I know. I feel bad."

"You've been independent since birth, I think she's expecting it."

"Yeah."

"I have a question."

"Uh oh."

"No. I have a roommate for you. It'll make the rent cheaper. Maybe make it more successful for you and if you ever need a little help I can?"

"It's Zoe, isn't it?"

"I can help with rent a little too if you need it. Just saying it would be a good way for you to spend less money while getting started."

"Donovan."

"She's not a smoker and has no pets."

"Donovan."

"And she is mostly clean, just bad with laundry."

"I'm sure she's great, but I barely know her."

"What better way to start?"

"Why? Why do this to me?"

"Come on."

"You know I'm introverted. I like my space."

"She can respect that."

"You've been together a month or something, right? You probably don't even know her yet. She's just putting out all the good stuff to lure you in, but if I live with her I'll see all the real stuff and I don't want to be the bad guy."

"Please? For me? If it doesn't work out I'll be the bad guy."

I ran down all possible outcomes and scenarios while he breathed into the phone. He let me think, knowing I'd say yes. I couldn't say no to people I loved and he knew that. He used it against me in the nicest way possible.

"I know you mean well, but—"

"Oh, right," he said. "You know you're gonna say that it's okay."

"Fine." I tapped my bobbin on the desk. "But if it's a nightmare you owe me."

"Course. And hey, go tell your Mom now. Moving day is in two days."

"Yeah."

"Don't sound too thrilled. It's too much for me."

"Bye, Donovan."

He laughed. "See ya, girl."

A knock on my door.

"Come in," I said.

Dad came in, stopped at my dresser, settled his gaze on a picture of himself carrying a two-year-old version of me on his shoulders, then tapped my dresser and walked over to where I sat, staring, waiting for him to ask me what was going on because that's what he did after coming into my room and stalling. Every time. Never failed.

He sat on the edge of my bed and folded his hands over his knees. "What's going on, Jane? Is there something you need to tell us?"

My chair creaked when I moved. He cleared his throat and waited. Deep breath. In and out it goes. I looked at him. He looked back.

"I wanted to tell Mom, but the timing never seemed right."

"Honey, you know we won't think any less of you if you're pregnant."

I coughed. "What?"

"We won't think any less of you."

"What? No. Dad, I'm not pregnant." I laughed.

"Gay?"

"Um ... if you mean happy, then yes. What the? I'm just moving out. That's all. Wow. Well, that made it easier."

"Moving into your own place?"

"Yeah."

"We figured you would. You've been like a wild horse stuck in a stable for too long. We're ready to watch you run." He refolded his hands and looked down. "Jane, you really need to learn how to handle difficult conversations better."

"Difficult things in general, so I'm told."

"You can't always avoid conflict. It's part of life. Learning to deal with it and keep a smile on your face may be difficult at first, but once you get the hang of it you'll realize that it's better to embrace even the negative aspects of life than it is to ignore them." He looked at me again. "It's part of life. Part of being alive."

"I'm trying."

"So, that's it? Or do you need to tell me something else?"

"Just that, um..." I picked at the spool of thread in my hands. "I ... I'm going to try to find my biological mother. I want to see her just once ... at least."

He smiled and laughed under his breath. "We expected this too."

"I just know how Mom gets."

"She loves you. A lot. You may be adopted, but your mother

breastfed you like you were her own and spent days and nights holding you. She didn't even like when I asked to cuddle you. Well, she did, but she secretly couldn't wait to get you back in her arms. I've never seen a mother love a daughter like she loves you."

"I know. I really do. Which is why I didn't want to hurt her."

"She is sensitive, but she's also realistic. She knows what you need to do and she's okay with that." He stood. "Talk to her, okay? She wants to be there for you."

I nodded. "No accent for you?"

"Oh, bollocks." He smiled. "I forgot."

Chapter 8

MOVING DAY CAME FAST. I TOOK CHOPIN OUT OF MY ears—or, um, my headphones out of my ears to be more exact—and stood in the middle of my room. My box-covered room. No more pictures scattered on my walls. No more mirror covered in more pictures and notes and ticket stubs. No more fabric and thread strewn across my bed. No more Batman paintings above my bed. No more blankets and sheets or clothes in the closet.

Autumn came in and put her hands on her hips. "Well, it's real now."

"We're growing up, Autumn. It's weird."

"But good."

"Good in a weird way." I sat on my bare mattress. "I'm kinda getting emotional. Is that normal?"

"Don't know, but it's not normal for you."

"True."

"Lots of memories here," she said, turning around to take in the emptiness. "It's definitely sad to me too."

"Next I'll be helping you move to Virginia. That's really going to be hard."

She stared at her feet. "It will be." She looked at me again. "But it'll go fast."

"Promise me we won't grow apart."

She hugged me. "Impossible."

"Never say impossible. Everything is possible. Good and bad."

"Thank you for that wisdom of the day. Can I add that to my quote book?"

I laughed. "Sure. I'd like credit though."

"Of course." She smiled and picked up a box. "Let's do this."

I picked up another and followed her to the moving truck.

"Is this it?" she said, setting the box down near the back.

"I got the smallest truck I could. I don't have much to bring. Keeping the bed here. I'll probably need a trip to Ikea after this."

"Definitely." She jumped out of the truck. "Can't believe your parent's decided to go on vacation on your moving day."

"I feel like Mom was trying to avoid it. I don't know. They said they don't mind, but I get the feeling it's upset her."

"Maybe it's just hard to see your daughter leave."

"Not for my real mom."

"Don't be depressing." She walked toward the house. "Come on. Let's beat Donovan and Zoe."

"Zoe...." I trailed behind.

"Excited?"

"Can't you tell?" I made the most serious face possible.

"It's written all over your face."

"Really though, how could a mother just give up her child?"

She shrugged. "Sometimes they don't feel like they can take care of the kid and the best thing is to let her go."

"But—"

"You can make up a million reasons why that's not enough, but to her it was. What's the matter anyway? You have amazing parents who just gave you a crap load of money."

"Crap load. I always hated that term."

WE UNLOADED A FEW BOXES AT THE NEW APARTMENT WHEN Donovan showed up with his arm around Zoe. I seriously couldn't stand when couples were all starry-eyed and inseparable in public. I would tell myself they wouldn't last like that much longer, but then be proven wrong every day when I saw Mom and Dad staring at each other over their tea cups. Tea, not coffee. Always tea. Even though I made sure they were aware of the fact that British people do, indeed, drink coffee too.

"Please don't make out in front of me," I begged as Donovan wet her lips.

He didn't stop kissing her. Autumn looked at me and smiled, her chest jerking with one of those bursts of quiet laughter. I shook my head. Finally Donovan stopped and put his forehead against Zoe's.

"Wow, this is intense," Autumn said.

I walked to the door and slapped Donovan's shoulder on the way out. "Time to work."

Autumn and I picked up another box and headed to the stairs. Donovan jogged down as we went up.

"Where's Zoe?" Autumn said. "Isn't she helping?"

"Nah. She's got painful joints."

Autumn raised her eyebrows and mouthed, "Okay."

I laughed. "Are you serious?"

He nodded. "Yeah, she's sensitive to hard labor."

"You're not serious."

He glanced at the two of us. "What?"

I laughed again. "Nothing. We'll help with her stuff too."

ONLY TOOK ABOUT AN HOUR AND A HALF TO UNLOAD AND even unpack quite a few boxes. Apparently Zoe liked to accumulate things, because she had twice as much as me and I was a little freaked out about it. Her rent was cheaper since she had the smaller loft, so I imagined her weird artwork on the living room walls and I wish I could say it didn't bother me.

Donovan and Zoe curled up on the floor and watched a movie on his iPad while Autumn and I unpacked the stuff for my room. I didn't have a bed yet, but I hoped to change that with an Ikea visit tomorrow.

We set up my sewing corner in silence until Autumn interrupted. "Um." She pointed to a large box beside the table. "I didn't even know you wore makeup, much less an entire box full."

"Whoa." I picked it up. "Totally not mine. Ever. How could someone own this much makeup? I mean, what are you trying to hi—"

Autumn shook her hands as she looked over my shoulder.

I mouthed, "She's standing behind me," then turned around to face her.

"I'm not trying to hide anything." She smiled and tossed her hair behind her shoulder. "Just accentuating my already beautiful features." She snapped her fingers. "Donovan, sweetie, could you put this box in my room for me?"

116

His footsteps already echoed off the stairs as I walked by her and said, "I'll take care of it. My joints hurt, but what the hell."

This was going to be a long, long summer.

I set the box down as she entered with Donovan kissing her neck as he walked behind her. Sickening. Even my parents knew where to draw the line.

I brushed by them again and an odd image of Alistair's face inching toward me took over my mind. *I should've kissed him.*

"But then it would've been more complicated," I said to myself.

Autumn said something.

I stared at the corner where the ceiling met the walls. "And I don't need complications."

"Are you talking to yourself again?"

I tuned back to her. "What?"

"So weird."

Chapter 9

SO MY ORIGINAL PLANS NEVER WORK OUT. I WAS BEGINNING to think maybe I should stop planning anything at all. Not that I'd be able to resist the beauty of my calendar, but still. The plan was to go to Ikea. Alone. Then to come back and put furniture together. Alone. Like a total single woman who enjoyed being a single woman and using single woman screwdrivers while screaming at the Ikea instruction manuals and wondering why, why, why they made everything so complicated.

But here I was. Standing in the middle of an array of Ikea couches. With Donovan and Zoe making out on the one I liked. The one I wanted to sit on until now. Okay, so they weren't making out, but man ... couldn't they go one-point-seven seconds without running their hands through each other's hair?

Sheesh.

I penciled in the number of the couch and walked away, like a third wheel who wanted to be a unicycle. Completely content in my unicycledom. But they realized I left and came after me.

They whispered and laughed behind me as I searched for a bed, wondering why I agreed to let them come with me.

Donovan sat on a bed and pulled Zoe onto his lap.

"Guys, seriously?" I looked around me. "There are people here.

People who don't want to see a make out fest during their Saturday shopping sprees."

Oblivious. Completely oblivious. *That's it*, I thought as I scurried away to the tent in the bedroom section for kids and hid inside. I figured they'd pass me and I could wait until all was clear, then go back to the bedroom section in peace. Good thing we drove separately. They could actually leave if they wanted to. I hoped they'd want to.

I pulled my knees to my chest and peeked out of the tent again as a mother and her two kids came toward me. Oh, great. The woman squeezed her eyebrows together and snatched her kids away, enveloping them in her arms as she moved them to the next section while glaring over her shoulder at me.

"What?" I whispered. "Not that big of a deal."

I heard Zoe's giggle coming around the corner, so I waited a few seconds and checked.

"Hey." Zoe pointed. "There she is."

Donovan linked his hand with hers and walked toward me. I closed my eyes.

Only me.

"What are you doing?" Donovan tapped the top of the tent and leaned down to look inside. "This is the kids section."

"I know," I grumbled. "Was thinking of getting this for when you stay over."

He smiled. "No, really, what are you doing?"

I stood up and walked away. "I'm just looking around. Shopping, you know, because that's what you do in stores. What are *you* doing? That's the real question."

He laughed. Zoe didn't.

She pulled his hand back and they stayed behind, surely about to kiss each other's lips until they turned blue. And I would be alone, wheeling away on my beloved, comforting, very nice unicycle, thank you very much.

I finished my shopping in peace and asked an Ikea employee if he could help me load the truck I bought.

"Sorry," he said. "There are people outside that do that. Not me."

"Kay." I maneuvered my cart thingies to the side of the exit and pushed one outside. Don't know what he was talking about because there were no Ikea employees anywhere to be found, so I wheeled the cart to the yellow poles and went to get the moving truck, then parked it and stared at the stuff.

Kay....

I brought the other three carts out.

Stared at them.

Kay.

Okay.

Okay!

I could do this.

Oh, wait! Out of thin air, he appeared! The blue shirt I so wanted to see. I walked up to him and smiled. "Hey, um, the guy in there told me that you help load?"

He didn't speak. But he moved toward the truck and began throwing—yes, throwing—my new stuff into the car.

"Um, I can do it. Don't worry about it."

The lips on his face seemed real, but they didn't move at all. He threw another box in. The wood inside banged against the truck and probably shattered into a million pieces.

"Right," I said. "So, I can take care of it, but thanks."

He didn't make eye contact with me, just stood there reaching his hand out. I looked at his sweaty palm.

"Yes?" I stepped back.

He picked up another box.

"Do you speak English?"

He tipped it on to the back of the truck so that half of it was hanging toward me, then reached out his palm again. "Tip."

"Hark, he speaks!"

He narrowed his eyes and chewed his gum. "Tip."

"Isn't this your job?"

He extended his hand closer to me.

I shoved a five into his hand just to get him the hell away.

I swear, only me.

He disappeared into a secret door and I turned back to grab the box, but it fell on my foot. I seized up and grabbed the edge of the truck, leaning over as stars danced inside my head.

"That hurt," I said, looking down at my toe. It felt broken. Thankfully it only looked a little red, but as I loaded the rest of the enormous heavy boxes into the truck without the slightest bit of ease, the pain turned into hot prickly needles stabbing my toe from the inside out.

I worked fast, shoving the damn things into the truck and contemplating suing Ikea. When I got everything settled I closed the truck and wobbled inside, careful to put pressure on the side of my foot to relieve the pressure from my big toe. I went to the customer service desk and told them my story. They shrugged. More gum chewing.

"Is there a manager here?" I said.

"That would be me." Ryan pointed to his name tag.

"Right. Thanks. Okay." I turned and walked back to the truck, sat down in the driver's seat, and held my toe which was now turning black.

Great.

This unicycle didn't have medical insurance now that she was supposed to be eighteen and responsible with her own money.

So, I took myself home, driving with the outer edge of my foot pressing on the pedal and even then it hurt like, oh, about nine thousand wasps stinging me at once while setting my foot on fire for kicks.

I breathed in and out, cringing with each throb, until finally parking behind my lovely new apartment. There was no way I could move the rest of the boxes in myself. Not now. Not when I needed to figure out how to deal with a possibly broken and definitely excruciating toe.

I hobbled to the back door and did what I always do when life sucks. I popped my earphones in and played my favorite music. From my favorite movie. From my favorite hero ever.

Batman.

Batman Begins. The Dark Knight. The Dark Knight Rises. I played the *Batman Begins* soundtrack by the incredible Hans Zimmerman and James Newton Howard. Some girls fangirl over Chris Pinetree or whatever and I obsess over film composers. Or any composer really. If I were ever to fall in love it would definitely be possible for me to fall in love with a composer before even meeting him. Okay, I take that back, but I guess what I'm trying to say is I adore classical music and film scores get me a little too excited. Hence the reason I play them when I feel like burying my face in my pillow and screaming my head off.

Donovan's car wasn't parked anywhere around yet. Whew. Some peace and quiet for a bit would be nice, especially while I researched how to heal a crushed toe without the hospital.

I opened the back door and hummed along with the music, using my hands like a composer. For a second, I forgot about my toe, closed my eyes, and let the music fill me as I stepped inside and pretended I was standing in front of an orchestra with welcoming ears behind me.

I got pretty into it, if I do say so myself. Someone tapped me. I opened my eyes, hands still hanging in mid air, and saw dozens of eyes staring back at me with a "SURPRISE!" banner hanging over their heads. Donovan laughed as I took the headphones out of my ears, my other hand still hanging in the air to complete the song.

"Surprise," Mom said, walking toward me with open arms and glassy eyes perched right above her red nose. "I'm sorry I couldn't help you move. We were planning this and I wanted to make sure everything was prepared in time." She hugged me and sniffed. "I'm so proud of you, Janie."

"I ... I don't know what to say." I squeezed her back. "Thank you."

She let go, then Granny wrapped her arms around me and stepped on my toe.

"Ahhhh!!!!" I howled into the air and hopped on one foot.

Granny stepped back, shaking.

"Oh, shi—I mean, shoot. Shoot." I strained my neck while my friends and family looked at me like I was as nuts as I apparently was.

Granny trembled and looked back and forth. "I ... I ...."

"No, Granny," I said. "You're fine. I just hurt my toe. I'm sorry I scared you." I breathed in and out as the pain shot up to my thigh.

"Are you okay?" Donovan teetered between a laugh and genuine concern.

"My toe," I said between clenched teeth, pretending to smile for the others still staring at me. "Make them eat. Make them do something."

"All right everyone." Donovan clapped. "Let's go ahead and eat. Mrs. Austen created some fantastic food you're all gonna love." He gestured toward the dining room, my dining room, which now had a table sitting in the middle of it where I planned to put the table I just bought. And the couch. The couch I just bought was sitting in the living room along with a coffee table. The entire place was now filled with my favorite furniture.

Dad and Mom lingered near me. I exhaled. Dad glanced at my foot. I shook my head as though it were nothing. Mom knelt down and peered up at me with those motherly eyes. I waved my hands.

"It's nothing," I said. "Just a little bruise."

"When did this happen?" Dad said. "It looks brutal."

"It's okay. Really." I nodded toward the living room. "You guys did this? The furniture?"

Mom blushed as she stood up.

"How did you remember which furniture I liked?" I couldn't tell them I just bought every last one of those things. Man ... could've saved myself a toe.

"I just know you," Mom said.

"She pays attention." Dad pulled her into him and kissed the top of her head. "She's always paying attention to you guys."

My. Freaking. Toe. Was. Now. Radiating. Extreme. Pain. To. My. Brain.

"Excuse me," I said, trying not to limp away. "I just need to use the bathroom real quick."

Away I went. Pretending as though everything was normal as best as I could. All of these sweet people here to see me, to welcome me into my new place. I didn't want to let them down.

Autumn crossed her arms and stood in my path. "Care to explain?"

I shook my head and bit my lip. "Toe. Smashed it."

"Why didn't you go to the ER?"

"Shhhhh..."

"What if it's broken?"

"It's not. It's just smashed."

"Smashed? Into a billion broken pieces? It looks really bad."

I brushed by hair. "Bathroom. I need a pillow to scream into."

"Afraid you won't find that on the toilet."

"Right." I cringed. "What should I do then?"

"Um, seek medical attention?"

"No insurance."

"I have some arnica."

"Quack sugar pills?"

"If you say so."

I brushed by her. "Ibuprofen."

"If you say so."

I sat in the bathroom only to realize that I was sitting, fully clothed, on an open toilet seat that gladly soaked my tunic as it draped down into the water. I took a deep breath and whispered to myself, "This is seriously the worst best day ever."

THE IBUPROFEN HELPED ME GET THROUGH THE PARTY, BUT by the time everyone left I was about to fall on the floor and cry myself to sleep. Thing is ... I didn't sleep. Couldn't sleep. I took as much as ibuprofen as I could and still couldn't close my eyes without seeing bright dots flashing in my eyelids. The sound of Zoe giggling woke me up in the morning. Not that I had been sleeping. Just rolling around on my bed, twisting the covers around my face, and contorting my body into all sorts of strange positions that somehow eased the pain for a millisecond.

So, I guess what I mean is her giggle made me realize that I made it to another dawn. And if I didn't get my toe checked out soon, I'd never make it to another.

Mom texted me. *Everything okay? You seemed unusual last night.*

I decided to be honest. *Think I broke my toe or at least smashed it into pieces.*

Well, go to the ER then. Can you drive?

I think I can. But I don't have insurance.

You're still on our insurance. We aren't canceling it until you set up your own plan.

I shoved my phone in my purse and limped as I ran to the door, then limped back to get my flip flops on. And back to the door while yelling, "The night is darkest just before the dawn. And I promise you, the dawn is coming.?

Batman. Ever-inspiring.

This was cause for rejoicing.

I didn't lose a toe after all.

Chapter 10

I NEVER THOUGHT I'D SAY THIS, BUT I ACTUALLY DREADED when Donovan came over. It became one of those things where he sorta morphed into this other being when he was around Zoe. An obnoxious being. And no, I'm not just being mean here. I admit I can be a little cynical and meanish, but this is just reality.

I made myself comfortable on my new couch, elevated my foot, took my pain meds, and sketched some jacket designs while Donovan and Zoe watched a movie all cuddled on the other couch. That's normal. I'm totally okay with cuddling. What starts to creep me out is when girls or guys snap their fingers and their partners jump to serve them. It's nice and all to sacrifice for each other, but the keyword there is "each other," okay? That means both people jump to serve *each other.*

Not so with Don. Zoe this. Zoe that. She wanted a drink, he got it. She wanted an Oreo, he went out and bought some. She wanted milk, he bought a freaking cow.

Pen to paper, I watched Zoe out of the corner of my eye as she started moving her shoulders around. Then she rubbed her neck. *Wait for it, wait for it....*

"My back hurts so bad," she said. I knew it. Called that one a mile away.

And next, the inevitable....

"Want me to massage it?" Donovan said as expected.

She'd deny it at least once. *And ... action!*

"Oh, you're sweet, but you don't have to do that."

"No, I want to. I don't mind."

"No. It's okay." Oooh. A double denial.

"Come on. Turn over."

"Are you sure?"

"Of course he's sure," I said. "Just turn over already."

They stopped and looked at me.

I looked at my paper and shrugged. "Just trying to help move things along here."

"Don't be jealous because you have no one to rub your back for you," Zoe said.

I pointed my pencil toward her. "Pegged me."

"Okay," Donovan interjected. "Calm down."

"I'm calm," I said as I drew another pocket on the jacket design.

"Ugh." Zoe flipped over to her stomach, obviously not calm. When Donovan began to rub her shoulders, she whined and told him to go lower or higher or press his thumbs in more. "Donny, really? You call this a massage?"

"I'm trying," he said.

"Try harder. This feels like something a first grader would do."

I sincerely hoped he had thrown that diamond ring out the window by now. What was he thinking?

"Donny!" she shrieked. "That's too rough." She sat up and motioned for him to lie down. "Let me show you how it's done."

He leaned down on his stomach and smirked at me. I smiled back, hiding my laughter. "Score," he mouthed. I shook my head, thankful that he was aware of how ridiculous she was acting.

He smiled during the entire massage as she instructed him on how and why her methods were so much better. "Can you show me that one again? I'm not sure I got it," he said about fifteen times.

I never understood his taste in girls.

Never would apparently.

"So," I said. "I'd like to go to Boston before I get the boutique started. I was thinking this weekend."

"With your toe?" Donovan sat up and looked at his very agitated girlfriend.

"I planned on bringing my toe, yes." I smiled.

Zoe rolled her eyes. "I thought I told you I didn't feel comfortable with that unless I could come?" She inched away from him and looked at her lap. "What's more important to you? Her? Or me?"

He did *not* want to answer that, but I nodded for him to say what she wanted to hear.

"You, babe," he said. "Of course."

"Then I want to come."

"You know," I said. "I've been having doubts about it anyway. Maybe I should just stay home."

"Really?" He searched my eyes for sincerity.

I gave him the most real fake sincerity I could manage. "Yeah. I don't want to upset Mom."

"Well." He eyed me up again, squinting. "Think about it a few days and let us know."

Oh, I'd think about it all right. And he'd forgive me when I left without them.

No freaking way I'd go on a car trip with Zoe. Absolutely not. I'd rather lose my toe for good.

I PLANNED TO LEAVE SATURDAY MORNING. SO I SPENT
Friday night at Autumn's house so I could leave without anyone bothering me or asking about it. Anyone meaning ... the entity I now referred to as D and Z.

Autumn grabbed her iPad to rent a movie while I attempted to
warm myself in her bed. She brought an enormous bowl of ice cream
to me.

I pulled the blankets to my chin. "How in the hell do you expect
me to eat ice cream when your air conditioner has made it, oh, below
ten degrees in here?"

"Hell wouldn't be that cold."

"Huh?"

"You said how in the hell, but hell isn't cold."

"How would you know? Maybe hell is nothing like you imagine.
Maybe it's worse. Maybe it's everything you hate about your life but
fifty thousand times worse. Maybe it's the absence of everything
good. Maybe it's—"

"Whoa. Put the horses back in the stable!"

"Sorry." I picked up the iPad. "Horses have been reigned back in
and stabled. What shall we rent?"

"How about—"

"Really, though. What do you think hell is?"

She smacked the bed between us. "I knew it."

I blinked.

"I so knew you'd bring it back up. Horses may be in the stable, but
they still won't stop yapping." She took a generous bite of ice cream

and waved her spoon at me. "You're too deep for me."

I laughed. "Okay, okay. I'll let you pick the movie this time."

"Yeah, since you made me sit through another man flick."

"Not a man flick."

"Anything on National Geographic or the History Channel isn't considered a chick flick." She tapped the device a few times and brought up what I hoped, but knew, she would bring up. "This"—she clicked the rent button—"is gonna be so good."

I dropped my jaw and pretended to snore.

She whacked my arm. "Come on. It'll remind you of Alistair."

I snored louder.

She pinched my nose.

"Ow!"

"That's what my mom does to my dad." She laughed. "We'll be watching movies and when he falls asleep he snores so loud we can't hear. So she taps him, but nothing happens. The only thing that works is when she knees him in the shin or pinches his nose."

I laughed. "Sounds romantic."

"Well, they may not be Mr. and Mrs. Austen, but I like to think it's romantic in their own little way."

Something about those words stuck with me. For some reason I had never thought of it before. I always felt this pressure to be like the kind of romance my parents had, but maybe I needed to find my own romance. Maybe love wasn't Jane Austeny to me. Maybe it was something I hadn't discovered yet.

That kinda intrigued me.

"Ready?" She hit play.

"Ready as I'll ever be." I sighed as the movie started. Some indie film called *Like Crazy* about two peeps loving each other ... like crazy, I assumed. But as the movie progressed I felt something I'd never felt before. I felt my cheeks pulling my lips into a smile as the couple fell in love on screen. It was natural. It was real. It wasn't Jane Austeny or bursting with sparks. It was so ... nice.

The credits came up and I smiled as big as possible.

Autumn flopped back into her pillow and grunted. "Horrible ending." She looked back at the screen as though it would suddenly reveal the ending she hoped for. "Worst ever." She landed in the pillows again.

I crossed my arms over my chest and smiled. "Loved it."

"Are you serious?"

I nodded. "Loved it a lot."

"But that ending...."

"Was real."

"Annoying."

"Beautiful."

And so I learned ... beauty is annoying to some people. My beauty, at least.

Is it bad that I liked that?

Chapter 11

MAYBE IT WAS THE MOVIE THAT I COULDN'T STOP THINKing about or maybe the emotional sound of *Secrets* by Jennifer Thomas as it serenaded me from my car's speakers. Whatever it was, I was now sitting in my car as gas poured into it and I was doing the thing.

The thing girls do when they like someone.

I was looking up every picture imaginable. Of Alistair. And zooming in. And feeling feelings. But not *the feels*. Just ... feelings.

A rap on my window and a boisterous laugh. What the?

Donovan pointed at my phone. "I told you!"

Great. I shoved the phone away. "I was—"

"You were just what?"

"What are you doing here?"

"Just got back from Autumn's house. Stalked you here."

The pump clicked. I got out and scooted around him. "But why were you at Autumn's?"

"I'm not dumb."

"You can't come with me."

"I can do whatever the hell I want, Jane. She doesn't own me."

"But...."

He opened my trunk and put his bag in. "I'm coming."

"When you're in love the person may not own you, but aren't they part of you? A part you don't want to piss off?"

He smiled. "Too late for that."

"You pissed her off?"

"Almost daily."

"So ... it's over?"

"I don't know."

"You bought a ring, Donovan." I shook my head. "See, this is exactly why I don't trust emotions."

"I didn't buy that ring." He grabbed my shoulders and pushed me around the car and into the passenger's seat. "Not recently anyway."

"Huh?"

He sat down in the driver's seat and turned the ignition. "Bought it for you."

He said it so casually. Like what the heck? He just said that and was he serious?

"Oh." I slapped his arm. "One of your dumb jokes again. I'm not falling for it this time."

He accelerated the car and turned out of the gas station. "I'm serious."

"No you're not."

He laughed. "I bought it when I was fifteen."

"What?" I laughed. "Now I know you're full of it."

He stopped at the red light and turned serious on me. "No, Jane. I really did."

I cleared my throat. "You what?"

"I bought it for you. I just figured it would be you and I saved up everything I could when I worked at the grocery store."

"Donovan James Slovak."

"Jane Maryanne Austen."

"Oooh. Not the middle name too."

He smiled. Playfully smiled at me like he smiled at his girlfriends. "I'm serious, you know."

I looked out the window. "I know."

We drove all the way to New York without saying another word. And I didn't feel the need to. Neither did he. The music filled in where we lacked and it filled in perfectly. Everything was comfortable with Donovan. Everything. Even awkward moments. That's how close we were.

He turned to me as we crossed the bridge over the Hudson River. "Wanna stay in New York for a night?"

I shrugged. "Why not?"

"That's exactly why I love you."

The words stayed there. In the air. Staring at me in a way only words could.

I nodded. "And ... suddenly this is strange."

"I didn't mean that." He shrugged it off. "I got over you years ago when you rejected me for the seventh time."

"Me? Rejected you? You never asked!"

"I implied."

"Well, either way it doesn't matter. You know how I am about guys."

"Yeah. I guess I was hoping you'd change."

"Maybe I will." I watched the sun glisten in the rippling water below. "Maybe I already am."

"If you were looking at that dude's pictures, you're changing."

I laughed. "Don't keep bringing it up."

"Oh, you know I will. Right after I bring up some different normal people music."

"Normal is as normal does and I'm not doing it."

I TOOK A SHOWER IN THE HOTEL WHILE DONOVAN WATCHED reruns of our favorite show, *The Office*, on Netflix. Part of me couldn't wait to get back out there and watch it with him. But part five of me—because I have many parts—had this weird nervous, sinking, trembly feeling rising in my stomach. Not like butterflies. Like worms.

Sorry, that was kinda sick.

What I mean is I was nervous. The end. Nervous to watch *The Office* with my best friend. And that nervousness made me nervous. So I took a long shower, hoping to rinse away the nausea.

It didn't rinse away, but I don't really need to tell you that, do I?

I stepped out of the shower and stared at my bag. I brought the entire thing into the bathroom so I'd have options. Because out of nowhere, I needed options. I never needed options before. I never cared. Now I cared.

Again. Nausea.

I shoved on a pair of pajamas. The ugliest I could find. Well, ugliest to Donovan. My Batman pajamas were pretty sweet, if you ask me. I got the fabric and made them myself and although they were kinda nerdy—I admit it, yeah—I still loved them. But I love nerdy people. Nerdy people are always more interesting.

So, Batman pajamas and all, I finally went out to the bedroom.

"Oh, no." He covered his eyes. "Not the Batman ones."

"What do you mean?" I dropped my bag in the corner. "They're

138

all Batman."

"Some are ... better than those."

"These are my favorite."

"I think it's just the cape that steps it up into weirdo range."

I sat on the edge of the bed. "You know you love it."

"Actually." He poked my rib. "I always did think you looked cute in these."

Donovan called me "cute" a trillion times in my life, but now it sounded real. For the first time.

"Are you and Zoe still technically together?" I said.

"No. I don't think so."

"How can you not think so? Why don't you know so?"

"We haven't officially said it, but I don't want to be with her anymore. I think we drove each other nuts."

"Why don't you ever listen to me?"

He took my arm into his hand and pulled me near him. "Cuddle me and watch Michael Scott make an idiot of himself."

"But you never listen to me." I slipped under the covers beside his warm body. "You always date girls that are horrible for you and then you think every single one of them is the one you want to marry, only to realize by week two that you're done." I sighed. "Now what am I gonna do about her living with me?"

He pressed my head against his chest. "Shhhh...."

"Let me pick your next girlfriend."

His chest jerked with a quiet laugh. "Maybe if you stop talking now."

Ear against his t-shirt, I settled my hand on his chest. Right above my eyes, right over his heart. I missed this. I really did. But it was getting weirder, because I was getting weirder. That Alistair really messed me up.

I pretended to laugh at *The Office* whenever Donovan laughed, but I was so distracted by his breath hitting the top of my head and his heartbeat under my palm that I couldn't look away from my hand as it rose and fell with every inhale and exhale.

What if I did love Donovan all along? What if Alistair walked into my life to awaken my heart so that I could finally see my best friend the way I was meant to?

He laughed, shaking us both until it subsided into a whimper. He reached his arm over me so that it pressed against my head as he wiped his eyes. We always laughed so hard we cried whenever *The Office* was on.

I reached up and wiped his eyes for him. He didn't notice. It was normal. Everything was normal to him.

But it was different to me now.

So different. So weird.

I WOKE UP IN THE MIDDLE OF THE NIGHT TO HIS TYPICAL snore fest and all I could think about was Autumn's mom kicking her husband's shin to make him quiet up. I laughed into the pillow as I imagined doing the same thing to Donovan, but couldn't bring myself to do it. No matter how many times the prank master pulled stuff on me. But ... I could do something else.

I turned to face him and he continued to snore, unaffected by my movements. So I tickled his nose with the ends of my hair and even tugged on his eyelashes and lifted his eyes. Man, I wished I had those kind of sleeping powers. He still didn't budge so I flipped my arms back and screamed at the top of my lungs, realizing in that split second that I was in a hotel, not the wilderness, and someone was probably going to call the cops.

Donovan flailed and shot up on his knees, his eyes darting in every direction possible. He clutched his chest and caught my suppressed laughter.

"What the hell was that?" He yanked the covers away from my face and pressed my arms above my head. "Now you're getting it."

He pinned me down, climbed on top of me, and tickled me until I couldn't breathe. Our faces were inches from each other and his chest was touching mine.

Feelings. Not worms. Butterflies.

I didn't like the feeling.

I stared into his eyes and saw little glimmers of light from the window behind us. He looked at me. Everything stood quiet and still. Time, us, the buzzing air conditioner. Everything stopped.

Does he know?

His smile officially disappeared.

Another comfortable awkward moment.

Maybe too comfortable.

He opened his mouth ever so slightly and moved toward me, then moved back and stared at me for a reaction that I didn't give. He was so close I could only stare at one eye at a time. So I chose the right one. Then the left.

Then he rolled over to his side of the bed and moved my hair to the side of my face. I curled up on my side and faced him. He faced me. The moonlight poured in from the windows and flickered on his skin.

I watched him.

He watched me.

And I fell asleep like that. With his fingers tangled in my hair and his eyes roaming my face. And I liked it. Like *that*, I mean.

Can you believe it?

I actually liked it.

I WOKE TO THE SUN BEATING ON MY FACE AND DONOVAN snoring in my ear. Again. Pet peeve of mine and it always drove me crazy before. But that was before. And now ... now was bizarro. Now I watched him sleep for a few minutes. I thought of Alistair and wondered if I should contact him. Maybe all of this Alistair stuff was making me crazy and a quick email with him would calm me down. I couldn't possibly have feelings—*those* kind of feelings—for Donovan.

His eyelids fluttered a little before he opened them, then saw the sun beaming into his eyes and pulled the blankets over his head.

"What do you wanna do today?" His voice was muffled through the blankets.

"Don't know. Any ideas?"

"Um." He flipped the blankets off and squinted. "For starters, food. A big, huge breakfast at a nice diner. A real diner."

"Okay. We came all the way to New York for a breakfast we could have at home. Sounds like us."

"Well, we could ride the subway and take a walk in Central Park."

"Sounds exciting." I laughed. "How about a Broadway show? Or a symphony? Or how about we walk the boutiques so I can get some inspiration?"

"Right." He pulled the blankets back up. "What you said."

"Man." Donovan stepped out into the hustle and bustle of New York City's gum-covered sidewalk. "It's raining now."

"Oh." I jumped out into the rain. "I love it. Rain is perfect for a New York tour."

"Not without an umbrella."

"Look at you." I moved a single curl from his forehead. "Hair wet. See." I spun in a circle with my arms outstretched. "This is perfect."

"If you say so." He laughed. "Where to?"

"Follow me."

We walked the streets of SoHo as people hurried by us, tucked under umbrellas or newspapers. Donovan looked up and commented on how enormous the buildings were. They felt monstrous even compared to the bigger ones from Philly. Something about New York seems bigger, like you can reach out and touch it, feel it, but it will always keep a piece of itself hidden, incapable of being found. I liked that about it.

"I want to be like New York," I said as the rain trickled down my face.

"Busy, dirty, and overrated?"

I smiled. "Romantic, worn, and mysterious."

"Romantic?"

"Yeah."

"Worn?"

"Yeah, like ... well-lived. Kinda like a favorite pair of shoes."

"Or Batman pajamas."

"Or those."

"You're definitely mysterious."

"I try."

Donovan's nose led us into a bakery. Fine-crafted breads sat on counters, waiting to be torn open and eaten. But they were almost too beautiful to eat.

Almost.

We got two. They were gone before we walked out. Then we ended up at a quaint little place called Spring Street Natural. Cute. We sat at a table for two and I ordered French toast while he got some sort of monstrous breakfast dish.

He rubbed his stomach and leaned back in his chair. "Can't wait for that."

I put my elbows on the table and put my chin in my hands. "So."

"So?"

"Heard from Zoe? What am I supposed to do when we get back?"

"She texted me. Said she was sorry and that she knows how important you are to me and that she trusts us both."

I nodded, thinking back to our tickle fight last night.

"She knows I don't have feelings for you anymore, but I guess it's just been eating at her all this time."

Why did it feel like someone just threw ice water on my chest? "Okay," I said. "So you're getting back together? When will you realize that she's not good for you?"

"I'm not getting back with her." He sipped his orange juice. "I know what I want in a woman."

"And what's that? Boobs and legs?"

He laughed. "I prefer the other body parts too."

"You always date girls who are super pretty and super annoying."

"Not Ursula."

"No. She was nice."

"But the name...."

"The name was beautiful in its own way."

His steamy plate of everything was placed in front of him and my yummy French toast was set in front of me. We both dug right in and didn't speak. So hungry. When we finished sharing each other's meals, he pushed his plate toward me and asked what I wanted in a man.

I laughed.

"Alistair Anonymous?"

"Maybe." I caught an old couple across the room while they were staring at us. I smiled. They waved and smiled back.

Donovan turned around and waved too. "What was that all about?"

"Just friendly, I guess."

We finished our drinks and asked for the bill, but the waitress said it was taken care of and handed Donovan a paper. He read it, smiled, and handed it to me. In scratchy, barely legible writing it said:

You make a beautiful young couple and we can see the love so strong in your eyes when you smile at each other. It reminded us of when we first met in 1953. When you find someone that makes you smile like that you don't ever let them go. Thank you for the reminder of our early days in love. This breakfast is our treat. Enjoy!

"Awww...." I said.

"I knew you'd say that."

"I'm a girl in some ways."

He laughed. "Ready to go, my young love?"

I looked at my phone. "Yeah. Plenty of time to check out some boutiques before the orchestra is on."

He offered me his arm. I linked mine and thought of Alistair. The time he elbowed my boob and looked like a poor, stuttery Hugh Grant character.

Maybe I'd send him an email tonight. Maybe I wouldn't.

I figured I'd let the symphony decide for me. Music had a way of helping me realize how I felt when I couldn't understand myself.

The rain calmed a little, but still sent droplets down our cheeks as we walked in and out of fine boutiques.

Inspired doesn't do it justice.

I was ready to take on the world—of design, I mean.

Chapter 12

NEW YORK WAS FUN, BUT BOSTON WAS GORGEOUS. OH, MAN. I fell in love as soon as we hit the little town streets. Donovan liked it better than NYC, but I think the rain played a part in his decision.

We enjoyed a nice morning walk, then made our way to the address we found for my ... mother. I wasn't even sure if it was her, but it was one of two people with her name and age range (thank you scary Internet) and the other was in California. So naturally we went with the easiest option first.

"Your mom just sent me a text," Donovan said.

"Oops." I pulled my phone out of my bag. "Forgot to reply to her last night."

"Does she know you came here?"

"They know about it, but they don't know we're here now. I didn't want them thinking about it. I'll tell them when I get back."

"Should I text her?"

"Nah, I'm doing it right now."

Donovan stopped as I finished up my text and I didn't realize it, so I kept walking. He whistled and I turned.

"What are you doing?" I yelled.

He pointed. "This is the address."

I swallowed and took a step. Or at least I thought I did. But I hadn't moved. He walked toward me and touched my wrists, just barely, with his fingers.

I nodded. "Is this weird? Maybe I shouldn't...."

"You'll always think about it if you don't. Just like Alistair." He tried to wink and failed, and tried again with a more exaggerated failed attempt.

I laughed. "I can't believe you don't know how to wink."

He put his arm around me like an older brother would and it immediately took me back to the time I busted my knee in first grade. Donovan ran over to me in the playground, scooped me up, and carried me in to the nurse. The kid was in first grade and not much taller than me. He struggled up the steps, but bit his lip and endured. When we reached the top he tripped and skinned my knee even more. I didn't tell him that though. How could I? He sprained his ankle when we fell and never said a word. But I knew.

He held my hand the rest of the way to the nurse, trying to hide his limp. After school that day he told me he would marry me and give me bandaids forever, if I wanted.

He always scared me when he talked like that. Maybe he considered that one of the times I rejected him.

He held my hand again. This time walking me up the steps to my real mother's front door. We knocked and no one answered. So Donovan opened the mail box.

"What are you doing?" I whispered, checking around for curious eyeballs.

"Seeing if her name is on the mail."

"Stop." I shoved the letters back in. "That's illegal, isn't it?"

"Not hurting anyone. I saw it. Wasn't her name. Some guy."

"Boyfriend?"

"Maybe."

I knocked again, less nervous now that I figured no one was home. Or we had the wrong house altogether.

But the handle jiggled, then turned.

I held my stomach to suppress that feeling again. The worms.

My mouth dried up as the door opened in slow motion. Donovan held my hand. I just kinda stood there.

A man stuck his head out, looked around us, then opened the door a little more. "Can I help you?"

"I'm here to see Julia. Does she live here?"

The man looked around us again and shook his head. The door started to close, but Donovan put his foot out to stop it.

"Do you know her? Or where she might live?" I asked.

"Why?" He hid most of himself behind the door. "Who's asking?"

I shrugged and looked myself up and down. "Me?"

"She don't live here no more." I noticed bruises on his arms. "California last I heard."

Donovan and I looked at each other. The guy finally closed the door on us. We stayed there. Looking at each other. Processing. Wondering.

"California?" I finally said.

"Let's do it," he said.

I smiled. "That's a huge trip."

"And you're gonna say yes."

"You know me."

"Let's enjoy Boston one more night and find a plane ticket tomorrow."

"Want to drive?"

"Don't wanna waste more money than we need to, but that would be a lot of fun."

"Come on. Let's drive."

"Let's get off this guy's steps first and figure it out later."

PLANE IT WAS. MAINLY BECAUSE DONOVAN COULDN'T GET off work anymore than three more days. We'd fly out and back and he could keep his job.

He went to the bathroom while I pulled out my iPad in the airport and looked up her address. A wee tad freaky that you can find out so much about a person online. It showed everything from her shopping preferences to criminal records and phone numbers.

Donovan sat beside me and crunched on a granola bar.

"Hey." I pointed to the screen. "I found all this information on her. Paid for this report thingy and I have an email address." He handed me his half-eaten granola bar. "Should I just email?"

"Up to you."

"I know. But what do you think?"

"Depends how you want your first meeting to go."

"I could try emailing and we can still go out there. See if she responds first."

"Go for it."

I pulled out my Bluetooth keyboard and typed, "Hello." Then I stared at that intimating cursor as it blinked and blinked and blinked. Donovan meandered off again in search of more food and somehow I ended up looking at Alistair again.

It was nice to see his face. A picture to go with the fading memory. I could almost picture his smile as he asked to kiss me. What an odd day.

"Jane is in love," Donovan teased as he handed me a water bottle and a slice of pizza. "If there's anyone you should email, it's lover boy."

"Stop calling him lover boy." I closed the iPad and smelled the pizza. "Mmm..."

"Why don't you just email him?"

"Can you imagine me dating someone? Like for real dating?" I took another bite of pizza and laughed as the cheese attached to my chin.

Donovan picked it up and pulled it toward his mouth.

"Ew!" I pulled it back and put it on my plate. "Gross!"

"Remember when I used to eat the gum you chewed? I think it was seventh grade."

"I remember." I wiped my face. "Sick."

He finished his second slice of pizza before I finished my first. When I finally took the last bite he threw our plates away and we made our way to the gates. They were now calling letters and numbers.

Donovan leaned into my shoulder. "Email him."

I leaned back into his shoulder. "I can't."

"You can." They called us and we walked forward, handed them our tickets, and headed down the terminal. "Do you want to?"

I shrugged.

"You pretend like you don't want a relationship, but I know you do."

"No." I tapped the side of the terminal three times before getting into the plane. Weird habit for good luck. Probably didn't do a thing, but I hated flying. Being superstitious was worth it in this case.

"Yes," he said. "I know you better than you know yourself."

"Apparently not." We shoved our bags above our heads and sat down. He took the window seat, knowing I didn't want anything to do with it. "I really don't. I'm not opposed to it, but at the same time I'm not ready for it."

"Will you ever be ready?"

"I think so." I set my iPad on my lap and looked at him. "Come on. I'm only eighteen! I have plenty of time."

He tapped on the window. "Unless you die on this plane as we're flying over Chicago."

"Thanks."

"Plummeting thousands of feet as the oxygen mask flings toward your face. No escape. Only the end. Waiting."

"Thanks for the mental image I've been trying to avoid for the last hour."

He folded his hands over his lap, leaned back, and closed his eyes. "That's what I'm here for, sweetheart."

WE LANDED IN LA. THANK THE STARS ABOVE. IF THEY CAN be thanked, of course. I don't need to tell you that the first thing Donovan insisted we do was immediately find food. Good food. Not airport food.

We picked up our rental car after navigating the airport and my phone beeped. I ignored it, but it kept beeping and buzzing in my bag.

"You should check that," he said as we drove off to find food.

I pulled the phone out. A bunch of calls from Eddie.

"It's Eddie," I said. "He called. A lot."

"Must be important. Eddie only texts. I didn't even know his phone worked like a normal phone."

I called back. "Hey," I said. "Everything okay?"

"No." I could barely hear him. "Mahidinahizpitooh."

"What? You're mumbling, Ed. I can't hear you."

"Oh, sorry." Finally could hear him. "Had my finger over the thing."

"Is something wrong?"

"Where are you?"

"I'm out with Donovan."

"No one could get in touch with you. Dad's in the hospital."

"For what?"

"We aren't sure yet." Something jumbled and then he spoke clear again, "Are you coming?"

"Eddie, what happened?"

Donovan was already heading back to the airport. Guess he noticed the tone of my voice.

"I don't know. Dad's acting weird. They're doing tests now. Mom is freeeeeaking out. You need to get here now."

"I'll get there as soon as I can. Might be a while. We kinda took a vacation."

"Yeah, well while you're out there looking for a mother who left you your real mother needs you."

"Hark! He speaks!"

"Hanging up now."

"Sorry. I'll be there when I can."

I hung up and looked at Donovan. "Leave it to Eddie to spend most of his life mute and then slam you with random bursts of intensity."

"What happened?"

"Dad. They don't know. Mom's having a nervous breakdown and Eddie is reprimanding me for looking for this mom while my real mom is in need of someone."

"Not like you could've known."

"Yeah. I don't think he likes that I'm looking into this. He doesn't express himself, so who knows, but I just feel like everyone thinks I'm betraying them."

"You're not."

I nodded. "Hope Dad's okay."

Donovan squeezed my hand and held it until he parked.

I was thankful for that hand.

BY THE TIME WE GOT ON A PLANE AND BACK TO PHILLY IT had been twenty-two hours since Eddie first called. That's a lot of time when you're dad is in the hospital for something unknown. It's also a lot of time when you have too much to think about. Like family, love, friends, mothers, roommates. Too much.

Donovan took me to the hospital and given his place in our family, he came inside with me too.

I inhaled as we walked in. Donovan gave me a weird look.

"What?" I sniffed again. "I love the smell of hospitals."

"Yeah." He smirked. "You and one percent of the population."

"It's clean and plasticy. Like Office Max without the paper smell."

"Mmmhmm."

We found our way to Dad's ICU room and Mom hugged both of us as soon as she saw us. Her tears totally covered my shoulder, but I didn't mind. She was always the strong one unless something happened to Dad. Can't tell you how many times I heard her half-jokingly but mostly seriously say to him, "Don't die. Don't ever die."

She finally let go of us, looked back to Dad, wiped her face, then stared at the floor.

"Dad's sleeping?" I said. "So, any news?"

She chewed the inside of her cheek and shook her head.

"Not sleeping," Eddie said from across the room, waking Granny in the process. "He's in a coma."

"Oh, Jane." Granny wobbled to her feet and walked toward me. I met her ninety-percent of the way. "So glad you made it, honey. It's going to be okay. Everything will be fine."

"Everything's not fine," Eddie said, rubbing his eyebrows. "It's not, Granny."

"Edward Darcy Austen!" Mom's tears dried right up as her face reddened.

"It's true." He hadn't looked up from his phone since I walked in.

"Eddie, why do you speak when you shouldn't and refuse to when you should?" I hugged Granny.

"Why do you go off and—"

"Enough you two," Mom said, now holding Dad's hand. "Your father could very well be dying. Maybe you two can find it within yourselves to stop arguing."

"Dying?" I looked from Mom to Granny, then noticed Donovan's bummed out face across the room. "Why is Dad dying?"

"He's not dying," Granny said.

Mom leaned into the hospital bed and sobbed into his hand.

"What's going on?" I pleaded. "What happened?"

"He was cleaning out the shed," Granny said. "He thought a bird flew at him, but he got a flu that wouldn't quite go away for the last week or so. When he came here they ran some tests and think he was bit by a bat and now has rabies."

"Rabies? There's a cure for that. People don't die from rabies."

Mom let out a loud cry again.

"Do they?" I whispered.

Donovan put his hand on Mom's shoulder and Granny put hers on mine. "He's in a medically induced coma. They are doing everything they can."

"But..." I couldn't lose it. Not in front of Mom. Not now. "He'll be okay." My voice shook. I steadied myself and tried again, "He's going to be okay. He will. There was an *Office* episode about this." Images of Michael Scott running down the sidewalk covered in sweat flashed through my mind. "Everyone was fine."

"This is real life," Eddie chimed in again.

"Put your phone away." I flicked his head.

He swatted my hand.

"Stop acting like you're toddlers," Mom said. "As you can see, your father is in a coma and doctors have warned me that this could be fatal." She sniffed. "Do you understand?"

I inched closer to Granny and whispered, "Has she left his side at all?"

"Of course not."

"Mom," I said. "Do you want to go get something to eat while I spend some time with Dad?"

"No." She ran her fingers along his jaw. "I'm not leaving his side."

"Mom, you—"

"I'm not leaving, Jane. I can't leave his side. You never know. You just never know...."

Donovan waved at me to let it go. I pulled a chair beside the hospital bed and sat beside him, mentally prepared for an Internet search extravaganza all about rabies. That would be later.

I kept staring at Mom. The pain on her face reminded me of a scene from *Batman Begins*, and I figured I probably shouldn't be thinking about Batman, so I focused on Dad's closed eyes. But Mom distracted me back to her face with every sniffle.

I don't know.

That level of love kind of freaked me out. I couldn't imagine loving a person like that. Where losing them is the most excruciating thing imaginable. I didn't like that. I didn't want another life to have that kind of power over me.

Donovan sat down beside me and held Dad's hand. The right side of my mouth pulled up into a jittery smile. He drummed on my knee and squeezed Dad's hand.

I imagined losing him. Standing over his casket as they lowered it into the earth. Then I quickly stopped imagining it because it was exactly what I feared.

The slightest inkling of what Mom felt. Creeping right in.

Don't die, I said inside. *Don't you ever die, Donovan.*

Chapter 13

I TRIED TO FOCUS ON THE BOUTIQUE, MY BUSINESS PLAN, the designs I needed to sew, decor, my obnoxious roommate, but it was too much. Just too much all at once and with Mom refusing to shower or leave Dad's side, I felt horrible trying to maintain a normal life while he was still in a coma. They said maybe he'd come out soon, but once they try to get them to wake up it really depends on the person. Doctors were happy with the results of his anti-viral meds though. They seemed optimistic, but I think all of us feared optimism because of the let down it could bring.

Fear or not, I refused to avoid optimism purely because of a *potential* let down. I believed and hoped Dad would be fine. Because he would.

That's all I needed to know.

Zoe ate a bowl of yogurt with blueberries on top as I poured cereal at the counter. I couldn't believe she was still living with me, but with their recent break up she seemed to become a little stalkeresque.

"How's Donny?" she asked for the six millionth time.

"Good." I crunched. "I'm good too. I mean, in case you were wondering."

"I thought maybe I heard him in your room last night."

"Nope." I crunched again. "He was on speaker phone though. So

159

if you count his voice being in my room, then yeah, I guess he was."

She nodded and stared off for a second, then said, "So ... um ... have you guys ever like ... has he kissed you?"

I laughed a bit of milk right to my arm. And crunched. "No."

"Never? But you guys are so close." She blushed. "And he's so hot."

"He's okay."

"Whatever. His arms. His back. Those eyes and that messy hair. He's like perfect."

"He snores. Loud. He's horrible at laundry, pretty much lives out of his basket. He has a third nipple. Yes, it's true. And prominent. He constantly bangs the spoon against his teeth when he eats and always, always, always gets something stuck in his facial hair even if it's just a tiny bit of hair peeking through." I crunched. "So. Yeah. He's okay."

She laughed a little. "You swear you never kissed?"

"Not once. He's kissed the top of my head. I've kissed his cheek. In a school play he kissed my hand. That's about it."

Technically, I wasn't lying. Because he kissed me.

"Well, it's clear he's not into you like that, but I just figured you were into him."

"Why?"

"Because everyone is."

"I'm not everyone." I really wanted to know why it was so clear that he wasn't into me though. Clear? Why clear?

"That's an understatement." She put her bowl in the sink. "Mind washing that for me? I'm late for work."

I glanced at her bowl and nodded.

"Donny coming over tonight?" she said.

"Donny boy will not be coming over tonight. I'll be sure to let you know."

She stepped closer to me. Too close for comfort. And sniffed.

I stepped back. "Did I forget deodorant?"

She shook her head. "Sorry. I thought for a second that I smelled his cologne on you." She sighed. "I'm going to marry him, you know. He was looking for a ring. He wants to be with me."

"Hmm. Yeah. I hope it works out for you."

"Do you? I know you have to be jealous, being single for your entire life and all."

"Shouldn't you be at work?"

She grabbed her purse, checked her reflection in her phone, and opened the door. "Sorry if I upset you. You're time will come."

I laughed when she left and drank the milk in my bowl, washed our dishes, and wondered if people like Zoe realized they were so rude or if it just came so naturally that they genuinely believed they were being nice. I'm a believer in skepticism so I say ... rude. Just plain rude.

I loved my apartment. Minus the Zoe part, but she wouldn't stay forever. Would she? It was so bright. Mornings. Afternoons. Evenings. Bright, bright, bright. I tried to sit down at the dining room table and plan stuff for the boutique, but Dad kept popping into my mind and I felt bad leaving Mom there to cry at his side.

So I took a quick shower and called Autumn.

"Hey," I said. "I'm gonna cancel lunch plans. I think I'm gonna go visit my dad for a while and then come back and try to figure out a name for this boutique."

"Can I come over later? I'll help."

"Of course. What's mine is yours."

"Even Alistair Anonymous?"

"If he were mine, sure. But he's not."

She laughed. "I'll see you at seven?"

"Perfect."

"Send my love to your family."

"Will do."

MOM BARELY MOVED WHEN I WALKED INTO THE HOSPITAL room. I hadn't seen her sleep since he got there, so it was nice to see her conked out by Dad's bed, fingers locked with his. I watched them both, careful not to wake her. And I noticed Dad's eyelids flutter. At the same time as hers. I imagined them dancing together in their sleep.

I admit ... their love was beautiful, as over the top as it was. They were best friends *and* lovers. The ideal marriage, really. I figured I'd be more of the "I married my best friend type"—I know what you're thinking and I do *not* mean Donovan—but I could appreciate those who had what my parent's had. Of course they were pretty much the only people I knew who had what they had. The staring into each other's eyes was a bit much though. And the emotional decay when something happens to the other one. Not so much a fan.

I would be stronger than that.

Donovan texted me. *How's Dad?*

Me: *His eyelids are fluttering. Maybe that's a good sign? Mom is asleep beside him. Please don't ever let me fall apart if my husband gets sick. I want to be stronger.*

Donovan:*Haha! :) Well, first you need a husband and secondly ... who said its not a strength to love someone that much?*

Me:*Hmmmmm*

Donovan:;)

Me:*I don't know. It seems weak to have your emotional stability depend on someone else being there.*

Donovan:*I think it's a strength. When will you see love as something to admire?*

Me:*Oh stop! I do see that.*

Donovan:*Riiiiight. Email lover boy?*

I slipped my phone back into my purse and ignored him. A nurse walked in and checked Dad, then typed some stuff on a computer next to the bed. Mom stirred and jumped when she saw me.

"How long have you been here?" She rubbed her eyes, then placed her hand right back on Dad's. Before I could answer she looked at the nurse. "Everything okay?"

"Yes, Mrs. Austen. He should be waking up soon. Remember it will be fuzzy for him and things may not make sense."

They also told us that he may be paralyzed or have speech impairments. If he did walk again, he would need physical therapy to retrain his body. All because of a bat.

Mom turned back to me and pulled me down to the chair beside her. "How've you been, Jane? Is the apartment working out for you?"

"It's going okay. Hard to focus with Dad in here."

"I know." She looked at him. "I know."

"Have you eaten?"

"A little. The nurses are so kind."

"Mom. You need to eat. Dad would want you to take care of

yourself."

"I'm eating." She almost laughed. "How's Donovan? Autumn?"

"Good."

"Has Don decided what to do next year?"

"Not that I know of. I'm gonna guess he ends up doing whatever his girlfriend of the moment is doing."

Mom flew into the air and scared the shibbles out of me. She hovered over Dad and I panicked, ran to the door, and screamed for the nurse. People rushed into the room, then backed away from the bed. Smiling.

What?

I went back to Mom's side and saw Dad's eyes flickering open. She caressed his forehead and hair as he slowly came back to life. I stepped back with the nurses and stood quietly. Another nurse clicked on the computer again while the rest of us watched Mom's tears dropped to Dad's sheets. A few minutes of blinking and sniffling later, Dad lifted his hand and brushed a tear from Mom's cheek. She cried harder. I even held back a tear. Or maybe even two.

They stayed like that for a while. Staring at each other like old times. I wondered how bad he was. He obviously moved his arm. What about his legs? What about his brain?

He tried to speak, but it was raspy, deep, and muffled.

"I love you too," Mom said. "I love you too, my dear, sweet husband."

I didn't want to interrupt their time together, so I followed the nurses back into the hall and found a seat in the waiting area at the end, across from the elevators.

Feeling a little inspired and slightly less cynical, I got on my phone and brought up Hatchenfield's website. After looking at Alistair's picture for thirty seconds too long, I went to the contact form and typed.

HEY HATCHERS!

I am a US girl wondering when you'll be in Philly. Would love to see you play at TLA. Maybe even make you trip at the airport so I can get a free latte out of it. Let me know.

Jane Austen

No... not that Jane Austen

I totally pulled one of those cliche moments in movies where your hand hovers over the send button. The clock ticks in the background. The hand hovers. So mysterious. Will she click or not? Of course I would. They always do. I don't know what the point of the hovering hand is, but I managed to do it myself.

Then ... CLICK!

Swoosh. Send. Buh-bye.

A minute passed and I checked my inbox. I had become *that* girl.

I turned my phone off and swore to myself not to look again until I got home, but I was already checking it as I walked back to Dad's room.

So. Not. Good.

So not good.

Donovan would have a party if he found out. Which is why he wouldn't find out.

Eddie and Granny were with Dad when I came in. Mom too, obviously. The nurse looked at me, stuttered, and finally said, "Typically we only allow three at a time, but I'll ask if this is okay."

"Oh, um, I can—"

"No." Granny took my hand. "You're staying here, young lady. When will you learn to say no? You don't get anywhere in life by saying yes all the time."

"Trust me, I don't always say yes."

Mom smiled. "It's true. She can say no when she's really uncomfortable, she just has a hard time saying no to people she loves or strangers. If you're an enemy or acquaintance?"

"Watch out!" I said. "Then you'll get my real opinion."

"No." Eddie laughed. "We get that all the time."

"Hark! He smiles!"

He glared up at me through his scrunched eye balls. Brothers. Man. Love him and all, but man....

Eddie and I went through stages. Super close as babies. Enemies when he turned four. Pretty much stayed that way until I turned five. Then we were best friends. Played army men, Super Nintendo, and even Barbies (shhh...don't tell) together for years. Then, I'd say around the time he entered sixth grade, maybe a few months before that, he hated me again. We annoyed the hell out of each other until ... well, I guess we still did sometimes. But we also loved each other. Even liked each other. Our teasing was all in jest and although it agitated Mom it was all in good fun.

I wrapped my arm around him and put my head on his shoulder. He pretended to shove me off, then put his head against mine. We stayed like that as Mom smiled at Dad.

See. We could be friends sometimes too.

AUTUMN STARED AT ME LIKE I WAS CRAZY, BECAUSE FACT IS

... I was.

"Let me see," she said.

"Stop." I waved her away. "You're practically squealing and I haven't even opened the email yet."

"Been staring at it for like ten minutes. Let me open it." She clasped her hands in front of her chest. "Please, please, please."

"No, no, no." I swallowed. Butterflies—or possibly worms—made my stomach do that thing I hate. "I'm opening it now."

She tapped her foot like crazy.

I laughed. "Calm down. You're freaking me out."

I read through it. Then looked at her.

"What?"

I stared as blankly as possible.

"What? What? Is it bad?"

"Autumn." I slid the phone toward her. "He wants to get married."

"Are you frickin' kidding me? What will you say?" She picked up the phone and read. "Ugh. You're so annoying."

I laughed. "Intriguing email, huh?"

"What will you say?"

"It's just his manager thinking I'm some fan. I'm not gonna reply and ask for his info. They'll just think I'm a stalker."

"But you are!"

"Uh oh." I clicked on the email. "This just came in. Dear Jane," I read aloud as my hands started to sweat. "Sorry about that last email. My manager copies me on all emails that go out and I saw this. Jane ..." My voice cracked. I read the rest silently.

"Jane?" Autumn practically yelled. "Jane what?"

I cleared my throat, but couldn't read the rest out loud. I handed the phone to her.

"Jane," she read, then looked up at me, then back down. "I can't stop thinking about you. Your twenty-first birthday is too far away. Write me back at this email." She squealed.

I held my ears. "Not the screeching!"

"What are you going to say?" She gave me the phone. "Respond. Now."

"No." I shoved the phone into the couch cushion. "No. I can't."

"You so, so can." She pulled the phone out of the couch.

I hid it under the pillow behind me. "I can't, Autumn. Seriously."

"You're never going to respond?"

"Don't look so bummed." I laughed. "I'm not a chick flick for your entertainment."

"But it's so interesting. And he's so adorable. Do it. Promise you'll respond at some point?"

"No, but I'll try."

"You are the weirdest ever."

"I go through great lengths to ensure that."

The phone beeped under the pillow. An email. She stared at me and I couldn't help but wonder what it said.

Zoe came into the apartment, sat down between us, and majorly disrupted my thoughts. She gave Autumn a hug, then me. Autumn and I looked at each other like ... uhhhh....

"I got you something," Zoe said, handing me a wrapped box.

Oh, great. Trying to get to Donov—

"And no, it's not my way of kissing your ass so Donovan comes back."

"Took the words right outta my ass."

Autumn tried to hide her smile and ended up stuffing her face into a pillow as she erupted into laughter. I laughed a little.

"I'm trying to be nice," Zoe said. "I'm really thankful for ev—"

Autumn popped up, holding her stomach and howling with laughter. I couldn't hold back anymore and cracked up as I opened the box, my hands shaking as I tried to control my laughter, and then I saw it.

I stopped laughing.

"Zoe...." I held the gift to my chest. "How...."

She blushed and folded her hands in her lap.

"How did you know?"

Autumn was still laughing in short bursts.

"I pay attention to what you say," she said. "And I noticed in your room that you had like all the Batman collectible figures, except this one. I'm not a huge fan, but my ex was and he got this for me as a gift one year. He's one of those people that like buys whatever he would like and gives them as gifts, instead of figuring out what they might like."

"I don't know what to say."

"I really didn't do it for any reason other than to let you know how thankful I am to be here. I kinda have a bad situation at my house with my brother. I don't know if Donny told you." She looked at me as though that was a question. I shook my head and she continued, "Anyway, it's not good there so this has really helped me."

"I ... I'm...."

Zoe squeezed the life out of me, then walked back to her room.

Autumn slapped her thighs and turned to me. "What the hell just happened?"

"Uh." I looked at the collectible in my hand. The in-the-box-excellent-condition-collectible-of-my-wildest-dreams. "Um ... yeah."

And Zoe? Of all people?

Speechless.

Chapter 14

ASTOUNDED BY DAD'S RECOVERY, HIS DOCTOR RELEASED him two weeks later. He could walk on his own and his speech was a little off, but nothing that would keep him from getting back to life.

Mom served him with even more enthusiasm. Bringing him drinks and snacks and tea while he rested on the couch. He kept telling her to sit down and just be with him. After the fifth time, she sat beside him and they spoke to each other with their eyes.

I understood the speaking with the eyes thing. Autumn and I could do that. Donovan too. But for that long? I couldn't imagine staring into someone's eyes for an hour and not getting bored. Or hungry.

I went to the kitchen and grabbed a tea cake, then made myself some warm milk with nutmeg and vanilla. Weird to be back home and not call it home. I left the love birds to themselves and knocked on Eddie's door.

"Yeah?" he said.

"Made you some milk."

"Come in."

I opened the door. "Technically the cow made the milk, but I warmed it up and added spices."

"Not nutmeg, right?"

"No. Put cinnamon in yours."

"Thanks." He set it on his desk and sat back down.

I sat on the bed and looked around the room. So different from my room. Mine was modern. Bright walls. Yellow and white chevron blanket. Black frames with modern Batman art. Watercolors on canvas. Photos of classical composers. His room, on the other hand, was moody and earthy. Hunter green walls. Brown and tan bedding. No art. No photos. Just wooden shelves he made with his own hands and a bunch of furniture he also made with his own hands. Stained dark when I would've painted them a distressed white or grey. Weirdest part of all ... he collected those trolls from the 60's and 90's. Lines and lines of them decorated his shelves. So bizarre. I'm sure my Batman figures (still in boxes of course) were weird to some people too, but hey ... trolls? Just kidding. I found it endearing.

We finished our milk at the same time and he went back to writing something at his desk. I looked around the room, remembering when we he used to sleep on the top bunk and me on the bottom. We were so close then.

"I miss you, Eddie," I said, still rummaging through memories in my mind.

"Yeah," he said without looking up.

"Hey...."

He still didn't look up.

"Eddie, I want you to know that I'm not curious about my biological mother for any reason other than ... I'm just curious."

He looked up. And back down he went.

"Eddie."

"Whatever you want to do. It's your life."

"See."

"No."

"Wouldn't you want to meet your mother?"

"Mom is your mother. That lady just got pregnant with you, then abandoned you."

"But I was a part of her body. That's gotta mean something. What would my life be like if she kept me?"

"Probably similar to something resembling a shit hole."

I laughed. "Thanks."

"Anytime." He continued writing.

"I love Mom. I love Dad and you. You guys are my family. I'm just curious."

"I heard you." He finally looked up. "Talking to your friends I always hear you saying 'real mom,' like this mom is fake or something. This mom gave everything for you. That one gave you nothing."

"I know. Trust me, I know."

"I don't get it." Writing again.

"Curiosity. What's so hard to get about it?"

"It killed the cat."

Mom came in and handed me an index card.

"What's this?" I said.

"Read it." She stood in the doorway.

The note said:

Between men and women there is no friendship possible. There is passion, enmity, worship, love, but no friendship.

Oscar Wilde

"I saw the way you looked at him," she said.

"Not this again." Eddie put earphones in and ignored us.

"Mom. How many times do I have to tell you? Donovan and I aren't in love. We really are just friends."

"Something's changed in you, Jane. I've been distracted with your housewarming surprise party and then Dad's hospital visit, but not too distracted to see the change in your eyes when you look at him."

"Mom."

She smiled. "Sometimes it's easier to just let love in. Otherwise it might break down your door and you'll either need to fix the door, which takes a lot of effort, or clean up the mess, which takes a long time. Why not just open the door and say hello? Worst thing that could happen is that it doesn't work and you say goodbye."

"Not with Donovan. He doesn't feel that way anymore, anyway. He got over me years ago."

"If you say so."

"I know so."

But I really didn't. Zoe said it was clear as the sun on a blazing August day, but it wasn't. Don and I had a weird friendship. Everything was always blurred and the only way to really know how he felt would had been to profess my love to him and see how he'd react.

Except I wasn't in love with him. Or anyone. And I definitely wasn't the "professing my love" type.

ROSALIND'S.

That's what I decided to call my boutique and fashion line. I had a million and three designs I created over the years. Some I'd scrap, some I'd ponder, and some I'd get started on right away.

This was my dream.

Like ... little girl dream.

And beginning to bring my little girl dream to life scared the crap out of me. I didn't fear failure, I hated it. What if the store flopped? What if everyone laughed at my designs? What if no one bought the stuff? Scary.

But I pressed on, hired two seamstresses, and went nuts. We sat together in the empty boutique and sewed our hearts out. That sounds weird....

Anyway, Autumn came over the day before to help with decor. Donovan offered his hand tonight, knowing Zoe would be at work. She'd probably be sniffing the place after he left.

He did some manlyish things, like hanging pictures and setting up the sales desks and furniture. We barely talked, but I needed to get him alone. Something was bothering him and so long as Brooke and Han, my two seamstress girls, were around, he'd stay like that. Walking around like a half-dead person with his shoulders all slumped.

"He's not always so lively," I said to the girls.

Han, sweetest person ever, chuckled modestly, but Brooke didn't hide her unmistakable laugh.

"Lively?" Brooke said. "Hate to see what he's like when he's tired."

"Hardy har," Donovan said. "Actually, I am tired."

Code word. He wanted me to make them leave. Since about fourth grade we had code words. "I'm tired," was our code for, "We need to talk. Alone."

I waited a few minutes and told the girls we could pack up and keep going tomorrow. Brooke winked at Donovan as she walked away. Han, on the other hand, hid behind her purse and completely avoided him.

When the back door swung to a close he put his hands over his face and whined.

"What now?" I said. "Please don't tell me it's another girl."

"I didn't get it." He peeked at me through his fingers. "It's done, Jane."

"Zoe? She'll take you back in a second."

"I applied for lacrosse scholarships, but I didn't get any of them. Got my last official rejection today."

"Why though? Can't a coach notice you at a summer tournament still?"

"I give up."

I gave him a hug and pat his back. "There, there, boy."

He pinched my back.

"What if I lend you the money?" I stepped back. "How much is it?"

"No way."

"It's mine to use as I please, sir."

"I'm not accepting that." He slumped into the chair and knocked over a container of bobbins and needles.

We both knelt down to clean them up when something pierced my knee. I flipped over and grabbed my leg.

"Um, there's a sewing pin stuck in my knee."

Donovan looked at it. "I'll go get the pliers."

"Pliers?"

He sat beside me and held up the tool. "Pliers," he said. "I'll pull it out. Real quick."

"No!" I scooted away, unable to stand because my tendon freaked out every time I moved. "I don't see the ball in there. It went in ball side first."

He touched his chin to his neck. "The ... ball?"

I laughed and squeezed my knee. "There are balls on the tops of pins. This went into my leg ball first. If we pull it out I'm gonna get a ball stuck in my leg and get infected or something." I clenched my teeth. "It hurts."

He waved the pliers. "Just one second and it'll all be over."

"The ball. And look." I pointed. "It's bent in there. The pin is this big." I held up my fingers. "What if it went into my bone? Oh my gosh ... what if it's in my bone, Donovan?"

He pushed his lips to the side of his face.

"It's not funny." I tried to move. "I need to go to the ER."

"Can you walk?"

I attempted to stand. "It hurts. If I move that tendon it kills."

"Here." He put my arms around his neck. "I'll carry you to my car."

And he did.

We stopped at one of those quickie emergency places, but they were closed. To the real deal ER we went. Only weeks after my toe incident. Thankfully the toe wasn't broken, just crushed at the tip and healed pretty fast. Otherwise I would've looked like an idiot coming in with a foot wrapped up and a sewing pin sticking out of my knee.

Donovan carried me into the ER and sat me next to someone with blood soaked on his shirt and a child with a gaping hole between her eyes. And so basically ... I felt like an idiot anyway.

Once we finally got to my room the doctor or nurse or whatever he was came in, pressed on it, and came back with ... pliers.

No joke.

Donovan pushed his lips around again, trying his hardest not to laugh in my face.

"Um." I put my hand between the pliers and my leg. "What if it's in my bone?"

The doctor guy shook the pliers. "This'll do it. It's not in the bone. I can feel right where it is."

"Is it possible to numb it first?"

"Are you serious?" Donovan said. "Give me that thing."

"I can numb it," the guy said. "It won't hurt but a second though."

"Numb, please."

"The needle to numb you will hurt worse than pulling this one out. Come on." Donovan held my hands. "Squeeze my hands, close your eyes, and let's go to Wendy's for a junior bacon cheeseburger, shake, and fries with nacho cheese."

"You're horrible."

"Or the diner."

"Ready?" the doctor said.

"Are you a doctor?"

"Physician's Assistant."

"Okay." I gripped Donovan's hands and closed my eyes. "Go!"

Out it came.

And Donovan shook his head. "Shoulda let me use the pliers."

I laughed. "Sorry." I felt all around my knee. "What if the ba—"

"There's no ball in your knee." He laughed. "Let's go. I'll even carry you out for fun."

He carried me back to the car and we laughed about the pin during our entire Wendy's excursion. Then he took me home and gave me a hug goodbye.

"You wanna have a sleepover?" I pointed toward the door. "I've got Batman sleeping bags."

"Tempting." He smiled. "But I've got work in the morning and I don't want to see Zoe until she's moved on. Oh"—he tried to wink and failed—"who's the shy girl you've got working for you? She's cute."

"Yeah. That's Han. She's from Korea. Brilliant. Talented. Creative. She's really sweet too. Not your type."

"Han?"

I nodded.

"I want to ask her to dinner or something. Will she do it?"

I glanced down and picked at my overgrown cuticles. "Probably. Everyone loves you."

"Not everyone." He tapped my chin.

"Heh." I almost managed a smile. "Yeah."

Chapter 15

AFTER A WEEK OF INTENSE SEWING—I'M TALKING FOUR-TEEN hours straight every day—I took a break to paint the walls. Han and Brooke kept up the sewing for me while Donovan, Autumn, and I painted the interior a nice cool grey.

Thankfully Zoe was at work, because I doubt she would've appreciated the way Donovan flirted with Han the entire time. Only in America two years, she brought with her this charm from Korea that made her impossible to dislike. Even I loved her and that's pretty strange when it comes to the girls Donovan likes.

Autumn dipped her roller into the bucket and slathered more paint on the wall while I worked on taping the other half of the room. Donovan disappeared again. With Han. Somewhere in the back.

I waited for Autumn to say something about his girl of the week, but she didn't.

"So," she finally cleared the air. "I decided to stay home this year."

"What?" I stopped taping. "Why would you do that?"

She twirled her hair and accidentally dropped a glob of paint on her foot. "I kinda met this guy."

"No." I went back to taping. "I'm not even acknowledging this."

"He's perfect for me, Jane."

"I wish I could explain to all of you that we are eighteen year olds and marriage should be the last thing on our agenda. Go to school. It's your dream to become a doctor. You've wanted to help people since you were a kid. So do it and if he's still around when it's done, then maybe he's the one."

"Don't be so negative."

"I'm being pretty positive actually. You have a free ride to the college of your choice. Don't ruin it for some guy who may not love you in a few years."

She painted in silence for a few minutes, then said, "So that Han girl and Don?"

"Yes. They're dating. Or going on dates. Not sure I know the difference, if there is one."

"She's like your twin."

I laughed and looked to make sure they weren't around. "She's Korean. We don't look anything alike. Just our hair maybe."

"No," she said. "She's so much like you. Only more shy and...."

"Go ahead and say sweet." I smiled. "I know it's true."

"You're just a little feistier and opinionated."

"Sweetness has never been my best trait."

"You're sweet." She laughed. "Seriously."

Han and Donovan came back into the room, eyes on each other Mom and Dad style. Don's eyes were brighter and Han's smile matched the brightness perfectly. They looked cute together. And they_were_cute together. She was the first girl to actually appreciate him and that made me feel like crap.

I was no longer the only girl who knew him, really knew him. They'd been dating a few short weeks, but she already knew things about him only I knew.

I thought back to the day in the hospital where I silently told him not to die. It felt like that now. Like he was dying. I was losing him.

Donovan went back to painting. Han sat down at her sewing machine. And they glanced at each other every few minutes. Her smile, all simple and surrounded by blushing cheeks, was killing him. In a good way. I could just tell.

He never looked at a girl like that before. Just me.

I finished taping the room and pretended not to watch them as I painted. Last time Donovan looked at me like that was in eleventh grade. We were cuddling on top of his car as the sun went down and he said something he shouldn't had promised.

"I'll wait forever for you or die waiting."

I'll never forget his face as I said, "You'll die alone then. Don't do that to yourself."

He lost the light in his eyes. He never told me that he gave up, but I could tell. His spark was gone. I killed it. He started dating all kinds of girls and the dynamic between us changed. Still good. Still close. But it changed. I knew I could bring the light back though. If I ever fell in love with him I knew he'd still love me. But now I doubted it because Han brought the sparkle in his eyes back. She beat me to it.

"You told him to die trying. What did you expect?" I whispered while spacing out at the wall.

Autumn tapped my shoulder. "You're talking to yourself in public again."

I slapped my hand over my mouth. "Did anyone hear me?" I quickly looked around the room and everyone was working. Everyone except Donovan. His eyes were on me.

"I heard you," Autumn said. "Not sure what it meant though."

We stared at each other. Donovan. Me. The rest of the room didn't disappear like I thought it was supposed to. The sewing machine hummed in the background. Rain dripped down the windows and tapped the sills. Autumn kept talking. Cars beeped outside. My phone buzzed across the room. Someone else's phone rang with a ridiculous pop song. Chaos. Absolute chaos around us.

But we stood there. Completely still.

I tried to smile.

He shrugged and crinkled his brow.

Comfortable awkwardness.

My phone vibrated itself right off the counter and hit the floor. Great timing. I needed an escape from the weirdities. I picked up the phone and opened the email.

Jane,

Did you get my last email? I hope I didn't scare you off. If you'd rather I hadn't been thinking of you, just pretend I didn't say that. ;-)

Jane?

I read it again as Han and Donovan kissed under an umbrella in front of the building. Looked like a freaking Nicholas Sparks cover.

I sighed and tried to reply.

Why wouldn't the words come?

"Hello, blinking cursor," I said. "Would you like some eye drops?"

"Don't mind her," Autumn said to Brooke. "You'll get used to it."

"I already am." Brooke laughed. "Hey, Jane. I've got another one finished. Wanna check it?"

"One sec."

Time to declare war with the blank email.

Dear Alistair,

I stopped. Inhaled. Exhaled. And tried to tell myself this was NOT a love letter. Just a friendly letter.

I continued:

Sorry. I've been super busy.

Well, that was painless. I thought about telling him that I was thinking of him too or at the very least acknowledging his declaration, but....

How are things in England?

That came out instead. So I kept going, promising myself I'd try.

I thought of you the other day when I was at the airport.

There. That should do.

Hope all is well!

Jane

And send.

Away it went. I checked Brooke's dress and approved it. "You're so good at this, Brooke," I said as my phone buzzed off the counter again. "If we make money with this place you're definitely getting a raise."

"I'm just happy to be here," she said. "I never thought my boss would be five years younger than me, but I have to say it's been fun. Your energy and passion for this has inspired me to start sewing again."

"That's so good to hear."

I picked the phone up again.

"Who's that? Mr. Anonymous?" Autumn teased. "I'm done with this wall. What's next?"

"We can start the trim where the walls are already dry."

Another email. So soon. With barely any contents.

Jane ...

That was all it said, but it was enough to bring those dreadful butterflies back.

I wrote his name, added some dots at the end, and hit send.

Another minute and he popped up again.

I got us a show booked at TLA like you said. October 27th. I know it's months away, but can I see you?

I wrote back:

That should be fun.

Good thing I wasn't trying to win an award for most flirtatious or anything. He emailed one last time and said he needed to practice. The guys were waiting for him, but he'd email me as soon as he finished.

Han came back into the store. Glowing. Then, in her cute little accent, she said, "He is very nice guy. Ah joh-eun."

"He is," Autumn said. "Are you in love with him?"

"Autumn!" I cut in.

"I don't know." The girl lit the room on fire with her radiance and she didn't know? "My father taught me to_be_in love, not to fall in love. He told me love is not something we feel. It is something we do. I have always been careful about feeling things. There must be harmony and peace around two people who marry. Everything make sense, you know?"

Autumn nodded. Brooke nodded. I figured I should nod too. So I did.

Han went back to her machine and smiled as she worked. I looked over a few times over the course of the day and I can assure you the smile was now a permanent part of her face.

For the first time ever—that I could remember, anyway—I knew what people meant by a pang of jealousy. Except it's kinda more than a pang. More like a twisting knife-in-the-chest desire to have something someone else has.

Of course.

No matter how much I never wanted to admit it ... Mom was right. She was always right.

Chapter 16

I LIKED HAN. REALLY LIKED HER. MAYBE MORE THAN Donovan liked her. Okay, that wasn't possible, but she had to be the sweetest person to ever walk the earth. She always stayed late to help me out and she worked so fast and rarely made mistakes. If I asked her to come in and help at nine in the morning she would show up at eight. What I loved most was that she did it out of genuine care and not to kiss up to Donovan's best friend. She smiled. All day. Even on bad days. She always went out of her way for others and put herself last. She amazed me.

Zoe, in other news, did not share these sentiments. So I sat her down with a big bowl of ice cream and let her vent. The first thirty minutes sounded like insanity and I barely understood a word, but finally she calmed down a little and made more sense.

"It's not like we weren't serious," she said. "We were talking about getting married."

"Zoe, you have to remember that he's never committed to anyone. Ever. He thinks he's in love whenever a girl smiles at him. It's an illness."

She stared at her ice cream.

"Don't take it personally. Someone better for you will come along."

"He was the best." A tear took a stroll down her face. "For me."

"This is exactly why I don't like this stuff."

She blew her nose. "What stuff?"

"Romantic relationships. My life is perfectly fine right now. Guys bring nothing but drama, tears, and confusion."

"There are good things that make the pain worth it."

"No." I shook my head. "No break up is worth this many sleepless nights. No guy is worth that, I don't care who he is. If he was willing to leave you, then you need to move on. The only one worth crying for is the one who never leaves you."

"I just really thought Donny was the one."

"You and seven thousand other girls."

She set her empty bowl on the table beside the couch. "Want to watch a movie?"

"Absolutely. How about *Shutter Island*?"

"What's that? I was thinking *The Best of Me* or *If I Stay*."

"Romance movies?"

She nodded.

"No way." I pretended to hide the remote behind me. "I am not interested in deepening your depression."

She smiled. "It's inspiring."

"Right. Ten minutes in and I'll be carrying a heap of sadness to her bed."

"Fine. Let's do your manly one."

I laughed and started to bring the movie up.

"Jane," she said.

"Yeah?"

"Thank you."

Chapter 17

I. LOVED. MY. TATTOO.

So, let me just tell you. Dee was amazing. Wonderful. I mean, the first tattoo artist was cool and all, but Dee? It's like she assessed my entire personality and got me the perfect, most incredible tattoo I could ever get. It's so hard to explain just how beautiful it is. So, here's a picture:

I know what you're thinking. What's so amazing about that?

Thing is ... I didn't even think to consider a Batman tattoo. I was thinking more along the lines of nifty designs and intricate thingies. But this ... this was exactly what I wanted and I just didn't know it.

It really captured what I love about Batman and how it related to my own life. So many times I felt like my own worst enemy and I think the Joker and Batman relationship shows how a hero and a villain are so similar in so many ways, like the Joker says to Batman, "I don't want to kill you. You complete me." That part of me. The villainous side. It completed me as much as I hated it. I was two people—maybe even eleven people—and I wanted to be one.

Although I couldn't see the tattoo way back there on my shoulder, it reminded me not to give in to the other parts of myself, the parts that wanted to ruin me.

It was a good thing I got the tattoo on Friday because I doubt I would've wanted to sew. The healing process isn't that bad, but I needed a break. The boutique thing was wearing me out, plus I seriously feared the grand opening and what people would say. They'd probably hate it all and walk out and all that time and all of those dreams would be a waste.

Anyway, it was now Saturday at noon and Donovan wanted me to meet him at our place. So I drove separately and we sat on the trunk of his car. Like usual. He didn't say anything for a while. We both lay there, looking at the treetops against the blue backdrop. Minutes stacked on top of each other. The sky turned darker and darker until finally he broke the silence.

"Still wanna go to Cali?" he said.

"Is that why you wanted to meet up?"

"Well, no."

"Then what?"

He leaned back and stared into the cloudy summer sky. "I just miss you."

I reclined beside him and watched as black clouds appeared in the distance. Donovan never said that before. *I just miss you.* Not in that tone. Normally when he dated girls I saw him a little less, but we were still best friends. This scared me. This scared me because I could tell that he felt it too. The inevitable change in our friendship.

I wondered what he'd do if I told him I wanted to be with him. If I actually did want to be with him. Like ... a serious thing. A real thing.

I turned and watched him. Eyes closed. He knew I was looking at him. His eyelids always struggled to stay closed when he knew. But I kept looking anyway.

"Jane," he said, eyes still fighting to stay shut.

"Yeah, Don?" I wanted to reach out and hold his hand, but instead I just stared at it and imagined his fingers with mine. What would it be like? To really be with someone? Was I even capable of real love?

"When we were fifteen I swore I'd open you up one day even if I had to cut you into pieces."

I somewhat laughed. "You were mad that day."

"I was." He turned his face toward me and pierced me with his serious eyes. "It was the last time you rejected me."

I looked away. "Why do you always talk about the past? Why can't we live right now without that stuff always popping up?"

"It's a part of us, Jane. It's got us here."

"Maybe I don't want to be here."

He grazed my arm with his thumb. "Jazzy."

My eyes stung and my nose got that tingly feeling that happened when I refused to let myself cry. I didn't even know why I was being emotional. It's not like I loved him like that. And my period wasn't due for another two weeks.

"Jazzy," he said. "This is exactly what I mean."

Gray clouds. Coming our way. I focused. Intensely focused. Big. Gray. Clouds. In the sky. Over me.

"You have to stop." He tapped my foot with his. "You need to stop avoiding things."

"I'd like to avoid this storm over our heads, but..."

"I promised myself and you that I wouldn't leave you until you found someone you loved more than a friend, some guy who finally won you over, or until you gave in and opened up everything you've been keeping inside." A raindrop landed on his lips. He licked it and smiled. "Jazz, I know you don't believe anything I say about girls, but I like Han."

"She's Korean. I know she's super sweet and all, but she told me she's concerned about her family's acceptance of you." I glanced at him out of the corner of my eye. "You're not exactly Korean."

"I don't need to think that far ahead?"

"So the future is off limits, but not the past?"

"Why does it bother you? It's not like it would be any different today. There's a reason—a hell of a lot of reasons—that I forced myself to get over you and you know that. The present is the past."

I pressed my lips together and focused on the looming storm again. I liked storms ... from inside a house. Being caught in the midst of bolts of lightning, tornadoes, or any kind of crazy disastrous weather was a major fear of mine.

"This storm," I said as my entire body seized with tension. "Maybe we should go."

"I guess what I'm saying is I want to make sure you're okay. If things change between us, will you be okay?"

"I'm fine, Donovan."

"I need to know that yo?"

"I said I'm fine."

"Fine." He sat up and swung his legs over the edge. "Just trying to love you, but obviously that's a frickin' waste of my time as usual." He jumped off the car and walked into the woods behind us.

It took me a second, but of course I went after him. I knew exactly where he'd be. Rain drops hit the leaves around me as the wind picked up. I jogged to get there faster and beat those black clouds back to my car. The rain trickled down my face and soaked into my shirt. Then it pelted the trees as their leaves unhooked and tossed to the ground. I ran faster, scared out of my mind. But I had to find him. I ran full speed, jumping over homeless branches and puddles of rain.

Thunder drummed in the background of nature's symphony. A steady, slow beat for now. I slowed down as I approached Donovan's hiding spot, but he wasn't there. Hands on my hips, lungs exhausted, I searched the area.

No Donovan.

Lightning cracked and shot through the sky, hitting a tree maybe fifty yards away from me. I breathed rapidly and froze in place. My fear wasn't irrational. I could *die*. Thunder rocked the sky. *Move legs, move.* I closed my eyes and told myself to *run* the hell out of there. Too many trees. Too many prime targets for a bolt of lightning. *Will power, will power. One, two, GO!* I sprinted for my car. Rubber tires. Roof. Just needed to make it to the car.

I tripped and landed on my hands and knees, then grabbed my knee as the wind shoved the rain sideways at my face. I stood and tried to jog, but it looked more like I was bouncing like a cracked up Tigger. I just wanted to get to the rubber tires before another streak of lightning decided to come down and electrocute my head.

But Donovan....

Maybe he was waiting for me back at the car.

I wobbled out of the woods and stopped. Right there in my tracks. A zig-zag of light flashed in the distance, lighting the clouds as it killed the arms of another poor tree. And more thunder. Quicker now. Closer together.

But I couldn't move.

I stared at the tracks the tires made when he left....

When he left me.

In the storm.

Alone.

Hands still at my sides, I walked to my car and saw a note on the window. Ink seeped through the drenched paper, forming blue rivers that poured from each letter.

You said you were fine.

I sighed as I sat in my car and dried the note with the heater. I would save it. Just like I saved everything Donovan ever gave me. Good or bad. Sweet or angry.

I turned my wipers on and waited, hands in my lap. My phone beeped with an email. Then a text. Then another text. I turned the music up. And up. And up. Until the phone could no longer be heard.

Then I drove away, over the same mud tracks Donovan's car created when he left.

Nicholas Sparks, my ass.

All of his girls get kissed in the rain.

Jane Austen?

She gets abandoned.

Chapter 18

I SAT ON THE FLOOR IN THE CORNER OF MY ROOM. IN ONE hand I held the letter Donovan put on my car, in the other I held the shoe box filled with stuff he'd given or written me over the years. I hadn't moved from that position since I got home. Three hours ago.

I hurt him so many times and he was the last person I wanted to hurt. Something told me I hurt him again, but I didn't understand why. He didn't love me anymore. That's what he said over and over. He got over me years ago. I remember when it happened. Things between us became more natural and comfortable. When he had a thing for me he was a little more shy and way more protective of me. If a guy so much as looked in my direction, Donovan was poised and ready for action. Not that I'd give them the time of day either.

See, I kinda lied a little.

To Alistair, I mean.

I told him I'd kissed plenty of guys, but it's not true. My first kiss was with Donovan. The summer before ninth grade. We were in his pool all day until the street lights came on, then we got out and sat on the edge with one towel wrapped around both of us. He shivered and laughed about it, then I laughed at him laughing at himself.

Next thing I knew he wasn't laughing anymore. His face moved closer to mine. Mirrored in the waves of the pool, the night sky sparkled and the almost full moon lit the tops of the trees.

And his face.

He forced my to look at him. I turned, but kept my eyes on the pool.

"Jazz," he whispered. "I'm going to kiss you right now, whether you like it or not."

My pulse probably stopped for a few seconds. I just kept looking at that water.

He moved closer and put his hand on my neck. I wanted to jump into the pool and avoid it. But then his thumb touched my cheek and his lips landed gracefully on mine. He tasted good. Really good. And I liked it.

He pulled away. "I couldn't stop myself."

I shivered. He gave me the rest of the towel, but I wasn't shivering from the cold. It was the heat.

"Sorry," he said. "I won't do it again unless you want me to."

That was my first and last kiss. I know a few modest girls from school who prided themselves on saving their first kiss for their wedding day. But for me? It was embarrassing. Everyone, including Donovan, believed I had kissed at least ten other guys. One of those mumbling, "Oh, yeah, yeah ... no, really ... yeah, I've kissed *plenty* of guys," kinda things.

So add liar to the list of horrible things about Jane Austen.

No, not *that* Jane Austen.

I sighed. Why did I suddenly hate myself?

I wanted to enjoy my first kiss with an amazing guy. I wanted to kiss other guys. I really wanted to be different. Better. I wanted to be normal, you know. Either that or confident enough to stop lying about my life.

But it's like I had this huge concrete wall between me and guys and not enough desire to break it down.

Zoe tapped on the wall that separated our otherwise completely opened rooms.

"Hey," I said, quickly hiding the box under my bed and standing as though I didn't have anything to hide.

She moved the curtain out of the way and walked in. "Just checking in on you. Is everything going okay with the sewing stuff?"

"The boutique is fine." I nodded and sat on my bed. "How are you?"

"I'm doing better. My parents had this bright idea to do family counseling and it was an absolute nightmare. Why are you all wet?"

"Got caught in the storm." I pulled my hair into a loose bun. "You said you have issues with your brother, but what about your parents?"

"They're okay. They just ... they like side with him a lot and so that's never fun."

"How's their marriage?"

"Normal."

"Wish I were normal."

She laughed quietly. "What?"

"People always assume that I'm going to be some kind of boy crazy nutcase because my parents are insanely romantic and ... then there's my name. Sometimes having really good parents is hard too."

"Why?"

"Just all these expectations. My own expectations, but they literally haunt me."

"When your guy comes he'll be even better than whatever you expect."

"No." I laughed. "It's not that. It's that I have such high expectations for whatever being in love should be like that I don't even want to try. I can't let people in. The perfect guy could come along and I'll lose him. I can't do it. It's weird."

"That is weird." She shook her head. "Really weird."

"Okay, it's not that weird. I'm just saying."

"It's funny you always say that about your name."

"Why?"

"Well, you read about Jane Austen in school, right?"

"A little."

She stared at me for a second, then smiled. "You're totally serious."

I nodded.

"You're pretty similar to Jane though. She was all tomboyish and believed women shouldn't be all crazy about love."

"I'm not a tomboy. I wear dresses and stuff." Speaking of that, I needed to get out of my wet clothes.

She smiled and pointed to my chest. "I mean that."

"Huh? You're saying I'm flat chested?"

She laughed. "No. Your heart. You're a little wild. It just means ... like ... how do I say it ... it's like you're the type of girl to be more insecure about your personality and stuff than your looks."

I laughed. "Oh. Okay. I guess that's true."

"And ... your underwear is Batman underwear." She shook her head. "Wow."

I tossed my shirt to the hamper and grabbed my pajamas. Yes, the Batman.

"Your bra too?" she said. "They actually make Batman bras. Okay, so yeah, wow."

I smiled. "And now." I slipped my pants on. "Time for the Batman pajamas, baby."

"Whoever you find, if you find someone, will need to be a Batman fan, because if not they are *not* going to find you attractive."

"Zoe." I tried not to laugh. "You do realize that seventy-five percent of the things you say are extremely rude?"

She shrugged. "Like what?"

I waved it off. "Never mind."

"Hey, I got something for you." She handed me a jar. "Stick your finger in there and taste it."

I opened it and put some honey on my tongue. "Uh ... what?" I ate another hefty finger full. "What is this heavenly thing?"

"My friend Nicole gave me some local honey. I knew you'd like it."

I licked my lips. "It's incredible. Seriously the best honey I've ever tasted. I'm not even kidding."

"It's really good."

"Man, those must be some bees." I sat on my bed again. "Thank you."

"No problem." She slapped her leg. "I better get going. Meeting Nicole for dinner in a few. Want me to bring leftovers? Or better yet, want to come?"

"Nah. I think I've decided to stay home tonight and write my bucket list."

"Okay, I'll see you later tonight then."

I grabbed my sketch pad and followed her down the steps. She left and I got comfy on the couch, then started writing in no real order:

1.) Learn the violin

2.) Write and—

My phone beeped. An email.

Jane.

Alistair again. Not tonight. Not after everything with Donovan. I wanted to focus on my bucket list. On the way home from being abandoned by Donovan I had this intense urge to accomplish something and I thought ... what if I died tomorrow? I never liked the idea of a bucket list before. Some list to taunt you while you try to survive. Always making you feel like a failure. Then you die.

I wasn't so interested in that, but now I had a different perspective. Now I wanted to enjoy life and make time for new things, new adventures.

So, back to my list:

2.) Write and compose—

Beep. Buzz.

I know you think about me too. Sometimes. It's my accent, isn't it?

I smiled and picked up my phone, then wrote: *Don't waste your time with me.*

I waited, hovered above *send* again, then erased. What if I tried? Just once. Maybe test the waters of flirting. I didn't need to marry him. Just a little fun.

I stared at the empty email. And ... realized I had no clue how to flirt.

So, what does one do when one knows nothing?

Trusty Internet search.

How to flirt with a guy.

A ton of options came up for flirting without making it obvious. So I clicked on the fourth. For some reason I don't trust the first result in a search engine. I read a few and pretty much decided I never wanted to be a flirt. With advice like "trip into him and say, 'Woowee, those pecs are so hard I felt like it was a wall," and sit in a chair, arch your back, and run your fingers through your hair ... um ... definitely not for me.

People actually do that?

Back to my blank email. I mumbled aloud, "How can I be myself without being myself?"

"Pretend he's Donovan," I responded to myself.

"Ah, yes!" I said. "Wait, no. I can't do that. I'll pretend he's Autumn."

"Autumn! How is she? Haven't seen her in a few days."

"Yeah, that's because everyone around you is dating someone while you sit at home and write your bucket list."

"Point taken."

"Not like I could date him anyway, he lives across the ocean."

Another voice cut in, "Jane?"

My dazed stare shot down to my phone screen. I did what anyone would do when caught talking to herself. I hung up the phone.

Then, she called back.

"Hey, Mom," I said, as normal as possible.

"Jane? You called, but it was all muffled. I thought it was Edward at first."

"Oh, yeah, I was?"

"You were talking to yourself again, weren't you?"

"Maybe."

"How are things going? Do you need any help?"

"Things are good. Maybe you could stop by when I decide to open the place up."

"You know I'll be there. Dad too. How much longer?"

"Maybe two weeks. Waiting for some graphic tees to get here and need to do a few last minute things. Oh, also I wanted to meet with the lawyer friend of Dad's. Can you text me his number when we hang up?"

We casually talked a few more minutes, then I was in the quiet again, staring at my phone screen, at Alistair's email address, at that pesky blank email, at that iPhone keyboard with endless possibilities.

Then ... my thumbs started.

And this is what came out:

Dear Alistair,

Have you ever made a bucket list? I've never done it before. Always thought they were so stupid, but I'm making one now. Curious what five things you'd like to do before you die.

Can't wait to see you when the leaves start to change colors. ;) Are you still coming?

Love,

Jane

Did you see it? I put a winky face *and* said I couldn't wait to meet him *and* signed it *Love, Jane.* That is hardcore flirting in my world and it made me nervous as hell as I hit send.

But I hit send. I did it.

I flirted.

Moving on.

I almost finished writing number two on my list, but a sudden urge for sweets sent me to the refrigerator for a tall glass of milk and the chocolate chip cookies Zoe made the other day. Oh. Man. The girl may had been one of the most "out there" people I knew, but she could bake like you wouldn't believe.

Cookies and milk in hand, I went back to the couch and started to write when the phone beeped.

Dear Jane,
No bucket list for me, but top five would be:
1.) Write an album I'm proud of
2.) Meet Bob Dylan and have a long talk
3.) Stop stressing out and trying to fix stuff (and myself) all the time
4.) Visit a beach with clear water and white sand
5.) Learn to change the oil in my car
What about you? And hey, how's the tattoo? Get any more??
-Alistair ;)

Dead Alistair,
My top 5:
1.) Learn violin
2.) Write and compose a symphony
3.) Write a screenplay and star in it
4.) Direct a film
5.) Have my own successful fashion line with Batman-inspired clothes

Yep! Got another tattoo! I'll attach a picture.

How's everything over there? What have you been doing?
Love,
Jane :)

Jane,
I'm not dead! Haha!
Your top five is quite lofty. Write and compose a symphony?? Do you have any musical training?
And that tattoo! Blooming hell! You just got fifty times more amazing in my book. I'm a HUGE Batman fan! I love that tattoo. It's brill! Favorite Joker!
Jane....
-Alistair

What do you mean you're not dead?
No, no musical training.... I know I'm crazy. Dream big ... worst you can do is fail!
I don't just like Batman. I'm obsessed. My friend Zoe told me guys won't find that attractive lol... Oh well!
So what's this about you not being dead??

You typed Dead Alistair instead of Dear. I'm obsessed with Batman too. We should quiz each other on trivia and see who is the biggest fan!

Damn autocorrect. Why is it never correct???
Oh, I'll totally beat you in a Batman trivia show down.

Haha!!! Hey, I'm glad you messaged me back this time.

Sorry. So busy getting my boutique up and running.

Boutique?

Yeah. I'm in my own apartment now. In the city. Got my own store underneath. Haven't opened yet, but I'm working on it. Just selling my own clothing designs and stuff.

Wow. Wish I was that ambitious at eighteen!

It's been my dream since I was little. I've always wanted to do it, so I kept a notebook filled with plans. Everything from how to make a business plan to what to call it. It's been a long, long plan of mine. So it's not that admirable.

Yes it is.

Jane, my eyes are closing. Let's talk tomorrow. Download the app I'm gonna send a link for. Then we can text instead.

Love,

Me ;)

PS- I'm ready to beat you in the showdown tomorrow. Prepare thyself!

Oh, I forgot it was late there. Okay. Talk soon! No need to prepare!

I CONTINUED MY BUCKET LIST WITH A SMILE I DIDN'T KNOW was on my face until Zoe came in said, "What are you so happy about?"

"Oh." I twirled my pen beside my face. "Just Batman."

"Batman?"

I nodded.

She handed me a container that smelled amazing. "Dinner."

I lifted the lid. "Thank you." I didn't realize I was hungry until I opened that container and stared at the lasagna waiting to be consumed. "You didn't have to."

"If I had to I probably wouldn't."

I laughed. "That doesn't sound nice."

"Why? I just mean I like doing it because I want to, not because I feel like I need to."

"I know, I know. Well, thank you. It's sweet."

I ate the yummy dinner as Zoe went to her bedroom. Then I took quick shower and settled into bed myself around 11pm. When I set my phone in the charge it beeped.

Another email. It said:

Jane....

I wrote back, *Alistair....*

And fell asleep with a smile.

So unbelievably odd for me.

But good too.

Chapter 19

THE GRAPHIC TEES CAME IN AND LOOKED EXACTLY LIKE I wanted them too. I hung them on a rack in the store while Han helped set up some last minute things. Autumn was off with her person I hadn't even met and I told Brooke to take the day off for her daughter. Donovan hadn't spoken to me since the last incident, so it was just Han and me. Which I liked. She was peaceful and didn't seem capable of getting stressed. Which I was.

I was very, very stressed.

"Okay," I said as I put the last of the shirts on the rack. "I think we're done."

The bells on the front door rang and Donovan walked in, somewhat nodded to me, then took Han's hands. "Hey, I made reservations for dinner tonight. Are you ready to go?"

She looked at me. He didn't.

"Sure," I said. "No worries. I think I'm done here."

My phone beeped. A text from Alistair. *What was Alfred's original family name?*

I typed back, smiling uncontrollably. *EASY. Beagle!*

Him: *Dammit Jane! I thought I had you!*

Me: *Ok. Give me a sex to think of a question.*

Him: *I'll ignore the typo.*

Me: *Lol. Autocorrect likes sex. Every time I write sec!*
Him: *Autocorrect has good taste.*
Me: *Thinking...*

Han smiled when I looked up. Donovan didn't.

"Oh, just some Batman trivia with lover boy." I looked at Donovan.

His eyes narrowed. He was still pissed at me. I wasn't the one who abandoned him though. I should've been mad!

"Let's go," he said to Han.

She smiled as she walked by me and said, "Have a good night, Jane. See you Monday for big day!"

I nodded, keeping my eyes on Donovan as they walked outside. He normally turned to look at me whenever he left. Not this time.

I sent him a quick text. *Don't be a jerk, Don. Our friendship is more important. I still love you. I'm sorry I hurt you.*

I waited for it to say "read" just below the text, but it only said "delivered" for the next five hours.

Alistair and I ended the night with him leading 34 to 32. I told him I would come back with a vengeance tomorrow, prepared with even more difficult questions, then we said goodnight.

I didn't go to sleep though. I used my iPad to search for the most obscure questions and answers I could find, then finally decided to go to bed about an hour later.

Just as I found that sleepy place between relaxed and dead asleep, a text came through.

Jane....
Me:*Alistair...*
Him:*Go to bed. Stop studying. You won't win.*

Me:*It's later there. You go to bed!*

Him:*Jane.*

Me:*Alistair.*

Him:*Goodnight.*

Me:*Goodnight. :)*

I WOKE TO A TEXT AT 4AM. HALF ASLEEP, I REACHED OVER and grabbed the phone. Squinting my eyes, I turned the contrast down and opened the messages.

Donovan: *It's all good jazz.... just stop being so annoying.*

I smiled and went back to sleep, finally waking to a text from Alistair.

Should be 9am there. You ready or what?

I rubbed my eyes and sent, *Just woke up.*

I don't have a show tonight. First Saturday off in a while. How would you like to continue this challenge on the phone tonight?

Butterflies. Worms. Whatever they were ... they were intense. I wanted to throw up.

I typed back, *I have plans with Autumn tonight but maybe if it's not too late there when I get back.*

I didn't have plans. Told you I lied to avoid things. Ugh. Donovan wasn't the only one I annoyed. Totally annoyed myself on a daily basis.

"No," I told myself as I typed. "I'm not going to lie this time."

I typed back to him, *Actually I'm lying because it makes me nervous. Let's talk tonight. Break me out of my shell.*

He said: *Don't be nervous. Actually, be nervous. That means there's some-*

thing between us. If not you wouldn't care enough to be nervous.

I waited a few seconds, then typed, *All that's between us is an ocean.*

I erased that and said, *I'm just nervous to lose the challenge.*

Him: *I'll pretend to believe you just so I don't scare you away. Now go prepare for your demise!*

Me: *Oooh....nervous! :) Talk to ya soon, Alistair!*

SO ... IS IT POSSIBLE FOR A DAY TO FEEL LIKE THE LONGEST and shortest day all at the same time? I dreaded and looked forward to talking to him. Both. I think what scared me the most was that I knew he liked me. He made it obvious. I guess the scariest thing was that I kinda liked him too. When I woke up to a random middle of the night text that just said "Jane" it comforted and excited me all at once. I think I spent the last few nights sleeping with a smile on my face. And the Batman thing....

Autumn told me not to worry about it so much and just take things one step at a time, but I think what worried me more than potentially falling for someone and getting stepped on, was losing Donovan. I never felt it as strongly as I did now, because I didn't need to. We were best friends. We talked all the time. About everything.

Since Han started seeing him, I hadn't talked to him in days and Alistair now texted me every night. Han took my place. Alistair stole his. Our best friend status would soon be demoted to "Hey, it's been a while. How ya doing?"

Maybe even?gasp!?brother and sister status.

I didn't want that.

So I made Autumn come over before Alistair called. She helped me get my mind off of it for a while. We laughed and talked and watched *The Office*. Donovan's favorite show. Mine too. We watched so many episodes together. I kept thinking about him and I guess it showed.

"Worried about the call again?" Autumn said.

"You know what's weird?"

"Besides you?"

"Besides that."

"What?"

"I ... I can't ... well, one of the reasons I'm worried about this is because of Don."

"He'd be thrilled if you found someone."

"No. I mean, yeah. Maybe he would, but I meant that I'm worried I'll lose him for good. Alistair is nice and all, but Donovan is my best friend. I don't want to lose him."

"One of your best friends, I might add."

"Yeah." I laughed. "Autumn...."

She stared at me. My heart rate picked up as the words entered my mind. I think my heart just tossed 'em up there without my consent, because they very idea of admitting it seemed torturous.

"Jane...." she finally said.

"I think I..." I cringed.

She smiled. "I know what you're gonna say and I'll just be ready to tell you I told you so."

"What?"

"No. I want to hear you say it."

"I don't know. This is stupid. I'm being stupid. I just miss

215

Donovan, that's all. We were close for years. It was bound to happen. Just so soon? We're only eighteen. Could Han really end up being the one he marries?"

"Who knows. Plenty of people find their spouse even in high school." She smirked and poked my knee. "Question is, why does it bother you?"

"Answer is, I miss him."

"Question is, why?"

"Answer is," I mocked. "I lov?"

Her eyebrows raised.

"I didn't mean it like that. You know I love him like I love you."

"Do you miss me when I get a boyfriend? Which, by the way, that other guy ... I'm not dating him anymore."

"Actually I do miss you when you have a guy."

"Are you nervous to talk to someone you may have feelings for because you're worried you might lose me for good?"

"How'd you know?" I teased, then wanted to bury my head in the couch like a four-year-old.

"I told you so." She beamed brighter than an obnoxious fluorescent light. "That's all I'm gonna say."

AFTER AUTUMN LEFT I GOT COMFORTABLE WITH MY Batman trivia questions and waited in bed for him to call. He said he'd call at 7pm. It was 6:54 and the worms and butterflies decided to have a war inside of me. Zoe wasn't home. If so, I would've been sitting in my car somewhere. But bed it was. I kicked the blankets off.

Sweat galore.

I rushed downstairs to the thermostat and cranked the A/C down to 64. Just till the call was over and my body stopped its unappealing antics.

I got back into bed. Sat up. Then down. Up. Down.

My phone rang.

I stared at the screen as it lit up with his name.

It rang again.

I held it in my hand.

Third ring.

I wiped my hands on my sheet, then answered the call.

"Alistair," I said.

"Jane," he whispered. My name sounded fifty times better when he said it. I like how he held the A.

"Who got shot during *The Killing Joke* story?"

"Barbara Gordon." He chuckled under his breath. "Which Robin got killed by the Joker?"

"Um ... is it Dick Grayson? No, Todd? Wait..."

He laughed. "Jane ... it's good to hear your voice again."

"Yeah." Cue the nervous laugh. And cut. "You too."

Long pause. "Jane?"

"Ye-yeah?"

"Let's have a new day. In my note I called it The Big Day. Let's make it in October."

"Okay, but aren't we planning to see each other in October anyway?"

"Yes. But I would like to finish what I started."

"Oh." Butterflies. *Definitely* not worms. "You mean ... the ... the kiss?"

"October 14th. The airport. I'll wait at the table where we last sat." He paused. "If you're there, I'll assume you want me to kiss you. Not in the airport, obviously, but somewhere ... somewhere around there."

"But you're not flying into Philly again, are you?" Like how I avoided the kiss thing? Sigh....

"No. We will be driving about, but ... well, where else could we meet?"

"At the top of the steps that Sylvester Stallone ran up in Rocky." Why did I just say that?

"Sounds absolutely perfect."

I laughed.

"What?"

"I don't know if you just talk so proper or if it's your accent, or both combined, but it's kinda funny. I feel like I'm listening to a BBC drama sometimes. Or Hugh Grant."

"Thanks." He laughed. "Now I can cross that one off of my bucket list. Always wanted to sound like a BBC drama and Hugh Grant."

"I'm glad I pointed it out to you then."

"Me too."

A few minutes of silence snuck by us. Like the time we sat in the car together. Like so many times with Donovan. Comfortable awkward silence.

I loved it.

Listening to him breathe as he listened to me.

"Ahhhhhh," Zoe screamed as she bolted up the steps and into her room. "What the hell, Jane? It's a freaking igloo in here." The springs in her bed creaked when she jumped on her bed. So loud I heard through the wall. "Jane!"

"What was that?" Alistair's voice was wearing out. He was tired.

"My roommate." I laughed under my breath. "I forgot I had turned the A/C down and I'm all under the blankets. It probably feels like she walked into a freezer."

He didn't respond and his breathing became heavy and slow.

"Alistair," I whispered.

"Jane."

"You're tired."

"I am."

"Go to bed. We'll talk tomorrow."

"Promise?"

I hesitated, then gave him my promise. "Yes."

"Goodnight, duck."

"Duck?" I smiled. "Is that supposed to be a good thing?"

He laughed a little, but it sounded like he was already half asleep. "It's not so proper."

"Okay ... well, quack, quack, and goodnight."

"Heh ... goodnight."

Poor guy. I hung up the phone since he probably didn't even realize we were still talking in real life, then I ran downstairs and turned the A/C back to normal. When I got back to my bed I sent Autumn a quick text. She sent me fifteen texts as I was on the phone. All pretty much saying, "What's happening? Is it good? How do you feel? Do you like him? Does he like you?" And on and on it went.

I responded with a very simple answer.

:-)

That little smiley face would torture her till morning, but there are some experiences that don't need to be shared, you know? I feel like it almost ruins them. When you give a little piece of it to someone else it's not only yours anymore. I wanted to keep this one safe. For many reasons. And Autumn would text me first thing in the morning and do everything in her power to make me tell her, but I wouldn't.

Donovan and I had many memories locked inside of us. Memories only we knew and loved.

And now he was making new ones with someone who lit up his life in ways I never could.

The smile Alistair planted on my face disappeared.

I pulled the blankets to my ears and thought about Monday. One more day between me and a new adventure. Can we say nervous?

I stared at the window knowing I would never sleep and as much as my mind kept drifting to Donovan, thoughts of Alistair interrupted constantly.

They interrupted. And won.

It's probably just the Batman thing...

Eventually—surprise, surprise—I fell asleep with thoughts of him and woke in the middle of a dream about us—Alistair and me—walking around as ducks. It should've been a nightmare, but there was something oddly peaceful about it. Strange, though. I'm not denying the strangeness.

Half asleep, I turned to my phone expecting to see a text that said nothing more than my name, but instead it was Mom. At 3:47am.

Just wanted you to know that I love you and I miss you, Janie. -Mom

Sometimes a mother's love is even better than a boy's. It's a love that—at least in my case—could never be ruined. I didn't need to grow in her womb to know that. She meant the world to me. She always would.

Love you too, Mom. -Janie

Chapter 20

WELL, THE BIG DAY ARRIVED. NO, NOT *THE* BIG DAY WITH capitals as Alistair liked to write. The grand opening of my shop!

Han and Brooke came in at 7am to help. We officially turned the sign on the door to *open* at 9am and waited for someone to come in.

At 10am the door bells finally rang as ... Autumn walked in.

"How's it going?" she said. "Any sales yet?"

I shook my head. "Maybe I should've done more advertising."

"Haven't people been walking by?"

She turned to the window as two women passed.

"Yeah," I said. "And they keep right on walking."

"Do not worry," Han said with a smile. "They will come. They will come in right time."

I swallowed. "We hope."

"Don't be pessimistic again, Jane," Autumn said. "It's the first hour you've been open."

The bells rang again.

"Oh, thank you for coming." I gave her a hug. "Hey, Autumn, Brooke, Han, this is Dee. She's the one who gave me the awesome Batman tattoo."

Dee nodded and tugged on one of her many earrings. "I love this place. Wow. You did a great job." She ran her hands along some of the graphic tees. "Did you make these?"

"I designed the prints, but had them made."

"I love it." She thumbed through the rack and placed two of them over her forearm. "I'll get these."

"Thank you so much. Just come over to the register real quick." I rang up her order and gave her the receipt. "Seriously, thank you for coming."

"Anytime." She took her bag. "Ella and some of her friends should be stopping in later. Knowing Ella she'll buy a ton just to help a sister out, but she will love this style. She's like Audrey Hepburn meets, well, Jane Austen." She laughed. "Still can't get over that."

"Don't remind me."

Someone walked in the door. I assumed only friends and family would come in today, but these two college-age looking girls walked in. Strangers.

Brooke greeted them kindly as I tried *not* to stare at them while they perused the clothes. I pretended to busy myself with something behind the counter, but I was listening to everything they said. Autumn pretended to be a shopper, which I thought was hilarious. She scooted next to them and sifted through a rack of dresses, commenting out loud about how nice they were.

"Really?" the one girl said quietly. "This stuff is strange."

"Yeah," her friend agreed, not so quietly. "Don't like it. Let's go."

"Strange?" I said as the bells clanged against the door and the girls disappeared. "What's that supposed to mean?"

"Do not worry," Han said. "They just have more modern taste."

"Your stuff is fresh and awesome," Autumn said. "Some people just won't get it. Pretty sure it's unlike any other line of clothes in major stores. It's unusual, yeah, but that's a good thing."

Door opened again and I honestly wished it were a friend, but it was a man and his wife who held a baby.

"Hi, welcome to *Rosalind's*," I tried to sound cheery. Good thing I had theatre classes. "Let me know if I can help with anything."

What was I *thinking*? I felt like a child trying to run a candy store. I should've waited. Everyone was going to hate everything. So dumb. Such a waste of my time and my parent's money.

"Hey, you must be Jane," the woman said. "I'm Sarah." She stood closer to the counter and swayed her baby in her arms. "I'm Ella's friend. The woman you met who teaches violin." She gestured toward the man. "And this is my husband, Vasili."

"Oh, right." I held out my hand and shook both of theirs. "So nice to meet you."

She looked around. "This place is beautiful."

Her husband put his arm around her and looked around too. "You started this place? By yourself?"

"I've had a lot of help."

The door opened and Ella came with a man I assumed was her husband.

"Hey, Ella," I said, coming around the counter to greet her. "Thanks so much for coming."

I stuck my hand out, but she pulled me into a warm hug and held it for a few seconds longer than acquaintances normally do.

"This is even better than I imagined." She tapped the man's chest. "This is my love, Gavin. Kids are with my brother and sister-in-law."

"Nice to meet you." I waved my hand toward the clothes. "Do you like the clothes? Be honest."

"Wow," she said.

"She may be a little biased," Gavin said. "This stuff is right up her alley."

"I *love* it," she said, already looking through several racks and handing a few things to Gavin, then stacking more on her arm. "If I could afford it, I'd buy this entire store."

I blushed. "Thank you."

Brooke stepped toward me and nudged my shoulder. "See. Just takes the right person."

Ella and her friend checked out with Han. I met them at the door and thanked them again for coming and buying five bags of stuff.

Ella gave me another hug and looked around the room again. "Such a nice place. With Jane Austen as your name and taste like this, I bet you have one lucky boyfriend."

Aha! Expectations!

"No boyfriend," Autumn chimed in. "She's like anti-love. Totally feminist."

I raised my eyebrows. "I'm not anti-love. In fact, I think I love someone right now. And feminist's aren't anti-love anyway. They're anti being treated like trash just because they're women."

Everyone stared at me. The music in the background suddenly got much louder. Autumn's mouth gaped open like she was frozen in place while saying, "What?"

Ella hugged me again and whispered, "If you have to think about being in love, you aren't. When it's the right one you just know."

I smiled and nodded. "That's what my mom says, but I don't know. That kind of love is for certain people, not me."

"It's for everyone," Sarah said. "If they want it." She linked her fingers with her husband's. "Good luck with everything, Jane. I'm really impressed."

"Thank you."

When they finally left I exhaled. I must've held my breath without realizing it. I turned toward the door and bumped into Donovan.

"Oh." My hand was on his chest. "I ... um ... hey."

My hand was still on his chest and I couldn't move it. *Why* couldn't I move it?

Move, hand. Move!

He stepped to the side and my hand fell. I stood there. Uncomfortable awkwardness. Yes, UNcomfortable.

"How's it going?" He looked in Han's direction. Not mine. Me, you know, who owned the boutique.

When did he come in? Did he go through the back door? My heart rate sped up. Did he hear what I said?

Autumn hadn't moved.

"What?" I mouthed.

Donovan and Han disappeared in the back and Autumn grabbed my arm and forced me to the back of the store.

"What did you say?" she whispered a little too loud.

"I was just kidding. I don't know. I think maybe I was embarrassed and said whatever came to mind." I turned to walk away.

She grabbed my arm. "Jane. Just tell me this. Donovan or Alistair?"

I shrugged. "Someone just came in. We'll talk later."

"It's Alistair, isn't it?" She followed me. "You guys have been talking a lot."

"I'm not talking about this. I didn't mean what I said. I don't even know what love is."

I made it to the front of the store. Autumn said goodbye to every-one and left. A few customers came in and left within seconds. Mom sent me a text that she was bringing Dad, Granny, and even Eddie around lunch time. Then another couple came in, holding hands. The man asked the woman if she wanted anything, she scrunched her nose and shook her head.

They left.

I tried not to let it get to me, but after four more customers came in and seemed to either hate or be completely disinterested in my clothing line ... well ... let's just say I felt small in a big world and it wasn't a good feeling anymore.

The Batman quote by Brad Meltzer came to mind. The one from the 2004 comic Identity Crisis.

People think it's an obsession. A compulsion. As if there were an irresistible impulse to act. It's never been like that. I chose this life. I know what I'm doing. And on any given day, I could stop doing it. Today, however, isn't that day. And tomorrow won't be either.

It didn't help though. Not like I thought it would. I never cried, but my eyes were warm and wet and my chest tightened every time I breathed in. Brooke touched my shoulder. I closed my eyes and inhaled, shaking.

This was my dream.

My dream from forever ago.

Failing.

"It's just the first day." Brooke tried. She wanted to encourage me, I guess. "More people will come in and love this place. The styles are amazing. Don't let it get to you."

"You know what bothers me the most about this?" I sniffed. "I really tried to create a line I knew people would like. I analyzed the industry for years to see where it was going, to try to be ahead of the game, but still make something people would love."

"People will love it. Don't get so down. It's only been open a few hours."

"We shall see."

Another set of young girls came in, walked around, and left.

I stared at Brooke.

"Give it some time," she said.

I nodded.

Donovan and Han walked in from the back. Holding hands. Smiling.

My eyes twitched as I held the tears in. *Don't cry, Jane. Don't do it.*

Han looked at me, then Brooke. "Is everything okay?"

I nodded emphatically while pinching my lips together. Don finally looked at me. I looked down and tapped my foot. Another group of two older men and a business-looking woman came in. I greeted them, they walked around for a half of a second, and out they went.

I wanted to hold myself together. Seriously wanted to be mature and businessy and deal with setbacks.

But I literally dreaded this very thing happening. And it happened.

I casually walked to the front door, turned the sign to *closed*, and looked at Brooke, doing my best to avoid Donovan's eyes.

"Change of plans," I said. "Meet me here tomorrow." I still avoided his eyes, but felt them burning a hole into me. "Whoever wants to help. I'm changing things. I need a change." I shrugged again and walked to the back, up the stairs to my apartment, inside, plopped on the couch, and inhaled the deepest breath ever.

I would not give up. Imagine if Batman gave up. Imagine if he said, "Hey, guys, this is hard and I've got psychos on my ass. Yep. I give up. Not worth it."

Giving up would not be in my vocabulary. And I had a plan.

A text came through. From Alistair. *How's it going ducky?*

I laughed and typed back, *Can I call?*

The phone rang. I picked up.

"Jane." That voice.

"Alistair."

"What's wrong?" he said. "Are you okay?"

"Why do you ask?"

"I can tell by the tone of your voice."

I tried to find something to say.

"Jane? What's going on?"

My bottom lip trembled. "It's just...."

"Listen to me." He paused. "Listening?"

"Mmmhmm." I pulled my lip into my mouth and bit down.

"Failures don't make us who we are, right? My biggest dream is to write an amazing album, something I'm proud of. And I'm shit at it, Jane. Can't do it." He sounded out of breath. "I'm playing drums for a band I can't stand and I hate it. Perhaps...." His tone lightened. "Jane, perhaps we have failed at these things because we should be doing something else. Yes." I heard the smile in his voice. "Let's do what we want to do. Let's check it off our bucket list."

I couldn't help but laugh. "What do you mean? Which ones?"

"Bad day with the store, right? Plan B, Jane. Open back up with your Batman-inspired line."

His excitement erased my desire to disappear or give up or give in and replaced it with my own excitement.

"Alistair...." I wanted to cry happy tears. "This is exactly what I needed."

"I'm quitting the bloody band."

I almost laughed at the way he said it, but he was serious, so... "You are? When? Are you sure?"

"Batman made the climb in *The Dark Knight Rises*. Now it's our turn. If I fall, pick me up. If you fall, I'm here." He paused. "I'm going to start now. I'll call you back later."

"Wait. So you're quitting the band? And I'm doing a Batman-inspired clothing line?"

"Precisely."

"Alistair."

"Jane."

"Thank you."

THAT HELPED. THAT REALLY HELPED. I STAYED UP ALMOST all night sketching new designs and pulling out old ideas. I planned on doing outfits inspired by all Batman movies and even the comics and I hadn't been so excited to set my pencil to paper in years.

Here are my two favorites:

Zoe came downstairs to take a shower before work. "Please tell me you slept on the couch."

"No sleep for me. I'm too excited."

"Excited? Thought you were depressed?"

"I was bummed out, but Alistair cheered me up."

"Gonna keep going with the store?"

"Kinda. You'll see." I closed the sketch pad and stood. "Think I'm gonna go sleep now for a little bit."

"Good idea. Hey, how's Donny?"

"I guess he's pretty good. Haven't talked to him in a while."

"I can't believe he chose someone like that over me."

"I don't think he chose. I think he just moved on, then found her.

Don goes through girls so fast though. He'll be single again in no time."

"She barely speaks English and she's so short."

I shook my head. "Now you're being rude again."

She covered her mouth with her hand, then walked toward the bathroom and turned around. "Oh, my clothes need to go in the dryer now. Thanks!"

Sometimes with Zoe all you could do was just stare and wonder if people are born like that or if they are somehow conditioned to be so oblivious of their own words and actions. I didn't like her at first. She annoyed me. She came across as extremely self-centered and mean. Plus she's a little too Cher from Clueless for my tastes. Majorly. But I guess we all annoy others with our flaws and weird antics. I loved Zoe now. She made me laugh. Plus how could I be upset with someone who had a past like hers? She didn't talk about it much, but I could tell she longed for the kind of family I had. As weird as my family could be, it was still a loving and encouraging situation. I don't think she ever had that.

I tossed her clothes in the dryer, did the dishes, then got comfy in bed. It wouldn't surprise you that I woke up around noon to a text from Alistair. We talked all the time now.

He quit the band.

It's weird and good all at once, he typed.

I responded, half asleep, by typing an incoherent string of words, then fell back asleep before sending.

He woke me up again. *Jane?*

Then he called.

I forced my eyes to stay open and finally answered. "Sorry, I had typed a mess of words and fell asleep before I sent it. I stayed up all night drawing. What did the guys say when you quit?"

"The guys are okay. They don't enjoy it much either. It's always been so contrived, but my manager had a fit about it. It's over now and I'm feeling good about it. Already started messing around with some melodies. I'll play it for you tonight."

"Tonight, huh? What makes you so confident that we will talk tonight?"

"The smile on your face right now."

I touched the corner of my mouth. "How'd you know?"

"I always know. Your voice gets a little higher. It's cute."

"Oh." I blushed.

Zoe tapped on my bedroom wall as her shadow moved behind the curtain.

"Come in," I said.

Donovan stood in the doorway. I sat up as fast as possible and dropped the phone.

"Donovan?" I whispered. "What are you doing here?"

He held up the spare key I gave him. "Checking on you."

Oh! Alistair! I picked the phone back up. "Hey," I said. "Sorry. My friend just randomly showed up and I dropped the phone."

"Who is he?" Crap, he was on speaker.

I fumbled to get it off of speaker as Donovan waited patiently.

"He's my ... um ... just a friend." I watched Donovan's reaction.

"Why do you say it like that?" Alistair said.

"Like what?"

"Nervously."

"I don't know." Donovan put his hands in his pockets and kicked

234

his feet around as he waited. "He's in love with someone and don't worry, it's not me."

"Are you in love with someone?"

I watched Donovan and hoped he couldn't hear the conversation.

"Jane?"

"How do you know when you are?" I said.

"I'll let you go. I don't want to be rude to your friend."

"No, it's okay."

"Go ahead. We'll talk later."

"Okay. Yes, call me tonight."

"Will do. Have a nice time with him."

"Alistair?"

"Yes."

"Alistair."

"Jane."

I smiled and we hung up after arguing about who should hang up first. When I finally ended the call Donovan continued to look at the ground.

"Why are you checking on me?" I said. "The boutique thing?"

"You sound pretty serious with him." He nodded to my phone. "Are you?"

"He's a friend. I've been going through a lot lately and he's been there for me. Vice versa too."

"Jazz..."

"Yeah, Don."

"Sorry for being a jerk."

"Don't worry about it."

He sat at the edge of my bed. "I'm glad things are going well with Alistair. Finally some guy has broken through your indomitable barrier."

I laughed. "He hasn't broken through yet."

"Yes he has. I can tell."

"How?"

"You still haven't stopped smiling."

"I don't know."

"You don't know what? You've been smiling since I came in and when you hung up the phone you paused, stared at it, and sighed. Jazzy's finally in love," he teased.

"I am not." I slapped his arm. "Stop with that."

"Lover boy's accent won you over, didn't it?"

"Annnyway, Don. How are things with Han?"

He smiled and stared off for a few seconds. The longer he stared the brighter his eyes got.

I swallowed. "Gonna propose?"

"No." He turned back to me. "It's not like that with her. It's different. Less of an emotional ride and more of a ... well, it's all things. Mental, physical, emotional. She hits every part of me, Jazz. She's amazing."

"She is pretty amazing. Very sweet."

"And smart, cute, funny. She's got this naive childlike part to her that makes her adorable." He gazed off into dreamland again. "She's perfect."

"No one is perfect."

"You know what I mean."

"This is different for you."

"Yeah." He smiled. "Yeah. It is."

"Is she okay with you being here? You're in my bed."

He nodded. "She's sitting in the living room. I just needed to talk to you. Wanted to tell you that Han and I are here if you need help. Don't give up the shop."

Han and I. He was officially becoming one half of a whole.

"I'm not giving up," I said. "Regrouping. I'll tell Han all about it."

"Why can't you tell me?"

Good question. I didn't even realize I said that. See, we were drifting. "I'm keeping it as a surprise from everyone," I tried to redeem myself.

He searched my eyes.

"Fine," I said. "I'm trying not to hide from the truth anymore. So the truth is ... we're growing apart, Don," I whispered. "This friendship is changing. Han is good for you. She's changing us though."

"What about Alistair?"

"Him too."

"I guess it was bound to happen. I always knew when I found the one that our friendship would take a few steps back. There's only room for one girl in my heart, Jazz, but I'll always be here for you."

I nodded and kept a straight face, tried to smile, tried to pretend like that last one didn't shoot an arrow through some sort of festering wound I had. "I know," I said. "And there's only room for one guy in mine."

But it's you, Donovan. It's you that I love. I've always loved you.

We looked at each other for a few seconds. I couldn't tell if he saw pain in my eyes or affection, because I felt both and without a mirror I had no idea which one I had painted on my face.

He squeezed my hand and stood. "I better get going."

"Yeah." I stared at my blanket. "Yeah, you better."

And he walked away. Hands in his pockets, heart in the palm of her hands. I listened as his footsteps met Han's, then a pause, a kiss maybe. The curtain continued to sway as two sets of feet clapped across the floor below, then the front door opened. And closed.

Do you ever feel like prolonging a chapter of your life? Just drawing it out, maybe rewinding and reliving it to make sure you feel and experience every detail fully and deeper. Maybe dying in the middle of it so that it never ends. The next chapter doesn't have to unfold. It doesn't have to bring something you don't want to experience. It can end right here. Before everything changes. Before you can never get it back.

What if? What if I could stop it? Make it so he doesn't walk out the door. He doesn't leave. He's right there on the edge of my bed.

And the page never turns.

Chapter 21

IT NEVER WORKS OUT THE WAY WE WANT IT TO. LIFE. THE
page always turns when we want to pause and it seems they get stuck
together when we desperately want to know what happens next.
Then, there are those times when the wind picks up and the pages
flip and flip and flip until we're completely lost. It's in those times, like
now, that I felt like giving up.

But he called.

And I picked the book back up, turned the page, and began to
read.

"Alistair."

"Jane.

"If I gave you a pen and told you it was magic, you could write
the story of your life, make it anything you want ... what would you
write?"

"Hmm ... well, that's not a little question."

I laughed. "I like the way you say little without the T's. Lih-ul."

"I know, I know. Mum always tells me to stop doing that. It's not
proper."

"It's cute."

"Oh, really? Then I should make sure to say it a lih-ul more
often."

"Don't let it lose its charm."

"Good point. So how was your time with the guy?"

"It was Donovan. I've told you about him."

"He's with someone now? Again? Does he not like to be single?"

"Not anymore. We kinda have a history together. I mean, we never dated, but he wanted to and when I finally pushed him away he just went full force into dating. One girl after another after another after another. This one's different though. She's normal and sweet and beautiful."

"But he's still your friend, you say?"

"He is. We've always been close."

"You sound sad."

"You always know how I'm really feeling."

"It's not hard. I just listen. Pay attention."

"I like you, Alistair."

He paused and I almost regretted letting that slip, until he finally said, "I like you too."

"So ... the story of your life ... what would you write?"

"I guess I would start by writing a plane to the States so I could provide this strange girl with the best kiss she's ever had in her life, from there I don't really care what's written. That'll be enough, thanks."

I laughed. "What if you're a horrible kisser?"

"Then it will be the worst kiss you've ever had, which will be equally as memorable."

I laughed again. "Thank you."

"For?"

"For being a morsel of happiness in a cookie of crap."

He laughed. "Sounds nice. Vulgar but nice. You're welcome, I suppose." He paused. "What would you write, Jane?"

"I'd write a new me."

"Not at all. I wouldn't change a thing about you."

"I've got flaws. Too many."

"That's okay. We all do. Part of what makes us real."

"I emailed my mom a few times. She hasn't responded."

"Maybe it's the wrong email."

"It's not."

"How do you know?"

"I have a few different ones. Tried them all and a Facebook account. She just hasn't responded."

"Don't let it get you down, okay? She may not be ready to face you."

We spent the next ten minutes in a content and warm silence. He fiddled with his guitar, then played a song for me. I used my iPad to send him pictures of my latest sketches. We talked and listened and breathed for another hour until he finally needed to sleep.

Before we first talked on the phone I dreaded it. My nervous and anxiety-stricken side got the best of me. Now I dreaded hanging up with him, but honestly ... I felt horrible. Like I was using him to deal with the hole Donovan was leaving in my heart.

I didn't want to be *that* girl.

So I watched the shadows on my ceiling as the streetlight flickered outside. The air conditioner hummed in the background. And I considered telling Alistair I needed some time to think and process things. Then, maybe if I felt better we could still meet in October.

Our long conversations at night made it impossible to think

clearly. My heart was so messed up. For years I avoided my feelings for Donovan. I could avoid them because he was always there. His arms around me without the threat of a kiss or a relationship. Now, though, Alistair awakened this part of me. I swear the boy slapped some wires on my heart and brought me back to life. I felt things. Things I never felt before. I smiled more. Laughed more. Loved more. Because of that sweet British boy.

But I could no longer deny the feelings I had for my best friend. Those endless summer nights as we watched the sun go down. Snow days full of hot cocoa and Frosty the snowman wars, where we challenged each other to see who could build the ultimate snowman. Being an artist and him a sports guy, I always won and it ended in snowball fight tickle wars. He was the first person I called when I passed my drivers license test and the last person who'd ever hurt me. Really hurt me.

There's one memory that sticks out the most to me though. I think I was sixteen and he was seventeen. He joked around about wanting to be with me and I told him it just didn't feel right. I loved him, but wasn't *in* love with him. When he asked what would make it feel right I said, "I don't know. If I ever feel that way I'll tell you that I've fallen and can't get up. Then you'll know."

He laughed, but he knew I'd never say it. Locked in my dungeon of relational fears, I sat alone. Content to be alone. Donovan learned to accept it.

But things change. People change. When they actually want to.

I changed.

Alistair revived me.

I'm sure that wasn't his intention and I wasn't being fair to either of them. I knew that. I knew I needed to tell Donovan the truth and if he no longer felt the same, well, then maybe I could move on.

Han made it difficult though. I didn't want to lose her friendship or hurt her in anyway. Or him. What if he really loved her and my proclamation—after years of pushing him away—made her go away? That would kill me too.

After going back and forth, pondering this option and that solution, over and over again, I finally made a decision. Wasn't the best decision in the world, but it was something I really, really needed to do as soon as possible.

Chapter 22

MOM AND DAD STARED AT ME LIKE I WAS CRAZY. I WAS. I WAS definitely crazy. Eddie played around on his phone, probably some weird brain teaser app to test and strengthen his intellect, but he stopped when I told them my latest decision.

"I know it sounds impulsive," I said. "But I feel like I need to do this right now."

Mom glanced at Dad. He nodded, then she said, complete with British accent, "Honey, if you feel this is important, then I am willing to do it. As long as Eddie and Granny can watch over your father." She looked at Dad.

"I'm just concerned," Dad's voice of reason entered the scene. "Not about me. About you Jane. Are you trying to run away again? I don't understand. And it's a lot of money." He paused, cleared his throat, and folded his hands on his lap. "I know the shop didn't go as planned, but you need to handle this like an adult."

"Dad." I sighed.

"I'm serious. You're eighteen now. You live on your own. You successfully created your own store, which is unheard of for many kids your—"

"Now I'm a kid." I laughed. "I thought I was an adult?"

Eddie's eyes shot up. "Jane!"

"What?" I nearly jumped out of my chair. "What did I do?"

"You just responded in a British accent." Mom smiled. "Maybe you really are changing."

"Okay, guys." I took a bite of Mom's homemade peach pie which was dee-freaking-licious, then continued, "You're all overreacting. I'm not running away. I'm not being immature. I just want to go somewhere with Mom. And these are places I've always wanted to go. Every Batman fan's dream. Plus, I need a vacation. Badly. I need to get away from everyone and I want my mother's support. That's all." I looked at Mom's glowing face as Dad's hand disappeared under the table. Then hers. "Mom, you're my real best friend. The best best friend. Remember when everything went haywire so many times in the past and I'd stay home and watch movies with you?"

Her smile grew.

"And remember how happy I was? Those are some of my best memories. This is something I've always wanted to do and I want you there."

"I'll come." Even her eyes smiled. "But we can't be gone long. Two weeks at the most. Where's the first destination?"

"This will wipe a lot of your money out." Dad. Again. Who else?

"Don't pop bubbles," I said. "Join in on the fun of blowing them."

He shook his head. "I'm just worried this is a bit irrational and when you come back to an empty bank account you're going to regret it. What if you lose your apartment and the shop, Jane? You put so much hard work into it."

"Dad, look, I've got it all planned to make it as cheap as possible. And quick. I need this. It will inspire me for the new direction I'm taking with the shop aaaand I can write it off as a business expense."

"Yes, but—"

"Husband." Mom gently touched his hair and wound it around her finger. "It will be fine. She wants to do this and I would love to spend some extra time with her. It'll be okay, dear."

He took her hand, kissed it, and there they went into La La Land. Eyes locked on each other's, smiles easing their cheeks up toward cloud nine. Oh, man.

I stood. "Okay. So let's plan to leave Friday."

Eddie looked up again. "Meet me in my room before you go. Give me five minutes." He stood and disappeared around the corner.

Mom and Dad looked at me.

I shrugged. "He's Eddie. Who knows."

"I know," Mom said. "He may not be the most expressive person—like someone else I know—but if you just listen and watch you can intimately know any person in the world, regardless of how much they tell you."

"How can you listen if they don't tell you?"

"People speak in all sorts of ways, Jane. It's just that most people only listen with the intention of speaking, not knowing. If you want to know someone you just need to be with them. Listen to the way they breathe, the way they talk."

Dad nodded. "She's right."

"I know someone like that," I said.

"How is Donovan?" Mom asked.

"Don't talk to him much anymore." I focused on my hands. "But it's not him actually. Alistair. He always knows what I'm feeling by the tone of my voice." I could almost hear his voice. "I don't know if I know anyone well enough to do that all the time, but I feel like I listen. I try to."

"Alistair?" Mom said. "Who's Alistair?"

"Oh ... I ... didn't I tell you?" I fidgeted with the *Pride and Prejudice* art on the wall beside me. "It's ... well, you know, he's a friend. A, uh ... a guy."

"Hm." Dad stood and put his plate in the sink. "And here I was thinking it was a girl friend."

Mom laughed. "So?"

"Oh!" I pivoted. "I think I heard Eddie call for me. Be right back."

They looked at each other as I dashed away. Then I stopped, walked backwards, peeked around the wall to the kitchen, and said, "I'm not avoiding." Even though I totally was and they totally knew it. "We'll talk later."

I jogged upstairs to Eddie's room. Door was open so I went in. He sat on the bed with his hands behind his back. Smiling. Eddie. Smiling. Prolific moment in the history of all moments.

"What are you up to?" I said. "Better not be hiding crack back there."

He laughed the tiniest laugh, then handed me a wrapped box. "Sorry this is late. Meant to give it to you on your birthday, but it wasn't ready."

"Oh, you didn't have to do anything." I smiled at the box. "Wow. Impressive wrapping."

He shrugged. "You're stalling. Just open it."

I didn't like opening presents in front of people. He was right. I always stalled. Peeling back the paper as slow as possible, like now. Not only was I horrible at pretending to like a gift when I couldn't figure out what it was, but I also had trouble getting excited when I really liked something. Most times I'd smile and stare and mutter a word of thanks and smile and stare again. Autumn jumped up and down like a two-year-old when she opened a gift and Donovan did this thing where you just knew he was sincerely grateful even if he was quiet about it. Something in his eyes.

I missed him.

"At this rate you might as well spend the night here," he said. "It's nothing big."

I finally got the paper off and folded it neatly as Eddie rolled his eyes. Then I lifted the lid while staring at him.

"You're such a jerk," I said, laughing, as I pulled another wrapped box out.

"Figured if I wrapped it twice it would take three times as long to open."

"Funny."

I peeled the paper off and found another wrapped box. I shook my head and unwrapped it. Then saw the gift.

"Ed..." I ran my fingers along the top. "You made this?"

A slight smile brightened his face. "It was my first wood carving project. Took me a while. I wanted it to be perfect."

"Ed." I couldn't get over it. "Eddie..." I waved my hand in front of me, thensat beside him, cross-legged, and wrapped my arms around his neck. He hugged me and tapped my back. I was his older sister, but his strength both physically and mentally always made me feel younger. He was smart, calculated, and extremely fit. I could feel his masculinity even when he tapped my back. That same strength always made me feel safe when Mom and Dad left us home alone. Or the time he rescued me when I tried to do a back flip off of the pool and knocked my head on the side. He was only fourteen at the time, but managed to pull me to the surface and out of the pool, then ran with my unconscious body all the way inside and up to Mom.

Still, to this day, he hadn't said, "I love you," to me. But he didn't say it to Mom or Dad either. He was the most internal person I'd ever known.

I pulled away from the hug and looked at the box again. It was a beautifully stained wooden box with a lock on the front, almost identical to the one Donovan found in the woods. Except the top was engraved with an amazing—I mean, seriously amazing—carving of my face split up like Two Face from Batman and underneath a quote from Harvey Dent in *The Dark Knight*:

You either die a hero or you live long enough to see yourself become the villain.

"Ed, I love this so much." I couldn't take my eyes off of it.

"I know it's weird. Harvey becomes a villain and everything, but you're always saying you feel like you have two sides of you and one side is worse than the other. Maybe this could remind you to be the hero."

"I love it." I looked at him, but he blushed and looked down. "It's so perfect. Thank you."

"All right, all right." He pushed me off of the bed. "Now let me get back to work."

I poked his rib. "I looooove youuu, Eddie."

He laughed. "Kay. See ya later then."

I turned into the hallway and walked into—

"What the?" I looked up at him and felt my face fill with heat. "Don ... what are you doing here?"

He looked over his shoulder and pointed down the steps. "Your mom called and said she needed plumbing repair. Dad's here and asked me to come and help."

She definitely set this up. Ugh.

"So ... how are you?" he said.

"I'm good. Yeah. How about you?"

"Good." He swung his arms and snapped his fingers. "Things are good."

"Right ... so..." I looked around. "I'm going on vacation. Going to travel the world to the different locations they shot *The Dark Knight* trilogy."

He held back a laugh. "You're so strange, Jazz."

"That I am. That ... I definitely am."

"I'll come."

My face contorted.

"Can I come, I mean—"

"No." I squinted. "Wait. Huh?"

"On the trip. Can I come?"

"Han wouldn't like that."

"We're taking a break."

"What?"

He nodded.

"Why?"

"It's a lot. I can tell you on the plane."

"Don..." I so badly wanted him to come, but I didn't want to hurt Mom. "Let me think about it."

He shoved his hands into his pockets. "Fair enough."

"If you want her back..." What am I saying? "Do you want her back?"

He sucked in his bottom lip. "Yeah."

"You okay?"

"Fine. Need a vacation. Sounds like you do too."

"Okay. You can come."

What?!

Great, I said inside. *What the hell was I thinking? Now I needed to tell Mom I changed my mind and what would Alistair say?*

"Donovan."

"Yeah."

"I don't know if it's a good idea."

"Please, Jazz." He pouted. Totally fake. "I miss you and I really need to get away. Plus, don't know if you heard, but I lost my job. Lay offs."

"Oh, no. You love that job."

"Yeah. Loved. Not love." He exhaled. "Oh well."

"I just ... I'm worried about Han."

"She broke up with me. I don't think she's the one you need to worry about."

I hated myself for saying this. But I needed to be there for him like a true best friend would, regardless of my own feelings. "Don, if you love her you'll chase her."

"It's complicated. Not to mention she's in Korea right now."

"Why? Is she coming back to work?"

"She's only there a few days. She said that you needed a few weeks to regroup, so she took the money you gave her and used it for a plane ticket."

"But she ... you ... weren't you guys so happy together?"

"Jazz ... can I come or what?"

I inhaled. A lot of air. And held it there.

"Were you just going to go alone?" he said.

"I had some options."

He tapped my head and walked around me. "Let me know."

He knew I couldn't say no to him and I hated that. But what I hated more was conflict and I didn't want to deal with telling Mom that I changed plans. She expected it to be mother-daughter time and I honestly didn't want both of them there. One or the other. It could only be Mom or Donovan traveling the world and staying in cozy hotel rooms with me.

Mom.

Or the boy.

Eenie-meanie-miney....

No. Didn't trust that.

Okay.

"Jane?" Eddie popped out of his room. "Why are you banging your head against the wall? Wait." He popped back out of sight and said from his room, "Don't want to know."

Chapter 23

ZOE'S ADVICE WAS TO TAKE MOM, OBVIOUSLY. AUTUMN told me to take Donovan, obviously. So I held a quarter in my hand, flipped it over several times, and named Donovan tails and Mom heads.

Did I mention that I hated making decisions like this?

I flopped on my bed and sighed, wishing something would happen and one of them would just back out.

It was 6:15pm when my phone rang and I literally—because what would it be like if it was *not* literally—thanked it for doing so.

"Alistair!"

"Wow. Happy to hear from me, little duck."

"Yes. I'm in a predicament."

"Oh, yes? Is this about your trip? Need someone to go with you?"

"Actually I kinda told two people they could come, but I only want one. Not both."

"So, just go with the first person you told."

"How reasonable. That's what I'll do. Thank you."

"Of course." Something banged in the background. "Want to hear a song I'm writing?"

"I can't wait."

My head hit the pillow and I expected to hear a guitar strumming through the phone, but it started with piano, then violins, and drums, and ... he was messing around. I knew it was a recording. Probably a YouTube video. But I leaned back and let the beautiful sound fill my mind anyway. I didn't recognize it. Which was odd. I knew a lot of classical music and even love the Piano Guys who do all of those classical covers of modern songs, but I hadn't heard this.

I loved it though. So reflective, moody, and swelling with emotion, yet bold and transcendent all at the same time.

Eyes closed, I soaked it all in, completely forgetting that I was on the phone until Alistair brought me back to reality with his voice, saying my name, drawing out the A.

I think I almost fell asleep.

"Did you like it?" he said.

"Yeah. Who wrote it?"

"Me," he said. "I know it's not perfect and I've got a long way to go, but I wanted to share it with you now. I'm really excited about this one, Jane."

"You didn't write it." I laughed. "Nice try. I'm used to Donovan's pranks."

"Well," he said. "I'm not Donovan and I'm not pretending. I really did write it. I used GarageBand for now."

I sat up in bed and squinted at the wall. "You did not write that."

"I'm not sure whether to take your disbelief as a compliment or an insult."

"Alistair, I'm so jealous. You seriously wrote that?"

"I ... um..." He cleared his throat. "I did, yes. I wrote it."

"Wow." I shook my head. He could compose classical music. He wrote a song just as beautiful as any other real life composer. Life long dream of mine. "Can I hear it again?"

He stuttered and finally got out the words, "Sure, sure. Yes ... yes, one second."

I listened with more intensity this time, focusing on every instrument as it entered and exited and brought the song to life. His song. The melody of his own mind and heart. I loved it. Adored it. Wanted to wrap it up and stuff it into my mind so I never lost it.

Or ask for a CD.

"Do you like it?" he said as it faded into the background.

"Like it? It's amazing. I thought you were a rock band type guy, drummer and all."

"I told you I wasn't enjoying what I did. I hated that. It was okay, but I've always loved writing songs and as a drummer you don't get much say in the matter. I tried my hand at writing a few songs on my guitar, adding lyrics and all, but your love for classical music inspired me to try it out, so I used GarageBand for the instruments and just went with it." I listened like Mom said, to every stammer and breath. I listened to him pour a piece of himself into the phone and into my life. And I heard a smile. Excitement. "Jane?" he said. "Part of it is that I want to finish the ... actually I was ... I was sort of hoping I'd finish it with you. Together we could write it." He coughed. "You know, check a little box off that list of yours."

The mirror on my closet door, directly across from where I sat on my bed, reflected my raised eyebrows. I actually slapped my hands on the bed beside me and mouthed to my reflection, "Are. You. Kidding. Me?"

Then I nodded to myself and my grin stretched wider and wider until my cheeks begged for mercy.

Alistair's voice trailed up to me from the floor. Apparently I dropped the phone.

I picked it back up. "I don't know what to say."

"Say yes," he whispered in a breathy, sexy tone.

"How? You live all the way over there."

"Well, one of us could visit. Or ... we could send GarageBand files back and forth."

"What if I suck at it?"

"You won't."

"And how do you know?"

"How do you not?"

I shrugged at my reflection. "Good question."

"Are you coming here on your trip? There are some Batman locations here. There's Nottinghamshire, Buckinghamshire, Essex. I'd love to show you around."

"I can hear the smirk in your voice, you know."

"Not trying to hide it, my lady."

I laughed. "Well, the first person I asked to come with me ... it was my mom. So she'll be there."

"That's fine." He paused. "Who was the second person?"

"My friend Donovan. The one that was here the other day when we were on the phone."

"You said you two are close. Isn't that a little weird? I never believed friendships like that could stay platonic."

"I don't know. I guess it is a little weird. We've cuddled and stuff. He was my first kiss. He always said he would marry me, but I rejected him so many times that he gave up."

"Why did you reject him?"

"I don't know." I thought for a minute as Alistair breathed into the phone. A minute turned into another minute. Comfortable silence. Again.

Many memories with Donovan spiraled through my mind as I tried to keep up. Tons of laughter and a few not-so-fun moments of anger and tears, like the time he told me that I needed to be with him or he could never talk to me again. I didn't want to lose him, but I was still so attached to myself that I couldn't give in. So I let him go and he turned at the last minute and said, "I can't stand you, Jane." He wasn't being funny and not an ounce of sparkle shined in his eyes. He was serious. And it hurt.

But I suppose in the end he never hurt me as much as I hurt him.

"Do you love him?" Alistair interrupted.

"Everyone has always asked me this and I've always said the same thing ... I don't know what love feels like. I've been raised by parents who display this overly affectionate stuff, staring into each other's eyes and bending over backward for each other. Mom and Dad don't fight, they discuss. Donovan and I fought a lot. Not a lot, a lot. But ... enough. When we disagreed it got heated and when things leaned the slightest bit oogly googly romantic I backed off. I didn't like it."

"Maybe you love him, but you just don't know it because you're expecting it to feel like what you imagine your parents to experience."

I pictured Mom and Dad in my head, talking in those sweet voices reserved only for each other. And both of them not being able to handle more than thirteen hours apart.

"I don't know," I said. "I'm eighteen. What do I know about love anyway?"

"How old were your parents when they met?"

I smiled. "Seventeen."

"Well, there you have it. Age doesn't matter so much, now does it?"

"I guess not."

"So maybe you love him." His voice turned down for the night. Quiet, relaxed. I pictured him under his blankets, one arm behind his head, phone in the other hand.

"Maybe." I inhaled and exhaled loudly. "I don't like thinking about it. Someone told me that you'll just know when it happens. You won't have to think about it. I wish that were true because I don't like this thinking stuff."

"Don't think then. Just experience him and see what happens." He paused. "I think it's true. When you know, you know." His voice trailed off into a sleepy row of words I couldn't understand, then he whispered, "It's easy. I knew I'd love her." He mumbled more nonsense. "Don't have to know to feel."

"Alistair?" I whispered. "Are you sleep talking?"

"Every piano has a key."

"Huh?"

"For them to find it."

"Alistair?" I held the phone away and laughed.

"Even Beethoven couldn't hear, but he could feel."

I stopped laughing and held on to those words. Maybe I was the opposite. Maybe I could hear, but not feel. Think, but not know.

I wanted to feel.

To know.

"Alistair," I said again.

"Jane."

"I'm gonna go now, okay?"

"Love you too. Goodnight."

I stared at the phone. What?

Did he mean that?

The phone made a weird sound. The Skype call was still on, but now the video was up. My heart raced and I had no idea why. All I could see was a candle flickering on a nightstand. A tea cup sat next to it, along with his iPad and *The Killing Joke* Batman comic book.

He rustled.

My pulse quickened so much it made me nauseous. I should had ended the call, but I couldn't stop looking at my screen. He moved again. The phone moved. For a second I couldn't see anything, then I saw his bare chest, covered in tattoos, rising and falling in the candle light. At this point any decent girl would've ended the call, but I guess I wasn't decent. I watched. And I found myself next to him, my arm draped over his chest as the candle lit our bodies.

I imagined his arm around me as his fingers ran up and down my arm. My ear against his heart, there between the two tattoos I couldn't make out.

I moved my head as though it would help the phone show me his face. I so wanted to see his face.

He twitched.

I jumped and my heart almost fell out of my chest.

Must've been one of those dreamy twitchy things. He didn't move after that.

Poor guy was so tired when we talked. It was only 7:24pm in my room, plenty of light still coming from the window, and it was already tomorrow where he slept.

The curtain that separated my bedroom from the outside world thrust open and Zoe flew inside.

I screamed.

She stopped and looked at me, her eyes nervously darting around the room. "Sorry, I just have to talk to you. Oh. My—"

"Zoe." I held up my hand. "I'll meet you downstairs."

"Jane, I think Donovan and I might be getting back together. He totally touched my arm today. I mean, it was quick, but I saw him when I was kinda sorta like driving down his street fifteen times today, and he went to the gas station so I followed. I'm like in shock because I was pumping and he talked to me and touched my arm. That's gotta mean something, right? I mean ... right?"

"Tell her not to be daft," his voice came from my phone.

"Who's that?" Zoe pointed.

I stared at the screen. His face, just ever so unshaven and tired, stared back at me. The candle was to his right, casting shadows on the left side of his face for this dramatic, dare I say ... sexy look.

"Who is that?" Zoe said louder.

"It's...."

"Me. It's me, Jane." He smiled.

"Uh-huh. It's Me," I said to Zoe. "It's just Me."

He smiled, laughed a little. I could still see the top of his chest. My eyes darted toward my own reflection to see what he saw, then I moved the phone so my little Skype image looked better.

And I realized I cared. I actually cared what he thought of my looks. What the *hell* was happening to me?

"I should go to bed." He hadn't stopped smiling. "And you should talk to your friend."

I nodded, trying to savor the image of his messy hair and the slow blink of his eyes as sleep called his name.

"Goodnight, Jane," he whispered.

"Night," I managed to say before Skype ended our call.

I fell back into my bed and held the phone to my chest.

"Um ... what was that?" Zoe said as my other hand fell to my face.

I covered my eyes with my fingers and shook my head. "I have no idea." I laughed. "Wow. I ... I have no idea what that was."

Chapter 24

SO, A WEE TAD OF A PREDICAMENT. ALISTAIR AND I PLANNED to meet in England and then Mom cancelled on me because Dad got sick and she felt like it was a sign to stay with him. It didn't upset me. Honestly, being across the ocean scared her, she just didn't want to admit it. A different time zone from Dad? Yeah. Nightmarish for her. So ... now Donovan was my traveling buddy and that would make for an interesting visit with Alistair. So interesting that I wasn't interested in going anymore.

Han came back from Korea and Donovan didn't tell me. Neither did she. But I could tell.

I knew as I cooked dinner for Don and Autumn that he wasn't actually with us. His mind was somewhere else. Thinking of her probably. So unusual for him. After a breakup Don would find another girl within weeks. I got used to his dating patterns only to be shaken up by Han.

"Got a new girlfriend yet?" I joked with him.

Autumn turned from the the dough she was shaping into dinner rolls. He looked over at her, then me, with that annoyed look on his face.

"Well, it's only normal for you," Autumn said, turning back to the rolls. "How many girls have you gone out with now? Eight thousand?

Or was it nine?"

"Technically it was seven thousand," he said. "And I'm afraid that's where it's going to end."

I threw a few potatoes into a pot of water and ignored that.

"So, Jane's been talking a lot to Alistair. She thinks he's sexy."

I chopped and tossed more potatoes into the pot, still ignoring.

"I'm sure he is," Donovan said. "When do we get to meet him?"

"Never." I dropped the last few potatoes and turned the heat up on the stove, then wiped my hands on my jeans and turned to him. "I was supposed to meet him in England during this trip, but I don't know if I can do that with you there. Kinda weird."

He smiled. "I can go out alone for a night."

My phone beeped from the kitchen counter where it sat on top of a huge container of coconut oil. I picked it up and froze in place. My hands trembled as I stared at the screen.

"What?" Autumn said, leaning toward me and reading the notification. "No way."

I set the phone on the kitchen table as though it were a bomb, and slowly backed away.

Donovan raised his eyebrows like Jim always did in *The Office*. "Want me to read it for you?"

I nodded as Autumn glanced from me to him over and over again.

He slid the phone toward himself and raised his eyebrows again. "Welp, there we have it." He peered up at me. "You're sure?"

I nodded.

"Okay, then." He clicked a few buttons and cleared his throat. "Hi Jane, It took me a long time to email you back and I'm sorry about that. I don't check my email very much and when I read this I wasn't sure how to respond. Do Anna and Laurence know you emailed? I don't know what to say or how to answer your questions, but I'll try." Donovan looked up at me as I bit my nails. I nodded and he went on, "I guess the reason I had Anna raise you instead is because she raised me and I trusted her. I'm not like her at all, even though we were raised by the same people and I just knew she was more responsible." Donovan stopped again. Autumn looked at me. I nodded, he inhaled and continued, "Let's see ... you also asked how old I was when I got pregnant. I was fourteen when I was raped and I know who the father is, but I'll let Anna tell you about that. Anyway, I'm sorry if this upsets you. Anna always told me she would keep it a secret because I pretty much begged her. She never breaks promises. I wish I was more like her. So ... Oh, your last question. You asked if I named you before they adopted you. Yes I did. I named you Jane Elizabeth Kelley and when Anna took you they only changed the last name and then decided to change your middle name at the last minute. Anna said you seemed more like a Maryanna than an Elizabeth. Anna thought I would come back one day, but my life isn't the best. I hope you understand. I'm in rehab again right now and I don't know if it would be a good idea to meet in person. I'm sorry. I don't want to hurt you, that's why I gave you to Anna and Laurence. I knew they wouldn't hurt you like I would. I'm sorry, Jane. I was so young, but I think about you all the time and Anna sends me pictures. I don't know what else to say...."

Donovan slid the phone back toward me, clasped his hands on the table, and stared at the phone. Autumn also stared at it. And me.

My real mother was my mother's little sister? My aunt?

Raped?

Autumn squeezed me into her arms and kissed my cheek. "I love you, Jane." She squeezed harder. "And yes, Jane. Looks like you've been Jane all this time after all."

Out of the corner of my eye I saw Donovan mouth, "Don't joke right now," and I almost laughed, but I couldn't. My mind was still fixated on the words he read. Reeling through them over and over, trying to make sense of it all. Why didn't Mom tell me she had a sibling? That I was the result of a crime? That my mother spent her life in rehab without anyone to help her?

I wanted to help. I wanted to meet her. Maybe if she saw me it would help. Or maybe it would just remind her of her own pain. I didn't want that.

"Maybe you should call your mom," Donovan said.

"Yeah," I said. "I'll probably visit. I don't want to do that over the phone."

"Don't shove it inside, okay?" he said. "Deal with it. If you need anything you know Autumn and I would do anything for you."

"As long as Han isn't around." Autumn smiled. "Donovan, go find her, would you? You're reminding me of a lost puppy dog. Or you could have this fine Jane Austen right here." She waved her hands in front of me. "She comes with nerdy Batman shoes, shirts, pants, belts, and decor. You'll love her."

"Tempting." He stood and walked over to us, then pulled me into his chest. "But unfortunately this one doesn't let people love her. Poor Alistair will find out soon."

I pulled away. "That was a jerkish thing to say right now, Don."

"Sorry." He took my hands and looked right into my eyes. "I'm here if you need me, but it's true ... you try to handle everything on your own and you push people away when they love you."

"I don't push you away." I snapped my hands from his. "I don't push anyone away. You just say this because I never kissed you back. I never let romance in, Don. That's different than love."

"Not when you romantically love someone."

"I didn't romantically love you."

"Oh, shit," Autumn said. "The potatoes are over-cooked and looks like you two are gonna start boiling too."

"You pushed me away the other day. I was just looking out for you. As a friend. No romance."

"Please go, okay?" I felt the tears coming. "It's too much."

"I'm trying to be here for you. Just let me for once."

"It's true," Autumn said. "You've always pushed him away when he tries to love you even like a friend."

"I'm not leaving." Don crossed his arms over his chest and leaned against the counter. "I'm too hungry for that anyway."

I shook my head and sighed. "Fine." I turned back to the counter and started dicing up an onion. "Just don't talk to me for a while. I need to think." The onion juice dropped on my fingers and its potency seriously made my eyes sting. Good excuse, I thought. It'll hide the tears.

"WANT ME TO STAY THE NIGHT?" AUTUMN SAID AS SHE draped her purse over her shoulder. "I can if you need someone here."

"It's really not a big deal," I said. "I'll be fine. Seriously."

"You always say that." She sighed. "I don't believe you."

"I'll be fine. It's fine."

She closed her eyes and scrunched her lips toward her nose.

"Okay. Call me if you need me."

Donovan stood next to me. Hands deep in his pockets. We listened as Autumn's footsteps disappeared down the steps. The back door opened and closed.

And he turned to me, moved the hair from my eyes, and tapped my nose. "This gets red when you're trying not to cry."

I shook my head. "It'll be okay."

"It will. Yes. *It* always is. But will *you* be okay?"

"I think so."

"You really want me to go?"

I nodded.

Zoe was at the beach with her family and he knew I'd be alone, but I needed to be alone. I'd be okay. Mom probably waited too long to tell me the truth knowing I wouldn't have been able to handle it at a younger age. But now ... I thought I could. I believed in myself.

Until he closed the front door.

I finally collapsed on the floor and let the rib-hurting, stomach-twisting sob fest begin. I rocked on my knees with my face in my hands. Tears didn't fall. They poured. And poured.

The door flung back open, banging against the wall. His body knelt beside mine and the warmth of his chest against my cheek soothed me. It really did. His hands cradled me with strength and gentleness all at the same time as my wet face soaked into his shirt. He kissed the top of my head and ran his fingers through my hair. I cried until it was all out of me. Every last drop. It felt so good to let him love me. And we stayed like that. Right there on the living room floor. Forever.

Chapter 25

I HATE CRYING. AND I HAVE A LOT OF REASONS FOR IT. ONE, the next day you wake up with a migraine. Two, it never really seems to change anything. Three, it opens the dam for more crying. And I hate crying. I tried to avoid reasons to cry, but sometimes it just happened.

I woke up around sunrise with Donovan curled up on the other side of the bed. Snoring. All too familiar of a sight. I remembered back to the time our families went on vacation together and we slept in the same room. Probably the summer before third grade. He didn't snore then, but he popped up randomly and had conversations that made no sense. Completely freaked me out as a kid and he didn't remember anything about it when he woke up. Every now and then he'd still do that. Shoot straight up and talk to you like he was awake, only it rarely made sense and he definitely wasn't awake.

I tapped his shoulder and made him turn toward me.

He rubbed his eyes. "Morning, Jazz. You doing okay?"

"Don't you need to work with your dad today?"

"Oh, man." He pulled the blanket over his head. "I hate plumbing."

"Well, it's a job for now and your dad's expecting you."

"Yeah, I know."

271

Birds chirped on the window ledge as their silhouettes danced on the shades. He kept the blanket over his head and within a few seconds began to snore again. I poked his shoulder about six times until he flipped the blankets off and sighed.

"Doesn't it feel better to cry and get it out?" he said, still groggy.

I nodded, but I guess it was another lie because I honestly felt like crap after that. But it's okay. At least I could visit Mom and Dad without the emotional volcano bubbling inside.

I planned on leaving after breakfast and a shower. I half-dreaded it though. But really wanted to start facing things head on instead of avoiding all odd and conflicty type situations. Is conflicty a word? If not, it should be.

Donovan forced himself out of bed and rolled over me to do so, then flipped down on top of me with all of his weight.

"Ow!" I shoved at him. "You're on my boob! It hurts, dork!"

He didn't budge and pretended to snore. I kicked and pushed him with all I had, but couldn't get him off. I did manage to free my boob from his shoulder though.

He held back a laugh when I kneed his leg.

"Come on, Batgirl," he said. "You can do better than that."

I laughed. "You're so dumb."

"If I'm dumb, then you're a fool." He rolled on to the floor with a thump. "Ouch. What the hell was that?"

I peeked over the edge. "Looks like a curling iron went up your ass. Who's the fool now?"

He laughed and pulled it from under him, then sat up. "I might be a fool, but you're the best of fools."

"Not gonna argue that." I threw my pillow down to him and

272

rolled over. "Now go meet your dad so I can sleep before I need to leave."

"Yes, Queen Jane." He smothered me with the pillow, then disappeared.

AFTER I PARKED OUT FRONT, I LOOKED AT THEIR HOUSE from my car. Their house. Used to be my house too. For eighteen years. Or maybe seventeen. Not sure how old I was when Mom took me from ... my mom.

Time for answers.

Mom answered the door before I knocked, hugged me, and had me come into the living room where Dad rested on the couch.

"He's not feeling so well and we just want to make sure everything is okay after his hospital stay and everything," Mom said as she motioned for me to sit on the smaller couch.

I did.

"Ready for your big trip with Donny?" Mom said, sitting next to Dad and taking his hand into hers. "Oh, sorry, I mean Donovan," she teased, knowing I'm the only person who never called him Donny, another reason she thought we were destined for marriage and baby land.

"Not ready, but we're still leaving tomorrow."

"What's wrong? Everything okay?"

"Are my feelings always that apparent?"

"I'm afraid so. You always show exactly how you feel even when you don't want to."

"Hm. Another thing I need to work on."

"What's wrong, honey?"

"Oh, geez, I don't know." I rubbed my forehead. "This is awkward."

"Did you finally meet Julia?"

"No." I took a deep breath. "Just ... she emailed me back."

Dad readjusted himself and wrapped both hands around Mom's. "So you know the truth now?" he said.

"I know a lot. I know she was Mom's sister." I looked at Mom. "She's in rehab. She was raped. That stuff."

"Did she tell you about our parents?" Mom said.

"No. Why? I thought they both died?"

"Yes." She paused and sat next to me, then continued, "But before that, well, I was adopted too, Jane. Our parents couldn't have kids and Julia was a surprise. She's quite a few years younger than me. Our mother died a few years after having her and our father abused us after that. I tried to take care of her and raise her, but it was hard. Your dad and I got married as soon as we turned eighteen and he helped me report my dad. We got guardianship of Julia after that, but it was too late. She had already been raped by him."

"Wait a minute." I held the arm of the couch as heat rose inside of me. "My grandfather raped his own daughter and that's how I got here?"

"Jane." Dad sat up with a pained expression pressing his eyebrows toward his nose. "This is why we waited until you were older. It's complicated. Your mom and I have a good marriage, but it takes work. Not everything in life is perfect and we wanted you to be old enough to handle these things without getting overwhelmed."

Mom held my hand. I moved away.

"I'm trying not to be overwhelmed," I said, almost to myself. "But this ... this is a lot."

"I know the feeling." Mom choked on her words and wiped her face. "Jane, I love you." She wiped her face again. "You are my daughter, regardless of how, and I love you."

"When did you adopt me?"

"You were a baby," Dad said as Mom cried into her shoulder. "Your mother nursed you as though you were her own child. Got her milk production going with some herbs and pumping and you were nursed just like Eddie was. She loved you. Barely left your side. You were in our bed sleeping on your mother's chest for the first year of your life."

"I know." Tears teased my eyes. "Mom." I took her hand. "Mom." She looked at me. "I know being a mother is more than a womb and a pregnancy. You are my mother." Her chest heaved as she sucked in the air and clenched her eyelids shut. A tear ran down my cheek. "You're my mother and I'm so thankful. This isn't about me feeling unloved or like I need a mother. You're more than perfect, Mom. You're beautiful and I couldn't have asked for someone better to look up to."

She fell into my arms and cried on my shoulder. "I love you so much, Jane. I always feared that you would?"

"No," I said, holding my mother as she held me. "I would never. I love you. I love you so much."

We held each other. Mom cried as Dad grinned from across the room. I needed that moment. I needed to remember that no matter what my biological mother may have been like or done ... she wasn't my real mother.

This woman, this beautiful woman who gave so much of herself and rarely got anything in return, she was my real mother. My role model. The very reason love scared the hell out of me.

I could never compete with a heart like hers. But I was starting to realize that I didn't need to. I could love just as big and just as deep as she did. And I was doing that very thing as I cried on her shoulder. I was loving and being loved. I was being me.

Jane Maryanne Austen.

"Mom," I said as she finally pulled back and moved the wet hair from her face. "I love you. My biggest hope is that one day maybe I can love my own child as much as you love me."

She pursed her lips together, caught Dad's smile across the room, and waved away more tears as she laughed. "I'm a mess."

"A beautiful mess," Dad said. "Most beautiful mess I've ever seen."

"Oh, no," I said. "Don't start, you guys."

We all laughed. And I looked at them, beaming at each other through glassy eyes. I figured it wouldn't be so bad. To have something like that, I mean. To love someone like they loved each other. Just ... maybe a few clicks more normal.

But there was definitely something beautiful about what they had.

And I was thankful I got to be a part of it. As their daughter.

Their *real* daughter.

Chapter 26

I CHECKED MY BAGS A FEW MORE TIMES AND A TEXT FROM Alistair popped up.

Haven't talked to you in a while. Busy little duck?

I responded: *Quack, quack. We have a lot of catching up to do. My biological mom emailed and I talked with my parents. Actually kinda cleansing.*

Alistair: *Can you talk on the phone?*

Me: *Can't right now. Super busy and running late. Maybe soon though.*

Alistair: *Jane.*

Me: *Yeah?*

Alistair: *Jane....*

Me: *Yeah...*

Alistair: *Ok... Talk soon.*

I didn't tell him I was on my way to the Mentmore Towers in Buckinghamshire as my first stop and that Donovan would be traveling with me. Didn't tell him that I'd be just over two hours from his home in Bristol, where we originally intended to meet and spend time making music together. Music I didn't know how to create, but he promised to teach me.

Zoe poked her head into my room. "Need a ride to the airport?"

I shook my head as I mentally checked off everything I needed. "Nope. Autumn is taking us."

"Is, um ... is Donovan waiting outside in the car?"

"I would hope so."

"Oh, um, then..." She ran down the stairs and down the next set of stairs before the apartment door even closed behind her. I shook my head. I swear that guy had a love potion stacked somewhere that he desperately needed to provide a cure for so that girls could handle the aftermath.

I straightened my bed and did one last mental run through, then picked up my two bags—I pack light—and headed outside.

Zoe turned into a ten-year-old boy band fan as Donovan soaked up the attention from the car. So utterly annoying. I shoved my stuff into Autumn's trunk as she laughed, then I got in the backseat. Autumn drove away from Zoe before she climbed into the car and Donovan climbed into the backseat.

"Ladies first," he said.

"Huh?"

"I mean, ladies get shotgun."

"Oh." I pointed. "You want me to climb up there and take that seat?"

He gestured for me to do just that.

"Uh ... okay..." I managed to get up there and buckle up. Autumn smirked at me.

"I can see your face in the rear view, you know," Donovan said.

I laughed. "She'll always think we're in love and destined to be together. It'll never end."

"Unless you both marry someone else," she said. "Then maybe I'll believe it."

"We've had a close friendship and some intense times, but that doesn't mean we're meant to be," Donovan said. "Right, Jazz?"

I stared out the window. "Mmmhmm."

"How do you know when you're meant to be with someone?" Autumn asked.

"The way I feel about Han. It's like. my heart walks away whenever she leaves the room. If I want to stay alive, I gotta follow it."

My head bobbed in the side mirror as I pretended not to hear that.

"You think Han is the one?" Autumn laughed. "Come on! You say that about everyone."

"It's different this time," I said, eyes still on the passing trees.

Neither of them responded.

I turned and looked at them both. "What? It is."

"It is," Donovan said somberly. "But it's also complicated."

"Why?" Autumn said.

"Because..." He tapped the car door. "She has a strict and conservative family and they believe in arranged marriages or at least something similar. I'm not exactly the arrangement they're looking for."

"Donovan." I looked over my shoulder at him. "You're an amazing guy and I'm sure Han thinks the same. One day at a time. We have years ahead of us. You're always rushing to get to tomorrow when you've got today right here."

"I could die tomorrow and I want to die with her as my girl." His voice deepened as he lowered his chin, something he did when he was agitated. "You keep saying we're too young to know real love, but speak for yourself. Maybe I got a little crazy with some of my exes, but I had a good reason for that. There's only two people I've ever loved, Jane."

I glanced at Autumn who tried to keep her smile from making a grand entrance.

"What reason is good enough to go crazy thinking every single girl you meet is the one?"

"You." He clenched his jaw.

"Trying to make you jealous," Autumn interjected.

"Thanks for the clarification, Dr. Phil," I turned back to the window. "I'm sorry I hurt you, Don. I don't know how many times I can say this. And I do believe love can exist for teenagers, maybe just not this one."

"You're too guarded," Don said. "If you died tomorrow wouldn't you regret being so closed up?"

"Not at all. I'm not as closed up as you think. I'm just cautious. Guys aren't my biggest desire. I have other dreams to live and if that happens along the way, great." I sighed. So tired of explaining myself. "And I do let people in."

"You've let Alistair in?"

"Maybe."

"Then why aren't we visiting him on this trip?"

"Maybe we are."

Autumn turned on some music.

And that was that. We didn't speak again until we boarded the plane. We weren't mad. We were thinking. Processing. Doing that thing we do in our comfortable awkward moments.

The time would come. Maybe halfway across the ocean. We'd finish processing, look at each other, and laugh.

Chapter 27

DONOVAN AND I WERE EXHAUSTED BEYOND COMPREHEN-
sion and passed out as soon as we got to the hotel. Neither of us slept
on the flight. We just can't. We hate flying and that was a loooong
flight with about fifty million bursts of turbulence—also known as,
moments when your life flashes before your eyes and you wonder
what the hell the oxygen mask is for anyway. Personally, if I'm gonna
die in a plane crash I'd rather forego the oxygen and pass out first.

I woke up in the middle of the night and Donovan, surprisingly,
was up. I was facing away from him, but the wall glowed from his
phone and his arms moved near my back.

I tried to blink myself back to sleep, but everything about my
birth situation kept my eyes open as I replayed my conversation with
Mom over and over.

I was raped. My dead grandfather was my father. My aunt was
my mother. Those kinds of twisted perversions only happened in
movies, not real life. Not my life.

A wave of major sadness tightened my chest as it swept over me. I
wanted to be strong and not care about how I came into the world and
just be thankful for *being* in the world. You know, live in the moment.

But my moment didn't appeal to me. I remember the day I overheard Mom and Dad talking about my adoption. I remember the day

I planted that box and vowed to never think of it again. So clearly, I remember crying myself to sleep feeling like I didn't fit in anywhere, with anyone. Except Don.

I was never the type to have many friends. Real friends. I had a ton of people I hung out with, but I always felt alone. Like a puzzle piece that got stuck in the wrong box. I didn't fit. At the end of the puzzle there sat a beautiful picture and then me ... off to the side ... nowhere to fit.

I turned to Don. His phone lit his face as he typed on the screen.

"Hey," I whispered.

He jumped and threw his phone across the room.

I mumbled somewhat of a laugh.

"Scared the crap out of me," he said, getting up to grab his phone.

"Sorry."

He got back into bed. "It's Han. She emailed me and said she wants to give it some time and maybe I can meet her family."

"Sounds scary."

"Sure as hell does."

"Gonna do it?"

"Sure as hell am."

I watched as his thumbs typed their little hearts out. Because thumbs definitely have hearts and I love to be literal.

My lungs collapsed or something, because I needed to inhale as deep as possible to get enough air and even then I felt like I couldn't breathe. I grabbed my chest as my eyes watered. Don glanced at me, then touched my arm as though I were having a heart attack.

"I'm fine," I said between breaths, while wondering what was happening. The room blurred as I squeezed Donovan's arm.

"Jane? You're not okay." He forced me up and held me. "Stop fighting your heart. It wants to feel pain and you keep telling it not to."

I swallowed. My nose burned. My eyes closed.

"I don't know," I said. "My chest hurts. I can't breathe. I want to be strong. I want to be the hero."

"Even hero's have hearts, Jazz." He pulled my shirt down to show my shoulder. "Remember why you got this tattoo." His fingers grazed my tattoo. "It's not who I am underneath, but what I do that defines me. Batman dealt with pain. And so did The Joker. Just in different ways. You can be a hero by loving. Anyone and everyone. Not just romantically. You know this. You know you're already a hero to me."

I leaned against the bed frame and pulled the blankets to my chin, then looked at his concerned face.

"Don't fight the tears, okay?"

"I am my own worst enemy."

"Fight it out with yourself. But don't fight your pain. Let it come. It's only part of you 'till you let it go, then it's gone. You're free."

"I feel like I'll never be able to love," I finally said. "I'm torn between the ideals of my parents and the fear of...."

"Of being hurt?"

"No." I imagined my teenage mother giving birth to me and handing me to her older sister, then disappearing. Not caring about my first words or first steps or first anythings. "Of being abandoned. Of letting someone love me and then watching them walk away one day when they realize it's too hard and I'm not worth it."

He pulled my chin toward him and made me look into his serious, yet gentle eyes. "Listen to me." His eyes searched mine. "If anyone ever feels like you aren't worth a fight, then they're not worth crying over. Your past doesn't define you."

"I know. This is why I always loved the relationship between Batman and Joker. We can't choose our circumstances, but we can choose how we react to them and that shapes our lives. I get it, I get it. But that doesn't change the fact that for whatever reason it hurts to know I was a child of rape just given up so easily and that one day I could finally love someone and give myself to them only to have them walk away."

"Isn't love worth it though? To you?"

"That's the thing, Don. I don't think it is."

"It's worth it to me. I'll take the pain because it shows that I really loved. Whether the person ever loved me back or not, at least I did my part. If Bruce didn't have pain when his parents died, it meant he didn't love them. And if he didn't love them, never had the pain, maybe he would've just been a pointless playboy for the rest of his life instead of a hero."

I watched the green light flicker on the light switch across the room. The air conditioner kicked on and created a comforting hum. Donovan began to fall asleep while sitting up. I pushed him down to the pillow and watched as he folded his hands under his cheek and drifted off into a dream. So peaceful. I always envied his peace. All those times I shoved him away and he never stopped trying, he never lost his sense of calm.

I spent my life wondering who I really was. Who my parents really were and how that shaped me.

Maybe Don was right though. Well, I knew he was right, but try convincing a broken heart of what's right. Pain was a good thing. This dull ache in my chest that turned into a nauseating knife-like searing pain, was a good thing. Because it proved I was alive. It proved I had a heart. And given the right time … maybe I could love and be loved.

Donovan snorted so loud he woke himself up, then immediately closed his eyes and fell back into a soft snore.

Figures. I finally pour myself out and when I feel a little better … he snores.

I watched him sleep for a while and I knew it was finally the right time. I felt it as I watched him sleep. He loved me for years. Faithfully without question.

For once, I felt the same. I loved him. My best friend. The only one who knew me. Really, really knew me. And I thought maybe … maybe I'd finally fallen in love with him.

And maybe I could finally tell him.

Chapter 28

AFTER BREAKFAST, DONOVAN AND I TRAVELED TO THE MEN-
tmore Towers, used in *Batman Begins*, only to find out that I was wrong.
We couldn't visit, but a local guy told us we could visit Mentmore Golf
and Country Club, then walk parts of the Rothschild Course near the
fourteenth and fifteenth holes to get a closer look and maybe snap a
picture. Can't say it didn't bum me out, but I had been so distracted
with Donovan that it didn't bother me that much. He wanted to go
out to dinner later and I planned to tell him the truth over our meal,
but throughout the day he kept checking his phone for messages from
Han and I was starting to question if it was the right time. And as I
questioned ... I felt less in love with him by the minute, to the point
that I wondered if I had only dreamed that I was. But no. I knew what
I felt. I just didn't understand why the feelings never lingered around.

Not that I believed love was totally based on feelings, but they
should have some kind of place in the mix, right?

Donovan and I pretended to play golf throughout the morning
as we made it to the view of the house. He took a picture of me with
it in the background, then a picture of the back of me as I stared at
it. This probably sounds ultra dorky, I know. Not too many people
understand my Batman obsession or why it felt so amazing to look at
that house, but I loved every second of it and so badly wanted to go

inside.

Donovan pulled me toward him and snapped a picture of us both. I smiled as I wondered if it would be our last adventure together as friends. Maybe we'd finally be more.

My phone beeped. Alistair and I used a special app for international texting and I knew that beep was him.

"I know that's lover boy," Don said as we sat in the grass. "Go ahead and answer it."

"How do you know?"

"Know the sound. You kinda smile whenever it beeps. Hard not to notice."

"Did I just smile?"

"Wasn't looking. Just know the sound now."

I opened the message so that I wouldn't seem too weird and read, *Got another song done. I hope everything is okay. I miss our talks.*

I responded, *Can't wait to hear it!*

Alistair: *Wow. You're up early!*

Me: *I am? It's already 10!*

Alistair: *Right, but in the States it's only 5am right?*

I shoved the phone back in my purse and looked at the house.

Donovan yawned. "Could this be any more boring? We are traveling the world to do this? Stare at mansions?"

I laughed. "Wanna go take a nap before dinner? I'm exhausted."

"Definitely."

WE MADE IT TO THE BED AND BREAKFAST IN ONE PIECE. Driving on the opposite side was extremely weird, plus Donovan kept checking his email. No, he wasn't driving, but every time he checked I had to keep myself from watching for his reaction as he read whatever she had written.

If he was doing this to make me jealous, it was the first time it actually worked.

After waiting for him to finish another message, we finally walked up to the porch of the bed and breakfast.

"Let's sit out in the garden," he said. "Out back."

I followed him to the back where we got comfortable in a few lounge chairs under the shade of a tall tree. It's arms reached down, pretty low actually, and nearly touched the tops of the chairs.

A built-in pool that looked like a pond reflected the sun. I loved the fake lily pads and the flower petals they scattered on top of the water. Truly a natural feeling pool setting. Amazing.

"I'm glad," he said as he finally slid his phone into his pocket.

"To talk to Han?"

He shook his head. "Well, that too, but...."

"To see Batman's house?"

"Hands down the best experience ever." He laughed. "No. That you're finally getting honest with yourself. Feeling stuff. Dealing with your past and your fears."

"I am."

Tiny rays of sunlight shot through the tree branches and leaves. Whoever said England is always rainy got their facts mixed up. It was a beautiful summer day and this quaint little poolside garden was the perfect setting for it. Completely peaceful.

Something jostled the bush behind me.

I jumped. "Some kind of animal is in the bush."

He looked over his shoulder. "Probably just a rabbit." His eyes widened. "Or Edward Cullen."

"Huh?" I settled back in the chair. "Who's that?"

"Pretty sad that I know and you don't."

"If that's the case, let's keep it that way."

We laughed, then sat for a while without speaking, when finally he broke the silence.

"So," he said. "Do you think maybe you're ready to let love in now? Maybe if someone told you they wanted to kiss you ... maybe you'd let him?"

I swallowed and told myself to breathe. *Stay still*, Jane, I said to myself. *Don't panic.*

"Actually," I said. "I ... there's something ... um ... yeah."

"I hope you'll say yes, Jane, because I have something for you. Close your eyes."

Butterflies. Whew. Good. Was starting to doubt the validity of my feelings.

"Don." Something rustled the bush again. I ignored it and tried to focus on him. "This is really hard for me."

His face brightened, but he seemed distracted. "Close your eyes, Jazz."

"Wait." Breathe. Breathe. Breathe. "I know it's been years and we've had our ups and downs and a lot of in betweens. I know I've hurt you a lot and I've been closed off, but I'm not that girl anymore. Maybe I am. Well, I probably am still a tiny bit closed off. It's hard to change over night, but these things have been changing me and I feel ready." I searched his eyes for clues to see if he was prepared to hear what I needed to say. He couldn't have looked any happier, so I went on, stuttered a few times, then said, "You waited long enough. I just need to say it." *Say it, Jane. Go on.* "Donovan. I ... I've fallen for you." His eyes darkened. Not the reaction I imagined. "I mean, I've fallen and I can't get up."

His palm flung toward his forehead. Warmth filled my hands as sweat began to form. Then, the bush cracked and shook and a huge thing came out. My heart dropped as I backed away, but it wasn't an animal.

It was....

Shit.

Donovan's hand still covered his eyes as he shook his head.

"Alistair?" I said. "What ... what is...?" I looked from Donovan to him, wondering why I was standing there feeling stupid as hell for pouring my heart out.

"Wasn't how I planned this," Don said. "I sent him a message from your phone while you were showering. I thought I'd surprise you. I thought you didn't want to see him because of me being here. And you're always smiling at his messages. I just thought...."

I panicked and tried to run into the house, but Donovan reached for my arm and gave me the eyes. The serious eyes. The don't-you-act-like-a-baby-and-run-off eyes.

Yes. I was an adult. But this ... this was terribly humiliating. My palms held a thick layer of sweat and my face was catching up. The pool was looking mighty nice. Mighty thrilling.

"I feel a bit out of place," Alistair said as he clumsily set a bouquet of black and yellow roses on the chair next to me. Batman roses. "I should let, um ... I'll just be going now."

His arm brushed mine as he walked by me.

I shivered.

And shook it off.

"Wait," I said. "Alistair."

He turned back, sighed, and walked away. I needed to apologize to him. Or something. But first I needed to finish what I started with Don.

He stared at me with droopy eyes. A smile-less Donovan isn't a normal Donovan, so I wasn't too excited to hear what he had to say. I wanted to crawl into a hole and disappear.

"Well." I clasped my hands in front of me and swayed them. "Looks like I really am the best of fools."

"Jane." Donovan sat down and motioned for me to do the same. "I don't know what to say. I waited years to hear those words..."

Don't say but, don't say but.

"But..."

"But you love Han."

"It's not just that. I do love her, yeah, but even if I didn't I still wouldn't be able to let you believe that you love me."

I'm sure I looked confused as I waited for him to continue.

"Somewhere along the lines I realized that I wanted to be with you because it was familiar. We know each other so well and I've opened up to you during the roughest times of my life. So obviously I thought you were the one for me. You were there for me constantly and I think the fact that you made yourself unattainable just made me want you more." He touched my knee. "Jane, I love you so much and I know you love me too, but you're not in love with me. You're in love with the idea of me. This last week has been a breaking point for you. I watched you have an anxiety attack last night as you emptied your heart out. I was there for you and you're confusing your vulnerability with me with love."

"But..."

He scooted toward me so that our knees touched, then he held my chin. "But I'm glad you feel like you can be in love now."

I shook my head. "This is ... I don't know ... can I have some time to myself? I just need to think."

He pat my knee and stood, then went into the B&B through the back door.

"Poor Alistair," I whispered, then jumped into the pool fully clothed. Don't know why. Sometimes random acts of oddness do the soul good. The cool water refreshed me, so I stayed there, floating among the lily pads, staring at the fluffy clouds. And I laughed. I laughed until I could no longer float on top the water. Because really ... what the hell?

Some people write love stories and some people live love stories. Then, there are the ones who do neither.

That would be this Jane Austen. Not the other one.

Chapter 29

WHEN I WENT BACK INTO OUR ROOM DONOVAN WAS GONE, so I took a quick shower and he still wasn't back. I wondered if he went after Alistair, then I wondered how I should act when he came back. Would things be different? Worse?

I braided my hair into two long braids, then flipped them back into a bun when a note caught my eye. On my pillow. His handwriting.

I closed my eyes, braced myself, then read:

Jazz,

I decided to head back home now. I'll be fine. Go after Alistair, okay? I think you guys need to talk. Sorry for messing up your Batman plans, or maybe you'll finish it with him. ;-) He's a good guy. I really like him and as your best friend I can tell that he's good for you. Try to talk to him, okay? See ya when you get home.

Love ya, Don

Well, I guess the positive is that I didn't need to figure out what to do when he walked back through the door.

The negative ... I was alone in a foreign country.

He assumed I'd go find Alistair and ride off into the sunset, but I figured Alistair wanted nothing to do with me and I was way too embarrassed to go find him and pretend like I never meant what I said. What would I say anyway? "Oh, hey, sorry I just professed my love to my best friend. Wanna go out to eat?"

The flowers!

The Batman roses!

I quickly ran back outside and sure enough they were still where he left them. I brought them to my room and got comfortable again.

I did mean it. What I said to Don. Whether I was right or not. Maybe I didn't *really* love Donovan. Maybe he was right. I don't know. But what I *did* know was that I didn't want to think about it.

I tried, you know....

I tried to be all "true to my heart" and whatever, but look what happened. Exactly why I thought it was better to avoid it all together. Keep the heart locked up and it can never be broken, unlock the door and there you go. Unpleasant feelings.

Amazing how fast excitement can bleed into the blues when it comes to matters of love. The heart is too fickle. Too sensitive.

Not sure I liked that.

I relaxed in bed, pulled up *The Green Mile* on my iPad, and ignored reality while watching Tom Hanks astound me once again. Incredible actor.

Then I reached over to turn the light off and noticed a card inside the Batman roses. I suppose they were ordinary black and yellow roses, but they would forever be Batman roses to me. Lovely, really. Such a cute idea.

I pulled the card out of its trusty envelope and read:

Jane.

It's hard to write a comma after your name because whenever I say it or write it I need to stop. Just stop right there and let it sink in.

Jane.

Jane.

Jane.

I hope this is only the beginning of sinking in. And I don't know ... I think perhaps I'm sinking into you too?

What is this rubbish anyway?

I'm blubbering. A fool.

Thank you for ... just being you.

I like knowing you.

-Alistair

I sighed and held the letter to my chest. Just a few months ago he tripped into my life. It was a beautiful day actually. He was so charming and fun. The Big Day. The day we were supposed to meet and kiss. If we were single. Guess that idea was over now.

A headache started between my eyes. I put the card next to the flowers and turned the light off. Sleep sounded like a great idea, but a little far-fetched.

I tossed, turned, stared, blinked, massaged my head, tossed, turned, and picked up my phone.

Blink. Blink.

It stared back.

I opened my texts to Alistair and began to type. I got out the word "hey," then shut my phone off and continued the staring contest with the wall.

I felt horrible. And my Batman trip was nowhere near as fun.

So, yeah. I decided to take the next flight out to America. Can you blame me?

Waking up alone, looking at the notes from Alistair and Donovan, imagining the rest of my trip alone ... right ... home appealed to me more.

I sat in the airport for a while. My flight would be another two hours and believe me ... I considered saying the hell with it and visiting Alistair. I opened my texts to him, started to type, stopped, started, stopped. Then I'd annoy myself and pull my sketch pad out, only to be completely uninspired.

Finally, I sent him a text. A simple one. I said, *I'm sorry.*

An hour passed. No response.

Another hour. No response.

I wished I could see the "read receipt" like iMessage, but nope. Nothing.

I boarded the plane, sat down away from the window, and closed my eyes.

"Excuse me," a voice said. "Could I scoot by you?"

I opened my eyes and stood so the pregnant woman could take the window seat. Pregnant. I stared at her stomach and wondered if my biological mom would've aborted me. Maybe she considered it. Maybe I was never meant to live and that's why I failed at so many things I tried.

The woman draped her arm over her stomach and smiled at me. I forced a smile, then leaned back and closed my eyes.

"Ladies and gentlemen," the flight attendant started as the plan began to move.

I zoned out. Didn't hear a word she said, then the plane began to lift off the ground.

My phone beeped. Oops. I forgot to turn it off.

A text. From him.

Don't be sorry, Jane. The heart feels what it wants to and I'm just glad you're feeling something. Still friends? Still want to do the music with me? I'm here if you want to visit. As friends of course.

I glanced out the window as the plane climbed toward the clouds.

"Oh, I, can someone..." The woman next to me tried to stand and—

Vomit. All over me.

I cringed and held my breath.

And yup ... that's my life for ya.

Right place at the right time.

Never failed.

Chapter 30

AUTUMN PICKED ME UP FROM THE AIRPORT. I WAS
surprised that she didn't ask why I came home early. Or why Donovan
wasn't with me. But I guess I shouldn't have been too surprised,
because as soon as we entered my apartment she finally said, "So.
What happened?"

"I thought you weren't going to ask." I walked up the stairs as she
followed.

"Figured I'd let you talk first, but since that's not happening..."

I rolled my suitcase toward the closet and grabbed pajamas from
a drawer.

"So?"

"I need a shower. Some lady threw up on me during the flight."

"Ew! Are you serious?"

"Unfortunately, yeah. I changed at the airport, but still."

"I need to head back home anyway," she said. "But tell me what's
going on first. Real quick."

I sighed. "It's not even worth talking about."

"But Don is still there?"

"He came back before me."

"He left you there? That's unlike him. Was he jealous of Alistair?"

I laughed. "You need to let it go now."

"Let what go?"

"Him. Me. Together. Not happening."

"It would if you'd just let him love you."

"Yeah." I walked toward the steps. "If only I'd let him love me. I should go right now. I'll find him, tell him that I'm in love with him, and then we can finally be together."

"Or just keep delaying the inevitable."

"Or that." I started down the steps. "Definitely that."

She jogged behind me. "Jane, I'm not kidding. You need to open up and let him in! How long have we been friends? And you've never once dated a guy. At all. Ever. That's not normal anymore."

We reached the bottom of the steps and stood there. She looked at me. I looked at her. And I considered telling her, but I didn't have the energy right now.

"I love you." I hugged her, then walked toward the bathroom while saying, "Stay the night. I'll tell you what happened after this shower zaps some life into me."

It didn't actually make me any less tired, but after the shower I made a quick blueberry crumble thingy that Zoe always made, grabbed two plates, and met Autumn on the couch where she was watching some weird romance movie. Course they're all weird to me, but this one was about a girl who constantly dyed her hair and a guy who seemed to have depression coming together, hating each other, erasing their memories, then regretting it as they relived the memories while each one disappeared. So weird. Autumn's favorite romance movie. Of the moment. Apparently.

When it ended she turned the television off and looked at me. The candle I had lit earlier flickered on the table, reminding me of the time I watched Alistair via that Skype video. Alistair!

"Hold on a sec," I said, then ran upstairs to get my phone. But ... couldn't find it. "Autumn, is my phone down there?"

"Uh ... don't see it."

I searched everything. Even things my phone couldn't possibly fit in.

Nothing.

I jogged back to Autumn and sat beside her. "Can I see your phone?"

"Yeah, why?" She handed it to me.

"Need to text Don and get Alistair's number. I lost my phone and have no idea what his number is. He's gonna think I'm ignoring him."

"Calm down," she said as I texted Don from her phone.

A few minutes later he responded. *I didn't save the number. I just messaged him from your phone. Are you back?*

I gave her the phone without answering him, then watched the candle flame tilt and sway through the glass.

Autumn's hand waved in front of my face. "Jane!"

"Huh?" I kept staring.

"What's going on?"

"Be right back."

I went back to my room, pulled my iPad out, downloaded Skype, and signed in.

Wrong password.

I tried as many combinations as I could think of, then hit the password reset button. After refreshing my email seven million times, I realized it was sending to my old address. The one I didn't have anymore.

I went to his old band's website. "This domain is for sale."

I looked up his Facebook. Twitter. Any remnant of him on the Internet.

Nothing. Nothing. Nothing.

Zoe sat beside me. "Hey, just got in and heard you flipping out in here as I was walking to my room. What's up?"

Autumn sat on the other side of me.

"Nothing," I said. "I'm fine."

"It's just a phone," Autumn said. "You can get a new one."

"I can, yeah."

"I'd probably flip if I lost my phone too," Zoe said as she checked her purse.

I stood and paced the room. There had to be a way to reach him. Oh! His address. I could mail a letter.

Oh....

My shoulders slumped. I saved his address in my ... drum roll please ... phone!

"Jane, you're seriously freaking out about your phone?" Autumn pushed me back to the bed and made me sit. "What is wrong with you?"

"I'm a failure, that's what. I should've never been born. I wasn't even supposed to be alive, you know. I came into the world through rape and here I am, messing up everywhere I turn. I spent my life ignoring love when my best friend devoted his life to me. I never really let myself enjoy my family because I couldn't stop obsessing over who my real mom was and thinking this endless thought that I didn't belong. I've used up a ton of the money my parent's gave me and I have nothing to show for it except a pointless trip and a shop that failed. Finally, I pour my heart out and tell the only person who ever loved me that, guess what, I loved him too. Really loved him. And he tells me that I'm delusional and don't really love him and that he got over me a long time ago. As if that's not bad enough, out of the bushes comes a sweet guy holding a bouquet of flowers—Batman flowers—and he walks away. Then I lose my freaking phone and can't tell him that I'm not ignoring him and that even if I can't let him kiss me right now, I still care." I buried my face in my hands. "I shouldn't even be here."

Hands warmed my back and shoulders. Someone ran their fingers through my hair. I lifted my face from my hands and shook my head.

"Just so you know," Autumn whispered. "I'm glad you're here."

She sniffed and wiped her face as Zoe rubbed circles on my back.

"I didn't know..." Autumn wiped more tears. "I'm sorry. I feel like a horrible friend."

"No, no," I said, taking her hand. "I never let you in. Just like everyone always says. I kept it all inside, tried to deal with it myself. Well, I'm not fine." I straightened my posture and exhaled. Felt good to say it. "I'm. Not. Fine."

"Got that right," Zoe said. "More like a hot mess."

Autumn shook her head and I stared at Zoe with a really-did-you-actually-just-say-that face.

"Just saying." She shrugged. "So, my Donny rejected you?"

"Oh my freaking hell," Autumn said. "Get the crap out of here, Zoe." She pointed to the door. "Now."

"No." I waved my hand. "It's okay."

"It's just that I think we're meant to be," Zoe said.

"Get the hell out of here now!" Autumn screamed at the top of her lungs, making both of us jump.

"Geez. Chill out. I'll leave." Zoe stood. "I'm tired anyway."

Zoe made her grand exit and Autumn and I looked at each other as a slight smile started on my face, then hers. I laughed a little. And within seconds we were laughing so hard tears squeezed their way to both of our faces, cleansing our eyes and my heart in the process.

Laughter is truly the best medicine.

"I love you, Autumn," I whispered in between breaths. "Thank you."

"I don't care how you got here," she said. "My life wouldn't be the same without you."

"What am I gonna do?" I curled up with my head on my pillow. "Everything is falling apart. I'm afraid to wake up tomorrow and get more bad news."

"There won't be anymore bad news," she said as she got under the blankets. "And I'm staying the night, so if there's anymore bad news or if Zoe comes in being stupid, I'll be here to help."

"That was hilarious." I laughed into my pillow. "You really screamed at her. Your hair and everything was shaking."

She laughed. "I was pissed. I mean, who the hell says that to someone who just emptied their heart all over the place?"

"She doesn't know how horrible the stuff she says is. She's got a lot of issues too. A lot of pain in her life."

"I know." She closed her eyes. "I'll apologize in the morning. For now, I'm ready for bed."

"Night, Autumn."

"Good. Night."

She was out cold within two minutes flat. And I think it's safe to say ... I didn't sleep at all.

Alistair was my friend. I liked him. I liked our talks. I didn't want him to think I never wanted to talk to him again.

"Autumn," I whispered.

"Hmm."

"Can I use for phone real quick?"

"Mmhmm." She rolled away from me.

I grabbed her phone from my nightstand and dialed my own number. It rang until the voicemail picked up. I hit a few buttons and accessed my messages. Two voicemails from Mom. One from Autumn. And none from Alistair. I figured that would be the case anyway. He would've called my Skype account, which I couldn't access without my phone.

I tried the iPad again. Put in every password I'd ever used in the last five years. Nothing worked. I always told myself to 1.) save my passwords somewhere off of my phone of 2.) always use the same password, but I did neither.

My passwords were always a Batman character mixed with some kind of number combination, like my birthday or the month and year a certain film was released. I swear I tried every possible one, but I had to be missing something right in front of my face.

I tried passwords until after midnight, then finally fell asleep and dreamed of giving birth to a bird. It honestly horrified me and I couldn't sleep well after that.

When the light of the morning finally entered the room, I immediately got up and walked to the cafe across from Dee's tattoo place. Quietly, I ordered three latte's and bagels and walked back outside. The golden sun was still low in the east, not high enough to rid the sidewalk of shadows, but not low enough to be forgotten. Cars swished by with windows half down as drivers held phones or coffee in one hand. I stopped and leaned against the wall of my closed boutique, then sipped my creamy latte.

A woman stopped in front of me. "Is it true what the paper said about you?"

"The paper?" I said. "What paper?"

"You own *Rosalind's*, right?"

I looked over my shoulder. "Um, I did. Why?"

"I read that you're getting sued for $142,000. Is it true? Is that why you're closing down?"

I laughed. "No. I'm not closing down, just revamping and going with a new style. Something for me, instead of the world."

She glanced at her watch. "Oh, good for you. Good luck with that."

I nodded, watched a few more people pass, then went inside. Zoe was still sleeping and Autumn just walked out of the bathroom.

"Please tell me you didn't go looking for your phone at the airport," she said.

I set the coffee and bagels on the kitchen table. "I needed caffeine. Couldn't sleep."

"So you never told me why you ended up on a plane alone. Where did Donovan go?"

"He just left me because he thought I should go talk to Alistair."

"But you didn't?"

"It was awkward. I felt stupid. Now I feel even more stupid as each day passes."

We sat down and ate our bagels as I went through my mail. About halfway through the stash I noticed a large envelope near the bottom. I tore the seal and read the document. My jaw tensed. I reread it just to be sure, flipping through pages as fast as possible, then backward again.

"What's going on?" Autumn said.

The lady was right.

I scanned each line two more times, reading the claim against me.

"This clothing boutique was a bad idea," I said. "Everything's been a bad idea. Why did I even try to be an adult? I just want to go back home and forget any of this ever happened."

"What now?"

"I'm being sued." I slapped the document back to the table. "Apparently someone had an allergy to the clothing they bought. She's claiming it wasn't properly labeled and that some chemical in the synthetic fabric caused a severe allergic reaction."

Autumn looked at me, unable to process what I said.

"I'm being sued. For a lot of money. More than I have." I closed my eyes. "Hopefully they can't go after me personally. The business has no worth anyway."

"But what about the new one? That Batman thing? Will they just take all the money you make?"

My stomach churned as I ran my fingers along my necklace. "I don't know. Is this as bad as I think it is?"

"You need to call your lawyer guy or your parents."

"Why did I do this? I should've used the money for school or a simple apartment. Now I need a job."

"Take a deep breath," she said, but I could tell even she was nervous for me. "You'll figure something out."

She wasn't so sure. Neither was I.

I imagined myself moving back in with my parents and feeling ridiculous. I couldn't let that happen. I wouldn't.

All I wanted was to follow my dreams. To be responsible and start a career in something I was passionate about.

Maybe I dreamed too big.

Maybe ... maybe I shouldn't have dreamed at all.

Chapter 31

MOM SERVED BURGERS ON HOMEMADE BUNS, SALT AND vinegar fries, and hand-squeezed strawberry lemonade. They knew *something* was wrong. Just not *what* was wrong. I came home early from my two-week trip. That's all they knew.

As we ate dinner I considered how to tell them everything. The lawsuit. The money. The store. But by the end of the meal I decided not to. Not yet at least. Maybe I could turn things around. Maybe I could open up a new place and people would come and actually like it.

Most likely not. But I could try.

I helped Mom with the dishes while Eddie and Dad did something in the living room. We worked in silence until the very end, when she turned to me and said, "We know about the lawsuit."

"I was going to tell you." I focused on the dishes. "Waiting for the right time."

"Funny how the right time never comes when it's something you don't want to do."

"I just want to fix this without worrying you guys."

"How will you make sure it doesn't happen again?"

"I can't. The lawyer told me that some people are sue happy and will look for reasons to sue me. Could be anything from someone slipping on the floor to tripping over a clothing rack. He thinks I can win this one because the shirt she bought was one-hundred percent organic cotton and had no ink on it, so I don't know. We'll see how it goes."

"How's the new shop idea coming?"

"I've got most of my designs ready. Just need to get Han and Brooke back in to help sew them."

"You're not telling anyone what it is?"

"I want it to be a surprise."

She forced a smile. "I'm worried about you."

"If you weren't, I'd be concerned."

"Just promise me that if you need help, you'll ask."

"I will."

I finished the last dish, she dried it, and we met Dad and Ed in the living room for family game night. I could remember family game night all the way back to when I was four and we played Go Fish, then a little later when we got obsessed with Uno. There was a Risk stage, a Twister stage, a Poker stage, a chess stage, and now we were in Monopoly mode, which Ed seemed to dominate. What did I dominate? Guess. No, not Go Fish.

Chess.

I know, right? Chess of all things. I was horrible at Poker because I couldn't keep a straight face when I had a good hand. Twister, not my thing. Chess though? I rocked the chess board.

Just kidding. I actually sucked at all of them, but it was fun anyway. Mom and I played to laugh at ourselves. Dad and Ed, on the other hand, flexed their competition skills no matter what the game was. And when they'd get intense and insist someone cheated Mom and I would always laugh.

The Monopoly board was ready and Dad and Ed had their game faces on. It would be a long night, but a needed one. I loved my family.

I spent so much of my childhood looking at them and wondering if I belonged, but I knew now ... I didn't just belong. I was part of them. We were all part of each other. Whether we liked it or not.

But I liked it. I really, really liked it.

WHEN I GOT HOME I GRABBED MY SKETCH PAD, MADE A LATE night cuppa, and drew my little heart out until I had way too many designs for my new clothing line. I wanted it to work. So bad. And I was determined to turn that desire into reality.

I finished around one in the morning and got in bed just as Zoe walked in. I listened to her footsteps click throughout the apartment until finally she went to her room. The light snapped on. Then off. Her bed springs creaked. And she sniffed. And whimpered.

I rolled out of bed and peeked into her room. "Zoe?"

"Go away," she said.

So I did what most people would do. I walked in and sat on her bed. She shoved her head under the pillow, but it was too late. I already saw the bruise and cut on her face.

"What happened?" I didn't touch her, knowing she probably didn't want another hand on her.

Something banged the window. I jumped off the bed and held my chest.

"What the hell was that?" I said.

She kept her head under the pillow and said something I couldn't hear.

I looked outside. A man stood in the parking lot by Zoe's car, screaming something and throwing his hands in the air.

"Who's that?" I said.

She grunted.

"Did he hit you?" My adrenaline kicked in.

She didn't answer. The guy raised something into the air and held it above her car's window, then swung and shattered it.

"Zoe ... you need to tell me who this is. I'm calling the cops."

The guy waved for me to come down. He probably thought I was her.

I ripped the pillow off of her and checked her face. Blood oozed from her right temple and her nose looked broken.

"Give me your phone," I said. "I'm calling the cops and taking you to the hospital."

She pulled the blanket over her and sniffed again.

"Where's your phone, Zoe?"

The apartment's alarm went off.

"He's trying to break in here." My heart rate accelerated. "Where's your damn phone? Now!"

She didn't move. I looked through her stuff, but didn't see it. Ripped the blanket off of her. Nothing.

"Zoe, I'm not kidding. Do you want him to come in here?"

She buried herself in the blanket again. I ran down the steps and checked to make sure the front door was locked. There was no way he'd be able to get in, but I still needed to call the cops and I didn't have a phone.

Too much drama for one week. Seriously.

I paced the living room and finally decided to go out of the apartment and call the cops before he'd have a chance to try to pick the lock.

I made it halfway down the stairs when something smacked my head.

"Where do you think you're going, little thing?" He slurred his words together and the alcohol emanated from his breath so strong I could smell it without facing him.

I continued down the stairs, but he picked up his pace behind me and met me at the bottom, near the back door. Didn't any neighbors hear the alarm? Didn't someone call the cops with this whacko out there busting her car up?

Or was I alone?

He swaggered up to me with a slanted smile on his face. I stepped back to the wall and kept my eyes on him as he looked up and down my body and licked his lips. I pictured Julia's face when her father raped her and my hands naturally curled into fists.

"Get away from me," I said. "I'm not interested in entertaining perverts."

"I didn't ask what you wanted." He put his hand on the wall, just over my head, and leaned into my face. "And with a sexy outfit like that you can't expect not to be touched."

"My outfit is no excuse for your perversions, but thanks for trying to blame me. Perfect opportunity," I whispered in a sultry voice, "to start owning your issues. Don't you think?"

I kneed him as hard as possible. He grabbed himself and stepped back. I kicked again and he lost his balance, then fell into the stairs.

Moaning, he stood back up and charged me, but he was drunk

and I wasn't. When his fist rocketed toward my face I pulled his arm toward me and his own body weight shot him toward the corner of the wall.

"I am vengeance." I kicked again. "I am the night." I opened the door. "I am Batman."

He struggled to stand while I dashed outside and down the street. Out of breath, I ran into a twenty-four hour mini-mart and begged the man to call the cops.

He did.

When they finally arrived I explained everything. They escorted me back to the apartment, but Perv was gone, so they went up to question Zoe instead. I waited in the living room until they convinced her to go to the hospital. She hung her head as she left with two cops who told me it was her brother, Jayden, and to keep an eye out for him and call 911 if I saw him again.

I locked the door behind them, crossed my arms over my chest, and looked around the dark room with only one little thing on my mind.

I needed a new phone.

Pronto.

Chapter 32

HAN AND BROOKE GOT TO WORK ON MY DESIGNS WHILE I stopped to get a new phone. I knew exactly what I wanted, being a bit of an Apple snob, so the decision was easy until the guy showed me a newer model.

"Will I need to pay full price?" I said while holding the sleek new gadget in my hand.

He smiled and nudged my elbow with his. "I think I can work out a discount. Come on over here."

I followed him to a desk and waited while he clicked a few things, asked a few questions, and clicked a few more things.

He looked up and smiled. "Lucky you, I'm a manager here and just got you an early upgrade."

"Okay ... so, what's the total price?"

"I can get it down to $299 for you."

"That's fine. Thank you. Hey, um, is there anyway I can access the information from my old phone?"

"If you activate your new phone and connect to iTunes it should restore everything." He winked. "Anything else you need today? A glass protector? A case? Any extra cables?"

I shook my head. "I'm good, I think. Thanks."

"No problem." He clicked around again. "Silver, gold, or gray?"

"Ooh. Options now."

He laughed. "I'm guessing you're a silver kinda girl."

"You guessed right." Can we say weird?

He handed me a box and I handed him my card. "Jane Austen?" he said. "Really?"

"Yup." I nodded. "Really."

"Really? Is ... hey ..."

"No, not that Jane Austen. Obviously. But yes, Jane Austen is my name. There are approximately a hundred and seventy two people in the U.S. with the same name, so it's not *that* unusual, but I'm thankful you know ... because it's who I am. It's my name. It's me."

"No, no," he stammered. "No, it's nice. I like it."

"I didn't embarrass you, did I?"

He smiled. "No. It would take a lot to embarrass me." He handed me my card. "So, maybe you would like to go—"

"I'm sorry"—I looked at his name tag—"Greg. Look, I'm just not interested in dating right now. Or ... maybe ... ever."

"Ever? Wow. Bad history or something?"

"Not much of a history. I don't know if I'm even interested in a history. Why do people date so many people? Can't you tell right away whether someone is right for you or not? And if so, what's the point in dating someone if they aren't right for you?" I shook my head. "And here I am talking to a stranger about my personal life." I took the bag with my new phone. "So, on that note, I'll just be going then."

"I think the point"—he tapped the counter with a pen—"is just to have fun, enjoy life."

"Mm. Yeah. And dating a bunch of people is what you call enjoying life?"

"Whoa." He held up his hands. "Don't shoot the messenger."

I laughed. "You're not the messenger. It's your opinion that you gave."

"Yeah." He laughed.

I leaned in and whispered, "I've loved one guy in my life and honestly, so far he's the only one who deserves my heart and he doesn't want it. Dating," I said louder, "is not my idea of fun. For me, fun is owning my own fashion line, living my dreams, and maybe one day I'll have a partner to live those dreams with me, but right now ... I just want to do something right. I don't want to give up. A challenge. That's fun to me."

"Dating can be a challenge too." He raised his eyebrows. "Want me to show you?"

We turned to his employees on the other side of the desk, staring at us. I waved. He smiled.

"Well, that was interesting," I said. "I really should go now. Good luck with ... everything."

"You too, Jane." He waved shyly. "Thanks."

I walked out of there with my head held high. It felt good to vent, even if it was to a complete stranger who had my phone number right in front of his face right now.

That's okay though. It inspired me to have fun. To enjoy everything I did, no matter what. To get back to work and make things happen.

So I did just that.

When I got back to the shop, I even let Han and Brooke choose music to play. And we played it. Loud. Dancing in between sewing runs. They sang along and I tried, although I didn't know any of the words. We laughed so hard my cheeks and abs hurt and I loved every second of it.

Then I saw him at the back of the shop behind a rack of my old line of clothes, my rejected line. Time stopped for a second. His eyes brightened when he smiled. I smiled back. I missed him.

"Han," I said, nodding behind her. "Someone is here to see you."

She turned and smiled, then rushed over to him. He picked her up and swung her around. Like he did to me so many times in the past. But it was okay. I loved him. A lot. And when you love someone you want them to be happy, even if that means being with someone else. I wanted that for him. I really did.

They disappeared out back and after a while Han came back in alone.

"Donovan would like to see you," she said as she sat back down.

I meandered outside and found him leaning against the wall with his hands in his pockets.

"Jazz, what happened with Zoe? Is she okay?"

"She's fine. They found her brother." I stood beside him, my back against the wall too. "Poor girl."

"I'm glad you took care of her. Like a real life Batman."

"Right. I actually thought about that." I laughed and looked off into the distance. Anywhere but his eyes.

"I don't want this to be weird between us," he said. "And I want you to talk to Alistair. He may not be the one you marry, but he cared about you."

"Did you guys talk about me?"

"Of course." He touched my arm. "You're avoiding eye contact with me."

I turned my face toward him. "How's this for ya?"

"Better."

"I lost my phone. No way of contacting Mr. Alistair."

"He's gotta be online somewhere."

"Maybe. I looked. Can't find him anywhere."

We stood there quietly for a while. Silence leaned a little more awkward than comfortable this time, but maybe it would pass soon. Maybe all of this would pass.

"I should?"

"Yeah." He walked toward his car. "I'll see ya later, Jazz. Let me know when you need help with the store."

I almost stayed to watch him walk away, but walked inside instead. Maybe it was just me, but our friendship changed. Into a normal friendship. Like Autumn and me.

I went back to my sewing machine and we kept going with our sewing dance party until we slowed down. At midnight I asked them if they wanted to stop, but they both decided to stay. An hour later we were all exhausted.

"You guys are amazing," I said. "How about you stay the night? It's too late to drive."

"Oh, no," Han said. "I do not want to intrude."

"It's good," I said. "If you drive home right now Donovan will kill me."

"He's really into you," Brooke said. "Are you guys a couple now or what?"

"It's difficult situation." Han sighed. "My family wants me to marry someone else. They are very upset about it."

"Shouldn't you be able to do what makes you happy?" Brooke

said.

"My family is very important to me," she said. "But Donovan is..." She blushed. "He's very sweet man. He's definitely big part of my heart."

"I love your accent," I said. "Your English is so good for only learning recently."

"Thank you."

"Han, Donovan is a sweet guy who will love you until the day you die. If you think it's right, just tell your parents that you respect them, but you need to follow your heart."

"Very difficult," she said. "My family ... very conservative. Very important to them."

"Don't let him go." I held her hand and squeezed. "He loves you. And he's worth it."

She smiled. "Thank you very much. I like him a lot."

"Okay, girls. Let's go to bed. We can have breakfast and get to it again tomorrow."

Chapter 33

BROOKE, HAN, ZOE, AND I COOKED BREAKFAST IN PAJAMAS
while laughing and talking. Zoe made eggs. Han made toast. Brooke
made home fries. And I whipped up some pancakes. It was a crowded
kitchen, but fun.

"Have you talked to your parents?" Brooke asked Zoe.

She shook her head. "They love my brother and they'll just blame
me. It's not worth it."

"How long has he been like that?" I said. "Has he always abused
you?"

"Some stuff happened when I was a kid," she said. "But it got
worse when he started doing drugs and drinking. My parents don't
believe me though. They think he's perfect and if they happen to find
pot in his room they punish me for planting it there."

"Do you smoke pot?"

"Used to. Stopped though."

"But they still thought it was you?"

"They just believe whatever my brother says."

"Looks like the home fries are done," Brooke said as she pulled a
potato-filled cast iron pan out of the oven. "How's everything else?"

We all nodded and set the table. I couldn't keep my eyes off of
Han. Never in my life was I the jealous type, but she was so petite

and pretty and the way she glided around the kitchen reminded me of some kind of angelic dance. She never laughed super loud, like I did. It was always this soft whimper-like laugh that barely opened her mouth, but she had charm. Tons of it.

Honestly, I could not have imagined anyone better for Donovan. At all.

I loved Brooke and Zoe too. Each in their own way, they brought something new to my life. A year ago, or even months, I would never had imagined sitting in my own place with such a diverse group of girls. I never had many girl friends and Autumn was with boys and her other friends so much that we didn't spend day and night together. She's a true social butterfly. Cheerleader. Complete opposite of me in a lot of ways. So most of the time I was with Donovan, but I wasn't a tomboy. Not totally at least. Just never connected with people like I did with Don.

These girls I definitely connected with though. Even amidst our differences.

I smiled as I looked around the table, toast dangling from my hand. This was my life. Maybe it wasn't perfect and I sure did know a thing or two about obstacles, but as I glanced around the table, I realized we all had our own obstacles. Han's conservative family posed as a wall between Donovan and her. Brooke struggled as a single mom trying to pay the bills and her nanny. Zoe dealt with bruised cheeks way too often. But we all sat at the table. Together. Smiling. Sure, life may not be perfect, but maybe it's those twists and turns that merge our paths and bring us together. A room full of broken hearts with the drive to keep beating.

"I love you guys," I said. "I mean it."

Chapter 34

THE THING ABOUT THE *RIGHT* TIME IS YOU NEED TO GO through a lot of *wrong* times before finally discovering the right one. Just like dating, I wasn't a fan of wasting time on the wrong ones.

Especially because it's just plain embarrassing.

The end of August snuck up on me way too fast. Brooke and Han worked for free, helping me finish an entire store's worth of Batman-inspired clothes. I was so proud of these designs, yet I had no store to sell them in.

I spent almost the entire month looking for a job, with failing interview after failing interview. Some companies knew me as "the girl who got sued," and others weren't interested in an eighteen-year-old dreamer, no matter how sophisticated I tried to be. Every job that paid enough to sustain me and help me lease a store didn't work out. I wasn't qualified enough. My work history consisted of a swim school and an unsuccessful business venture. So I didn't blame them, but I was a week away from rent and I barely had enough money to eat.

Autumn knocked on my door. I let her in and she hugged me as hard as possible.

"I ... can't ... ribs ... ouch..."

"I'm leaving," she said. "Can you believe it? One more week and I'm miles and miles away."

"Are you ready to eat?"

She turned back to the door and walked into the hallway. I followed and called up to Zoe. "You okay?"

"Yeah," she yelled.

"Come lock the big lock. Just to be safe."

"I will."

"Has she gotten a restraining order yet?" Autumn said.

"Not sure. I think it involves court and stuff. I really don't know though. Zoe's a private person with that side of her life. I probably know more than anyone else. Even Donovan didn't know as much as she told me."

"How's Donny? Feel like I haven't seen him in forever."

"He's good, I guess."

We walked down to the car and talked about everything from college to job interviews as she drove. I told her to be careful. I was enduring a bad luck streak, even though I didn't believe in luck, and didn't want to get into an accident.

"Maybe you should believe in luck," she said as we entered the restaurant. "Maybe that's been the problem all along."

"Oh, no." I sighed as we walked in.

"What now?"

"That guy over there." I tried not to make eye contact, but he already saw me. "Don't look at him."

"Huh? What guy?"

"Party of two?" the hostess said.

"Yes," Autumn said. "Two, thanks."

The hostess led us toward the guys over there.

"Oh, actually would it be okay to sit on the other side of the restaurant?" I said.

"This is all I have open right now," she said. "Or that booth over there."

Even closer to him. "No, this is fine. Thank you."

Autumn sat down, set her purse on the bench beside her, and raised her chin. "Um...."

"That guy." I leaned in. "He hit on me at the phone store the other day and now he saw us."

She looked.

"No, no. Don't look. Don't encourage it ."

"Wow." She smiled and waved at him and his friend. "They're hot."

"You're leaving in a few days and I'm not interested." I hid my face in the menu. "So stop smiling and waving at them."

"They're coming. They're coming!"

"Ugh. Autumn. I'm gonna kill you."

I set the menu back down and faked a smile. "Oh, hey."

He smiled. "Hey, Jane. This is my friend Noah. And..." He looked at Autumn.

"I'm Autumn." Oh no. Autumn turned into another person around boys. Flipped her hair and did stupid stuff. I wasn't prepared for this tonight. She shook their hands. "So, Noah and...."

"Cameron," the guy said.

"Oh, I love that name." *Autumn. Please.*

I busied myself with the menu.

"Could we eat with you?" Cameron said. "We just got here too."

"Yes!" Autumn scooted over.

"N—" I tried to object.

"Yeah, sit down." She waved them in. "We could use the company."

"We could?" I said without looking up from the menu.

"Jane, since you're so interested in that menu," Noah said, "how about you just read it aloud to us?"

I glanced up, then back down.

"She's anti-men," Autumn teased, knowing it would provoke my defensive speech.

But I decided to go ahead and read the menu aloud. And I did. All the way down the wine list too. When I finished I looked up at Autumn and Noah. And Cameron who was laughing beside me.

"So." I closed my menu. "What'll it be guys?"

"It's your treat, right?" Noah said.

"Of course." I played along. I didn't like him.

"You'll have to excuse her," Autumn said. "She's been rejected by the only guy she's ever loved."

"According to him I didn't actually love him."

"What's that supposed to mean?" Noah said.

The waiter set a root beer in front of me and a water in front of Autumn, then asked everyone what they wanted. Noah ordered a chicken pasta thing, Cameron got the steak and potato meal, and Autumn went with a large salad and a soup.

Then me. "I'll have five orders of the brownie dessert. Extra caramel sauce, please." I handed her my menu. "Yes, I'm serious."

Cameron laughed while Autumn inched toward Noah. By the end of the night she'd be on his lap.

"So why are you anti-men?" Noah said.

"Well, really it depends on the size of the penis."

Noah spit his soda out and Cameron's took a journey through his nose.

"She's kidding." Autumn grinned. "I hope."

"I'm not anti-anything," I said. "I love all things. In moderation."

"Jane believes that to date a guy you need to give him your heart or fall in love."

"And what do you believe?" Noah said.

"I believe in cutting strings and having fun."

"What about you Noah?" I looked at Cameron. "And you. What do you guys believe?"

"I'm good with no strings," Noah said.

"I think it depends on the girl," Cameron said.

My five brownies were suddenly in front of my face. I picked up a spoon and wasted no time. Autumn flirted during the entire meal. Cameron asked if he could have one of my brownies. I slid it to his side of the table and spaced out. Memories of Autumn drifted in and out of my mind. Our friendship over the years. Her excitement for life. The way she danced even when there was no music and then, when asked, she'd say, "There's always music."

In a week she would be gone for nine months, only visiting on holidays. Then she'd be gone the next three years after that. I imagined her with new friends. New interests. And I genuinely worried we'd grow apart.

I watched her twirl her straw and bat her eyelashes across the table and I didn't even care about the two guys sitting with us. All I cared about was taking pictures with my mind. Of my Autumn. My friend. My sister.

"It won't change that much," I said to myself.

"What won't" Cameron said.

"Oh, just the brownies. Sometimes they're wrapped in new packages, but they're still the same brownies."

He thought I was crazy. I liked that.

We finished eating, Autumn, of course, wrote her number on a receipt and slipped it into Noah's pocket. Cameron shifted his weight from one foot to the other until he finally stuttered a string of words. If I was interested in dating people I knew weren't right for me, I would've given him a chance. He was a very clean type of attractive guy. Probably the kind of guy cast in a romance film. And he had charm to him, a gentle child-like quality, but he was extremely shy. Forward, but shy. Unsure of himself. Like me. I knew myself well enough to know that I needed someone confident in himself without being conceited. Someone like Donovan.

Or Alistair.

"Still not interested?" he said.

"It wouldn't work anyway."

"Okay."

Autumn finally pried herself from Noah and the guys got into Cameron's car. As they drove away she waved at them.

"So deliciously sexy," she said through her smile. "Wow."

"Aren't they a bit old for us?"

She put her hand down and laughed. "Really, Jane? There's no such thing. As long as it's not over ten years."

"So there is such a thing then. Ten years? That's like ... he's in college while you're in middle school. Creepy."

"The older we get the less creeper it'll be. Come on, those guys were ridiculously hot. I could just—"

"I'd prefer to leave that a mystery."

"Why didn't you just give Cameron one date? Just one little date."

"Waste of time."

"I'll never understand."

"Likewise."

"Before I leave I want you to go on one date for fun. No strings. No relationships. Nothing serious. Just one date."

"I don't get why you people think that's fun. I'd rather spend the night home alone drawing and actually accomplishing something."

"Just one."

"Nope."

"What was it about Alistair that made you give him a chance?"

"I didn't give him a chance."

"You like him."

"Probably that he didn't give up. He was sweet. I don't know. There's something there or there isn't. He has something." We walked to the car as I imagined the afternoon we spent together, the phone calls, and the Batman roses that wilted by my bedside. "He made me feel."

"And now you'll never talk to him again."

"If not, then it wasn't meant to be."

"Do you think there will ever be a right time with Don?" She sat down in the car.

I did too, shaking my head as I pulled the door closed.

"Why?"

"He's going to marry Han."

"But he really loved you."

"The heart can only love a broken heart so much until it breaks itself. She's healing him. She's putting his pieces back together." My eyes burned. "I want that for him."

"Is that why you're stopped at a green light?"

"Precisely."

Chapter 35

DAD NEVER WAS THE I-TOLD-YOU-SO TYPE, BUT I STILL EX-pected him to be disappointed in me, which is why I stalled during my entire visit with them.

"We're heading to Granny's in fifteen minutes," Mom said as Dad and Eddie focused on the end of their Monopoly battle. "Want to come?"

"Oh, I can't right now," I said. "But I did want to tell you guys something before I leave."

"No worries," Eddie said while counting fake money. "Mom already has your room ready for you."

"Edward!" Mom's hands went to her hips. "Don't be so insensitive."

"We figured you'd need a place to stay until you found a good job." Dad picked up a card, then stopped to look at me. "There's no shame in it, Jane. Things didn't work out, that's all."

"I can hear disappointment in your voice, Dad."

He sat up straighter and inhaled. "I'd be lying if I said I wasn't disappointed in your decisions, but I'm not disappointed in you."

"You blew a ton of money," Eddie said. "Fast."

"Thanks, Ed. I'm sure you'll be so much wiser when you get yours."

He counted his fake money aloud, then said, "Probably right."

I sighed. "I still want to make the shop work. We have a lot of clothes made already and I thought maybe I could sell them online until I save money for a place."

"That's a great idea." Mom smiled.

"I know I should of thought of that from the start."

"It's a good lesson though," Dad said. "Now you know what not to do."

"Yeah, I do."

"You never were the quitting type," Mom said as she stood. "You boys ready to go?" Then she hugged me. "You'll work things out. I've always believed in you, Janie."

I'm sure glad someone did.

ZOE AND I PACKED UP THE LAST OF OUR STUFF WHILE Autumn did the same at her house. Two days left. Then she'd be gone.

Brooke offered to let Zoe stay with her for a while and maybe we could find another place together when I saved some money. And Donovan, Dad, and Eddie offered to take my stuff to a storage unit, load it in and everything, so I could spend the night at Autumn's house before she left. Very kind of them and I was thankful for the help.

"This was short-lived," Zoe said as she taped a box of kitchen supplies.

"Too short-lived." I looked around at the stacks of boxes all over the place. "I really liked this place, too."

"Will Donny be here soon?"

"Probably. We should put the small stuff in our cars. Save the big stuff for the moving truck."

I'm not sure what felt worse. The first day I moved out. Or moving back in to my parent's house within the same season. I loved them, but it wasn't appealing.

Zoe and I jogged in and out, filling our cars with boxes upon boxes. At some point some guy ran by and she jumped.

"Did you get a restraining order?" I said. "You really should."

"I'm afraid to."

"Why?"

"I don't know. I have no family on my side."

"You have me."

"I could never be related to you. No offense."

I shook my head. "Wrong thing to say, but that's okay. You do realize that you are actually related to an extremely abusive brother, right?"

"That's different. He's blood. I can't help it."

I almost said something, but what's the point?

"This must be them," I said as a moving truck pulled into the parking lot.

Dad parked and jumped out of the driver's seat, then Eddie and they walked over to me while staring at Zoe.

"Where's Donny?" Zoe whined.

"He is in love with Han, you know." I waved Dad and Ed over. "He's not interested in getting back with you."

"He will. When something is meant to be it finds a way."

"Zoe..." I stopped myself and started again, "He's taken. If you love him, you'll respect that."

"Your brother is hot. Wow."

I ignored that as Dad and Eddie approached. Did I really want to move in with her again?

"So." Dad squinted his eyes to avoid the sun. "Eddie and I will get the bigger stuff. Donovan and Mike should be here soon."

"His dad's coming too?"

"Yes, I think his girlfriend wanted to help out too." He searched my eyes for a response they wouldn't provide. "They should be here soon."

Dad and Eddie loaded a few pieces of furniture while Zoe and I packed our cars as much as they could handle. Donovan, his dad—who I also called Dad—and Han showed up and began to help.

Han cleaned the apartment with Zoe and me as the men emptied the apartment. Every time Donovan came in Han's face sparkled when his eyes met hers.

He came in again and made his way to her. Zoe watched in disgust as his hand gently touched her back, but then quickly smiled as Eddie walked by. I tried not to watch Donovan's hands on Han, but I couldn't help myself. The way she grinned when he touched her. And the way he liked it, his smile matching hers in shyness.

There's only one person I looked at like that. Only one who made me weak when his hand grazed my back.

And it wasn't Donovan.

AUTUMN PICKED ME UP FROM MY PARENT'S HOUSE. WHICH was now my house again. She had her car all ready for a new adventure, stuffed to the limit. My stuff was all in storage and Dad even said he'd take the rest out of my car tonight and put it in my room.

"Your parents are the nicest parents in the world," Autumn said as we entered her house. "Wish mine were like that."

"Your parents are nice." I followed her inside. "Just bizarre."

"You can say that again. Can't wait to have my own dorm room."

"Not sharing it with someone?"

"Well, yeah." She tapped the stuffed bird on the entryway table. "Just mean away from all the dead animals."

Her parents filled the house with stuffed animals. Everything from real, dead snakes to real, dead elephant heads. They spent tons of money on these weird "decorations" and even raised their own birds and ducks to later stuff them when they died. Don't ask.

"Why, hello, Jane," Mr. and Mrs. Beverly said in unison.

"Can I get you something to drink?" Mrs. Bev said.

"No, thanks. I'm good."

They bowed as we walked by them. Autumn shook her head. I laughed. They weren't totally creepy. More like Weird Al type of people. Intentionally strange. You could hear them cracking up laughing whenever you left the room. Like now.

"And they wonder why I've never brought a boy home," she said.

"Can I be here when that finally happens?" She shut her bedroom door and I flopped on to the bed. "Exhaustion strikes."

"Our last night together and we're probably gonna spend it sleeping," she said.

What she *didn't* know was that we had a surprise going away party planned for her tomorrow. Donovan and Han took care of the details for me, since I couldn't be there to get everything ready. They found a place in the city and I was supposed to walk by tomorrow and nonchalantly decide to go into the building. I hadn't quite figured out how to make it happen, but I would.

My phone beeped.

"Who's that?" Autumn looked at her own phone.

"Looks like Ella. This woman I met at Dee's tattoo place. She wants to know if I can teach her some sewing tips in exchange for violin lessons."

"How many things do you have on your bucket list now?"

"Forgot about it, honestly. Alistair and I were going to help each other check off the first five, then make five more."

"Have you tried to find him again?"

"I've looked." Looked, meaning I'd wake up in the middle of the night hearing his voice say my name. Only to realize it was a dream. Then I'd spend a half hour looking for a sign of him on the grand ole Internet. I just missed my friend, that's all.

"Have you said goodbye to your cheerleader buddies yet?" I said, knowing she'd see them tomorrow at the party.

"Yeah. I got all that out of the way so I could be with you this last night. Plus, I need a break from people before I go."

"Oh. Why?"

"Just too much."

She was in for a real surprise then. Hopefully it didn't ruin her plans too much.

"Sure you don't wanna come to school with me now that Donovan isn't going to be around as much?"

"Don't say that."

"Well, he's not."

"No. I mean the 'school' word."

She smiled. "Can't hurt to have a degree even for cool people like you. Maybe a business degree so you don't fail again."

I slapped her arm. "Funny thing is Zoe would say something like that and be totally serious."

"She's funny. I can't believe she doesn't realize how rude she is sometimes."

"She's oblivious. Reminds me of Eddie. I'm not sure if that makes it better or worse."

"So ... since I'm the one leaving, you need to do what I want to do tonight."

"Please spare me the chick flick nonsense."

"I just want you to watch this one movie."

"You say that every time."

"I know, but it's different this time."

"How so?"

"Because you're different."

"Fine, fine," I said, and within thirty minutes she had nachos and cheese and root beer sitting in front of us. We propped ourselves up on our elbows as we lay next to each other, huddled under blankets with the iPad against the wall in front of us.

She made me watch a Korean film. Oddly enough. It was about a girl with a facial scar who locked herself in her room and created different online personas to vicariously live through. And a guy who lost everything and tried to kill himself, only to end up alive on a patch of land surrounded by water—with a fear of drowning. The two accept each other from a distance and eventually their love forces them to overcome their fears. Quirky, intriguing, and emotional.

Autumn wiped her eyes at the end. "I can't believe you didn't shed one tear."

"I don't cry at movies. Except *Amistad*. That one gets me going."

"Don't you want love like that?"

"Like *Amistad*?"

"Shut up." She laughed. "You know what I mean."

"All I kept thinking about was Donovan and Han."

"Oh! I'm so dumb. I forgot!"

"No." I ate another chip. "I'm happy for him. I really am. Just saying it's hard for me to put myself in those shoes, so I picture my friends instead."

"What would you do in that situation?"

"Huh?"

"If you thought you lost the love of your life, only to find him at the last minute?"

I thought for a few minutes.

"Would you cry?"

"Mmm ...I think I'd laugh."

"You'd laugh? Not even one tear would fall?"

"Maybe I'd laugh so hard I'd cry."

"Fair enough."

Chapter 36

THAT DAMN MOVIE MESSED WITH ME ALL NIGHT. I TRIED TO sleep, but I kept getting sweaty and anxious as I pictured Autumn leaving and starting her life. And me. Sitting at home with my parents and Eddie while failing at my dreams. I didn't toss and turn all night. I stared at her ceiling. For hours. I processed everything from my birth to my recent mistakes. Every major life event and every minor one too. It's true, I overthink things.

The sun finally poured into the room and Autumn stirred.

"I have two goals," I said before she opened her eyes.

"Am I supposed to have a serious conversation with you at the crack of dawn?"

"One, I'm going to make this Batman-inspired fashion line work, I don't care what the hell I have to do."

"Okay. I never doubted that one."

"Yeah, but I did."

"And what's number two?"

"I'm going on a date."

She sat up and rubbed her eyes, then leaned closer and analyzed my face. "Where's Jane and what have you done with her?"

"Maybe cell phone guy. Maybe even tonight."

"Wait. What? Are you serious?"

I nodded. I spent my life avoiding guys because I didn't *need* them. I didn't *need* the breakups. I didn't *need* the extra drama. I didn't *need* to force myself to get all worked up over someone if it wouldn't last. I didn't *need*, but that didn't mean I couldn't *want*. Besides, maybe it would be fun. Maybe it could even *relieve* stress. Maybe I just wanted a kiss.

Not need.

Want.

I wanted a kiss. That's it. No strings attached. No relationships. No drama.

A simple, fun kiss.

"On that note," Autumn said, "I'm getting in the shower. Smells like Mom cooked cereal for breakfast if you want some while you wait."

I laughed. Her family was notorious for convenience foods, while my mom made gourmet breakfasts whenever a guest came over.

"I'm afraid to venture out into stuffed animal land alone," I said.

"Just watch out for the elephant. I've bumped into the horn a few times and it hurts."

"So weird, Autumn." I shook my head. "And I remember when they stuffed the snake and we walked in thinking it was real."

"Then you got all Batman on it while I screamed and ran out of the house."

"I ripped that thing to shreds, thinking I was so brave and victorious."

She held her stomach in laughter. "Laugh. Out. Loud."

"I'm gonna miss you," I said, looking at my fingernails.

She sat back down and hugged me. We stayed like that for a few minutes as our laughter turned quiet.

"I'm gonna miss you too," she said. "Especially those Batman pajamas."

We went to lunch at some random place in the city. Her choice. Now I needed to get her to the surprise party, which was all the way across town, but I didn't want to make it obvious. So I let her go in and out of some shops on Walnut Street, this beautiful little shopping district in Philly.

We walked back out of another store and I checked the time.

"Got somewhere to be?" she said.

"No, just got an email." Technically I did just get an email. So I wasn't lying!

"Okay. One more store then? For me?"

"I hate window shopping. It's like dating. Why waste your time on stuff you can't buy?"

"For me?" she whined.

"Of course."

"And you said you're gonna go on a date and kiss that guy, maybe even tonight."

"That was this morning."

She walked into a store. I followed. We were definitely going to be late.

"Jane," she said. "Isn't this...." She held up a shirt. "This is just like yours."

Lungs. Heart. All of it stopped. I held the shirt in my hands and looked at the others on the rack, and the others, and the others.

"Can I help you?" someone said.

Autumn slowly took the shirt from my hands as I stared at the rest of them. My designs. My clothes. My Batman-inspired line! Someone stole it all!

"Excuse me," someone said. "Is there something I can help you with?"

I turned. "Where is your manager?"

"I'm sorry?" the girl said.

"I'd like to see your manager. I have a question about employment."

"Let me check and see if that's a possibility."

"It better be a freaking possibility."

She disappeared.

"Autumn, they totally stole my stuff!" I wanted to grab everything off the racks and run. "How is that even possible?"

The girl returned. "He's willing to see you, but he said there are no employment opportunities at this time."

"Come with me," I said to Autumn.

We followed the girl into the back of the store and into a tight hallway. She opened another door. "Go on in."

Fists clenched, pulse racing, palms sweating, I stepped in.

"SURPRISE!"

Mom. Dad. Donovan. Han. Zoe. Brooke. Eddie. Granny. Ella. Dee. Aunt Sandy. Uncle Kenny. And ... what?

I turned to Autumn. She held her hand over her growing smile as tears collected in her eyes.

"Everyone chipped in," Donovan said. "And we started a fund-raiser."

"Chipped ... what?" *Why is everyone smiling at me?* "Isn't this Autumn's party?"

She stepped up and hugged me. "No, dummy. There's no going away party. It was for you."

"But ... what's going on exactly?"

"This is your store," Mom said. "It's not technically opened yet. The girl at the front was a friend of Han's. We just opened the front door for now to make it seem real to you. The name on the front needs to be changed to whatever you decide to call it. We gathered enough to pay for five months of rent and your furniture is all moved into a new place a few blocks over."

"You've got five months, kiddo," Dad said. "Time to make it work."

I inhaled until my lungs couldn't take it anymore. "You guys are too nice to me. I don't deserve this."

"There's more," Donovan said. "I got you something." He handed me a rectangle wrapped in black and gold paper. "It's not much, but I think you'll like it."

"Open it now?" *In front of all these eyeballs?*

He nodded.

You can do this, Jane. I ripped the edge of the paper and peeled it back, then ripped and peeled more. A picture frame. I turned it over. Framed by black and gold, with a little Batman stamp on it, was the note Alistair first wrote me. The day we met.

Autumn played 1812 Overture from her phone. It was all a little ... queer, in Alistair's words.

I didn't know what to say. Especially to Donovan. Especially in front of a sea of glowing faces who wanted an emotional reaction I couldn't give.

Dad stepped aside. Then Donovan. Then Mom. Then, one by one, every person formed a path in the middle until it opened up and led to...

Him.

Chapter 37

HE STOOD THERE. HANDS IN HIS POCKETS, WEARING THE same outfit from the day we met. Black t-shirt. Fitted jeans. His lips twitched and turned up into a funny, nervous smile.

All eyes on me. On him. The song. The black and yellow roses tucked between his arm and his side.

I didn't know what to do.

In a romance movie she'd run up and jump into his arms, they'd twirl around the room as everyone cried in the background. The song would get louder, their hearts would beat faster, and it would be amazingly cheesy.

In a comedy, I'd stand there and someone would run in and ruin the moment.

In a tragedy, maybe I'd run off and kill myself. Then he'd follow after and do the same. Never understood that one.

He closed his eyes and his smiled turned up one side of his face. When he opened his eyes again I was a step closer. He pulled his hands from his pockets and took a step too.

"I ... I ..." I couldn't.

He took another step.

My turn. *You can do this, Jane. Don't hurt him in front of everyone.*

Another step.

And my turn again.

We stood a few inches apart. Close enough that I could smell the flowers and his minty breath.

"Jane," he whispered.

I closed my eyes. "Alistair."

Something welled inside me. Some foreign sensation. It wasn't butterflies or tears. I knew those already.

It wasn't nervousness or shyness. I felt those many times before too.

It was something else. Something that tightened my chest, warmed me from the inside out, and brought the slightest smile to my face.

He handed me the flowers, took my hand into his, brought it to his lips, and kissed, looking right at me the entire time.

I turned to everyone around us. They smiled like they were watching a chick flick, which didn't appeal to me.

I grabbed Alistair's hand, whispered, "Let's go," and ran toward the door with his hand in mine.

We dashed out the front and down the street, disappeared around the corner, and stopped. Panting, he leaned on his knees.

"What exactly just happened?" he said.

It started small. The slightest bubbling in my chest, then it increased and I couldn't hold back anymore.

Leaning against the wall of a store, I laughed. And he joined in. I laughed harder, louder, as the flowers trembled in my hands.

We shook our heads and held our stomachs, trying to speak between fits of laughter. People walked by, cocking their heads at us, but we didn't care. Not at all.

My eyes welled as our laughs subsided into soft bursts. He stood close to me. Really close.

Then silenced himself as he pulled a single rose from the bouquet.

My eyes continued to blur. "I tried to—"

He placed the rose on my lips. "I know what happened. I would've come after you, Jane, but Donovan found me first and told me to wait." He took the rose away and cupped my hand around it. "He said you needed more time and he wanted to surprise you."

"How did he find you? I tried everything."

"He looked up my old band on Facebook, searched through old comments, and there I was."

"Leave it to Don. I thought I tried everything at least."

"You really wanted to find me, eh?" He smirked. "Staying up all hours of the night to look for me?"

I tried as hard as humanely possible not to blush. Or lie. He was joking, but it was true. I stayed up many nights trying to find him.

"So tell me," he said. "What is it about me? The accent or the anticipation of the greatest kiss of your entire life?"

I hit his chest. "Shut up."

He laughed. "Hungry?"

"No, but you always are. So should we get something? Am I supposed to go back to the store?"

"I don't think they'll mind."

"I can't believe this. Any of it. There are so many people that deserve this more than me."

"When we don't feel like we deserve something we appreciate it even more." He held eye contact, then broke away. "Pizza?"

"Only if it's a date." I smiled.

He gave me the flowers. "No. I'm not ready for a date."

"Oh, well I just th—"

"Jane." He laughed. "I'm kidding."

I smelled the flowers as he began walking.

"Wait," I said.

He turned.

I looked at him, taking it all in. Hair made to be messy, t-shirt that exposed his strong arms, cute shoes, nice jeans ... and that face, that smile, and those eyes. I took a picture with my mind, held it there, and hoped the image would remain for a long time. "Okay," I said. "Let's go."

As hungry as he was, he sure did walk slow. Or maybe life just slowed down completely.

His hand brushed against me and I found myself longing to feel it happen again. A few seconds later, his fingers hit mine and stayed there. I moved my index finger toward his. He looked at me. No smile. Just serious eyes. I curled my finger around his hand and waited.

He let go.

Then took my hand into his.

And held it.

Our hands swayed between us as we continued down the street. It felt good. And right.

But I couldn't shake the fear that it wouldn't last. That it wouldn't work. He'd go back home and this moment—this comfortable, beautiful moment—would be nothing more than a memory to haunt me in my sleep.

"Jane," he whispered into my neck. "Stop thinking so much."

I double-looked at him.

"I can tell." He stopped in front of a pizza place and nodded toward the door.

"No." I tightened my grip on his hand. "Let's keep walking."

Every moment we let go of is replaced by another, which could be better ... but it could also be worse. I didn't want to risk it. I wanted this moment to last. And if I'm honest, I didn't want to let it go at all. Even to trade it for something "better."

Chapter 38

WE DIDN'T STOP HOLDING HANDS UNTIL WE MADE OUR way back to the pizza place and separated to go to the bathroom. I checked my phone before coming back out and had a message from pretty much everyone.

So I responded to Autumn by saying, *I'll stop by before you leave. Tell everyone I'm turning my phone off till tomorrow.*

Then I turned it off, walked back out of the bathroom, and jumped. I didn't expect him to be standing right outside the door waiting for me, but I liked it. He reached his hand out and mine naturally fell into his again.

"Hey," he said as we walked toward the front counter. "Are you going to let me be gentlemanly and pay for this meal?"

"If you can tell me who said that it's gentlemanly to pay for a meal and when it originated."

He smiled. "And that I can't tell you."

"Maybe at least tell me why *you* think it's gentlemanly?"

"Because..." He thought for a minute. "That's what I was told to do, I guess."

"But what do *you* want to do?"

"I want to pay for you."

"Because..."

"I like you." He smiled. "And I want to be kind-person-ly."

"I like that better. See, now you're doing it because you want to, not because you think it's the proper thing to do."

"But it is proper," he said. "It's proper for me to love you if I want to."

My mouth opened and stayed there. Did he just say *love*?

"I didn't ... it's only that ..." He nodded toward the counter. "Pizza and chips?"

"Extra chips." I forced a smile.

Love?

I couldn't do love.

Not yet.

He ordered for us and I attempted to stay focused, but the word kept flying into my mind like a gnat. I'd swat. And it would fly right in again.

We sat down across from each other and waited for our meal. I really tried to look at him.

"Jane." He laughed. "I suppose we're going to need to face this at some point."

I swallowed.

He reached his hand across the table and opened it, I slowly placed my hand in his.

"No," he said. "You know what?" He stood and scooted into my booth. "I'm going to sit next to you."

"I'm sorry, I just—"

"I completely understand, but listen to me"—he cupped my face in his hands—"I do love you. Yes, I may not know what it's like to kiss you, although I hope to find out soon. And perhaps I don't know you like Donovan does. Yet. But I love who you are, Jane. I love your fiery passion and your drive to really, really live life to the fullest. You're inspiring. I love that you don't give up easily. Hell, I even love that you try to run away or hang up on people when you're embarrassed. So, yes, it's true. And I'll say it because I want to. I love you."

I nodded and tried to process everything.

"Do you want to run away right now?"

Someone set a pizza, two fries, and two drinks at our table.

"Thank you," he said, then turned to me. "Am I not allowed to love you?"

"No, no. It's not like that. I'm sorry."

"Jane."

I finally looked into his eyes.

"You don't have to say it back," he said, smiling.

"It's just a lot all at once. The shop. The surprise. The people. You. This." I took his hand. "I like you. I like talking to you and being with you, but..."

He nodded. "Go on. It's okay."

"But you live in England."

He broke eye contact and turned toward the table. "You're thinking too far ahead."

"I have to." I opened two straws and gave him one. "Don't you see? What if we start this and it gets so deep and so beautiful and then it doesn't work? What if our hearts don't line up with reality? I can't pour myself into a sieve. It's not fair to either of us."

"Jane."

"Yes?"

"Just eat."

I picked up a fry. "Are you annoyed at me?"

"A little." He threw a fry at my face. "But you deserve it."

"Fair enough." I threw it back, but it soared right by him and smacked an older woman in the face.

I hid my face in his shoulder as her husband snapped his head toward us.

Alistair pat my head and smiled at them. "I apologize. She was aiming for me."

Their contorted eyebrows slowly eased and I held my laugh inside. The woman still looked horrified that anyone would do such a thing, but her husband was definitely suppressing a laugh.

Alistair leaned into me and whispered, "Do it again."

"No way." I moved back into place and picked up a slice of pizza. "I'm too hungry to waste anymore."

"That's right. I forgot you eat triple the amount of normal girls."

"I like food, what can I say?"

AFTER OUR MEAL, WE WALKED BACK TO THE SHOP AND DIS-cussed possible names. Anything related to Batman. And it was in that conversation that I realized I did love him. Who knows if it was real deal marriage type love, but I loved who he was. The way he glanced to the side at me without moving his head. And the way he used his free hand to speak so enthusiastically about Batman, a subject none of my friends and family could ever get that deep into. I loved his laugh and the way he made me laugh. His dreams and goals and passions.

But I couldn't tell him that. I didn't want him to take it the wrong way.

We stayed in the shop for a while as he rummaged through every last piece of clothing, commenting on all of them in detail. No one ever did that. Not even Don. Most people said, "Wow, this is nice. Good job." But Alistair spent at least a minute looking at the front, back, and inside of everything and then he'd say something like, "I love the asymmetrical pattern on this one and the way this knot ties here."

Finally, when we only had about three women's outfits to go, I said, "Are you really this into fashion or is it just because it's me?"

"Psssh..." He slapped my thigh with the back of his hand. "Don't be so full of yourself. It's because it's...." He lowered his voice and continued, "the Batman."

"Oh." I smiled. "Why, of course!"

We finished analyzing each thing, which was more fun than I ever thought it could be, when he turned to me and said, "I'm chuffed for you. It doesn't matter if people buy it or not, it's amazing and really well thought out."

I clasped my hands and lowered my head. "Thank you."

"I should probably get back to my hotel. Where did you park?"

"Wait. Where's my apartment? I didn't even stay to find out."

"Oh." He pulled an envelope out of his back pocket. "Donovan anticipated that. He gave me your key. Address is on the envelope."

"Wow." I took the envelope and read the address. "He knows me too well."

"He's a good friend."

"He is." I peeked around him. "Looks stormy out. We should go."

"Yeah, okay then."

I wanted him to ask to come over, but he didn't seem to want to and I wasn't about to ask and give him the wrong impression. "So ... how long will you be here?"

"I don't have any set plans."

"Let's, um..." I nodded toward the door.

"Right, well I'm parked in the back parking lot."

"Right. Should I walk you there?"

"Jane." He took my hand again.

"Alistair."

"I didn't get a hotel."

"Oh, so you need some—"

"Jane."

"Mmm?"

"I'm staying with you." He smiled. "If you don't mind."

Chapter 39

THE APARTMENT WAS ON THE SECOND FLOOR OF A HOUSE, with the first and third floors occupied as well. A note in the envelope said rent was paid for the next five months, but after that I'd pay $750. The door opened to the living room and dining room. One big room separated by the back of the couch. The enormous kitchen had a window to the dining room, a huge bay window, and a long counter-top. Zoe would love it. The hall led to two bedrooms, one half bath with a shower, and a master bath off the back room, complete with a jacuzzi tub. All wood floors, old with dings and scratches, and cream-covered walls that were in dire need of paint.

"What do you think?" Alistair said.

"I love it. The loft was more artsy, but this is nice in its own way."

"That's a crackin' tub." He nodded down the hall as we walked back to the living room.

"I know. I'm sure I'll use it a lot."

"What would you like to do?" He sat on the couch and pat the spot next to him. "I'm knackered after that flight. Want to watch Batman?"

"Really? I would love that. I'm ... what was it ... knackered? Too."

"Knackered. You don't say that here?"

I shook my head and bit back a laugh as I opened a window.

"Would you like a cuppa too?"

"That'd be nice, yeah. Why don't we go make us a brew, duck?"

"I'll go make us a brew. You get comfortable here. Duck."

I searched the kitchen for the tea kettle and found it in the oven. Odd. Had to remind myself that this was my place. Once I fired up the kettle, I leaned against the counter and noticed he turned the lights down and lit a candle. Rain tapped on the window as the vanilla scent warmed the room.

Oh! What if I didn't have tea?

I looked through all of the cabinets and the fridge, just in case, but didn't find much more than flour, rice, and a few cans of diced tomatoes.

"Um, Alistair?"

He didn't respond. I walked into the living room and started to say his name again, but he was sleeping. Dead asleep on the couch. A little disappointing, I must say, but hey, I didn't have tea anyway. I turned the stove off, changed into my pajamas, grabbed a blanket from my room, then held it as I watched him sleep.

I thought of the night he accidentally called me on Skype. The time I watched him sleep before getting caught. That was before I knew his favorite color was orange and that he liked to drink tea right before bed because his mom gave him a taste of hers when he was a kid. It was before I knew that his parent's divorce actually did hurt him, even though he tells everyone else it didn't. Before I knew the way he stumbled over words when he was excited. Or the way he had some uncanny musical ability to play any instrument he put his hands on.

It was before I knew him.

And now that I knew him better ... he graduated from sexy to adorable. Instead of focusing on the rise and fall of his chest like last time, I focused on the slightest flutter of his eyelids and the way he tucked his hand under his pillow. His other hand draped over his chest and his breathing was slow, but heavy. He didn't snore like Don though.

I unfolded the blanket and put it over him as gently as possible. Then I sat on the floor with my back against the couch and listened to him breathe. I leaned back and whispered to myself, "I don't think he'd mind."

"No," my other side responded. "It would be weird if I just..."

"He'd like it," I said.

His fingers ran down the back of my head and lingered on my neck.

"He'd like it if you came up here," he whispered. "You nutter."

I waited. Then turned. "Hey."

He touched my hair again, then moved over to make room for me. "Come here, duck."

Suddenly ... my heart decided to beat fifty thousand times faster. So fast I wondered if he could hear it. Or see it. Or feel it.

He pulled me toward his body and I slinked down beside him.

"Cute pajamas." He wrapped his arm around me and pressed my body against his. Our legs touched. Our fingers locked. And I wondered if he'd kiss me.

The anticipation, the fact that I didn't know if and when he would, created a major rush inside of me. Every touch of his skin against mine—his thumb rubbing my hand, his leg warm against mine, his heart under my ear. Every touch and sound intensified and sent electricity through me. I unlocked my hand from his and ran my fingers up and down his arm. His breathing increased in depth and speed. The rain picked up outside, loudly pelting the window. Moving my hand toward his neck, I watched his lips. Slightly open under closed eyes. His pulse throbbed in his neck as I ran my fingers up to his face, tracing his jaw down to his lips.

What am I doing?

I closed my eyes and felt his lips with the tips of my fingers, then opened my eyes as he took my hand into his and kissed each finger one at a time.

Thunder rumbled in the background as adrenaline took over every inch of my body. I couldn't wait for him to kiss me.

I propped myself up on his chest and looked down at his sweet smile. His eyes, barely open, stared up at me as my hair fell out of its braid and touched the side of his face. He took a strand of hair—eyes still on me—inhaled, then curled it around his hand.

My breathing grew as rapid as my heart rate. I moved closer, then pressed my hand against the one he held above his head. Closer. Our eyes met and stayed there. Fixated on each other.

Then his lips parted.

I licked mine and stopped centimeters from his. Lightning flashed, casting a blue tint on his face as a gust of wind snuffed the candle.

He titled his jaw upward and swallowed, then closed his eyes again.

The electricity heightened. Sparks. Definitely lots of sparks. My lips touched his, lingered there on the softness, unmoved. Still as can be, we just breathed. Heavy. Into each other.

"Alistair," I whispered against his lips.

"Jane."

And then it happened.

It felt like every summer day and every winter night all at once, passionately filled with heat as chills coursed my body. He gently sucked in my bottom lip and opened his eyes as I opened mine, ever so briefly, then closed them as he brushed his fingers through my hair and pushed me a few inches away.

We quietly read each other's eyes while his thumb traced the outline of my face.

"So," he whispered. "That was worth waiting for."

Thunder shrieked and the street light's went out. I jolted and fell off the couch, holding my erratic heart with shaky hands.

"You okay down there?" He laughed.

"Seriously scared me."

"Come back up here." He touched my hair. "I'll calm you down."

"No." I smiled as I climbed back to him. "I don't think calm is the right word."

Chapter 40

I WOKE UP BEFORE ALISTAIR AND STOOD UP AS QUIETLY AS possible. He stayed asleep as I wrote a note telling him I'd be back in a little bit, but opened his eyes as soon as I came out of my room.

"Good morning," he said.

"Hey, I'm gonna run out and get some groceries so we can make breakfast."

"Oh." He swung his legs off the couch and yawned. "I'll come."

"You can stay if you want. I don't mind."

"I can't stay more than a few days." He stood and pat his pockets while looking around, then grabbed his wallet off the couch. "I'd like to see you as much as I can while I'm here."

I wanted to say, "Then what?" But I didn't. Then you're over there and I'm over here and we experience that unbearable feeling of emptiness as we fall asleep alone. Exactly like I feared. How could this work? I'd have to move to England or he'd have to move to America just to have a normal dating relationship, and then what if it didn't work after all that?

"You're spaced out again," he said.

"Sorry."

We walked out to the car, drove to the grocery store and parked, when finally he broke the silence. "Do you regret last night?"

"No. Not at all. It was perfect."

"Best kiss you've ever had?" His voice didn't carry the same joy it always did.

"Best kiss I'll ever have." Bet that surprised him.

But he didn't show it. Maybe it was the sadness in my voice as I said it.

We went inside the grocery store and bought a bunch of food, which he insisted on paying for to be "kind-personly," plus he said I could remember him for weeks whenever I ate.

We finally got back home and attempted to make breakfast together, but we were both terrible at it.

"The eggs aren't the worst," he said as we finally started to eat.

"Pancakes taste like sponges. I need Zoe's recipe."

He laughed. "Eat sponges often?"

"Very."

"Okay, listen." He took my hand. "I know you're not going to be able to turn your brain off and every time I kiss you perhaps you will put a wall up to make sure you don't get hurt, but I'd like to enjoy this time together without worrying about tomorrow."

"It's hard for me, Alistair. And the fact that it's hard says how much I like you."

"Jane, I'll never hurt you."

"Don't say that. Even my mom and dad, of all people, hurt each other sometimes."

"I'll never hurt you on purpose."

"This just can't work. It's too good to work, like everything in my life."

He sighed. "I thought you didn't give up easily, but maybe I was wrong."

"I'm not giving up. I'm just afraid to start something I know I can't finish. Remember when we said that?"

He nodded and took his hand away. "The difference is I intend to finish what we've started and I'll do anything to make sure it happens."

"It's just not realistic."

"Then be unrealistic. Who said you have to live by the world's standards?"

I shoved the food around on my plate, then looked up at him. "Okay. I'll try to enjoy today without thinking about tomorrow."

He smiled, but the air between us was cold. I wished more than anything that I could change myself. Why couldn't I have fun and fall in love like normal people?

We threw out what we didn't eat, had a conversation about consumerism and wastefulness, then decided to go for a walk where we continued our conversation while holding hands and laughing. We even named the store, jokingly, *Caped Crusader*, but I didn't tell him I had a real name picked out. I chose it while I tried to fall asleep after our kiss. 1812. Just 1812. After the song that played the day we met. Had nothing to do with Batman, but that was fine. Room for growth.

On our way back to my apartment Alistair noticed a woman trying to climb the steps to her house. He motioned for me to stop and approached her.

"Good afternoon," he said, touching the rail. "Might you need some help?"

"Oh, oh." Her hands shook as she reached for his arm. "Thank you, dear. You know I'm ninety-two years old in three days."

"Is that right?" He helped her to the door and smiled back at me.

"Yes, and you know what?" The keys trembled as she tried to stick them in the keyhole. "I lost my husband only a few months ago." She focused on the keys as he held his hand over hers to help her unlock the door. "Heart attack."

"I'm very sorry to hear that. I'm sure he was a wonderful man."

"*Is*, honey. He still is to me." Her face shook and a tear fell. "Thank you for helping me."

And she disappeared.

Alistair turned back to me and we kept walking.

The lady looked great for ninety-two, but her spirit had obviously buried itself with her husband.

I stayed quiet for a while after that. Then we walked up to the porch and I pulled out my keys, but he took my hand and pulled me toward him. I thought he was going to kiss me, but he didn't. He cradled me in his arms, hard, like I'd disappear if he let go, then he pulled back and said, "I'm hungry."

I laughed. "I bet you are."

"Jane?" He said as I opened the door. "Thanks for being cautious."

"Really? Why?"

"Because it shows that you're careful about who you give your heart to. And if you give it to me one day I know it'll be that much more special."

"Or I could keep it locked up forever and then it's not so admirable, is it?"

"No." He grinned. "No, that's not admirable at all."

"I don't want to."

"I know." He shut the door behind him. "I know that."

Chapter 41

THE THIRD MORNING I WOKE UP NEXT TO HIM I COULDN'T go back to sleep. It was four in the morning, but I knew he planned to go home the next morning so he could go back to work. Exactly what I worried about had finally happened. I dreaded him leaving. As I watched him sleep with the early morning moonlight on his face, I played the scene in my head. Kissing me goodbye at the airport. Several times because one goodbye is never enough. The emptiness that would settle in as he walked away, then sink in even more as his plane landed across the ocean, then just pretty much reside in my heart from then on.

Was it all worth it? A few days of fun?

I tried to sleep. I really did. But my eyes were still open when the sun woke him up. Or maybe it was the ambulance that drove by.

"Morning beautiful girl," he whispered and kissed my head. "Sleep well?"

I ran my fingers along his arm and hand, then back up to his shoulder and along his chest, where I finally settled on the *Carpe Diem* tattoo near his heart. Locusts hissed in the background as a September breeze swept through the air, billowing the curtains as it cooled the room. It was crisp and comfortable. Perfect.

"Why so serious?" he said, turning to his side to face me.

Marilyn Grey

I tried to make eye contact, but the wall around my heart struggled to rebuild itself and I didn't know how to stop it.

He moved a strand of hair behind my ear and kept his arm against my neck. "Jane. It's okay."

"No." I shook my head. Was I really about to cry? "It's not okay. I can't do this."

"Do ... this?"

"This. Us. I knew this would happen."

"We'll make it work." He wiped the tear from my face. "We'll do this."

I closed my eyes. "I can't deal with missing you, Alistair. There's this pain in my chest just thinking about it. I don't know if—"

He kissed me, then pulled me into the crook of his arm. "I always finish what I start."

"That's just the thing ... I don't want it to finish."

"We're going to make it. Stop worrying." He kissed the top of my head again. "We're going to be okay."

THE DAY WASN'T NORMAL. AND IT WASN'T OKAY. NO MATTER how much both of us tried to pretend that it was. We met up with Donovan and Han at her apartment and I'm sure even Don knew something was up. At the same time, it felt nice to have somewhat of a boyfriend—was he my boyfriend?—while Don had a girlfriend. We spent most of the afternoon talking in the living room, then Donovan and Han decided to make us dinner.

I was thankful to have more alone time with Alistair.

He nodded toward her piano. An old, beaten piano taking up

most of her apartment. I shook my head. Didn't know how to play anything. At all.

You may listen to this scene by scanning the QR code below:

"You need to start somewhere," he said, nodding toward the intimidating thing. "Go on."

"I really can't play at all. I'm horrible."

"Try." He took my hand and led me to the piano bench. "Sit."

I sat down and placed my hands on the keys. "I really don't—"

He covered my eyes. "Keep them closed." He removed his hands. "Now find a note you like. Just one."

I pressed a few keys until I found one.

"Now. Relax." He shook my shoulders to loosen me up and kept his hands there. "Now play what you feel. Don't think. Don't open your eyes. Only play what you feel."

I pressed the single note again and zeroed in on the way his hands felt on my shoulders. I pressed again. The note was on the lower end of the piano and had a deep, sad resonance. Then I hit another key a few up from that. Alistair leaned over me. His chest warmed my back as he told me to keep my eyes closed and then placed his hands over mine. My right hand came into play. I replayed everything from the airport on my birthday to the surprise at the new shop. Our first kiss. The old woman. Batman marathons. Popcorn fights. Plenty of cuppas. And laughter. Lots of laughter.

He let go of my hands and held my shoulders again.

My hands moved left and right. The notes turned deeper again as I pictured saying goodbye. He said we'd make it work, but he lived off of hope and believed the glass was not only half full, but overflowing.

I stopped, breathed in and out, then continued playing until I felt Donovan and Han's presence near me. Embarrassed, I opened my eyes and stared at my hands. Alistair sat down beside me, placed his fingers on the keys, and started where I left off.

Only he took it further. Louder. Happier and sadder all at once. His eyes were closed and he played effortlessly. Drums, guitar, piano, singing, symphonies. What couldn't he do? I loved it. I felt it. Every high note and every low note. Every meaning behind it.

When he finished he looked at me, hands still on the keys. Our eyes searched each other's for a few seconds, then I kissed his cheek and whispered, "Why so serious?"

He nearly smiled, but didn't quite make it all the way.

I so wanted to know what he was thinking.

Donovan and Han must had disappeared into the kitchen again, leaving us alone to be so serious. We stared, barely blinking. I don't know about him, but I was holding on to the moment, capturing it and filing it in my mind. Memories always worried me too. I could take a thousand pictures with my mind, but what if I lost my mind and all of my memories with it? What if—one day—I couldn't remember him?

AFTER DINNER ALISTAIR EXCUSED HIMSELF TO GO TO THE bathroom and Don finally asked me how things were going with a goofy smile on his face.

Our friendship endured many ups and downs and I can honestly say that for the first time ever it felt like a friendship and nothing more. Except it felt right this time. Like it should've been that way all along.

I nodded and looked at my lap.

"Look at Han and me," he said, taking her hand. "A boat load of obstacles to overcome, but we're together and we'll face them together. That's all that matters."

She smiled that sweet smile of hers and leaned her head into his shoulder.

"But you two live in the same country," I said. "It's a lot different."

"Do you love him, Jazz?"

"Sometimes when you love someone the best thing you can do is let them go."

"Sometimes," he said. "But sometimes that's the worst thing too."

"Sometimes it's hard to tell the difference."

"And sometimes it's not."

Chapter 42

I TRIED, WITH EVERYTHING IN ME, TO ENJOY OUR LAST night together, but it was weird. Just no getting around it. All I could think about was ... what's next? A Skype relationship? I didn't want that. I also couldn't leave the shop after what everyone did for me. And ask him to move to America? I couldn't ask that of him either. Especially considering how complicated it seemed from my quick Internet search. Maybe if we got married it would be easier, but that wouldn't be happening anytime soon.

So, that left a Skype relationship and maybe a few visits when we could afford it.

Donovan said it was better than nothing. Not to me. Absence hurts like hell. I was already missing Autumn like crazy. I sent her so many texts and would hear back hours later. Something like, *I'm busy, but we'll talk soon. Promise.*

That promise hadn't decide to show up yet.

I didn't want to carry out a long-distance relationship over months and months only to be devastated when it ended. Everyone kept saying I was being immature. Even Mom and Dad told me to let it be and enjoy it for what it was, not that I fully trusted their opinions about romance with their heads being in the clouds and all, but still. Why didn't anyone realize how painful it is to let someone in only to watch them walk away without the promise of returning?

Actually he did promise. He said he'd come back and visit in a few months. He promised we'd make it work. But to me those promises felt empty, like Autumn's promise that we'd talk later. She had a new life. New friends. New boyfriend, knowing her. Her schedule was crazy and that promise wasn't something I held dear, because I knew better.

"Am I being immature?" I said to myself as Alistair took a shower before bed.

My other self couldn't respond, because no part of myself knew how to answer that question. Was I being immature? Was I being unreasonable? Difficult? Childish? Totally unromantic and boring?

"I?m just being me," I said.

I sent Autumn another text. *Hey. Hope you're doing well. Miss you lots.*

And of course I stared at the phone waiting for a response only to *not* receive one. So, I sent Donovan a message instead. *Why can't I just love him, Don? He's so amazing. He's so sweet to me. The way it feels when he's in the same room as me? It's all so good. Why can't I just be normal???*

He responded quickly and said, *Because you?re not.*

Me: *Thanks.*

Him: *I don't know, Jazz. I've heard you say "'no, no not that jane austen" so many times in your life. Maybe you've been so preoccupied with not being someone, that you haven't allowed yourself to just be you.*

Me: *What does that even mean???*

Him: *It means ... do what YOU want to do. If you want to overthink things and complicate it and make it like that, then do it with 100% of you and enjoy the little webs you get stuck in or ... if you want to live in the moment and fall in love with lover boy, then do it with 100% of you. Just figure out what you want and do it. 100%.*

    Me: *What if all I do is fail? Do that with 100% too?*

    Him: *Yup. Fail passionately if you're gonna fail!*

    Me: *I kinda like this advice.*

    Him: *Good. Now stop texting me and go find your lover boy.*

    Me: *He's in the shower.*

    Him: *Even more reason to find him. ;-)*

    Me: *Mmmhmmm ... thanks, D. Love you.*

    Him: *Love you too, DUCK! Hahaha!*

    Me: *Okay, done now.*

    Him: *Quack.*

    Me: *Byeeee Donovan.*

    Him: *:-D*

ALISTAIR CAME BACK INTO MY ROOM FULLY CLOTHED AND no, I did not take a shower with him. Tempting, but it was still afternoon and I was a little too self-conscious about my body to let him see it for the first time in the broad daylight. That would be during a nice candlelit moment when it just happened and was just right and the soft glow would make me look better than I actually was.

    Half-kidding.

    "I thought of a going away gift for you," he said as he ran his hand through his wet hair.

    "You've already bought me so much."

    "Just something little." He dropped his bag by my bed. "Also, I'm going to come back in October. It's only a month and a half away."

    "Only...."

He stood right in front of me and held my wrists. "We'll talk every day."

I grabbed his hands and pressed my forehead against his chest. "How does it happen so fast?"

"Time flies when you're having fun."

"No, I mean how did this ... happen so fast?" I looked at his bare feet next to mine. "One day I saw you in the airport, and the next I can't be without you."

He pulled my chin up and searched my eyes. "Well, actually it's been a few months."

"You know what I mean."

"Yes, I know what you mean, but I don't know the answer. "

He moved his hands down to my neck and held one there, while slipping the other one behind my back. I wrapped my arms around him and fell into his embrace. Maybe it had only been a few months, but at the same time it felt like we had known each other for a lifetime.

"It's definitely the kiss," he said into my hair.

"What?"

"I knew I'd win you over with that kiss."

"Probably practiced with your pillow, huh?"

"No. I'm too posh for that." He started kissing my neck, then stopped to say, "Taped your picture to my mirror and went to town."

I laughed, but quickly stopped as the warmth of his lips continued to take over my neck and shoulders. He pulled my shirt down a little and kissed me where I got my first tattoo. With him. Then he made a trail of kisses back to my lips. I'm not sure at what point we ended up on the floor against my bed, but we did.

The passion between us elevated so fast and yet it never felt rushed. He took his time and every kiss from him seemed to have meaning and emotion behind it. Not once did I feel used or groped or like just another body. I felt loved and enjoyed and desired. Every time.

And I didn't want it to end. I really, really, really didn't want it to end.

Chapter 43

THE DRIVE TO THE AIRPORT WAS AS FAST AS THE MORNING at my apartment. We didn't say much until it was too late. He needed to go and my heart was exploding with so many different emotions. My hands trembled and my voice cracked as he tried to pull away to say goodbye. But I pulled him back and everything I'd felt and thought the entire week needed to come out.

"You're killing me." He held my face. "Be strong for me. We can do this."

I sucked in my bottom lip and nodded. *Strong, yes. That's me. Jane. Strong. Totally strong. I can do this. Can. Do. This.*

"Alistair, I can't do this."

"You can." He looked over his shoulder. "I've really got to get on now. We can do this, Jane."

I didn't cry. I wanted to. I even felt a puddle of tears somewhere behind my eyes, but it didn't happen. It was too fast. We were late for his flight. Literally ran into the airport. It wasn't the goodbye I expected.

It was all a blur. Then he walked away, looking over his shoulder and crushing my heart with those eyes. I hated it. Whoever the hell said absence makes the heart grow fonder doesn't know a thing about the heart. Fonder is not the word. Crushed, broken, confused. Those would fit better. I didn't need time apart to grow closer to him. I needed time with him. I wanted time with him.

I could no longer see him, so I turned in a circle as dozens of people walked by me. I watched others say goodbye and some say hello, then I sent him a text, hoping he still had his phone turned on.

Take care of my heart while I'm gone.

Your heart is safe with me, he typed back.

Me:*I miss you.*

Him:*I miss you too, little duck.*

BACK TO WORK I WENT. IMMEDIATELY. IT'S WHAT I LIKE TO call "avoiding reality." Very healthy.

I left the airport and went straight to the shop, blared some Chopin, got familiar with everything, and ordered the sign for the front. 1812. Then I did a bunch of paperwork. I figured I'd work the shop myself until sales started to happen, then maybe hire Brooke and Han to help and come sew with me. *If* sales started to happen. Big*if* there.

I hadn't slept in my bed alone since I got the new apartment. Didn't want to go home for that very reason. Autumn still hadn't responded to me and I was getting a little frustrated. Donovan and Han were preparing for a trip to Korea so he could meet her family. Gulp. So I couldn't vent and whine to him. That left my parents and Eddie who I hadn't talked to since Alistair came and I was kinda avoiding that too. Their advice would be too idealistic for me to follow and I didn't want to feel like a romantic let down. But Eddie's advice ... I didn't even think of that one. He'd probably be ho-hum. And for whatever reason I felt like I could use a generous dose of ho-hum.

So I finished everything I needed to do and set next Monday as the grand opening for 1812. I was scared out of my ever-loving mind, but I figured if I failed again I could run away to an English countryside.

In the car I put on Carl Davis and the Royal Liverpool Philharmonic Orchestra's movie theme album, beginning with the *Forrest Gump* theme. My favorite theme song outside of Batman. Oh man. That climactic part of the song made me want to grab my cape and soar. So beautiful and triumphant. After that I moved back to Danny Elfman's *Spider-Man* and by the time it ended I was parked at my parent's house.

I glanced at my phone before I went inside. 5:12p.m. His flight was set to land at 6:30pm my time, 11:30pm his time.

Literally counting down the minutes to talk to him again, while also pretending that I wasn't.

Mom greeted me at the door. Dad and Eddie looked up from a game of Risk.

"Oh, no," I said. "Not Risk."

"Fourth day," Eddie said. "And I'm not backing down."

Dad laughed. "He's losing."

"No I'm not. I'm letting you think that so that when I win you'll be even more shocked."

"Okay," Mom said. "It's just a game."

They both stared at her like she had left her brain in the cake I could smell baking in the oven.

"Smells like..." I inhaled again. "Is it strawberry cake?"

"Wow," Eddie said. "Is that what meatloaf smells like to you?"

Mom shook her head. "It's strawberry cake, yes."

Somehow I needed to get Eddie alone to talk. I couldn't even believe my own brain for thinking such a thing, but I was curious to find out what he'd tell me. I sat beside Dad as they continued their game. After a few minutes in the kitchen Mom reappeared and sat on the other side of me.

"Did you pick a name for the store?" she said.

I told her and we talked about my plans for a little bit, but I could tell by the sparkle in her eyes that she desperately wanted to ask about my love life, because, well, for the first time ... I actually had one.

I tried to avoid the topic until she asked about Donovan and Han, which bled into her finally saying, "So...." with that smirk growing and growing.

"Yes?" I said.

"The handsome British boy." She lit up. "How did things go with him?"

"Why did I know you'd have to refer to him as the British boy?"

"Sorry." She straightened her back. "British *man*."

"No." I laughed. "I mean calling out the British thing."

"Well." She laughed. "How could I not?"

"He's fine. Our time together was nice."

She leaned forward and motioned for me to continue.

"What?"

"And...."

"And I had fun?"

"Will you be seeing this young man again?"

I nodded and inhaled through my teeth. "Yes, Mom."

Dad laughed. "Let her be, honey."

She made her way back to the kitchen and I waited a few minutes before asking Eddie to show me his latest wood project. I even double-winked, but he didn't look up from his game. At all.

"In a minute," he said.

Not wanting to seem strange, I let it go and told myself his advice would've been weird anyway. My younger brother? What was I thinking?

I pulled out my phone and sent Autumn another text. *Hey... Can we talk soon? I feel like you're drifting away.*

No response and she still hadn't acknowledged my other three messages. So I typed out how I really felt.

Soooo ... I know you're busy and all with your new school and friends, but there are people here ... eh em ME ... who still care about you and need you. Can you just call me tonight? I'm trying not to get annoyed, but Autumn ... this friendship is more to me than a high school thing. You're my sister and sisters don't leave each other for other people. Please call tonight. I'll be up.

Mom called us in for dinner and we ate, talked about normal stuff thankfully, and topped it off with cake. We laughed and for a few minutes here and there I even stopped looking at the time. But when 7:30pm hit and he hadn't messaged me I started to worry, but did a quick flight check and saw that it hadn't landed yet. They estimated twenty more minutes. So I helped Mom clean up real quick and parted ways, went home, drew a bath, which reminded me of Alistair just like every. thing. else.

I put the phone on a little table by the tub and put a towel there too just in case I needed to dry my hands to answer a call. Autumn or Alistair would call. One of them. Autumn I wasn't so sure about, but Alistair....

He'd call.

I almost fell asleep to the sound of crickets, but my phone rang.

"You're alive!" I said.

"Jane, I'm so sorry," Autumn said. "It's been so hectic and I do still care. I swear."

"I know. Maybe I overreacted because everyone is gone."

"Alistair finally left?"

"Yeah. He stayed a week and he's coming back in October. I think I might surprise him by coming at the end of this month if I can afford it."

"Those flights are like two thousand dollars."

"I know."

"How was it? You sound as depressed as you were when you told Don you loved him."

"I'm not depressed. Lonely. Confused."

"So emo. So unlike you."

"I know." I stared at the other side of the tub where Alistair sat, luring me over to him with his eyes. "Oh man. I'm so dumb."

"What are you guys gonna do?"

"He insists that we'll make it work, but I can already feel myself falling apart." I closed my eyes. "This *is* unlike me. But it is me at the same time. What the hell, right?"

She laughed. "One day at a time."

"Anyway, tell me about school."

"My dorm is small. Like a horse stable or something. My roommate is pretty much like Zoe, except without the random acts of being nice." She sighed. "I hate my classes. Seriously. The one class I thought I'd like could win an award for worst teacher ever."

"One day a time," I said.

She laughed. "I know, right? That's all we can do."

We kept talking until 10:24pm. Alistair hadn't called. His flight landed a while back and I figured he'd call as soon as he got home. Maybe before then.

I got into bed at 11:02 and watched my phone, opened the app, and repeated until, just after midnight, my eyes begged me to let them close.

"Only for a few minutes," I whispered, but I think I was asleep before finishing the sentence.

Chapter 44

I WOKE UP AT FOUR SOMETHING IN THE MORNING AND didn't see a single message from him, so I finally opened the app and messaged him first. Just sent, *Alistair.* And waited for my phone to alert me. Minutes. Eternity-like minutes. One. After. Another. After—

"Why isn't he messaging me?" I said to myself.

"Maybe he ran into an ex-girlfriend in the airport and went to a hotel," less enjoyable me said.

"Or maybe he died on the plane," less reasonable me said.

"Or maybe he doesn't like you anymore," less confident me said.

"Or maybe he fell asleep," more reasonable me said.

"Or maybe his phone died and then he fell asleep," most reasonable me said.

"Thank you," I said. "That's probably it."

My phone beeped and my pulse quickened as I opened his message.

Jane. I'm so sorry. My phone died and when I plugged it in I fell asleep. It's 9 here. Your text woke me up. I miss you.

I read the words several times, smiling.

You there? he said.

I typed, *Hey ... I miss you too. How was the flight?*

Him: *Long. Boring. Too much turbulence. Hate flying. Did I tell you I miss you?*

Me: *You may have mentioned it. :-)*

Him: *I can't wait to hear your voice. Can I call now?*

Me: *Yes.*

Buh-ter-flies. We talked on the phone dozens of times before. But it was different now and I was so nervous.

The phone rang.

"Jane," he whispered.

I closed my eyes and could almost imagine him beside me with his messy hair on my pillow.

"Can I come visit this weekend?" I said.

"Jane. Are you serious? How can you afford that?"

"I have an emergency credit card. I've never used it."

"Jane." He laughed. "I'm flattered, really." He laughed again. "It's not realistic. I can come in October."

"I want to come. You told me to be unrealistic, remember? I open the shop on Monday, so maybe I could come from Friday to Sunday?"

"You're something else."

"Am I being irrational? I don't even know what's come over me."

"I told you what it is. It's the—"

"I know, I know. So how about Friday? Maybe we can see a few more of the Batman places I wanted to see last time."

He breathed into the phone for a few seconds as I waited for him to answer.

"You said it yourself," I said. "Just jump in."

"First of all, you already know I can't possibly resist your immense longing for me?"

"Oh, stop." I laughed. "You wish you were so full of yourself."

"Secondly"—I could tell that he was talking through a smile—
"I would like to see you as much as possible, but I also don't want to
waste money when you need it. I want your dreams for the fashion
line to work out."

"Just for the weekend?" I couldn't believe I was begging to see
him. I was actually begging! "Okay, if you don't want me to...."

"That's not it at all." He quieted, then said, "I'm looking forward
to it."

"Will I get to meet your mom and dad?"

"We could do that if you would like, but Dad lives about an hour
south and Mum is two hours away."

"We'll see," I said. "So, Friday it is."

LATER THAT NIGHT, AFTER TALKING TO ALISTAIR BEFORE
he went to sleep, I tried to buy a plane ticket, but it kept saying invalid
card number. That's when I realized the expiration date expired two
months ago and as far as I knew I never received a replacement. I
called the company first thing the next morning, but they said there
was no way for me to use the credit line until I received the replacement card they were sending out. Seven to ten business days was too
long.

Alistair offered to pay for the plane ticket, but I couldn't let him
do that this time. So we decided to wait until October and instead of
him visiting me, I'd get to see his place.

So I stayed home and we talked every day and night instead.
When Sunday rolled around I realized I hadn't even thought to call

anyone else about the grand opening the next day. My mind was on Alistair so much that the shop didn't seem as important. Of course, Donovan and Han had already left for Gongju and Autumn was gone too, so they wouldn't be able to come anyway. And quite honestly, after that last experience I wasn't sure if I wanted to invite anyone. Maybe I could be embarrassed alone this time. So ... I called Mom and told her I was opening, but not making a big deal out of it and asked her to come by later in the week if she wanted.

Then Monday morning came and anxiety dawned right along with it. I went to the shop early, checked over everything, and messaged Alistair as I got ready. He tried to lighten my mood by joking around, and I'd laugh along well enough, but the closer it got to opening the more freaked out I got.

At nine on the dot, I flipped the sign to *open* and waited. No one came inside, but it was a busy shopping area and soon enough someone would come. I put a little chalkboard sign out front that said, "Grand Opening" and right below, "Gotham City Inspired Fashion."

I didn't expect a lot of interest right away given the fact that obsessive Batman fans didn't seem rampant or anything, but I wanted a few customers just so I could get some sort of idea.

Alistair sent another message. *Remember you're doing this for you... not the customers. If they love it, then great. If not, don't stress.*

Oh, oh, here comes someone, I typed.

A guy walked in, probably in his early twenties, and smiled while looking around. "Gotham City inspired?"

I smiled and clasped my hands in front of me, then put them in my pockets, then clasped them again.

"What are you wearing?" he said. "Is that Two Face?"

"Oh, um, yes." I looked at my outfit and smoothed the pants. "It's the female version. I have a male version too."

"You? Is this your store or you just work here?" He stopped in front of my favorite. It was The Joker outfit for women. Purple dress and jacket with a small green vest and green scarf.

"It's mine." I stepped out from the counter. "I had two other girls help me with the sewing and they'll probably be working here soon if it works out."

"If it works out?" He meandered over to the men's side. "There's no *if* here. This is cool as shit."

I laughed. "Thanks."

"I'm telling my friends about this. You know how many guys would love this shit for their women?"

"Well, I don't consider it shit. Personally." I smiled.

"I like that," he said, picking up a Nightwing outfit. "This is sweet. I wish I had enough to buy it all."

"Batman fan?"

"I like the movies, but not obsessed or anything. This is awesome though. And what are you only like twenty-one or something?"

"Eighteen." I smiled. "I failed once though and I've had a lot of help. It's a huge dream of mine."

He held eye contact a little too long before continuing, "Yeah, I think it'll work out." He pointed to the ceiling. "What's playing on the radio?"

"Oh, it's my iPod. It's Batman soundtracks."

"Are you a huge fan?" He held up his hand. "Stupid question. Hey, if you need any extra help around here I can help. No charge."

"Oh, I—"

"Or I could just ask you out. Dinner? Maybe, uh...."

"Thank you." I tried not to laugh. "That would be nice, but I have an amazing boyfriend who...."

"Who...?"

"I was gonna say he stole my heart, but he didn't steal it. Somewhere along the way ... I gave it to him."

"Lucky dude." He gestured toward the counter. "Okay. I'll buy this one for now, but I gotta bring my friend Dietz in here. He's gonna flip."

I helped him check out and texted Alistair as soon as the guy left.

He responded, *It was a bloke?*

Me: *Yeah, he seemed to really like it.*

Him: *A bloke? He was probably trying to win a date.*

Me: *Maybe. He did ask.*

Him: *What did you say?*

I smiled as I typed, *I told him I had a boyfriend who stole my heart, except he didn't actually steal it. I gave it to him.*

Him: *You have a boyfriend?*

Me: *Yeah. He's a terrible kisser, but it works for now.*

Him: *Jane....*

Me: *Alistair?*

Him: *Thank you.*

Someone else walked in, so I told him I'd text him soon. This time it was an older woman who did not look anything like someone who would like Batman stuff, but she seemed genuinely pleased as she thumbed through the clothes.

Finally, she looked over a rack of clothes and waved me over.

"Your sign out front caught my eye. See, my son is a very devoted comic book fan and this would make his day, but I'm looking for his favorite character, Jimmy Olsen."

"Oh. Actually that's from Superman. This line is only Batman-inspired."

"I apologize." She laughed quietly, embarrassed. "He likes Batman too. Some Harvey Bump character."

"Harvey Dent?" I chuckled. "He's one of my favorites too. Right over here." I showed her the Dent outfits for men. "And if he likes that he would probably like the Two Face one as well." I waved my hand over it. "My personal favorite design that we have."

"This is great. Thank you." She checked the price tags and didn't flinch. "Wonderful. I'll take both. He will be so pleased."

By the time I helped her to the door, another person showed up. This time an older man, maybe fifties or sixties. He looked around, then walked out without saying anything. Two outta three worked for me though. A few minutes later three girls walked in, maybe a little older than me. They loved everything, but somehow remained oblivious of the Batman-theme until one girl asked why the decorations around the store had bats. That's when I chimed in, explained things, and although they seemed to care less about Batman, they loved the clothes. Raved about The Joker dress and one of my Batman outfits for women. I had four variations of Batman ones in the front of the store, near the window. They said they'd be back for one as soon as payday came. I thanked them and texted Alistair. He could "hear" the excitement in my words. Could've been the four million exclamation marks at the end of everything I said. He was happy for me. And I was even happier knowing he was happy for me. But amidst all the happiness swelling inside me ... the biggest thing I wanted was to get back into his arms and fall asleep with his chest as my pillow. That's what I really, really wanted. Like, yesterday.

Chapter 45

SEPTEMBER WENT BY EXTREMELY FAST. I CLOSED UP THE register and handled a few things in the back while Han put some of our latest creations on the racks.

The shop wasn't overwhelmed with customers like I hoped it would be, but stuff was leaving the racks fast enough that I had to get Han and Brooke back in by the end of the month. We sewed and sewed and sewed. It was fun. And I got to see Don more again, since he came to visit her whenever he had a plumbing job in the area.

Autumn and I had random talks whenever we could, but with my busy schedule and her *very* busy schedule, it was rare. I definitely missed her, but my life got so busy that I didn't think about it as often as I thought I would. I'm sure she felt the same. And I hated that. I kept telling myself it would be just like old times when she came back for the summer, but my skepticism liked to have a say and it was never the most encouraging.

Don appeared from the back and wrapped Han in his arms. I can honestly say I no longer had *those* kind of feelings for Don, but seeing them together made me jealous in a completely different way now. It had been weeks since I felt Alistair's skin against mine and days since I heard his voice. We kept missing each other and I think he sensed my doubts about long distance relationships, because he wanted me to fly in the first weekend of October, which was two days from now, instead of waiting until late October like we originally planned.

"Wanna come to dinner with us?" Donovan said with his hand permanently glued to Han's.

I shook my head and smiled. It's not that I didn't want to spend time with them. They were super good about making me feel like I wasn't a third wheel, but I needed to get home to *hopefully* catch Alistair before he fell asleep. I looked at the clock. 7:15pm. I sent him a text, *You still awake?*

Waiting for you. Got my phone on as loud as possible so it wakes me up if I fall asleep, he responded.

Be home soon.

Donovan's keys jingled as he pulled them out of his pocket. "Still need a ride to the airport on Friday?"

"Yeah, if you can." I did one last look around the place before walking to the back door with them.

They went out first and I locked the door behind me.

"Are you guys going back to Korea soon?" I said as I pulled my keys out of my bag.

"We may do that soon," Han said. "My family wants to see Donovan again. They like him very much."

"I knew they would. So are they getting better about you marrying an American?"

Don pulled her into him.

"Yes," she said, elbowing him. "So long as he keep a good job, right?"

I loved the way she smiled at him. So sweet and real. Her family accepted him well enough according to my last conversation with

Don, but they also expected them to move to South Korea if they ever got married. I didn't want to think about that. Of course he said I'd be in the UK and it would be a little closer. It was a nice try.

Also couldn't imagine Don living in Korea and learning the language, but I knew he'd do it for Han. He'd do anything for anyone, but especially her.

He hadn't said one word to me about proposing, which told me he'd eventually ask her, unlike all of the other girls he fanatically obsessed over within a week. I wondered if he'd use the ring he got for me years ago, and if not, what would he do with it?

"How about we drive to your place first?" he said to Han. "Then I'll drive to dinner and we can stay at your place tonight?"

"Risqu !" I teased.

Han blushed, gave him a kiss on the cheek, and drove off. Don sat in his car and put the window down.

"Doing okay, Jazz?" he said while turning down the radio.

"Fine. Why?"

"Just making sure. Everything going okay with lover boy?"

"It's hard, but it's good. When are you gonna propose to Han? Are you just waiting for her family's approval?"

He put his arm on the window and looked ahead at the brick wall. "Nah. I don't know. I'm not in a hurry. It will happen if it's meant to."

"Wow." I flicked his temple. "Where's Donovan and *what* did you do with him?"

"I know. Weird." He made a funny face. "It's just not the right time. I want her to be comfortable if I do it."

"Will you tell her you almost proposed to eight million thousand other women?"

"Eight million thousand. Hm." He raised his eyebrows. "I learn new numbers every day." He laughed. "She knows everything about me. Well, everything that I know about me, she knows. Maybe more."

"Did that bother her?"

"No. I told her why I was like that."

"Which was ... why?"

He just looked at me.

"Oh. Right. Even with Zoe?"

"Not really. Not sure what the hell I was thinking there. Maybe just the fact that she needed so much help. I felt like I could protect her if I married her and got her out of that house. Then you moved out and it worked out." He pretended to wipe his brow. "Not that she's not a nice girl and all, but..." He laughed. "Well, you know."

I looked at the time. "I better go. I need to call Alistair. I hate this time difference stuff."

"He's doing okay? I like him, Jazz. You know I wouldn't say that about everyone."

"I know."

He smiled and put his car into reverse. "Go call lover boy," he said in his horrible British accent.

I ignored him and got into my car. I was going to wait until I was comfortable in bed, but I couldn't.

I called. And it rang. And rang. And ... look at that ... rang.

I hung up and tried again. And a third time before I got home. Nothing.

8:41pm my time. 1:41pm his time. I made myself leftovers and responded to a text from Zoe, who lived with Brooke, helping her clean and take care of her little one in exchange for free rent. Worked out great for both of them, but I missed having a roommate. Lonely as hell now that Alistair was falling asleep before I could call. He worked early mornings into the evening with a landscaping company. It was hard work and he was exhausted by the end of the day. But he wanted to save money so we could visit often. So I tried to let it go.

I tried to call again before I went to bed, but he didn't pick up. So I got comfortable, turned the light off, and gave it one more shot.

The screen turned black, then glowed.

"Alistair?" I whispered.

The screen showed a candle by his bedside, a tea cup, and a picture of me under his hand on top of his Carpe Diem tattoo.

"Alistair?" I whispered again, wishing I could reach through the screen and touch him.

He didn't stir.

I propped my phone on the pillow next to me and watched his chest rise and fall until I fell asleep.

When I woke up to my alarm going off, I read through the notifications on my phone. A bunch of nothing except he sent an email.

Dearest girl of mine,

I woke up for work to a beautiful, sleeping face on my phone. I don't remember talking last night. I can only imagine what sort of rubbish I said in my stupor. I'm so sorry, Jane. I hope you haven't forgotten the way it feels when we're together. It fades with each day, that intensity of being able to close our eyes and feel each other there, but I'll never forget. Don't forget. We need to hold on and we WILL have it again soon. Stay with me, girl. We will get through this. It's only an ocean between us, not like it's a universe, right? I loved waking up to your cute little face. I can tell you one thing, it was bloody hard to hang up the phone. I'm off to work now. Check

the attachment. I sent audio.
   Yours,
   Alistair

I opened up the attachment and hit *play.*

You may listen to this voicemail by scanning the QR code:

"Jane," he said. "I know we don't say this because it makes you uncomfortable, but I'm saying it now because if I don't I think I might regret going another day without being honest with myself and you. I love you, Jane Maryanne. I love you more than my own life. Stay with me."

Then he sang a song and ended it by saying, "I know you don't know many modern pop songs, but that was a song called *Stay with Me* by Sam Smith. I changed the words though, because I do know that I love you. And I'll always know, Jane." He paused, the audio crackled a bit, then he said, "Okay, I don't know what else to say now. This is a bit queer talking to my phone like it's you, but I had to say it and didn't want to write it out. All right, talk soon."

I replayed it at least seven times, then brought up my voice recorder, stared at the picture of him on my nightstand, and said, "Alistair. The Oxford English Dictionary has about 171,476 words, but there isn't a single word in there that can explain how I feel. So I'll keep it simple, although it's nowhere near what I really want to say." I waited, looked at his picture, then said, "I love you." I pressed my lips together and told myself *not* to cry. "I love you, Alistair. And I miss you so much it hurts."

You may listen to this voicemail
by scanning the QR code:

I sent it through as a text, set it beside my picture of him, and took a really long shower with a huge smile on my face. When I got out I checked my phone and he responded, "I can't tell you what that does to me."

It wasn't much.

But it was more than enough.

Chapter 46

IF I SAID I LOVE YOU, THEN TECHNICALLY I SHOULD'VE BEEN able to clearly define love, but throughout the rest of the day I found myself thinking and thinking of a definition without coming up with anything worthwhile. The dictionary says things like "deep affection for someone" and "sexual or intimate attraction," which I find kinda funny, because when you look up affection it says "a gentle feeling of fondness or liking." So that would mean, really, that love according to the dictionary is a deep, gentle feeling of "liking," which really doesn't do it justice. Then there's the definition of falling in love. Moving from neutrality to love for someone. I didn't get that either, because I never had feelings of neutrality toward Alistair. I went from a gentle fondness or liking of him to an aching love for him. Aching. Love.

I tried, but came up with nothing. I don't even know if words are capable of defining something you can't *know*. It's so much more than knowing and even feeling. It's almost like a state of being. Love changes you. I know that for a fact, mind you, because it changed me.

All of a sudden my days were filled with thoughts of him or oh-let-me-grab-my-phone-and-tell-him kind of moments. At the sewing machine I'd watch my hands run the fabric through and imagine his hand on top of mine. When I walked down the street I'd pull up the picture in my mind of him there on the sidewalk, and I'd stop, smile, and send him a text to tell him I missed him. Taking baths reminded me of passionate kisses and bed time reminded me of his arms. Pizza made me think of his quirky sense of humor and writing words like humor and color made me think of humour and colour and silly British things he said like "sod off" and "barmy" and "bollocks." Don't get me started on planes and tooth brushes and Tchaikovsky and Batman. Everything reminded me of him and everything I experienced—like the Monopoly game I finally won—I wanted to share it with him right away.

So I guess what I'm trying to say is that I can't fathom love being a "deep liking" for someone, because fondness doesn't change lives. Fondness doesn't take a girl scared of getting her heart broken, surrounded by extremely high walls, and turn her into a girl with her heart in someone else's hands, completely mesmerized by the way it feels to be mesmerized. Walls destroyed. Trusting. Devoted. Passionately excited to feel his fingers locked with hers. Fondness doesn't do that. But love ... this thing called love ... whatever it is ... it does. It changes you. It gives you life and makes you bleed all at once. How can a "deep liking" compete with that? It can't. Nothing can. Not even 171,476 words. Not even sex. Or passion. Or dreams. Just love. That's it. This undefinable, crazy, stubborn thing called love.

It's beautiful.

TIME AND ME. NOT FRIENDS. WHEN YOU ASK TIME TO HURRY, what happens? Time takes a freaking eternity and a half. Ask time to slow down so you can please, please, please savor a moment ... what happens? Time breaks the clock, fast forwards its hands, and turns it back on when it's satisfied with stealing your life. Now, I'm not normally so dramatic, but these are special circumstances. And special circumstances call for dramatic soap boxes.

Told you relationships bring drama, but I guess Donovan was right. It was worth it.

So ... I finally—after way too long—boarded a plane to the UK. Mom would be proud. The flight also decided to take forever and cause my life to flash before my eyes a zillion times. But that's okay. It was all worth it when I landed earlier than expected—I know, ironic, right?—and found him walking into the airport just as I was walking out. I dropped my bags on my toes, flung my arms around his neck, and possibly broke a few of his ribs.

"Don't joke about your amazing kiss being the reason I'm so happy," I said into his neck. "That joke is way old now."

"How did you know?" He laughed and tightened his arm around my back while holding the back of my head with his other hand. It felt incredibly good. So good I couldn't let go.

"Time is cooperating for once," I whispered.

"Time?"

"It's slow when I want it to be." I kissed his neck and finally stood back, taking in every last detail of the face I missed so much. "But I have a feeling as soon as we start walking it's going to stop cooperating."

"I missed you, little duck."

He smiled and put his hand on my hip, then pulled me back into him so that our lips naturally fell into place. When we stopped kissing, we started again. Someone yelled at us to get a room, but that didn't stop us. We just laughed into each other and after another minute or so we finally stopped again.

"Let's continue this at home," he said while picking up one of my bags and grinning almost as much as me. "So blooming glad to have you here, Ms. Austen."

I slung my bag over my shoulder. "Glad to be here, Mr. Gladwyn. So blooming glad."

Chapter 47

WE HELD HANDS ON THE DRIVE TO BRISTOL AND BARELY let go. About halfway he asked if I was tired. I was, but didn't want to ruin any plans he made. So he took a detour to show me the Clifton Suspension Bridge. Once again, no word in the dictionary could suffice. The bridge was a wee tad scary with the narrow road and what not. Plus, as much as I tried to get used to the driver being on the right side, it was strange.

Everything about the bridge was captivating though. From the water underneath to the rocks and trees surrounding it. The entire bridge was lit up and I can't say I'd ever seen something so magical in America. Not that I got around much, but in my little Philly world things like that didn't exist. I tried to sit higher to get a good look around and when I turned back to Alistair he gave me this smile that said everything I felt. Once we finally made it to the other side of the bridge, I looked behind us to see the beautiful lights stretch from one side to the other. I loved it. And I loved the boy next to me even more. He looked so cute, like he was proud to show me a piece of his home. A piece he knew I'd enjoy.

"There's more," he said. "Since it's late I thought we could stay at my flat tonight, but tomorrow I booked a stay in a thatched cottage."

"What's a thatched cottage?"

"You've never been to a thatched cottage?"

"Not sure I've ever heard of one."

"They're little houses with straw rooftops. You're going to love it."

"Interesting. I'm sure I will."

I enjoyed watching him get excited. He seemed like a little kid who loved to show and tell. As we drove he pointed to things, gave me little snippets of history or in some cases he'd say, "No idea what that is, but isn't it lovely?" Honestly, I didn't care what he said. I was just happy to have his hand in mine and his face smiling next to me.

We finally made it to his apartment—oops, I mean his flat, of course—and oh my flying flipping heaven! He opened the door with a sneaky little grin on his face, so I should've known. No, it wasn't a trillion rose petals and candles. It was a thousand times more romantic and so much better than that.

The flat had big, huge windows down to the clean wood floor. High ceilings. And the best part. Yellow rug. Grey couches. Black fireplace. Can you guess where I'm going here? Batman. A Batman living room done in a tasteful, modern way. Mainly using the colors and abstract art on the walls.

My jaw felt like Eddie's when he saw Autumn in her prom dress. Alistair walked to the mantle and pointed to the art on top, then I realized it wasn't art.

"Wow. Is that what—"

"Original editions. Bill Finger and Bob Kane." He handed me the framed comic book, one of my favorites ever. "I want you to have this."

"No." I held the frame and gawked at the sight before me. "I can't take this."

"I really want you to have it."

"Alistair." I ran my fingers over the glass. "I'd kill to open this and smell the pages."

He took it back. "Easy there."

We laughed.

"You know," I said, "this may sound ridiculous, but I think I love you even more now."

His fingers curled around my belt loops and he slowly stepped toward me until his chest was against mine. My heart raced as warmth rushed from my head to my toes. He looked down at me and moved his lips toward mine.

"Two dorks destined for dorkdom," he whispered along my neck, then kissed his way to my collar bone.

My hands somehow made their way to his shoulders while his held my hips. Then his lips met mine again so we could finish what we started at the airport. He kissed me right into the wall as my fingers dug into his shoulders.

A loud shrieking sound interrupted and we both jumped. He looked around with wide eyes, then ran toward the kitchen cursing himself.

"What happened?" I followed.

"Oven. I left the bloody oven on when I left." He stood on a chair to turn the smoke alarm off and his shirt lifted, revealing the tattoo just above his pants—or as he would say, trousers. I imagined kissing him there, but he hopped off the chair and brought me back to *right now*. Kitchen. Smoke alarm. Fire.

He pulled a pan out of the oven and I'm not sure what he intended it to be, but right now it was a dish filled with black stuff.

He set it on the counter and shrugged. "That didn't work out." He poked at it with a fork. "I tried to make you a dessert and apparently I forgot about it."

"I'm glad your flat is still here." I inched toward him and took his hands. "You can be my dessert."

"Mmm ... I like the sound of that."

PRETTY SURE WE SPENT HALF THE NIGHT SLEEPING AND the other half making out all over his flat. At some point after 2am we stopped kissing and cuddled in the low light of the nearly melted candle. I looked around the room I had only seen on Skype and wished I could stay longer than a weekend. His room was so different from mine. So masculine feeling. Darker colors, more wood. A picture of me beside his bed, now with two tea cups next to the candle. I loved being in his home, becoming part of his life.

He ran his fingers up and down my back as I twirled my fingers through his hair.

"Do you think one day this will get old?" I whispered.

"Staying up all night?"

"Being so passionate and excited to be together. Kissing. Cuddling. This feeling inside when we're like this."

He laughed quietly.

I turned to my back. "What?"

"I don't think it gets old. I'm sure we'll change and things will change, but it won't get old. If anything it will be new all over again."

He turned to his side, buried his face in my hair, and inhaled. "I love the way you smell."

"You mean you like my shampoo?"

"It's more than that." He kissed my neck and wrapped his arm around my stomach. "It's you."

A few seconds later he was out. I turned to my side and held his arm tight around me, then with his chest against my back I drifted off to sleep myself.

THE SUN WOKE US UP. TOLD YOU IT DOESN'T ALWAYS RAIN in England. We made breakfast together and lounged around all day. First we watched *The Dark Knight* because it was our favorite. Heath Ledger's performance is just ... wow. Then we discussed the comic, *The Killing Joke*, and the sad timing of Heath's death, which led us into a conversation about death and back to our bucket lists. We made a pact to write a complete album together within twelve months. Of course I told him it was wishful thinking with the long distance and my complete inability to play or write music. Then he pulled out his phone and said, "I don't think this is a complete inability."

Back at Han's apartment he recorded me when I played the piano. We listened and when it ended he said, "Not perfect, but pretty good for someone who literally played their first time."

"Yeah, I don't know."

"Don't doubt yourself," he said. "That's where failure begins."

"Well, I'll try my best."

He looked at his phone. "Ready?"

I nodded and we gathered a few things for our overnight stay in the cottage, then got in his car. By the time he parked at our first destination, which was a surprise for me, it was already dark outside.

"Is this a neighborhood?" I said as we got out of the car.

"Yes." He took my hand. "Want to show you something."

We walked down to the corner of the street.

"This," he said, "is a park I used to play in when I was boy." He pointed across the street. "And down that way is the house I grew up in. Care to see it?"

"Oh, I care all right."

I followed his lead as our hands swung in the cold October air. I tightened my scarf as he pulled me closer and put his arm around me. We stopped in front of a little stone house with ivy climbing the sides.

"This is it," he said. "And back there is a tree house with spiral stairs. When I was a kid and my parents would argue about this or that, I'd climb up there and fall asleep watching the stars. It was much more peaceful than the war inside the house."

"I thought they parted on peaceful terms?"

"They did, but they definitely had their moments." A light turned off in the house. "I've never shown a girl this house."

"How many girls have there been exactly?"

"One that matters."

I smiled. "Good one."

"We best be getting on. I have the key to the cottage, so we can check in whenever we'd like, but I have something there I want to show you."

"So many surprises." I nodded toward the house. "Can I see the tree house?"

"Oh, someone lives here. I don't know."

"Come on." I pulled his hand as I walked into the grass.

He pulled me back. "What if they see us? Last thing I want is for either of us to get in trouble for trespassing."

"It's an adventure," I whispered. "Come on."

He hesitated with each step, but eventually I got him to the back-yard. Thankfully no motion detector lights went off and it stayed dark enough to hide us. He wanted to show me and leave, but I insisted that we go up and see the inside. With major caution, constantly looking to the house and back to me, he climbed the steps behind me. The tree house was old, but I could tell it was beautiful in its prime. Spiral stairs leading up to the top. Tree branches spilling out of the enclosed house section. Miniature windows. It looked like a real wooden house that got stuck in a tree, but the inside was just a plain box tiny enough that he had to duck his head, but large enough that I still had an extra inch between the ceiling and mine.

He sat down in the corner and spread his legs so I could sit between them. We cuddled there for a few minutes in silence, then he whispered, "It's a lot smaller than I remember."

"What's this?" I pointed beside us.

"Oh, I forgot about that." He touched the carving. "I carved *Carpe Diem* into this in Latin."

"Is *Carpe Diem* something special to you?"

"Just jump in. That's what it means to me. Tomorrow may not be what you expect, so jump in before it's too late."

"Why did you write it as a kid?"

"Have you seen *Dead Poets Society*? Is that what it's called?"

"Of course. Classic line. I think it was even voted in the top movie quotes by the American Film Institute."

"My parents were too consumed in their own issues to pay much attention to me. Even now we're a bit estranged. So I sort of retreated into myself for a few years and when I started middle school I fancied this girl and didn't have the courage to tell her, then a queer little bloke snatched her up for the school dance and I never had the chance again. After that I decided to stop holding back and try to jump in, even if it didn't come natural in the moment."

"So it doesn't always come natural for you to seize the day?"

"Does it for anyone?"

"I guess not."

"Like now. You." He kissed the top of my head. "Remember when we were walking out of the airport and I walked away from you?"

"In the parking garage?"

"Right. Well, I wanted to come back and ask if you would like to get a bite, but I couldn't do it. Then you stopped me on the side of the road and I was kidnapped."

"Aren't you glad?"

"So, then I came home and got the tattoo over my heart. Carpe Diem." He paused and the rustling tree branches filled the silence, then he cleared his throat and continued, "I wanted to have a permanent reminder to always take chances. Not pile up regrets."

"I'm glad we found each other," I said, leaning my head back so my cheek touched his neck.

He looked down at me, his eyes darkened by the night as he cradled my head. The moonlight hit his face in all the right places, glistening in the whites of his eyes and setting a blue glow on his face. He licked his lips and held his bottom lip in, then moved toward me so I could taste him.

Our gentle kiss soon escalated into a passionate hair pulling embrace. Somehow I ended up straddling him as his hands moved from my hips, to my back, to my hips again. Then he stopped and stared at me with such gentle intensity that I wanted to melt right into him. My hair blew across my face and he pretended to snap a picture. I closed my eyes, willing my mind to store this one forever, vividly, so I'd always remember every detail about this moment. From the warmth of his lips against mine to the slightest sparkle in his eyes and the way it felt inside to be in love with him. Everything about him. And to be loved just as much in return.

He cupped my face in his hands and kissed me like it was the last time he'd ever kiss me. His hands slowly moved down to my jacket as he unzipped it without taking his lips off of mine. Without thinking, I took off his jacket and tossed it to the side. Then he moved my shirt down my shoulder and kissed every inch of exposed skin.

It was cold outside, but the treehouse was now filled with heat as our heavy breathing increased and our hands roamed every inch of each other. Part of me worried when he slowly pulled my shirt off, then gently lifted me and set my head on our jackets and shirts, but when he looked into my eyes I couldn't stop myself. Every part of me wanted to be with every part of him.

The moonlight bathed the muscles on his arms and chest as he lowered himself on to me and kissed me all over. I held my palm over his heart, over the inked *Carpe Diem*, and when I glanced up at him I saw his hand against the Latin carving he etched into the wood when he was a boy.

So many emotions flooded my heart. Deep affection. Curiosity. Intrigue. Passion. Excitement. Trust. Devotion. Attraction. Desire. Gratitude. Hope. Joy. Contentment. Love. I literally felt like I needed to open the floodgates and let it all pour out, but instead a single tear traveled down my cheek and into my hair while I whispered, "Alistair."

He stopped, looked deep into my eyes, and whispered back, "I don't want to use words. Close your eyes and feel my love for you."

I closed my eyes, wrapped my arms around his back, and felt the profoundness of his love as he melted into me.

Chapter 48

GOODBYES ARE THE WORST. TIME, THANK YOU VERY MUCH, did not cooperate. And before the weekend really had a chance to begin it was over. And it was painful to say goodbye to his sweet smile, knowing I wouldn't get to feel him for another few months.

When I got home Sunday, almost at midnight, Donovan picked me up and pried for details during the entire ride home. I didn't tell him everything. I had no idea how far his relationship with Han went and I wasn't about to open that up for conversation. Which was strange. It was the first time I couldn't tell Donovan about one of the most beautiful experiences in my entire life.

He parked in front of my apartment building, turned the car off, and of course, like his typical Donovan self, asked exactly what I didn't want to tell him.

I shook my head. "There's no way I'm talking this stuff with you. Or Autumn for that matter. Some things need to stay private."

"You did, didn't you?" He smiled, thankfully. I thought maybe he'd be mad or upset. "If you didn't, you would've slapped my arm and told me not to be ridiculous."

I slapped his arm. "Don't be ridiculous."

"Do you think you'll marry him?"

"*Carpe Diem.*"

"What's that mean?"

"Who knows what tomorrow brings." I stared out the window and imagined the treehouse, the moonlight, his face. "I don't need a ring or a paper from the government to confirm what my heart already feels."

"Which is?"

"Which is ... half of me lives in a little flat on the corner of a quiet Bristol street."

"Wow, Jazz." He leaned into the steering wheel and grinned. "I've never in my life seen you like this."

I laughed. "You look like a kid who's got cotton candy dangling in front of him."

"I'm happy for you." He glanced over his shoulder to the street, then back to me. "You finally let love in."

"Miracles occasionally happen."

"So now what?" he said.

"What?"

"What now?" he said.

"I don't know. What about you and Han?"

"Guess we'll take it one day at a time. She isn't as emotionally-driven as I am, so I'm just taking it slow to make sure she's comfortable."

"You were right, by the way."

"I always am." He smiled. "But why this time?"

"You're such an arse." I picked up my bag and opened the car door. "It's definitely worth it."

"Huh?"

"Love." I grinned as I stepped out of the car. "It's more than worth it."

UNFORTUNATELY, I WAS RIGHT BACK AT 1812 THE NEXT morning. Bright and early. And I hadn't spoken to Alistair, although he did sent me a good morning message while I was still sleeping.

Han and Brooke took care of the shop over the weekend and when Brooke walked in while I was drinking my coffee and hoping for the caffeine to kick in, she immediately said, "Jane. Did you see the sales?"

"Sales?" I sipped my coffee. "I didn't look yet."

"La la land," she said. "We sold a ton of clothes. Han sewed a bunch all weekend to keep up with sales. I helped in the evenings and we managed to make enough to restock the shelves."

"Like how many?"

"Over thirty. People are loving it more and more. Mostly men coming in and either getting stuff for themselves or their girlfriends and wives. It's really taking off."

"All that over one weekend? Are you messing with me?"

She handed me an envelope. "Cash sales are here. Credit card sales totaled $563.97 for the weekend."

"That's good. Not amazing yet, but I guess it's working this time."

"You're not as excited as I thought you'd be."

"Oh, no, no. I am, trust me. Just exhausted from jet lag and lack of sleep."

"How was your trip?"

My mind went back to our late night in the cute thatched cottage. Waking up later than we intended and falling back asleep in each other's arms. I missed him already. Our memories were already starting to feel like dreams. And this ... the store, work, oceans, time zones ... this was reality.

"Jane?" Brooke snapped her fingers in front of my eyes. "Earth to Jane."

"Sorry." I shook my head and set my coffee on the counter. "What did you say?"

"How was the trip?"

"It was perfect. Too perfect. I hope I can handle being away from him until December."

"Will he visit in December?"

"Yeah. He's not super close with his family, so he wanted to come and spend it with mine."

Speaking of Alistair, I hadn't heard from him since my last text two hours ago. I sent him another one, just a simple note to let him know I was thinking of him.

Brooke disappeared in the back as I turned the sign to *open* and put the chalkboard out front, which now had black and yellow balloons tied to it. Cute touch. Probably Brooke's idea. If the clothing continued to sell I would definitely need to consider hiring more people, but now I wondered if securing myself here would be wise. What if I needed to move there to be with him? Could I take the store?

I really didn't want to choose between the store and him. Of course I'd choose him, but I loved owning my own fashion line and I wanted to see where it would take me. Somehow maybe both could work out.

Han entered from the back and gave me a hug, which I didn't expect, but gladly accepted. After normal greetings she went to the back to find Brooke. I watched her walk away, wondering if one day I'd consider her a sister of sorts. Autumn said Donovan and Han were like sugar and Alistair and I were spice.

I kinda liked that.

Maybe I was never the sweet girl to steal Don's heart, but I happened to run away with someone else's.

Man, I missed him like crazy.

"Time," I said while staring at that dreadful second hand. "Please be my friend and skip ahead to December."

If only, right?

Chapter 49

FOUR WEEKS FROM MY TRIP TO ENGLAND AND IT FELT LIKE five years. Three entire days passed without Alistair and I connecting on the phone or video and our messages were rare too. I missed him. He missed me. It didn't feel good. At all. So I rushed home Friday night to talk to him, but by the time I closed the store and got home he was asleep. I tried calling him with Skype, hoping maybe he'd answer the call in his sleep and I'd get to listen to him breathe, but he didn't.

So I sent a quick message saying I was sorry and maybe we could talk tomorrow during the day. Saturday. Brooke and Han would both be at 1812 and I could probably sneak away to talk whenever he could.

It took my forever to fall asleep that night and when I did my dreams were pure nightmares. I mean, the hellish of all hellish nightmares. There was a fire and Alistair was stuck in the house. I tried to go in and save him, but ended up flying out of a window and crashing to the ground. When I woke up from the dream with my entire body shaking, I eventually went back to sleep only to dream that he died in the fire and when they found his body he was naked with another girl.

So, yeah ... I woke up wanting to stay awake and never sleep again.

He didn't message me in the morning and I hated that it affected me so much. A few months ago I was tough Jane. Resilient-ish. Able to *not* fall in love and get my heart broken. Now I worried, maybe unrealistically, but I couldn't help it. My boyfriend lived in another freaking country and our conversations were getting more and more infrequent. When we did sneak in a conversation it was often so quick and rushed ... so not romantic. We should've been together. Passionately intertwined with each other. Waking up to a warm body on the bed beside us.

My fears were coming to life and it made me become a person I didn't want to be. I was losing focus at work, tripping up the steps, stopping at streets that didn't have stop signs, eating way too much sugar, and going to bed much earlier than normal.

Then he called.

I rushed across my room and picked up the call.

"Jane," he said. "I'm eating lunch. A short break from work here. I miss you."

"Hey." It was only the beginning of the call, but I was already dreading the end.

"Why so serious?"

"You know why." I sighed. "This is horrible. It's only been a few weeks and things feel all weird."

"I'll be there soon. Christmas is right around the corner. Hold on for me, okay? We can make it."

"I can't do this, Alistair."

He breathed into the phone, but didn't speak.

"I need to see you or feel you or at the very least hear you. This is killing me."

"It's killing me too, Jane." I could barely hear him.

"I think your phone is breaking up or something. Maybe it's Skype?"

"Jane?"

"Hey. Are you there?" I said.

Crackling, buzzing, and ... "Jane? Can you hear me?"

"I'm here. Can you hear me?"

Static, his voice, more static.

"I can't hear you."

Silence.

I threw my phone on my bed and stared at it. Then picked it up and checked to see if he messaged me. Not yet. I tossed it back to the pillow and took a shower, hoping the water would wash away the pain in my chest.

LATER THAT NIGHT I STOPPED BY MY PARENT'S HOUSE. THE front door was unlocked, so I went right in and found Mom at the kitchen table with a friend.

"Jane." She jumped up, screeching her chair in the process. "I didn't expect you, honey."

"It's fine. I wanted to stop by and see Eddie, check on you and Dad. Nothing major. No need to bake or make tea."

"Jane?" her friend said, holding her cheeks in her hands. "Jane...."

I looked at Mom, then back to the creepy lady. "Yes?"

Mom came beside me and took my hand, sandwiching it between both of hers. "This is Julia. I didn't know you'd be here, but she planned to see you before she left."

I blinked at the woman and found my eyes naturally gazing down her chest to her stomach. My original home. Images flashed. Nightmares of my conception, of her pain, of my birth.

She didn't stand. She just sat there and she couldn't even look at me. Yes, he raped her. I wasn't making light of her painful experience at all, but she carried me inside of her, felt my feet in her ribs, and watched me take my first breath.

"How could you let me go?" I said. "How could you just leave me like that?"

"Jane." Mom touched my shoulder.

"I wanted better for you than I could give," the stranger said as she stared at her knees.

"But I'm your daughter. I know it's a messed up situation. Mom told me everything." That was awkward. "But still ... didn't you at least want to be in my life?"

"It's ... you don't ..." She looked to Mom, then finally made eye contact with me. "I just—"

"It's okay," Mom said, but it was too late. She was already running for the door. Mom almost went after her, but stayed with me instead.

"It's painful for her, Jane," Mom said. "You shouldn't have said that."

"Mom. Seriously? I was being honest. That's how I feel. I want to know."

"Just imagine being in her shoes. She was severely abused by her father. Her own flesh and blood, only to be raped and left in the basement to bleed on the floor until I came and called the cops. Imagine when she found out that she was pregnant. She wanted an abortion, Jane. She begged me to tell her it was okay to abort you, but I told her I'd take care of the baby and she could worry about herself. Try to get back on her feet. I knew if she aborted you that she would feel even worse. But just think what it might feel like to stare at the child that was conceived when you lost your virginity to your father in a cold, dark basement." She stopped to hug me and stayed there with her head against mine. "I know it's hard for you, sweetie, but you need to see things from her perspective too."

I held on to her and tried to process it all. Abort me? I didn't want to be selfish. I wanted to think of the poor woman who conceived me like that. But abort me? The words refused to leave my mind. I did my best to pretend like it was all okay. I told Mom I'd write a letter and apologize. But the entire time we played Pictionary, my mind was somewhere else.

Alistair sent me a message at 9:02pm asking if I was going to call because he was getting tired. I told him I'd call in a half hour and asked him to please stay awake, peel back his eyelids, whatever it took, I needed him. Yes. For once, I admit, I *needed* him.

I said goodbye to everyone as fast as possible, jogged to my car, and called him.

No answer.

I sent a text. *Hey, are you there? Please be there. It's only 9:24. Alistair? Please be awake.*

I called during my drive home. Over and over again. I called when I got home. Over and over again. I called in bed. Over. And over. And over. Again. I called fifty six times before midnight. Then I gave up, turned my face into my pillow, and used every ounce of willpower within me to keep myself from screaming.

Chapter 50

I WOKE UP AT 3AM FROM ANOTHER HORRIBLE DREAM. I tried to call Alistair, hoping maybe he was awake and would finally answer. After calling three times, I hung up and called Donovan.

He picked up on the second ring.

"Jazzy," he mumbled half asleep. "You okay?"

"No." I pressed my lips together and breathed deep through my nose.

"Jazz. What's wrong?"

I started to explain, but my mind couldn't catch up with my heart and I couldn't find the words.

"What happened? Tell me you're okay." He sounded wide awake now. "Should I come over?"

"No," I said quickly. "No, that's not fair to Han and Alistair."

"What's wrong? Talk to me."

"Why does it feel like whenever something goes well for me it all starts to fall apart? I can't hold on to happiness, Don. It doesn't like me."

"Happiness is overrated anyway. Did something happen?"

"Well, my biological mother was at my parent's house tonight aaand that was interesting and Alistair and I..." My lip quivered.

"Did you break up?"

"No. No we're still together, but it's only been like a month since I got back and it's been so hard to talk. We keep missing each other and I feel like he just doesn't make an effort and I don't know, Don ... what if he realizes this isn't worth it and..."

"And what? You get your heart broken?"

I nodded as though he could see me.

"Remember what I said? A broken heart is proof that the heart worked to begin with. I doubt Alistair would do that. He adores you just like any guy would if they had you. It's long distance, Jazz. That comes with the territory. You just need to work through it like anything else. Just be honest with him."

"I will if I can ever talk to him again."

"Leave it to you to be optimistic."

"Mmmhmm." I felt a little better. "Thank you for picking up the phone."

"Always."

"I wish Alistair would wake up when the phone rings. The guy has an alarm on his phone and a digital clock next to his bed and still oversleeps sometimes."

"But he doesn't snore."

"No." I laughed. "Not that."

"Try to get some rest, okay? Close your eyes and put the phone on speaker. I won't hang up until you're asleep."

"Thank you. You have no idea how much I needed this."

ABOUT THAT OVERSLEEPING THING.

I woke up ten minutes after 1812 was supposed to open and had

432

three missed calls from Brooke. I called her back and told her I'd be there soon, then got ready without taking a shower.

On the way to the shop I called Alistair.

"Jane," he said.

"Alistair. It's so good to finally hear your voice again."

"I tried to bloody stay awake. I feel rubbish. I'm so sorry."

"How are you? How's work?"

"Everything is all right. Hey, I tried to call you back earlier. It was around 4am your time and your phone gave a weird beep like you were talking to someone else."

"Oh, it was Don."

"You called Don?"

I parked in back of the store and turned the car off. "I called him, yeah. I needed someone to talk to."

He didn't say anything. Something slammed.

"Are you upset at me?"

"No."

"Yes you are."

"I'm driving. I'll call you back when I'm off the road."

"Oh." I hoped maybe he'd pull over and finish our talk. "Okay."

"Okay then."

We hung up and I leaned back in the driver's seat wondering what the hell just happened. What was happening to us?

I sent him a message. *Alistair, I hope you're not mad. You know Don is just a friend. I was upset about my birth mother and not talking to you as much.*

A minute went by, then he responded with, *He's not just a friend. There was a time when you chose him over me. Looks like you did again.*

Me: *I didn't choose him over you. You didn't pick up.*

Him: *Then why didn't you pick up when I called?*

Me: *I was sleeping. He just let the phone stay on while I fell asleep because he knew it would comfort me.*

Him: *Some other bloke comforting you. I see.*

Me: *He's not some other bloke. You know how I feel about him. Don't do this. Please.*

Five minutes later he still hadn't responded. I wiped my sweaty hands on my pants and tried to stop them from shaking, then sent another message.

Alistair. Please. I love you.

No answer.

I went into the store, dazed, nauseous, dizzy. Brooke and Han helped me sit down in the back and said they'd take care of things. Brooke told me to rest, but how could I?

How could I possibly rest until he told me everything was okay? We were still worth the fight. I considered hopping on a plane and showing up on his doorstep, but I couldn't leave. And I didn't have any money anyway.

Han touched my shoulder. "Jane, someone here to see you."

"I can't right now."

Brooke tapped on the doorframe. "You may want to come out."

I forced myself to my feet. One step at a time. A woman in a business suit stood at the front of the store. Why, for a second, did I think I was in a Nicholas Sparks film and Alistair would be the one standing at the door, holding a bouquet of black and yellow flowers? Why the *hell* did I think, for one freaking second, that maybe, just maybe, I could wrap my arms around him and make it go away?

The woman greeted me. So and so from such and such. I tried to focus. At the end she said, "You let me know," and I had to ask Han and Brooke what happened.

"She wants to hire you," Brooke said. "Spacing out again?"

"For what?"

"You weren't listening?"

I shook my head.

"She's from New York. Word got around. She wants to have your designs on the runway by the end of this year."

"What? Is that even possible? I'm not even sure I want that."

She pointed to the business card that I dropped on the floor. "Might wanna pick that up."

Maybe that should've been good news, but it wasn't because I couldn't share it with Alistair.

I texted and called over a hundred times before bed that day. Even sent a long email pouring my heart out to him.

He never responded.

Not. Even. Once.

Chapter 51

FOUR INSUFFERABLE DAYS. FOUR.

Day one, I was pissed. Day two, I was confused. Day three, I was worried. Today ... Thanksgiving ... sad. Not thankful. Not a fun person to be around, but I put on my happy face when I went to Mom's for dinner. Then, of course, as we're all sitting around the table listening to Granny talk about how Grandpa used to cook the perfect turkey, Mom passed me the sauerkraut and whispered, "Are you still upset about Julia?"

I traded the sauerkraut for cranberry sauce. "Not really. I sent her an apology, but haven't heard back."

"She went back to California. It's really difficult for her, Jane. I hope you understand. None of this is your fault." She handed me the mashed potatoes. "But I'm glad you're here and whether I gave birth to you or not, you're my daughter and I love you."

Eddie cleared his first plate within minutes and looked up for seconds.

"Slow down," I said to him. "Some people have nothing today." I looked around the table. "And here we are overeating all in the name of thankfulness."

"Well, I am thankful," he said, scooping a generous spoonful of stuffing on to his plate.

I sighed and pushed my plate away. "I can't eat."

"Jane," Dad said.

I stood and stared at the sweet potatoes covered in marshmallows, which took me back to the day I met Alistair. The day he tried to make me feel less awkward about my name by bringing up how weird he thought it was that we put marshmallows on our sweet potatoes. The day he walked into my life that I was now starting to wish hadn't happened.

Better to not know love than to find it and lose it.

"Sit down, dear," Granny said. "You look famished. Please tell her to eat, son."

Dad looked at me, then Mom, then back to me. "Jane, sit with us? Even if you aren't hungry?"

"I'll be back. I need to go to the bathroom."

I went to my old room instead and sat on the guest bed. Mom converted the room to a *Sense and Sensibility* theme.

"I used to be sensible," I said to myself. "Now I can't pull myself together."

I checked my phone again. Just in case. Last text from him was still, *Some other bloke comforting you. I see.*

How could he not forgive me? It was so trivial in the grand scheme of it all.

I opened up my voice recorder and said, "Alistair, I don't know what's wrong with us. I don't know how to fix it if you don't talk to me. It's been four days and you can't even respond to one of my messages? Just tell me you don't want to talk to me ever again. Anything. Something. Just not nothing. You always told me we'd make it. We'd work through anything that comes our way. You told me to stay with you. So I'm here, but you've gone away. Please just respond. I miss you. I love you. I hate this. Please." I then put my phone in my lap and sang "Stay with Me" to him. I'm not the best, not always in tune, but I felt every word. Then I ended the recording, messaged it to him, and hoped maybe he'd respond before he went to bed.

You may listen to this voicemail by clicking the QR code:

Eddie walked by the open doorway, stopped, walked backward, and peeked inside. "Jane?"

"Hey." I shrugged. "Nice room here. Fitting for Jane Austen, don't you think?"

He sat beside me and looked at the regency paintings. "A few days ago I heard Mom and Dad talking about your birth and adoption and everything. They didn't know I was listening because I had headphones on, but the song ended and I heard them saying how weird it was that the two of them met over a Jane Austen book in class, and his last name was Austen, but then their first child was named Jane without their input. Dad said it was meant to be. Mom agreed and cried, saying she could never imagine life without you." He rubbed the back of his head. "So, yeah, I don't know what's going on with you and I know all of this is pretty shitty, but today *is* Thanksgiving and I'm thankful you're my sister, no matter how it happened."

I pat his shoulder. "Thanks, Ed. I'm thankful too."

"Good." He slapped his legs and stood. "So can you please come down before you upset Granny?"

We walked downstairs together and I sat down, trying to pretend again. It wasn't my life that upset me. I could get over that. I had a good family and I *was* thankful, regardless of the weirdness of my birth story and those years of my childhood spent wondering where I fit in and who I was. But I wasn't thankful for Alistair's decision to ignore me without closure and I knew what I needed to do.

I needed to fly out to him. As soon as freaking possible.

"How's Alistair?" Mom said over dessert.

"He's good," I said.

"Things are going well with you two?" Granny smirked.

"Yeah," I lied. "Everything is good. We're good."

But Mom knew something was up. She gave me that look.

"I'm going back out sometime this week," I said. "I'm excited."

Mom looked back at her plate, then Dad. She wasn't buying it.

And of course she pulled me aside later and asked me what was going on, but I didn't want anyone to know. Last time Donovan got involved it didn't go well and the surprise party was nice, but overwhelming. I wanted to handle this on my own without everyone trying to step in and write my love story for me. No, I *needed* to figure this out on my own. I needed to show him I still loved him and wouldn't let this stuff come between us.

Chapter 52

ANOTHER WEEK AND STILL NOTHING, SO I BOOKED A FLIGHT to England for the first weekend in December and hired a temp to help Brooke and Han at the shop. It was getting busier and busier especially around Christmas. I didn't realize how many Batman fans existed in Philly, although quite a few people liked the uniqueness of the designs and the store even if they weren't fans.

But I couldn't fully enjoy the success without Alistair to share it with, so I boarded the plane and tried to avoid the nauseating emotions begging my mind to turn around and go back home. When I landed I promised myself I would stop flying so much sometime soon. Not my favorite thing.

I got the rental car I booked, did my best to drive on the right side while also following the map on my phone, and finally made it to his house around 3am his time. I figured if he was sleeping I'd just wait in my car, but first I knocked on the front door. Of course he didn't answer, so I went around to the side and tossed a few pebbles up there. Still nothing.

Back in my car I went. Where I tried to sleep—ha!—until morning. He normally worked Saturday's, leaving around 8am. So I woke at five and set my phone's alarm for 7:30am. When it woke me up I bunched my scarf around my neck and put the hood of my coat over me, then slipped my gloves on and sat on his front step. By 8:32 I gave up peeping through the windows and being a stalker, and walked to his car in the back. Which wasn't there.

But I wasn't giving up. I wasn't going to allow myself to feel or be defeated. Love fights. And that's exactly what I intended to do.

So I walked back around to the front and sat down on the step. The door clicked and opened.

Shoes clacked behind me.

"Can I help you?" someone, a female someone, said.

I stood. "I'm here to see Alistair."

"Who?" She stepped out of the doorway and locked it behind her. "I'm afraid you have the wrong address."

"No, this is his apartment. I mean, flat. He lives here. Who are you? His girlfriend?"

"Darling, I don't like boys like that so that's a bit impossible." She laughed as she rattled her keys while walking by me and down the steps.

I looked back at the door. The bright red door. It was the right address. Unmistakeable door. I turned back to her and walked down the steps.

"Where is he?" I pleaded. "Look, if you're his new thing that's fine, but I need to see him."

"Like I said, wrong address." She stood at the driver's side of her car. "My name is Arabella and I live there." She pulled something out of her purse. "See." She showed me her name above the address, his address, on her mail. "I just moved in a week ago. Maybe this Alistair lived here before then?"

"Maybe." I closed my eyes and breathed in as much air as pos-

444

sible, then released it. "Thank you, Arabella. Sorry to bother you."

She drove off and I stood there, staring at that stupid red door and wondering why he wasn't behind it, then I started to worry. What if he died? What if I would never know? I didn't know his parent's names or addresses. All of his friends lived in London where he spent the second half of his life. And I never met them or learned their last names.

His old band mates!

I shivered as a frigid breeze swept down the street, then looked up their website on my phone as I got into my car. Nothing came up and their old site had an error page. Their Facebook page was gone too. I tried to remember one of their names, but realized I didn't know any of them. I didn't know one person in his life.

"Maybe I don't know him at all," I said to myself. "Maybe he was a creep."

"I don't think so," I responded to myself. "You knew him. You loved him and you knew him."

"But I don't know any of his family or friends."

"Shut up!" I turned the car on. "Whatever side of my brain you are, stop being negative. I'm done. I'm thinking positively no matter what you say."

"But—"

"Nope."

I turned the radio up to ignore my thoughts and of course that *Stay with Me* song came on. I didn't turn the station though. Instead I sang my heart out as loud as possible while driving around aimlessly looking for him.

Too many questions. It was unlike him. Either he was seriously pissed off at me, he found someone else he liked better, or he died. But why would he move?

My heart beat was driving me nuts and my chest felt tight. I pressed down where it hurt and pulled over to catch my breath. Cars passed and I found myself hoping for a ridiculous Nicholas Sparks feeling scene. Anything would be better than whatever I was experiencing now.

I rummaged through my purse for some headache meds in my special, rarely used pocket reserved for pain meds. I pulled out arnica with a note in Autumn's handwriting that said, "Use this instead. If it doesn't work, use the chems." She called over-the-counter drugs "chemical drugs" and soon she just called them "chems." I popped the recommended dosage in and hoped they were more than sugar pills. Then I saw another note in there.

Alistair's handwriting.

Thanks for letting me stay at your flat this week. I had a lovely time, Ms. Austen. Here's a little gift for you. Put it to good use, okay?

It was a gift certificate to Dee's tattoo place. Somehow I never got the note. I guess he wanted me to be surprised, because he never mentioned it or asked about it.

I knew exactly what I wanted. Right above my heart on my chest. Maybe a small one, some pretty decorative border around the words.

Carpe Diem.

Because even if he never spoke to me again, he taught me that. And I'd always remember him for that. I'd never forget the way it felt to be against his body, looking into his eyes between kisses.

I'd never forget him.

Ever.

Chapter 53

DECEMBER PASSED. JANUARY PASSED. FEBRUARY. MARCH. April. Then May came.

I said I wouldn't give up, but I did. I tried everything imaginable. Even called his phone from a British number while I was there, so he wouldn't know it was me. But it rang and rang and rang, then went to his generic voicemail. I left a message and said, "If I don't hear from you I'll know you're done. I don't understand and this seems extremely immature, but I know a thing or two about that so I have no room to talk. I'll always remember you. Thank you for our time together. Goodbye, Alistair."

When I hung up I felt bad for being so straight, so I sent another one that said, "I love you and I think I always will. Just like the real Jane Austen, not that I'm not real. They say she never got over him either. The guy she loved. Anyway, I love you. Carpe Diem."

Five months passed since that voicemail though. And he was gone. Out of my life. I told everyone that we broke up. A mutual ending because of the distance. Donovan tried to convince me that he should intervene, but I convinced him otherwise. Autumn and I didn't talk much, but she thought I was still meant for Donovan anyway. Mom seemed sad, but I told her there are plenty more English fish in the sea. I tried to believe it myself, but figured life doesn't always work out the way you want it to. Stories don't always have good endings. Some are tragic, like the real Jane Austen who died alone, penning love stories without living them. But like me, maybe she felt that one, genuine love was enough. She didn't need anyone else. She needed that one. And if she couldn't have him, then no one would do.

That's what I chose to believe, although I hoped maybe I would one day find love again.

Carpe Diem, right?

I touched the tattoo on my chest and looked at the calendar. Almost one year exactly since the day we met.

Alistair left my life, left me, but he never left my heart. In fact, wherever he was ... whatever he was doing ... he still carried a piece of me with him, whether he liked it or not.

"SOME LOVE STORIES JUST AREN'T MEANT FOR GIRLS LIKE you," Zoe said as we sat down on the couch with bowls of ice cream. "Seriously did you actually think a guy like that would stay with you? I mean, he could like have any girl he wants."

"Nothing like a nice dose of Zoe for a pick me up." I dug into my ice cream and exaggerated an eye roll. "The anniversary of the first day we met is in a week and I just need to stop talking about this now. I can't keep reopening wounds just to watch myself bleed to death. I need to let them heal so I can get on with life."

"I'm just being real with you. The guy was a sexy as hell and that sent him over the top."

"He was sexy to me, don't get me wrong, but he wasn't that hot or anything. He was normal."

"Then what does that make you?"

I laughed. "You're lucky I love you anyway, because the things you say are pretty damn messed up."

"Some people sugar coat a pile of trash, but I just like to call it trash."

"Are you calling me trash now?"

"No. I'm just saying you're average and he's hot."

"Well, I think hotness has nothing to do with anything right now. Alistair isn't here. So whatever, put your stupid chick flick on so I can understand why girls like to depress themselves even more by watching this stuff."

"It should bring you hope," she said, walking over to my DVD player. "I picked it out just for you."

"Oh yeah? What is it?"

"*The Umbrellas of Cherbourg.*"

"Never heard of that."

"You'll love it."

THE MOVIE CAME TO A CLOSE AND I STARED AT THE CREDITS while Zoe stared at me. Did she honestly just make me watch that?

"So..." she pried.

"Are you trying to break me into a thousand and one pieces? Is a thousand not good enough for you?" I stood and took our bowls to the kitchen. "I think you need to find somewhere else to live."

She laughed and followed after me. "It was supposed to inspire you."

"Inspire my ass. " I pointed my spoon back to the television. "This is exactly why I can't stand romance movies."

"But it's realistic. It shows that your story is realistic, so it's not like it's your fault or anything."

"I never thought it was my fault," I said. "Oh, man. I need a long night of sleep with no dreams after that."

"You didn't like it?"

"Zoe." I brushed by her as I walked to the hallway.

"We could watch *Titanic* instead," she offered.

"Yeah. I'd rather take a shot to the head instead of the heart, thanks."

She laughed as she went into her room and I shook my head as I went into mine. I didn't bother closing my door. Zoe moved back in a few weeks ago and we were closer than ever. She was there and needed someone just as much as I did. Donovan and Han barely talked to me anymore. I mean, they did, but I couldn't always handle seeing them so happy together. Sometimes it was perfect and I was fine, other times everything would come rushing back and I couldn't bear to be in the same room with love like theirs.

Not that tragedies made me feel any better. What was Zoe thinking?

I plopped on my bed with my laptop and pulled up my emails, went through a bunch of ho-hum work stuff, and then decided to fill a few online orders, which I did from home at night since I didn't get as many online orders as I did in the store.

Business was perfect. I managed to make enough income to pay three employees, the lease, my rent, and even food. I wasn't rolling in the cash, but it was good and I knew it would be even better with some good marketing.

Three orders to fill. I packed the first two into a box, slapped on the mailing labels, and opened the third.

> New Order from 1812 Online Store
> The Joker/ DKT - Size 32, M
> Bruce Wayne/DKT - Size 32, M
> Alfred/EAG - Size 32, M
> Note from buyer: Gift wrap, please. This is for my son. Please mail it to the shipping address for him, not the billing address. Thank you. And include this note if you could:
>
> I found this store from the States and thought you would fancy it. If it's the wrong size, just return it for the right one. Tell Mum I said hello. I'll come visit soon. -Dad
>
> SHIPPING ADDRESS:
> Alistair Gladwyn
> 47 High Oakham Road
> Mansfield, Nottinghamshire NG18

My eyes closed, then reopened. Yes, it was really him. The mailing label quivered in my hands. Memories upon memories flickered in and out. So many. Then came the question that tormented me for months.

Why?

Why didn't he call?

Chapter 54

THERE ARE TWO WAYS OF LOOKING AT THIS. ONE, I WAS crazy. And two, I was out of my ever-loving mind. I preferred the latter so that I didn't have to take credit for my actions. Just blame it on the lack of sense, right?

See. It goes like this and if you've ever been in love then you know what I'm saying. When you grow up with a bunch of little girls planning their weddings at age eight and you think you'll never get married, there comes this point in your life when you get kissed by someone you really love and who really loves you, and it's nice and all, but not enough to keep you up at night wondering when it will happen again. Then, as you're going about your life, someone else walks in and he's funny and charming and different and beautiful. He promises you this kiss and you're thinking right whatever, but then it happens. He kisses you and you know that whoever you loved before that ... it wasn't real love. Not like this love. You know and feel and experience so deeply the difference in this one person's kiss that you can't possibly imagine never tasting it again. I guess, long story short, what I'm trying to say is that love isn't about finding people we can live with. We can get along with anyone. Even live with people who hurt us. But it's that one person, that one single person in an entire six billion population, that you can't live without. It's that person who's worth living for and dying for. It's that person I loved.

And so, to summarize plainly, I could now understand Romeo and Juliet. And that's all I'll say about that.

The plane lifted off the ground just as I started to doubt myself. He clearly didn't want to talk to me. To the point of moving away and changing his number. His new flat wasn't even in the same town. And yeah, maybe I was crazy, but isn't drowning your life in poison crazy? All because living without Romeo is unbearable? I guess love makes you a little crazy and I admit, I felt weird and nervous and got up to go pee about forty times. I couldn't sit still and the woman next to me probably thought I had an intense fear of flying. I had a mild fear of flying, but standing in front of him scared me more. Simply because I didn't know what to expect. Or why he did what he did to me. Or if he would still love me. Or if he ever loved me at all.

That's the one that really freaked me out.

SO, MY FLIGHT LANDED AT THE EAST MIDLANDS AIRPORT AT 7:21am Saturday morning, which was 2:21am my time. Originally I planned to go right to him, but my eyelids were heavy and I didn't want to drive a European car with tiredness looming over me, so I booked a room at a hotel near the airport and ... who was I kidding? I didn't sleep at all, but the rest helped. Plus the shower I took woke me up well enough to drive. Maybe with a complimentary coffee from the lobby I would be even better.

I finished up and stood in front of the mirror. I chose to wear my Dark Knight Trilogy Catwoman design. It was very similar to the outfit Anne Hathaway wore, but with my own twist. I tend to prefer asymmetrical designs, so the black dress was a little less tight, but still fitting, and had an asymmetrical pull from one shoulder to the other hip. I also wore the black tights, heels, and a wide-brimmed hat. But as I was looking in the mirror I thought maybe it was a little much. It leaned sexy and it was ultra classy, but I didn't bring anything else except my jeans and t-shirts.

I took a deep breath. "Just go," I said to my reflection. "Time to get this over with."

I grabbed a coffee before leaving and drove to Mansfield, which was way too close to the airport. Not super close, but not far enough to make it feel like I had enough time to prepare. Not that there could ever be enough time for such things. The rain started just as I turned on to Nottingham Road and by the time I turned left on High Oakham Road, his new street, it was pouring down.

I slowed down and squinted through the rain to read the numbers on the houses. The very nice houses. In a neighborhood. I expected an apartment, but these were real deal houses.

He bought a house?

Butterflies assaulted me. Yes, assaulted. It felt more like whacked out bats going to town inside of my stomach. I was excited and nervous and scared all at the same time. What if he slammed the door in my face? What if he was married to someone else? What if this wasn't even him? What if it was a different Alistair?

I never even thought of that.

And with my luck....

I slowed down and finally saw his house number. It was a large brick house. Two stories tall with pretty shutters and a nice garden. Big yard. Very well kept.

Breathe, Jane. Yep. You can do this and you WILL do this.

I parked and tried to slow down my breathing, but I couldn't focus. I watched the door and windows for any sign of life, worrying that I might be intruding into a new life he built for himself. I didn't want to upset him or his wife if he had one. I just wanted one last word from him. And a reason. I needed to know why he left. If it was deeper than our conversation. If it was me.

I opened the door and held my hat as I jogged through the rain to the front door. Frozen in place, my hands stayed at my sides as the droplets pelted my hat and soaked my shoes.

To knock or not to knock, that is the....

"Just do this already," I reprimanded myself and knocked loudly on the door. I gave three hard pounds and then stepped back as my throat closed up and my heart competed with the fast tap of the rain.

Definitely had my doubts. Definitely wanted to run back to the car. But definitely stood my ground.

The door opened.

Chapter 55

SHE LOOKED AT ME AND I LOOKED AT HER.

She looked nothing like me. Short blonde hair, longer in the front toward the shoulders. Trendy glasses and lots of makeup. No tattoos that I could see. Very professional. Mature. She looked more like a woman. More his age. Maybe that was it....

"Hello," she finally said, looking from my face to the package in my hands. "Do you have the right address?"

"I have a package for Alistair Gladwyn." I swallowed hard. "Does he live here?"

"Oh, I'm so sorry, please step inside." She grabbed my arm and pulled me in to the entryway. "Yes, Alistair is here. He's resting. Do you know him or is this some kind of special delivery service?"

"Oh, it's um...."

"My name is Emma. I'm so terrible with introductions, but you look so posh I hope I didn't offend you."

I *almost* laughed. "I'm not posh in the slightest. I'm not even sure I know what posh means. My name is Jane."

"Jane? That's odd. What's your last name?"

I coughed. "Austen."

"Jane Austen? Really? You're having me on, aren't you?"

"Having you on?"

"Is this a joke?" She clapped her hands in front of her as though she were excited. "Who put you up to this? He's going to love it."

"I don't, um, I'm not sure I know what you mean..."

"Oh, Alistair is always talking about how much he loved Jane Austen and we joke around that he must have experienced some interesting dreams."

"Dreams? I'm not sure I—"

"So you must be an actress? Singing telegram?"

"No, I'm ... I'm just Jane Austen. That's my real name." I handed her the package. "Anyway, this is a gift for him. Could you?"

"Oh, I hear him now." She leaned toward me. "He's a bit stroppy when he wakes up, but he will love this. Alistair," she called toward the hallway. "Someone is here to see you."

"No, I should go. I didn't mean to—"

"Shh, shh!" She waved at me while turned toward the hall. "Here he comes."

He turned the corner and caught my eyes as they were filling with tears.

"Alistair," Emma said. "This ... is Jane Austen."

My heart.

I grabbed my chest as a tear fell to my cheek. Alistair....

He gripped his walker and leaned more on the left side. His right foot turned in and his right arm dangled by his leg. The muscles in his face were more relaxed, drooping to the left and causing drool to slip from his mouth. My chest expanded rapidly and more tears collected. I blinked one to my cheek and looked at his eyes, they were still the same. But everything else....

A single tear zig-zagged down the right side of his face and fell to the hand that held the walker.

Emma stood and put her arm around his back. "Come and sit. Ms. Austen came for a visit. Isn't that fun?"

"Don't patronize me, Emma!" he yelled.

She raised her eyebrows at me and mouthed, "See."

"Leave." He looked at her. "Go now."

"But your mum won't be home until—"

"I said leave, Emma." He tried to shove his head toward the door, but it only caused drool to fling across him. "Sod off!"

She jerked back and forth, looking for her things and mumbling some kind of curse at him.

"I'm leaving a note for your mum," she said. "And you can fuss all ya want, but this is my job on the line." She looked at me. "Stay here with him until his mum gets home. I'm assuming you are friends?"

I nodded, dazed.

Who was this man?

She shut the door and I watched through the window as she ran to her car. He pushed the walker forward and made his way to a chair across from me, where he sloppily managed to flop into it without help.

He closed his eyes. "Jane."

I pursed my lips and held back more tears. "Alistair."

We sat there, five feet away from each other in complete silence except for the slight tap of the rain on the windows. He kept his eyes closed, but I watched him breathe. The same chest I used as a pillow so many times before. The same tattoo peeking out from his shirt. The one I held the night he made me his own. But his body was crippled, paralyzed or something, and he looked so much thinner. Less muscle and broadness. Less like himself, like the man I fell in love with.

"What happened?" I whispered.

He squeezed his eyes and tried to shake his head. "Jane," he cried, his chest jerking.

I got up and knelt down beside him, taking his hand into mine and losing myself in the softness of the skin I missed so much, but he moved it away from me and set it on his lap.

"What happened?" I said again.

"I don't remember much. They said I may have been on the phone or distracted, but I swerved and hit another car. I don't re-member that at all, but I was in the hospital for a long time. I didn't remember anyone when I woke up, but slowly memories began to come back to me. Memories of my childhood. Of the treehouse. Of you." He finally opened his eyes again, pulled a handkerchief from his pocket, and wiped his mouth. "I'm so embarrassed."

"I don't understand. One minute we were texting and the next you...."

He looked at me blankly.

"You crashed your car?"

"That's what they say. I'm lucky in many ways. It could have been much worse and my brain damage is minimal, although it's hard to tell because of my physical ability."

"Brain damage?"

"Traumatic Brain Injury from the accident. When I got out of the hospital I wanted to contact you, but Jane..." He closed his eyes. "I didn't want you to lose your life and dreams because of me."

"Alistair." I took his hand again. "I thought you hated me. I thought you were ignoring me because of a dumb argument we had.

I wish you told me. I wish I had known. I would've been right here with you from the start." I kissed his hand. "I had no way to know. No way to find you."

"Jane, I'm sorry. I know how you feel about being abandoned, but I—"

"Stop it." I placed my finger over his lips. "Stop apologizing."

"I can't take care of you anymore. I need therapists and caretakers and I have so many—"

"Please stop."

"I'm not a man anymore, Jane. I'm not who I used to be. I want better for you."

"Shut up." I sobbed into his hand. "You are the best, do you hear me? Just stop saying that ... that rubbish."

He moved his fingers toward my chin and ran them up my jaw, back down to my lips, and held them there as we looked at each other through tear-filled eyes. He was right. He was different. And from what I knew of brain injuries personalities and memories could often be distorted too, but he was still the man I wanted. The one I needed. The one single soul out of six billion that I couldn't live without. He was still my Alistair. And I loved him. So much.

Chapter 56

FOR THE NEXT HOUR ALISTAIR TOLD ME WHAT HE REMEM-
bered before the accident, which wasn't everything, but quite a bit.
He told me that he couldn't remember the accident itself at all or
waking up in the hospital, but he slowly regained his ability to remember bits and pieces as he recovered. He had surgery and a lot of
occupational and speech therapy and quickly went from a wheelchair
to a walker. When he described the pain he went through and still
endured I wanted to take it away from him. Go back in time and tell
him I loved him instead of getting upset. Or at the very least I wished
I told him not to text and drive. Instead I texted him. I was part of
this. And I wanted to take it all away, give his pain to myself, anything
to make him feel better.

He explained all of the logistics. His injury types, which for the
life of me I couldn't remember no matter how much I tried, and his
prospective healing and treatment plans. Doctors believed he could
one day regain all mobility with hard work, but it would take time and
patience that he often didn't feel like he had. He still had feeling in
his ... lower region. So he could go to the bathroom without the em-
barassment of needing help. And although he lost a lot of function on
one side of his body, it was mostly in his arm and it wasn't completely
gone. He could feel hot and cold and move his fingers. He could also

move his leg, but with the help of a walker.

When he stood and showed me how well he could get around it took all I had not to cry. We were so young. He was so full of life and we didn't have enough time to enjoy the bliss of falling in love before dealing with such a difficult obstacle. As he pushed his walker back to the couch I found myself torn between trying to help and letting him feel like he could do it without help and I wondered where I fit in now. Where I belonged in his life. Try to take care of him or love him as he struggles? Both?

How could I go back home and leave him here?

So many thoughts ran through my head, but more than anything I wanted to rewind. I just wanted to turn the hands back and change that one conversation. Maybe things would have been different.

"Carpe diem," I said as he sat back on the couch, looking majorly tired from his brief walk across the room and back.

He tried to smile. "Carpe diem."

I sat beside him and pulled my shirt down to reveal the tattoo. "I found your gift after ... after the accident. This is what I got."

He nodded and held my knee. "I'm so sorry. I wish I could—"

"I told you to stop apologizing."

"We can't be together, Jane." His eyes darkened and he turned his gaze toward the ground. "Perhaps if I get better, but not now."

"Alistair. We *are* together. We never stopped being together just because we were apart. Let me ask you this ... did you think of me?"

"You know I did." He refused to look at me. "You're all I've thought about. It's the one thing that's kept me going."

"Don't push me away because of this. I can't live without you. I can't deal with the feeling I had the last few months, thinking you were dead or with someone else or who knows what else."

"You deserve better. You know that. My short-term memory is terrible. If I go for a car ride I forget the street name before we turn on the next one. I'm always misplacing things and I'm not always happy. Sometimes I can be a bit crabby and angry and it nearly seems out of my control." He finally looked at me, but quickly reverted his gaze. "I just can't put you through this."

"I live in another country. Let's just take it one day at a time. Let's talk like we used to. Every night, okay? I'll visit as much as I can."

"I won't be able to provide for you as my wife. It's like you said before, why start something you can't finish?"

"We already started." I held his face in my hands. "And I'm gonna finish."

"What about—"

"The store is nowhere near as important to me as you. Not even close."

"What if I can't work again? What if it's always like this?"

"Carpe diem. One day at a time. Forget tomorrow, Alistair. We have today. We have right now."

"You're inspired now, but when it gets difficult you will be miserable. You need a husband, Jane. Not a child."

"Would you please stop telling me what I need? I know what I need and it's you. We can make it. I know we can." I cuddled into his shoulder and kissed his arm.

He breathed deeply and touched the scar on his neck. I knew he didn't want me to see him like this. I knew he felt like giving up. Letting me go along with the idea of ever having a normal life. But I didn't believe in giving up. And I wasn't about to let him do that to himself.

"Why do we fall, Bruce?" I whispered, hoping to see if he remembered the next line of Alfred's wise words to Bruce Wayne.

Alistair closed his eyes and breathed in. Then out. Silence hovered between us for a few minutes, then finally he touched my hand and whispered, "So we can learn to pick ourselves up."

Chapter 57

WHEN ALISTAIR AND I FELL ASLEEP ON HIS COUCH IT DIDN'T cross my mind that his mother could walk in before we woke up, but that's exactly what happened. And let's just say she wasn't happy. We woke to the sound of her cursing and throwing her hands in the air in front of us.

Before my brain caught up with everything, Alistair was explaining what happened in a very loud, agitated tone. A tone I had never heard from him.

"You need to get on," she said to me. "I don't care who you are."

"Mum," he said sternly. "If she leaves, I leave."

"Mm, right. And where exactly might you go?"

"Dad's. Like I wanted to from the start."

"I'd like to see that." She waved her finger at me. "Who do you think you are coming in here and kicking his—"

"She didn't kick her out. I did. I wanted to be with Jane."

His mom left in a huff and stormed up the stairs, cursing until we could no longer make out the words. Alistair used his more functional arm to pull himself up into a straighter sitting position. "I need to use to the loo," he said shyly. "Don't fret about Mum. She's cheesed off because her boyfriend couldn't handle me being here and left her."

"Not exactly how I imagined the first meeting," I said.

467

"No." He shook his head sadly. "Not at all. This entire thing is just bloody awful."

"Is there anything I can do for you? Right now, I mean?"

He reached for his walker. "I can manage." He pulled himself up and I got the impression he was struggling to show me that he was still a man inside.

Don't cry, Jane. He needs you to be strong.

"Alistair?" I said as he forced himself to his feet and looked down at me with those struggle-glossed eyes. "You can do this. You're going to overcome this."

"No, Jane," he said. "*We* are. We're going to do this."

When he came back from the bathroom almost thirty minutes later, he told me that no one ever told him that he would overcome it. They always said it was a "possibility." When I said that to him he felt something inside of himself click. Like a light switch had been turned back on after a long, lonely spell of darkness.

We embraced in odd positions, but comfortably, for five minutes and then his mother walked back in.

"I'm sorry," she said to me, reaching out her hand. "It's nice to meet you, Jane. All this time I thought Alistair had imagined you while in a coma."

I shook her hand as my entire body flushed with warmth. "Oh, yes. I'm real."

"I've never met someone actually named Jane Austen."

"Mum, please."

She rolled her eyes at him and put her hands on her hips. "We need to get your bath ready now."

"I'll take a bath when I bloody well feel like it," he snapped.

I gazed toward the floor, pretending and hoping not to notice the tension rising between them.

She exhaled loudly as he adjusted himself on the couch. I really wanted to stay the night with him, but definitely didn't see that happening in her house. Problem is ... I didn't want to say goodbye again. Ever.

"You can't sit here with your little mate and act like everything is normal."

"Mum, I said—"

"No, Alistair. This is my house and you haven't appreciated a thing I've done. I'm losing my life because of you and I'm exhausted. Do you expect me to let this girl sleep in your bed tonight? You need help and assistance and this is too much for you right now."

"If you don't stop, I'm going to leave."

"Over a girl?" She tossed her head back and laughed. "Give her a few months and she'll give up on you."

He grabbed a tea cup from the table and flung it by her head. It crashed against the wall and slid to the floor in dozens of pieces. She gasped. Her brow lowered and her knuckles whitened as they rolled into fists. Alistair stared at her with a steady locked jaw and serious eyes.

"I'm only speaking the truth," she continued to dig her grave. "What sort of pretty young girl like this would want to be with a cripple?"

"This one!" I stood, my stomach whirling about and my blood on fire. Alistair tried to pull my hand back to the couch, but I yanked it up and shoved it in the air between his mom and me. "I want him. I don't look at him and see what you see. I see..." I turned my face toward him and looked into his eyes as I said, "I see the person I want to spend my life with and when I look at you"—I faced her again—"I wonder what kind of nasty mother says such horrible things about her own child."

She stepped toward me, then stepped back. "If you don't leave within two minutes I'm goin—" She broke down and fell to her knees, sobbing into Alistair's pants. "I'm sorry. I'm sorry."

What. The. Hell. Seriously?

He shoved his foot at her. "Get up, Mum. I'm not playing this game again. I'm going to Dad's." He looked up at me. "Can you take me to my Dad's?"

"No!" she screamed and shot back to her feet. "It's dangerous. I will not allow it. Does she know how depressed you've been? Practically sleeping all day for months?"

"I've been depressed because I missed her, but I feel a bit better having seen her and now you—"

"Does she know that I had to change your diaper early on? Would she do that?"

I wanted to raise my hand and say, "*She* is standing right here, you know?" But I didn't.

"Mum, I'm going to say this as nice as I possibly can," he paused, then wrinkled his forehead and screamed at the top of his lungs, "Get the fuck away from me!"

"I will not allow it. See, you're unable to manage your emotions. No. You're staying here. You need my help. Your father doesn't know the—"

"I am not a fucking baby! Yes, my fucking arm feels like jelly, but I'm not a baby and I'm bloody tired of you thinking I need you every second of the day. I can do more if you just let me." He hid his face with his hand. "And stop talking to my girlfriend like that."

She looked at him, then me, and started to speak, but decided not to.

Whew.

I clasped my hands in front of me and sucked in air. "Yeah. Oh, um, okay..." I rubbed my necklace and swept the Batman charm up and down the chain. "Um, so..."

"Go away, Mum," he said, hand still covering his eyes. "I'm sorry, but go away."

She dropped her hands to her sides and looked at me like she expected me to rescue her from the grave she dug. And I guess I felt sorry for her because I tried to reach out for her arm to tell her it would all settle down soon. But she scowled at me and rushed out the front door, screeching tires against asphalt as she drove away. You'd think perhaps Alistair's situation would've caused her to buckle up and drive like a normal human being, but I suppose love, even love of our own selves, makes us a little crazy sometimes.

I knew all about that.

Though I hoped to never become a nutcase.

Chapter 58

I WALKED BESIDE ALISTAIR AS HE WENT TO HIS ROOM TO pack his things. He fumbled around with one hand as he tried to gather some of his stuff, then he lifted his pillow and pulled out a picture of ... me. He seemed like he was trying to hide it, tucking it behind him to keep it from my view.

"What are you doing?" I said.

He turned and shrugged.

"You put my picture under your pillow?"

"No. Well, sort of. I keep it there and put it on the other pillow when I can't sleep." He sighed. "I'm sorry if that—"

"Shhh..." I stepped closer and gently wrapped my arms around him, worried I might hurt him. "No. More. Apologizing."

The walker was cold against my lower stomach, keeping us from fully embracing. He lifted his left arm and placed his hand on my hip, then ... his right arm lifted. It wasn't much. But it was something.

"You still smell like you," he whispered into my hair.

I so badly wanted to kiss him like we did the last time. Walls, tree houses, baths, suddenly they all seemed like distant memories and an intense feeling of mourning came over me. That part of us was gone. Or at least temporarily gone. The conversation we had before came to mind. The time he held me in the middle of the night and I asked if it would always feel like that. He said it will change and be new every time. Like falling in love all over again.

I felt that now.

He sat on his bed and rummaged through a drawer in the night stand. I thought of his mother, albeit a little looney, and how I was raised to never go to bed angry.

"Maybe you should stay here," I said, hoping he wouldn't yell at me like he did to Emma and his mom. "I mean, it's going to be hard to transition to your dad's house and your mom's right. She knows the stuff you need."

He continued sorting through papers in the drawer.

"Alistair, our last conversation wasn't a good one. Not terrible, but not the best. Imagine if something happened to your mom right now. You'd feel so bad."

He stopped. "What was our conversation?"

"Us?"

He nodded.

"We hadn't talked in a few days. We were both getting upset about it and just not handling it well. Then you got in your car and we were texting and that was it."

"What did you do?"

"I don't know." I sat beside him. "I feel weird talking about it. You'll think I'm a psycho."

He laughed.

He ... laughed.

He actually just laughed.

I wanted to hear it again. To see him smile. I wanted him to feel alive again and be the man I knew he was.

"Tell me," he said.

"Well, I called about seven billion times. Sent emails. Messages. You didn't get any of them?"

He shook his head. "To this day I can't remember my old email address or password. Two months ago I got a new cell phone. Went months without one. It was lost in the accident, I think. I never saw it."

"I hate that this happened to you. I wish it were me."

"Don't say that," he said. "I wish it were neither of us, but definitely not you."

"I even flew over here and went to your apartment flat."

"My apartment flat?" He chuckled. "I like that. Apartment flat."

I tucked my hair behind my ear and blushed.

He leaned his head toward me and whispered, "Jane."

"Alistair." Butterflies still existed. Calmer and sweeter, but still there.

My hair fell back from my ear and created a curtain between him and me. He twirled a strand in his fingers, pressed it back behind my ear, and kissed my cheek.

With his lips still against my skin, he whispered, "I've missed you so much," and sent shivers down my neck just like the first time.

Only better. Deeper. And more real.

He listened to me. Thankfully. And decided to stay. When we heard his mom come back in, I asked him if I could go talk to her first. He said I could, but before I went out to her he explained that she's not always like that, but she endured a lot with the divorce, his accident, losing her job, then her boyfriend, and to top it off someone stole her dog. I told him to come out and apologize after about ten minutes. I just wanted to show her my heart. I needed her to see that I wasn't just some girl looking to play the selfless martyr. I was just a girl who loved a boy and I refused to let obstacles screw me over.

After he prepared me for her depression and volatile emotional mood swings, I meandered down the hall and back to the living room. She jumped when she saw me and put her hand over her heart.

"I'm sorry to scare you," I said, feeling like a freshman forced to stand in front of the entire school on the first day. "I just wanted to apologize. I know you've been through a lot and what I said wasn't kind. Alistair does appreciate what you do and I appreciate what you've done for him. He wants to stay. And I'd like to get to know you better."

"I'm glad you reacted that way," she said, motioning for me to sit next to her on the couch. "I don't know how much Alistair has told you about his other girlfriends, but I can tell you one thing ... they were all selfish little things. As a mother you can just tell when someone really loves your kid. Those girls loved him on the outside and maybe for his music, but when you stood up for him I could see it in your eyes. Maybe that even scared me. He's all I have right now and I worry that he's finally found someone who loves him in a deeper way than I ever can." She wiped a tear from her face. "He's my only baby and he was always wise beyond his years. Grew up much too fast and I miss him. Having him back like this ... it wasn't what I expected. Or wanted. And he certainly doesn't want to be here like this. He's been gone since he was eighteen. Moved back to Bristol and now he's forced to come back to Mansfield and have his mother care for him in his early twenties. I know he's embarrassed and I knew about you.

His nurses and I would joke that he was making it all up, thinking he fancied Jane Austen, but I saw the picture he keeps under his pillow and I knew. So I should apologize to you, Jane. I saw you in here and recognized you from the picture and I worried you would take the last thing I have." She cleared her throat. "I figured so long as he needs me, then I won't lose him. But it's not fair. I need to let him grow, even if that means away from me." She wiped another tear into her sleeve. "I'm sorry for rambling. I don't have many people to talk to."

"No, no, it's okay. I ... I don't know what to say."

"Say you'll love my son. Say you'll make him smile again. It's been too long."

"I ... I love him more than I've ever loved anything in my entire life. Being without him these last few months showed me that. I felt sick. Like a part of me died. I'm not stupid and I know I'm young and well, maybe I am stupid and don't know what I'm talking about, but I know that I love him." My voice trembled and cracked. "That I do know."

"I really am sorry for the things I said," she repeated. "I love him too. It hurts to see him go through something like this. I remember when he fell off of the bed when he was two and I put a little plaster on and kissed him to make it all better. And the first time he got his heart broken or got into a fight. I could help with those things. Make it better. I can't make this better. He may be a man now, but he'll always be my baby boy."

"My dad says the same thing to me. Well, except the boy part." I heard his bedroom door creak. "I don't want to take him from you. I have no desire to be his mother. I just want to be everything else." I smiled. "I'm half-kidding."

"Oh, I see why he likes you. That and the strange Batman obsession you two share."

"No," he said from the doorway. "I love her because she's everything I am and everything I'm not all at the same time."

We both looked at him, startled, and I smiled. It may not have been an image I imagined or could've fathomed a few months ago, but it was a beautiful one in its own broken way. I snapped a pretend picture with my hands and stored it away, hoping to add many, many more memories throughout the rest of my life.

His eyes turned up as his lips curved into a smile. His mom touched my shoulder and said, "Thank you." But I was still staring at the boy across the room. Who was still staring at me with a barely visible tear drop stuck in the corner of his eye. I stood, walked over to him, and kissed it away, tasting the salt of his tears as I closed my eyes and felt his love for me. No words needed. No kiss needed. Just ... him. We had officially fallen.

Chapter 59

HIS MOM INSISTED I CALL HER "MUM," WHICH WAS WEIRD at first for several reasons, but I got used to it before I had to go. She let me stay in the house, but made me sleep on the couch. I woke up in the middle of the night to his breath on my face and his body against mine and I can't describe how perfect if felt, no matter how imperfect we were. He was gone before the sun woke up and I thought it was a dream until he smiled at me in the morning with a mischievous little grin on his face.

Our goodbye was dreadful. Tears and heart-twisting pains in my chest. But he promised and I promised to talk every day at least once. No excuses. No way around it.

We texted while I waited for my flight and when I landed I immediately got an email from him.

Dearest Jane,

Thank you for this weekend. Thank you for finding me and caring enough to still come after all of those months of thinking I abandoned you. I'm still sorry whether you want me to be or not. I'm thinking of you. Hope the flight isn't too long. Can't wait to hear from you. (Takes forever to text with one hand, so this is a bit short, but my thoughts of you are anything but.)

Yours,

Alistair

PS- Don't know if I told you, but I thought it the entire time ... You are so beautiful. For so many reasons. In so many ways. That is all.

I emailed him back as everyone filed out of the plane.

My sweet Alistair,

You have bewitched me, body and soul, and I love, I love, I love you. I never wish to be parted from you from this day on.

Yours ALWAYS,

Jane

PS - you'll always be gorgeous to me. Those eyes...

AND THAT WAS THE START OF DAYS AND DAYS AND DAYS OF constant emails, texts, and phone calls. And I do mean constant.

Carpe Diem, right?

I couldn't visit during the entire summer. The shop had plenty of orders, but it was at a stage where it was too busy to leave and not busy enough to hire more people, but Alistair and I were faithful in our promise to speak every night. Looking back, I feel like that was one of the happiest times of my life. The joy of getting to fall in love not once, but twice, with the same person.

Occasionally he had some sort of emotional outburst, whether it was frustration, happiness, or sadness. But I read up on people recovering from TBI enough to know that it was the injury causing those reactions, not him.

In September I was finally able to visit again and he had significant more function in his leg and face. So his facial muscles had less spasms and his face was starting to look like his old self again. He was so proud and Mum was too. I met his Dad during that visit and when I left he gave me a really good hug and told me that Alistair had changed since I came back. He thanked me for loving him and told me to come back soon. They didn't know I had plans to move there in the spring. It was my birthday present to myself and I was planning to surprise Alistair on the day we met, which was my birthday.

So when I left his house that day I stayed a few extra days to sort out some details with a shop I found in London. I was hoping for Bristol or something a little less busy, but that's where it ended up working out. Before leaving I signed a lease for a place on Regent Street. It was *extremely* busy, a stream of people always on the sidewalk, and the rent was not cheap, but I thought the populated, heavy shopping area would work out well. Plus it was gorgeous. The building ... just wow. Stone buildings with large windows. I couldn't wait to show Alistair.

I applied for a work visa and was given a Tier 1 visa for being an entrepreneur or having special talents. It took a lot of work and help from Dad, but I prepared an amazing document and business plan when I got home. It helped that I already placed a deposit on the store too.

I was given two years to live and work in the UK and would apply again for a three year extension. At five years I could apply for an Indefinite Leave to Remain, which gave me chills just thinking about it.

Alistair would be so surprised and I couldn't wait for May to come. Of course it came as slow as possible. I spent Christmas in Mansfield with Alistair, Mum, Dad, and his aunts and uncles. Alistair's mobility was even better, but what I loved most was his smile. I felt like he smiled the entire time I visited and the passionate kisses we snuck in the middle of the night brought back old memories.

My next visit would be in May, as a new resident of London. And he had absolutely no idea. And I could absolutely not wait. Soon enough, I kept telling myself, and with every paper I filled out and every detail I planned the butterflies returned and my hands would literally shake. I really, really couldn't wait to see his face when I showed him and it brought tears to my eyes just thinking about it.

Chapter 60

MAY! BEAUTIFUL, SUNSHINEY, WARM, LOVELY MAY! TODAY was the big day. No, not that big day. My moving day. It was a little complicated, but I had a lot of stuff shipped over to London and decided that in some cases it would be cheaper to buy new stuff once I got there.

Dad, Mom, Eddie, Zoe, Donovan, and Han flew over with me to stay the first few days and help me get acclimated. Once we got there we set up some things in my *flat* and went out to eat in London. I was still weeks away from telling Alistair, but I couldn't focus during dinner and I could barely eat. I kept getting nervously excited that this. was. really. happening. Really, really happening. Really. Really. *Really.* Happening.

I leaned into Zoe while she finished her dessert and whispered, "I want to tell him now."

"I heard that," Don said from the other side of her. "Don't do it. Wait for The Big Day."

We had this fun surprise planned for The Big Day. It would be two years from the time we met, on the dot, and I wanted to bring Alistair on holiday to London, then causally walk by the store and show him.

I had three weeks left to torture myself waiting. I'm horrible at keeping secrets from Alistair. Horrible. Every time I got him a gift I ended up giving it to him early, unwrapped, because I just couldn't help myself.

But Don was right. I should wait.

I looked around the table during dessert and missed Autumn. Since she started college things never got back to normal. She started smoking pot and calling me while high, which annoyed the hell out of me. One, because she laughed the entire time and made no sense. Two, because she only talked about boys and didn't keep one long enough for me to remember who she was talking about. She was one of those sorority peeps too and way, way into her new girl friends. She was a different person and we grew apart more and more each day. Something I never imagined happening when we held each other on her bed before she left. But that's okay. I was okay with it. Broken promises change you for the better if you let them. It was all part of the plan.

"I think I should move here with you," Zoe said. "Would it be hard?"

"Maybe not. I could hire you and you could apply for a temporary work visa."

"Hm. I'll look into that."

Mom and Dad paid for dinner and we all went back to my new flat about forty minutes from the shop. It was a nice one bedroom flat on Floyd Street in Charlton. Even had stairs going up to the bedroom and bath. Unfortunately though, the bath wouldn't fit both of us in it. Yes, I considered that when looking for a place. I'd been wanting to repeat that memory ever since.

It wasn't a big place and everyone wanted to stay the night to make it easier and less expensive, which was fine with me, but cramped. Zoe and Han slept with me in my new queen size bed, Mom and Dad slept on the couches downstairs, and Donovan slept on the floor beside my bed.

Did I mention I loved every second of it?

OVER BREAKFAST MOM AND DAD TOLD FUNNY STORIES about Don and me. Eddie chimed in a few times too.

"Remember the time Don tried to throw a pebble at your window and it broke the window?" Eddie said. "You came running in my room thinking someone was trying to shoot you."

"Hey, man," Donovan said. "There comes a point in every boy's life where he realizes the difference between the pebble and the rock." He made a goofy face. "Some of us mature faster than others."

I shook my head. "You're seriously the biggest dork."

"I think he's adorkable," Zoe said, then looked at Han and flushed with pink.

Ah. Yeah. Awkward moment two point O.

"Well, if my opinion counts," Don said. "I know two huge geeks who have Batman pajamas, bathing suits, and tattoos, and throw movie and comic book quotes into serious conversations."

I held my hands up. "Guilty as charged."

"I'm so happy for you, Jane." Mom reached her hand across the table and held my wrist.

"Oh, not the tears, Mum," I said. "You're just happy I'm dating a British boy and living in your favorite place ever."

She held up her hands. "Guilty as charged." She smiled. "No, really, Jane," she said in her English accent. "I'm so proud of my little girl. You've grown so much in the last few years."

Dad crossed his arms over his chest, leaned back in his chair, and chewed the inside of his cheek.

"Dad? You're getting emotional too?"

He pinched the top of his nose. "Just going to miss you, honey."

"Oh, no," I said. "Don't make me cry guys."

Zoe scooted her chair back and hugged me. I stood and hugged her back as she cried into my shoulder. Then Donovan and Han joined in on the hug while Dad kissed Mom's tears away on the other side of the table, Eddie sitting oddly beside them.

"Guys, I'll be visiting and we'll talk," I said, but then it all hit me. My life was changing. These people helped me get to where I now stood. They were there for my first steps. And my first kiss. They raised me and supported me and taught me and ... loved me.

And now they were letting me fly.

Eddie walked over and pulled me from the group hug, took me into his arms, and said, "I admire you and always have. I'd say I'm gonna miss you, but you already know that."

A lonesome tear fell from my eye and into his shirt as I looked at Mom.

She smiled back at me and mouthed, "I love you."

And then the tears ... they were unstoppable.

Chapter 61

THE. BIG. DAY.

May 17th.

IT WAS FINALLY HERE!

AHHH!

Okay.

Yes.

Breathe. Breathe. Breathe.

It's safe to say I didn't sleep. Alistair didn't even know I lived in the UK now, much less owned a new store that would be opening in June and had my own flat. I knew it was going to make him so, so happy and I had this little paper taped to the door of the store that told him how I felt and what I did.

He still didn't feel comfortable driving, so he wanted me to come pick him up first. And since it was almost a four hour drive, I planned to stay the night there and then bring him to London for the surprise. I hadn't told Mum either. No one knew. It was going to be a long, long night of no sleep again.

When I pulled up to Mum's house I nearly ran to the door, so excited to see him. She was at work, so it was just him, but he didn't answer.

I tried knocking on the windows, but nothing. Last time he told me where the spare key was hidden, in the backyard under a stone, so I quickly ran back there and saw a note taped to the stone instead.

Jane ... meet me at the treehouse. I'll be waiting.

I held my hand over my mouth. He remembered my birthday. I didn't think he would. Since the accident he was horrible with numbers. He could barely remember his own birthday. What did he have planned? I wondered and had the fleeting thought that maybe, just maybe, maybe, maybe ... he'd propose.

But I didn't want to get my hopes up.

"Actually," I told myself. "Screw it. Get your hopes up."

"Yep," I said back to myself. "In the words of Nightwing, 'You'll never know if you can fly unless you take the risk of falling.'"

"Hopes. Are. Up."

I jogged back to my car, buckled up, and drove as fast as I could without being reckless. It was another few hours in the car, but it was worth it. He was worth it. Thankfully he was smart enough to put the address on the back of the note, otherwise he would've been waiting a heck of a long time.

By the time I pulled up in front of the house, it was dark, but I saw lights glowing from the backyard and I wondered ... could he really propose right now? And how would these people not notice the lights in the back? And ... who drove him?

I couldn't wait any longer.

Running to the back, hair in the cool spring breeze, my entire body filled with butterflies. I think even my mind was fluttering. Every inch of me felt like one twitchy, adrenaline-filled mess of a person.

Then I stopped.

And so did my heart.

I brought my hands to my face, closed my eyes, and although I desperately wanted to maintain a composed state of being ... I started to laugh.

He stood there, holding his cane instead of the walker, wearing the Alfred Pennyworth suit his dad bought from my store. His face was brighter than the thousands of candles surrounding him. So bright I barely noticed my friends and family standing around him. 1812 Overture played in the background, coming from the person's house it seemed.

I stood there for a few minutes, unable to move. Then he walked through everyone—he walked—and took my hand.

"Jane," he whispered.

I breathed in and let out a soft cry. "Alistair."

We stood in silence for a few minutes as the song hummed sweetly in the background.

"Happy birthday," he said against my ear.

Shivers. Shivers. Shivers.

I expected him to kneel down any minute, but he stayed there holding my hands and after another minute of looking into each other's eyes, he finally said, "I want you to know that the reason I'm standing here right now without that walker is because of you. Before you came back I had such little motivation to go on, to get better. But after that, after you came back that first time, I knew I needed to be strong for you, for us Jane. For us, do you hear me?" He held my face in his hands. "Us." He kissed me, then stepped back. "So, I was intending to propose to you today, because this is The Big Day as I'm sure you're well aware, but ... thing is ... what's the point of proposing when you know you're going to spend the rest of your life with someone?" A man, a stranger, stepped up to him, then Alistair took a box out of his pocket and gave it to me. "Open it."

I eagerly opened it and three rings sparkled in the flickering candlelight.

"This gentleman here is going to officiate our wedding. Right now."

I couldn't breathe. Or think. Or stop the tears from wetting my face.

My family, his family, my friends, and some of his friends I recognized from his photographs, moved closer and surrounded us as Donovan stepped up and took the rings.

More tears.

"Oh, wow," I said. "I need to compose myself here."

"I chose Donovan as the best man." Alistair smiled. "Without him, I don't know if we would be here today." He turned and gave Don a bro hug, thanked him for pushing me to do things I didn't feel comfortable doing, and turned back to me. "Jane, your love has healed me," he whispered sweetly as the candles showered him with a warm glow. "Your love has changed me. And I love you not only for that, but because of every little thing you are. Will you marry me?"

I would've jumped into his arms, but I was afraid to hurt him and I noticed his one arm still didn't move much at his side. So I gently wrapped my hands around him and held the back of his neck. He looked down at me, that sly grin on his face. I shook my head, kissed him, and said, "I love you."

We turned to the man who officiated our intimate wedding and right after we kissed, the first time as husband and wife, the cannons of 1812 Overture blasted. Alistair pulled me into him, pressing our *Carpe*

Diem tattoo's together as we laughed at the intense cannon ending.

"Couldn't have timed that better if I tried," he said, then pulled back from our embrace and whispered, "Jane Gladwyn, let's go home."

"Where's home?" I said.

"Floyd Street. London."

"Hey! You knew?!" I laughed. "What?"

"Yes. I knew all along." He turned to Don. "He knew about the proposal and told me I wouldn't have to worry about getting a new flat, that you were taking care of that part."

"Oh, you guys!" I smiled so much it hurt. "I don't deser—"

"Yes," Alistair whispered. "Yes, you do."

Don nodded in agreement, his eyes glistening too. Then everyone erupted in applause as Alistair and I turned toward their joy-painted faces.

There are things you deserve in life, but love isn't one of them. Every time you're given it, it's a gift. That's what Alistair was to me, no matter how much he thought I deserved it ... I didn't. And never would. As we stood there under the treehouse, our fingers intertwined and turning white from squeezing so hard, fireworks started. And I mean, they actually started. Spilling out in the sky above us. White and yellow against the dark blue star-speckled backdrop.

"Batman fireworks," I laughed.

He leaned into me and said, "Just wait till you see the fireworks tonight."

I blushed.

"I rented a thatched cottage," he said. "And it has a huge tub."

"Oh, fancy that." I grinned as the fireworks burst in his eyes.

Everyone watched as the crackling colors fizzled out. The song finally ended. But I knew it was only the beginning.

I whispered a Nightwing quote, "Whenever someone is asked what power they wish they had, flying is always at the top of the list. But I have to admit, I've learned to love the art of falling too."

Donovan handed Alistair his cane. He steadied himself on it, then looked at me with the most contented expression. "What do you say we get on?"

We said goodbye to everyone and drove away with "Love is Worth It" painted on the back window of my car. We barely spoke and didn't need to, but every few minutes we'd squeeze each other's hand and smile across the car.

When we got to the thatched cottage, he apologized for not being able to carry me inside and I told him to stop apologizing, as usual. Then we entered the bathroom without questioning. Black and yellow rose petals covered the floor and the water, which was warm.

"How'd you get it to be warm?" I said.

"You didn't notice, but Eddie left before us."

"You're something else, Mr. Gladwyn."

He set his cane down beside the tub and grinned. "I suppose we don't need a cozzie this time."

"A cozzie?" I laughed.

"A bathing costume."

"You mean a swimsuit?" I laughed again.

"Mmhmm." His lips were now distracted by my neck. He moved my dress sleeve down my shoulder and kissed across my collarbone. I closed my eyes and savored every sensation from the rush of excitement to the firmness of his hand on my hip. He slipped the other sleeve down and my dress dropped to the floor. It was a little more difficult to take his suit jacket and shirt off with the lack of motion in his right arm, but we managed while kissing and laughing and enjoying the ever-evolving chemistry between us.

Carefully, I helped him ease into the petal-covered water, then slid my body down beside his. Perhaps it would've been a convenient time to make love, but we held each other, making love with our eyes and deeply passionate kisses instead.

The water turned cold and we woke in each other's arms, only to end up on the bed, under the sheets, where we finished the night as one.

It's only one of the thousands of moments I've captured with my mind, safely holding them in a place I could return to time and time again whenever I needed to remember why love is worth it.

And will always be worth it.

We fell that night. But we also flew.

Trust me when I say, brokenness is proof that the heart works and when it's fixed it works better than it ever did before. You just need to find someone willing to fix and be fixed with you.

For me, that person was Alistair.

The English boy who captured my heart and made it new again.

epilogue

May 10, 2075

THE LAST TIME I SAW MY SISTER SHE HANDED ME A USB drive and said, "I'm not a writer, but this is my story. Edit it, call it *The Best of Fools,* and share it with the world. Love is too beautiful to keep to yourself." Then she handed me the CD of the music they composed together over the course of their lives.

The cancer ate away her body and she was hanging by a thread. Alistair never left her side, even though his frail eighty-two year old body was weighed down by the heart attack he survived five months before Jane's cancer started its vicious attack against her life.

I hated traveling and my bones were old and tired too, but I wouldn't miss my big sister's last days. So I stayed there, telling Alistair to please go eat something, but he no longer had the desire to push forward.

When Jane died May 12th on a rainy London morning, the lights in Alistair's eyes went out. I actually saw it happen when she took her last breath. He sobbed into her chest, convulsing, stopping for air, and then staring off with reddened eyes every few minutes. Same thing a few days later at her funeral. I had just walked away from her casket with Donovan and Zoe when Alistair walked up.

He stood for a few seconds, just looking at her. Then he placed his hand on her heart and his other hand on his own heart.

"The tattoo," Donovan whispered as we watched. "He's holding their Carpe Diem tattoos."

Then, without warning, he leaned into her casket and bawled like a baby, whispering something no one could hear.

Donovan walked back up to the casket, put his arm around Alistair, and cried with him as they stared together at Jane's lifeless body. It's an image I'll never forget. Ever.

My nieces?Jane's three daughters,?and their children, gathered around as well, hugging their dad with drenched faces.

Alistair was never the same after that.

Zoe and I decided to stay a few extra weeks, but our son and daughter flew back home right after the funeral. We just couldn't leave Alistair in such a state. Jane's last words to me were, "Don't let Alistair lose the will to live. Our children need him."

I needed to help, because I loved her and even though she was gone, I knew I still had a piece of her left in my brother-in-law.

Zoe and I cleaned and cooked for him, but he barely ate.

Then her birthday came around and he asked to visit her grave. Zoe and I drove him there and gave him some space. We sat under a tree and watched as he set his cane against her stone and cried on his knees. After an hour, he stood and put a letter against her grave, then walked back to the car with his shoulders reaching toward the ground.

"How will he ever go on?" Zoe said as she wiped her face.

I shook my head and walked to her grave. Zoe's hand in mine. We stood there with a cloud of heartbreak over us.

I read the altered *Dark Knight Rises* quote Alistair insisted on having etched into her stone.

A hero can be anyone. Even a girl doing something as simple as loving a boy ... to let him know that the world hadn't ended.

I peered over my shoulder to make sure he couldn't see me from the car, then stuffed the letter in my pocket.

"What are you doing?" Zoe said. "You can't do that."

"It's just going to get ruined in the rain anyway."

"You're terrible," she said, half-smiling, but of course she was the first to want to rip it open when we got back to their home.

So, since this was Jane's story, I thought it would only be fitting to let Alistair have the last word. Here it is. This is his letter, written in shaky letters and blotched with tears.

Dear Jane,

Happy Big Day.

I despise this feeling in my chest and I know it can only be seven thousand times worse than what you felt when I got into the accident. It's not fair that you went before me. You're the strong one. You're the one that kept me going. You were the real hero in my life, Jane. Truly.

Now I'm just a weak old man with a weak old heart. My body hurts, but my heart is worse. My real heart, not this ticker in my chest.

I know you told Donovan and Eddie to watch over me and I know our girls need a father, but I need you. And I won't be much of a father without you anyway.

Sixty years today. Sixty years since the day I fell into your life and five days since the day you fell out of mine. I can't be expected to go on. Please forgive me, and I know you'll say not to apologize as you did the many other times I failed you, but as always, I apologize anyway.

Marilyn Grey

I miss you. I love you. And I'll see you soon.
You came after me. Now it's my turn to come after you.
Carpe diem,
Yours

The End

from marilyn

Guys, I can't tell you how hard it was to write *The End* on this story. This one, of all the novels I've written, is my favourite. Yes, I spelled that with a U intentionally. :-)

I don't know why this is my favourite. Just as Jane didn't quite know how to explain what love was to her. It's hard to explain why I love this one more than the others. Maybe it's my love for all things British. Maybe it's my love for Jane and Alistair. Maybe it's Batman. I don't know. What I do know is that writing *The End* on this book felt like a depressing goodbye between Jane and Alistair at an overcrowded airport. It felt unnatural. No, it can't possibly end. These are my friends and I miss them. I want to spend more time with them!

But nothing ends. Every end is only the beginning of something else. While I plan to write little novella stories here and there to fill in the gaps of Alistair's recovery and show you some of their letters and other things that I couldn't fit into this book without making it an enormous read, I have plans for another book. A book of friendship and sacrifice called, "All You Need."

And although I am forced to move on from my beloved Jane and Alistair, I know that it's only the beginning of sharing them with the world. I hope you enjoyed them as much as I did. If not, well ... no two hearts beat the same. Perhaps you aren't a dork destined for dorkdom like I am and I congratulate you on such things. :-) But I truly loved writing this book and it will always be dear to my heart, regardless of how it's received by the world.

Thank you for reading. For sharing the beauty of words and stories with me. And most of all ... celebrating this thing called love.

Don't forget to visit me on Facebook or Marilyn-Grey.com to stay in touch! I adore my readers and many of you have become my closest friends. I love all of you. Thank you for inspiring me to write stories of life and love. Thank you for being a part of *my* life.

Just ... thank you.

And so ... it begins....

www.ingramcontent.com/pod-product-compliance
Lightning Source LLC
Chambersburg PA
CBHW030909050726
47498CB00003BA/662